STUART EVANS

Centres of Ritual

Hutchinson of London

Hutchinson & Co (Publishers) Ltd
3 Fitzroy Square, London WIP 6JD

London Melbourne Sydney Auckland
Wellington Johannesburg and agencies
throughout the world

First published 1978
© Stuart Evans 1978

Set in Monotype Imprint

Printed in Great Britain by The Anchor Press Ltd
and bound by Wm Brendon & Son Ltd
both of Tiptree, Essex

ISBN 0 09 133050 5

'The occupational debris implies temporary hearths and there is no evidence of permanent houses on the site.'

Stuart Piggott

I

The wasp droned inevitably into the room, after hovering for a second or so above a frond of fading wistaria. Candida became immediately nervous because she hated wasps. No one else seemed to notice. Roger was talking evenly and the others were all listening with rapt attention and little expectant smiles.

There was a bowl of fruit on the desk near Roger's left hand and the wasp settled on it. Candida loathed the creatures: she thought you could read greed and malice in their shapes, in their nasty black and yellow heads, in their movements whether creeping or flying. The wasp crawled out of sight behind a pear.

Roger, as usual, was sprawling back in his swivel chair. His immaculately white shirt was fastened at the wrists and he wore his customary plain dark tie. He did not seem to notice the excessive heat. The wasp reappeared, voraciously scouring the smooth surface of a nectarine. Candida watched it. Then Roger must have made some particularly telling or dramatic point, because he swivelled in the chair and shot out his left arm in the direction of the fruit bowl. The gesture disturbed the wasp which promptly stung him. He drew his hand abruptly away but did not interrupt the flow of his brilliant little discourse, and it was only Candida's shriek or squeal which made him pause and the others look around. Roger smiled at her and went on with what he was saying while inspecting the stung hand. The others all grinned. The wasp flew at Stephen Kent, who flicked it out of the window with a neatly athletic wave of his rolled-up essay. Candida felt silly: but she could not help it. She disliked all creeping things and had once, when she was little,

7

been stung nastily just above the eye by a wasp which had settled on a towel. She was naturally frightened of the beastly things.

She knew that she had flushed, but the others did not seem to notice. They were still eagerly listening to Roger, who was in a particularly mellifluous vein. Candida tried to tune into the elegantly phrased peroration – but her attention had been wandering before the wasp had intruded. She knew it was something to do with the political acumen of Maria Theresa in her domestic proceedings, but it was too late to pick up the argument. When the others laughed, Candida followed them – a second or so too late. It didn't matter: she doubted whether Roger Ingestre would be aware of it.

Perhaps she had been made inattentive by Stephen Kent's essay, which had been unusually long and boring even for him. The poor boy worked so dreadfully earnestly, terrified of leaving something significant out. Roger always saved the situation for him – as she supposed he did for the rest of them – by appearing to be desperately interested and almost impatient to take up this or that point in his eagerness to elaborate upon it and to relate it to their work in preceding weeks. This week, before he had even started his commentary, Candida had been day-dreaming, watching Roger swinging in his chair and wondering, once more, what it might be like to be in bed with him.

Candida wasn't quite silly enough to think that she was in love with Roger Ingestre, but she was certainly attracted to him, as was Sheila, the other girl in their tutorial group. It was difficult not to be: he was tall, neatly built, in very good physical shape; he had a pleasantly lined face which wasn't too handsome, thick dusty-reddish hair, a splendidly modulated voice, and endless good humour. The other girl was rather obvious: today, for example, she was wearing an unnecessarily tight cotton shirt and no bra – so that her heavy breasts were all too evident. Candida noticed a trickle of sweat along the girl's temple. She herself was and looked wonderfully cool, though none of the three men seemed to notice it. Michael Lumley glanced at her once, but then turned all his attention to the tutorial. Candida did not care about that: she thought he was probably *comme ci, comme ça*. She understood that he led a busy, male-orientated social life, very much along nineteen-thirties lines – carrying the sub-platonic, civilised notion of friendship on from school to college. Of course it was no longer possible to be as fashionable, as sybaritic: but to someone of her liberal upbringing it was surprising how many well-heeled young men maintained such standards even in the Oxford of 1976. At the same time, this particular man wanted to do well in his Schools, seeing a career in the diplomatic service as the best opportunity for pursuing the same pleasant way of life without too much interference from reality. And Stephen Kent: well, Stephen Kent was boringly and implacably, doggedly in love with Candida, which made him almost rude to Sheila.

Roger Ingestre for the most part was aware of them only as deserving his meticulous professional attention. The fact that he was a friend and political associate of Candida's parents was obviously an irrelevance, and the circumstance that she and several other girls in her year had been sent to him was a coincidence. The tutor at their own college who usually taught the eighteenth and nineteenth centuries was having a sabbatical: but since Roger Ingestre was absolutely brilliant on the Whig Supremacy and so on, everyone had been terribly pleased when he was able to take them on.

Candida was in no sense over-sexed. When she had met Roger in the past, at her parents' house, she had always found him charming, attractive and considerate. He was unfailingly kind to young people, did not patronise them and sought to include them in conversation when others tended to treat them as rather tiresome kittens. Gradually, however, she had admitted to herself that she was increasingly sexually aroused by him. At odd vacant moments, she had found herself having almost absent-minded fantasies about him;

9

and then at others, quite deliberate and delicious variations on these.

She had cautiously tested his reaction in several ways: by holding his gaze rather longer than necessary, smiling at a psychological moment, changing position, even by veiled little phrases introduced into friendly conversation before or after tutorials. When Sheila's display of her ample facilities had become a little too much, Candida had herself, again cautiously, made this or that provocative movement. While Stephen Kent missed nothing, Ingestre seemed to be blithely unaware of what was being offered. Not that Candida was absolutely sure that she was being so specific. She wondered if, in spite of quite a lot of minor experimentation over the years, the fact that she was still technically a virgin at the age of nineteen was beginning to bother her. Few of her parents' friends, surely, would have believed it. Then, there had been the appalling heat-wave of late May and June and Candida had concentrated on looking and being cool rather than sexy.

When the wasp had interrupted, she had been wondering about Roger's private life. From what she knew of him from her parents and their friends, he was certainly not queer. There was never much in the way of gossip in their home, but she had a distinct impression that he was thoroughly ordinary in his tastes. His divorce had been civilised and startlingly undramatic, even for that refined circle of people. So what did he do for sex? She remembered thinking during A-level English, when her attention had often wandered, that the hectic in the blood was not tamed with age. At least from what she could tell of her parents' generation. Yet Roger was almost notorious for abstinence.

It was in fact ridiculous. Here she was, after the wasp, brooding over the things she had been thinking of before it had interrupted. She had missed even the end of Roger's spiel. What a waste of time. Roger was standing up, smiling.

'Quite charming,' he said. 'They had been to the opera at Vienna and when the evening was over Maria Theresa remarked that so-and-so – I forget who it was – was the greatest actress who had ever lived. Francis, with husbandly perspicacity, said, "Next to you, Madam." And, of course, he was right – as husbands frequently are. Her sense of theatre was astounding.'

There was the customary appreciative amusement and noises of it.

'That wraps it up for this week, I think,' Roger said. 'Thank you, Steve. That was a good piece and obviously it's brought up a lot of interesting and worthwhile chat. If my internal clock is right, we have one more week of term. So whose turn is it?'

'Mine, I think,' said Michael Lumley.

'Good. Write us something elegant, Michael, on "The Pendulum and Pitt".'

Including Candida, they all laughed.

'All right, Roger,' said Michael Lumley. 'Explain, please.'

'The *entre deux guerres* years, 1748 to 1756, and what was going on in European politics. In fact, there were all kinds of deplorable things going on between us and the French in America and India and so on. Oh, it's fascinating stuff! What brought Pitt the Elder to power? Was it inevitable, or was it carefully plotted, or was it (like so much in politics) happenstance? Can you all stay for a glass of sherry?'

Lumley had a rather pressing appointment: this time, to buy wine for the dining club of which he was comptroller. Candida raised her eyebrows as she glanced at Roger, who received the information with his usual neutral composure. In 1976, for God's sake! Sheila said 'Lovely!' (of course) and sort of flexed her breasts. Stephen Kent waited for Candida. She knew that he had arranged to play tennis, but she was not surprised when she said she would stay, that he stayed too. For the first time she thought that Roger Ingestre showed awareness of this and it irritated her.

He poured them glasses of acceptably dry sherry. When asked, Candida affected the driest possible: but she did not really enjoy it much. Roger's was appropriate to the sensibilities of his most sophisticated pupils but at the same time drinkable. He was completely easy and relaxed. They talked nonsense: about the hot weather and what it might portend for Wimbledon in which everyone pretended to be interested. Sheila was fat and much too eager. Stephen Kent was preoccupied with Candida, with whatever she said, with when she might leave so she became thoroughly bad-tempered, wondering why everyone could be so stupid.

'I think that any historian's patience should be on the side of eternity,' Roger Ingestre said, 'but mine runs a little short with these tennis players.'

'I thought you were playing tonight, Stephen,' Candida said.

'Not until much later,' Kent said, lying and looking irrelevantly at his watch.

'I adored it last year when Ashe beat Connors,' Sheila said. 'It was so *just* in so many different ways. But I must say I have an absolute flaming passion for Nastase.'

'Indeed?' Roger said. 'I'm rather pleased to say I can't claim to share it.'

'Oh, Roger!'

'Well, apart from the most obvious reasons, I've always rather favoured the passionless in any art, or craft – whichever you prefer. It's all a matter of mastery and not of personal display.'

'I agree,' said Kent.

'Oh, but what about fire and soul and . . . oh, I don't know . . . guts for want of a better word?' said Sheila, to dog-paddling movements of her shoulders that made her unsupported torso surge and billow.

'Not for me,' said Roger. 'It is proving mastery that matters, not pleasing the audience. The applause of onlookers is almost always an irrelevance: about ninety per cent have no idea what is really happening.'

He smiled around them rather wanting to be challenged. Sheila was much too stupid and giggled ingratiatingly.

Stephen Kent looked towards Candida. Usually she would have said something: not necessarily clever but sharp enough to keep things going. She didn't, because she simply could not be bothered. Roger Ingestre seemed obscurely amused by them, as after a short pause he began to embroider around his own theme. Of course, they listened and laughed dutifully. Candida thought perhaps that Roger was quite remarkably conceited, but the idea didn't please her and she discarded it. She was being sour and unfair: he was a civilised don in his mid-forties trying to be friendly, talking just marginally below his own level, without exactly patronising anyone. Somehow he got onto the Liberal leadership problems and flair in politics. After a few wet lettuce exchanges, the conversation wilted.

When Ingestre offered them more sherry, Sheila declined and was chagrined when Candida, who almost always opted out first, took some. So she had to stay on with an empty glass. When Stephen Kent saw what Candida was doing, he also had his glass refilled.

'Anything exciting planned for the vac?' Roger said. 'I must say compared to my time I think your generation is much more enterprising. We were a frightfully stodgy lot. Any of you crossing Anatolia in an old ambulance?'

No one was doing anything interesting.

'I expect you're going to Venice, aren't you?' Candida said.

Ingestre glanced sharply at her. She seldom took advantage of the family friendship during tutorials, but she was irritated by the sheer limpness of the other two.

'Probably not,' Roger said. 'I was there in the spring and the friends I visit both happen to be coming to London. I don't think you've met them, have you? Clodia and Francesca Oricellari.'

She had not expected as much success in isolating him so easily from the general conversation, but followed it up quickly by esoteric, if hardly intimate, allusions to other people who would mean nothing to Sheila and Kent.

Accordingly, Sheila applied her bosom in Stephen Kent's direction and he responded as nervously as the scampering marmoset. Candida giggled inside. It was really quite unfair. Kent was a big, muscular young man – but so boring.

Roger said he was spending most of the summer in London where he expected to be seeing quite a lot of her parents, both of whom hoped to consolidate the activities of their 'group' during the Parliamentary recess when the politicians were less busy.

'Sounds exciting,' said Candida with calculated irony.

'We live in exciting times,' he said.

'That rather depends on what you mean by excitement,' Candida said.

'Oh well, I'm too old to sleep rough on some Aegean rock, or sniff arcane herbs in Juan les Pins,' Roger said. 'I have to opt for these less rigorous delights.'

'I can't think of anything more boring.'

'Than politics?'

'Oh no, Roger! I didn't mean that. After all, I'm the daughter of my parents. I mean dragging around tavernas and discos with a lot of tatty students.'

She spoke loudly enough for the other two to hear. They were ready to be distracted.

'I find people of my own age so bloody predictable,' Candida said.

'Happily that changes as you get older,' said Ingestre. 'I find my own generation more and more interesting, quite regardless of sex, class or nationality.'

'I'd have thought you found almost everybody interesting, Roger,' Sheila said.

He smiled. Candida stepped in quickly.

'Well, if you're going to be in London with the group I expect we'll see something of each other,' she said.

'Inevitably,' said Ingestre. 'How's Jessica?'

The banal inquiry about her younger sister infuriated Candida. She put her glass down unfinished.

'I understand she's being a nuisance,' she said. 'I think

she's discovered boys. And she has never been discriminating in her enthusiasms.'

'I imagine they will have discovered *her,*' said Ingestre. 'How old is she? Sixteen or so?'

'Just over fifteen,' Candida said.

She thought that there was the hint of a smirk between Sheila and Stephen Kent, cross with herself for showing evident pique. What the hell did *they* know about anything!

'I must go, Roger,' she said. 'I'm going to the theatre and there are a hundred things I have to do first.'

Kent gulped the rest of his sherry. Candida waited for him to glance at his watch and exclaim about the time, so that he could leave with her. Sheila's mind was lumbering around ways of hanging on, but Candida asked her if she was walking back to college. While still holding a hospitable glass, Roger Ingestre was tidying an already orderly desk. They all left. Sheila, as it turned out, had her bike.

They walked through two hot somnolent quads into Radcliffe Square, where there were more people lounging on the steps of the Camera than reading inside. Sheila mounted her bicycle, remained poised long enough to make sure Stephen Kent had a good preview of her crutch and then teetered away.

'Can I walk back with you, Candida?' Stephen Kent said.

'What about your tennis?'

'That doesn't matter. It's important that I talk to you.'

'Aren't you letting them down?'

'It was only a scratch game. Please, let me walk a little way.'

'If you think there's any point.'

As they walked in the direction of All Souls, Candida noticed two sweaty and scruffy characters eyeing her. At least, Stephen Kent had well-kept, freshly washed hair and a strong powerful body which smelt aggressively of soap. It wasn't that she found him physically unattractive: he was just earnest and dull and dogged. He was talking about the tutorial, no doubt hoping she might say something pleasant about his essay. She laughed about the wasp. He went into a customary paean of praise about Roger – his wit, his brilliance, his easy fluency, et cetera. He supposed that if he were a woman, Ingestre was the sort of man he'd find attractive. Not that he was or did, as she knew . . . if she knew what he meant.

The conversation lasted along Parks Road and ran out in front of the Pitt Rivers Museum. Candida let the silence last until he was screwed up to his purpose, which was to ask her to his College Commem Ball the week after term ended. She tried to turn him down as gently as possible, explaining that she had to go down immediately to look after her little sister. At the gate of the Parks, she asked him not to bother to walk further.

Candida walked around the edge of the cricket match rather dreamily. After the protracted sunshine of the last few weeks the grass was a curious beige colour in patches, but the trees were beautiful. Almost guiltily she realised that she had already dismissed Stephen Kent from her mind. For an instant she saw again his good-looking, disappointed face trying to compose itself, and felt sorry. Then she returned to the pleasantly diffuse excitement of how she might exploit a more intimate access to Roger Ingestre in the coming weeks.

*

I suppose that I have to face the fact that I am pretty immature in most ways. Perhaps keeping this journal is itself a symptom of immaturity: but it helps in some way that I can't quite define. There was a lot of talk last year, earnest late-night rubbish most of it, about maturity and I rather fancied myself as emotionally as well as physically more advanced than a lot of the others. But I'm not. And intellectually I come off worst of all. I know so bloody little. It's not that I'm stupider than Michael Lumley, for example: but he has read so much more and he's so much more familiar with ideas, however superficially.

Watkins once asked me, after I left school, whether I found that the education I'd had at Ashbridge Grammar was up to my coevals (as he put it). It was a sneaky way of getting at old Banks, and I saw through it: so I was much too fulsome. In fact, I *can't* compete with the best people from Winchester and Manchester Grammar and Edinburgh Academy and even Eton. They weren't just taught to pass examinations; they were taught to have intellectual curiosity – so that work is a pleasure. It's just finding out more all the time. And this lack of mine is almost entirely intellectual.

Socially it doesn't matter, because I don't care. I suppose I've done some pretty stupid things by trying to be correct when it would have been better just to behave naturally: but no one seems to give a damn nowadays. Ingestre was interesting about this: when he was an undergraduate after the war, and it still did matter. He was very funny about it. He took someone to dinner at a place called the Café de Paris and ordered wine. When the waiter poured some into his glass for him to try, he quietly reproached him for not serving the lady, who said, rather frostily: 'I think he means you to taste it.' Ingestre! I can't imagine him as anything but the confident, fluent, charming character that he is now. Stupidly, I said as much – though not in so many words. He said that he'd come straight up from school, when almost everybody tended to do National Service first, and he went on to describe some related story (I think originally told by Bowra) about the young John Betjeman fascinating a roomful of dons by the originality and eccentricity of his conversation, when he was still a new and relatively obscure under-graduate. Ingestre said that for all the Betjemans and Aldous Huxleys and so on who were able to do this, he thought that the vast majority of undergraduates suffered badly from awe and were content to look intelligent while someone else flaunted his epigrams. I asked him whether he had ever felt that he didn't belong. Never, he said.

Today he was on top form. We've arrived at the War of

17

Austrian Succession and it is one of his pet subjects. I read my essay which I'd put a lot of work into. Ingestre was generous about it, but it wasn't very inspired. Then he took over and he makes the whole thing come instantly alive. Not only Maria Theresa herself – but all the English Whigs: Walpole, Carteret and the Cobham group. (Curiously enough, he obviously much prefers Walpole to Pitt. I've always admired Pitt, but Ingestre doesn't find him amusing enough. Of course, he hasn't said anything quite as unscholarly as that, but I'm sure it's what he thinks.) Anyway, he went on for about an hour, without a note in sight and it was absolutely terrific. He did his usual thing of referring back all the time to the essay he's just heard – so that it might appear that all the good ideas are in some way coming from that, rather than from him. Nobody is fooled. Lumley made notes while I was reading, which is something of a compliment, because he is keen and pretty good himself. Sheila, who was wearing a sort of cotton shirt and nothing underneath it, seemed to be listening when she wasn't flashing her thighs at Ingestre. Candida looked desperately bored, except for one moment when some thoroughly disrespectful wasp stung him on the hand.

He offered us sherry afterwards and she managed to cut Sheila and me out of the conversation for a while by talking about people they both knew and we didn't. It's quite obvious that she fancies him and she'd quite happily leap into bed with him. So would Sheila! But she's a lot more obvious about it and anyway, from all accounts, isn't short of clients. (That is unfair, of course.) Ingestre himself doesn't seem to notice. He certainly does nothing to encourage either of them. In fact, I haven't seen him often with women. He doesn't seem to need them: although the one he brought to the Summer Ball last year was absolutely dazzling. I think someone told me she was a fashion model.

He certainly isn't queer, I should say. And I can usually tell them at quite a distance. I suppose, like everything else, he's got sex in perspective. He's a mature, well-adjusted man who takes his pleasures discreetly and expertly. Nothing in excess: the proper Apollonian.

I asked Candida to come to the Commem with me. She turned me down flat. So I don't suppose I shall go. I know that there are other people I could ask, but I don't really see the point. It's a lot of money and if it's to be any kind of occasion it should be spent with someone who matters. For a moment, I thought I'd ask Sheila – to annoy Candida. She'd come and I'd probably get it. But it would be childish and not really very fair to her, however easy she is.

I wonder what it is. I know bloody well that I'm not physically repulsive. Not to any other women. So why should I be to Candida? So it must be that I've overplayed my hand. I should *not* have told her that I love her. I suppose it's pathetic and she's much too sophisticated for anything like that. But, for God's sake, people do still fall in love and they do admit it. The trouble is that she meets so many clever, interesting, worldly people in that group of her parents that Ingestre belongs to, that I must seem very dull and ingenuous. She obviously wants the mature, sardonic type. And I think she does actually want him. I know that I've written in this that I thought she was frigid. Whenever I've kissed her – or whenever she's let herself be kissed – she's been tense and if she's touched me it's been more with restraint than anything remotely . . . even affectionate; fingertips against me ready to push me gently away as soon as it was polite. And since I've told her how I feel about her, not even that! Yet I've watched her looking at him and there is something speculative and, more than that, something lascivious in her eyes. I wonder if his indifference hurts her as much.

And my God she is so lovely! Today she was wearing a black silk shirt and a green skirt. So what with that wonderful red hair and those bright eyes, she was a bloody vision! I'm well past the 'pure' phase, too. She leaned forward at one point today when we were drinking sherry and I saw inside her blouse. She was wearing a little scrap of a lace bra and by Christ they were beautiful. I think of taking her clothes

19

off and some of the things I want to do to her and it's like a instant thump in the guts from a hammer. I don't think I've ever had fantasies about anyone else. Well, I'd better grow out of it, because I'm never going to get anywhere. And as much as I'd sometimes like to hurt her and violate her, I couldn't do anything like that. I'll try after next week's session with Ingestre to make some arrangement to see her in London in the vac, since I've got the job in a pub. Dad isn't too pleased about that.

If Ingestre's going to be in London, perhaps I can set up something through him. He'd see straight through it, probably; but I don't think he'd mind. I think he quite likes me and he's obviously not interested himself.

Jim Petheridge and Alec were annoyed about playing tennis: but fortunately Clegg didn't want to play so my failing to turn up didn't matter all that much. They wanted me to go on the piss with them after Hall, but I didn't feel like it. If I went drinking every time I felt miserable about Candida, I'd be on the way to being an alcoholic by now. I read a book by Waddington on the Seven Years War but I found it hard going. I don't think it was the book: it was me. Dad and his pals seem to think that students today are at it all the time like knives. If only they knew!

*

Blakemore refuses to understand Walpole. I suspect that this is a patrician affectation. He elaborates with all his icy wit on the theme that subtlety in public life is heinous and that the practical in politics is, *sub specie aeternitatis*, never truly efficacious. New College port is excellent, however. I define the nature of his affectation as: a Refusal to Mourn the Death by Pragmatism of Democracy in London. Blakemore smiles with thin lips. He digresses about Domitian's reign of terror. What has this to do with our own dear home-life? Consensus politics and the ensuing parliamentary farce will be destroyed, Blakemore prophesies, by the growing cynicism of the public in the face of immoral public subtlety. A brief spell of patrician power before subsequent and successive periods of misrule is now no longer possible: because there are no patricians, and those who remain are not true to their principles. There must follow chaos, in which men of honour, such as Blakemore, must do what they can. He half believes it.

Prompted by the information that Clodia is to arrive from Venice, he categorises the Highgate Group in terms of Machiavelli's circle. It appears that I, of all people, am cast as the phantom Machiavelli; Farrell (whom he loathes) is Guicciardini and Jeremy Taylor is Giulio de' Medici. Quite absurd but rather funny.

Lovely evening. Something of a breeze at last. Moon almost full. It all looks very pretty. Nice sweetness in the air. Not before time. Thank God, I'm not involved in Schools this year.

I rather think that Candida is giving poor Steve Kent a rough time. Pity. Because he is a nice lad and I should have thought very attractive to women. Candida has, in fact, the makings of a pretty fair bitch. At the same time, she is unquestioningly pretty. She is also clever. Cleverer than poor Kent, alas. And she is lazy; but she gets away with it. I think perhaps I'm a little too severe with her. Not absolutely sure it's not because I'm sorry for Kent and think she might tip him over. He seems balanced enough, but I've seen it happen before. He'd be better off with Sheila Grishkin who is the warm type and rather sweet. Lumley is probably homosexual. But bright.

Odd that Candida should have turned out quite like that.

Barbara, underneath the tough efficiency, is really rather a pussycat. And Jessica is a charming child. Still, mustn't be too harsh. Being young is always difficult. And she has all the impedimenta of the Highgates; and Jessica breathing down her neck. Candida wants to compete, but without effort.

And it can't be done. Perhaps I should talk to her. She really isn't turning into a nice young woman. . . .

Curious confession upon the Paddington train, occasioned by a fairly – no, extremely – pretty air-hostess, who got off at Reading. Smartly uniformed and perfectly *maquillée*. A traveller, not obviously drunk, leaned forward and confided an irresistible urge to grope (as he put it) air-hostesses. 'Those tight skirts hoisting up at just the right height,' said he, 'as they brace themselves to fiddle about in them lockers.' At which point, he made an expressive sort of sound.

I know exactly what he means and for the best part of the day have intermittently returned to his unlikely, sinful and wildly pleasant sensation of groping (complaisant!) air-hostesses as they go about their duties. Very silly.

The Highgates seem depressed by the smooth accession of Callaghan and the fact that the Labour lake is still wonderfully unruffled. But Highgate depression never lasts very long: they are all indefatigable optimists. I'm sure that Simon Farrell and Jeremy Taylor really do believe that they will become an unofficial All Souls to some future administration, or at the very worst a *fin de siècle* Cliveden. A good but non-committal sprinkling of honourable members, including the splendid Rachel Bailey, who seemed more worried about the unpleasantness below-stairs caused by Wilson's retirement honours list, as and when it appears, than by any likely rift over spending cuts. This rather surprises me: it is obviously trivial. She gives very little away but I think there is some conflict between her essential loyalty and her fears about the really wild bunch on the far left. After all Jenkins did not get the FO and Mrs Shirley W. (though it is said she is being groomed for the big time) didn't do as well as many hoped she might. The government has a homely tinge. Is it just a holding operation? How can it be? It's been a decade of hand-to-mouth politics: but perhaps all politics is hand-to-mouth. Discuss. So there is reason for Highgate depression and Blakemore's patrician woe.

Dimchurch is convinced that I am an irretrievable philistine because nothing bores me more than the history of cricket. Since he knows that I am quite fanatical about the modern game and an historian by profession, he finds this inexcusable. And I have to admit the attitude is unscholarly. Well, I didn't see Hobbs and Hendren and Woolley and I saw Bradman only in 1948. But that was good: so why should I begrudge an old clergyman his run stealers flickering to and fro. It's not that I am consistent: I think I remember an article by Philip Toynbee in which he said that he found more to interest him in minor writers of his own time than all but the very great writers of the past. Something of the sort. There I part company. I'm not sure that I've ever grown up. I am very much looking forward to Lord's on Saturday. Term over and the Lord's Test. . . . What more could the heart desire?

Francesca Oricellari is really quite stunning. I mean this objectively: but only in a way objectively. No one of any reasonable sexual persuasion could not want or, indeed, imagine the possession of such an exquisitely made woman. And she can only be about twenty-six or -seven. She enters even the most scruffy little bar with a kind of shining beauty and an elegance that immediately lifts it out of recognition. This convenient place is near the BBC and in the middle of the appropriately described 'rag-trade': it is regrettably full of young men with emblazoned brief-cases, obviously to do with 'pop', seriously dilapidated fashion mongers and a Juvenalian farrago of indeterminate function and sex. In all this there is Francesca in black and white. Unlike Clodia she charms and soothes and enlightens without actually speaking. Clodia has always said that her sister is a business woman first and a female later: so here she is, not in Bond Street, where one imagines she belongs, but in Langham Street, where there are (no doubt) bargains. I don't suppose I shall remember a word we say.

I am not sure that commitment is desirable, let alone necessary. Nor am I prepared to believe that the collapse of liberal democracy is all that imminent. Difficult though it may sometimes be to admit, we are still a more tolerant society than most. What worries me about the Highgates though is that they are not realistic.

At the same time they are sincere. At least Taylor and Barbara and one or two of the non-politicians in the group are. I suspect that Rachel, Hay, Connors and the other MPs are in it for what they can get out of it. At the same time we all believe that there is no alternative to civilised consensus politics with the broadest possible base.

Most of our problems seem to me to be capable of rational resolution, given a sufficiently flexible and diverse coalition – not of interests but of conscience. Blakemore may well be right and we are all Jacks-a-dreams: but we have to give it a go. Of course, however much whispered encouragement they may offer behind the arrases of power, none of the really big guns are going to support us publicly – so it is, as Taylor understands, a matter of the discreet exercise of influence.

*

Darling Olliphant,

We are sitting up late again because the Tories are keeping up their non-co-operation cabaret and are forcing a vote on a compulsory purchase order in Wales. They're also mucking up the Conference of Labour women that starts tomorrow and some of the arrangements have had to be changed – so that our party Mahomets can go to them and high-tail it back here in time to vote. Come to think of it, it's so hot at the moment they might quite properly travel by camel! Officially it's all chassis and confusion (and, in fact, must be

24

wearing for the old and halt – of whom we have more than they do at the moment); but at least I'm able to snatch a few moments to write properly to you.

Life, I am happy to report, is as boring as ever without you: but at least the experience of the International Women last year at Crapville-sur-Montagne was a glimpse of Hell itself and this is only Limbo. I suppose it is hardly fair but this leads me inevitably to Jeremy Taylor and his ginger group who seem to be the most prominent bunch wandering about in it, waving banners with indecipherable devices. We had a very good buffet supper at Highgate on Sunday. You would have loved the food and the wine, but I think the rest of the proceedings would have irritated you. Personae on view were Jeremy and Barbara; Roger Ingestre up from Oxford for the occasion, where he apparently teaches the elder Taylor girl; Jason Hay; Mears from the Environment, doing crossword puzzles all the time; Marie White in a sari; Tony Connors and Simon Farrell among others. I counted about a dozen MPs, all backbenchers. No Liberals: but I suppose they're preoccupied by the Punch and Judy show that has followed J. Thorpe's resignation.

The purpose of it all was to expand the group in the event of the forthcoming realignment of the centre: which Jeremy Taylor confidently predicts after the next cuts have scythed off, in passing, most of our left wing and the Tories have failed to take advantage of it – with Heath still sulking in his tent below the gangway. This is not the way I read it at all; but Bill Delahaye (the Once and Sometime Novelist) gave us a furrowed analysis of the situation. It went: cuts and uneasy rumblings until the recess, but frightful lightnings at the party conference; a new economic crisis in the autumn, more borrowing with IMF inspectors laying down the law. This will bring about the fall of the government and we shall do badly at the next election losing quite a lot of seats on our wing of the party. More, proportionally, than the Tribunites. The Tories will gain, especially from the Liberals, but so will the Scots Nats. And while the Tories will have a working majority, it will be by no means thumping. Nevertheless an upturn in the economy (as things improve) will mean another election pretty soon and this time they will trounce us. Thereupon the collapse of stout party, with the left getting really way out under W-Batman, and responsible opposition to a really reactionary Tory administration devolving (sorry it slipped out) upon a responsible centrist alliance drawing its membership from the Social Democratic wing of our party, the Liberals, the mavericks and the left of the Tory party. (What left? Apart from Jason Hay and three other possibles.) Roger Ingestre came in on cue and said something very neat about a coalition based less upon interests than conscience.

Well, as you can imagine, most of us were pretty guarded (for various motives) in our response. For my part, I thought that Bill Delahaye's analysis was just about feasible, but pretty unlikely. The only credible leader of a centrist union would be Roy Jenkins and the rumours are that he will become president of the European Commission and quit British politics, which will be a pity. At the same time, unless the scenario is in some way speeded up, these evolutions of Bill's would take two or three years and, in that time, there are enough skilful manipulators around to ensure the maintenance of chaos. It is all wishful thinking. The most unequivocal in support, from the MPs, were Connors and Jason Hay. I'm rather surprised at Connors: and what his motives are only God and he know. Jason Hay is a sort of resident Guy Fawkes in the Tory party and is constantly being searched for barrels whenever he goes anywhere near Central Office.

Barbara then, at her briskest and most efficient, took over and described how their little group had been meeting, as we all knew, over the years to discuss issues which were vital to the survival of a liberal democracy as we understand it. They were now proposing to subdivide into more specialised units, each to be concerned with a particular topic; for example, an economics unit with herself, Simon Farrell, me,

Fred Carey from the *FT*, and two people from Nuffield. There would be another group on welfare services, foreign policy, Europe, environment, law and order, and so on. Nothing was said about immigration or Ireland, by the way. The findings of these groups would be published, by Jeremy of course, in pamphlet form and would be intended to catalyse thinking on all these vital issues, while at the same time generating support for the ideas of the moderate centre in British politics. Someone grumbled that there were too many people producing too many reports, policy documents, surveys and forecasts already. Ingestre pointed out quickly that these were virtually all servants of sectional interests, or else were, by constitution, so politically neutral that they hardly represented a point of view at all. They merely interpreted what had happened in the light of what might be about to happen.

Now you understand why I think you would have been irritated. I don't think you'll approve, but I think I shall actually decide to participate in this particular folk-dance. I've thought about it and I can't see that it will do any harm. It may also do some good. We both know perfectly well where I stand and it is certainly on the right of the party: so that *if* there were re-alignment on the lines that Taverne and Levin were writing about a year or so ago, that is where I should re-align. Most of the other MPs, I might add, seem to be taking a similar line, with Connors and Hay openly enthusiastic. The idea is obviously to use us in the hope of catching bigger cod inside the limit: but I don't see why we shouldn't use them.

I've probably been going on a bit, haven't I? After all these intense proceedings, there was a certain amount of slightly self-conscious jollity, as though we had been asked to the party for ourselves and not for our harps. I think I am Ingestre's assignment, because he homed in like a bat out of Madame Tussaud's. And asked me to lunch.

We went to The Gay Hussar and Victor chose our lunch in the most persuasive way. Ingestre seemed inclined to laugh at the earnestness of the whole Highgate endeavour: but I think he's probably a lot more committed than he lets on. We talked most of the time about the presidency and the position of 'Jimmy Carter as the Supreme Example of the Letter C'. Ingestre improvised a Wallace Stevens sort of poem, which, in so far as I could tell, was very good. It was certainly very funny. Then we were briefly joined by a gossip writer from one of the Sundays, called Simeon Pike, who asked us if we had anything on the most recent rumours of a homosexual scandal. Ingestre, who didn't know him, was almost discomposed in an evident, Oxford way – though quite interested when it was obvious Pike meant someone in the Labour Party. I've heard nothing and told Pike it was probably a cloud no bigger than a man's arse. He giggled and went away. Ingestre enjoyed it.

So, I must admit, did I: the lunch I mean. He is a pleasant man who accepts that a married woman, even in politics, doesn't want to slip between illicit sheets at the first opportunity. He was attentive without the slightest hint of lechery. It seems, furthermore, that he is expecting an Italian friend called Clodia Oricellari, who is a sort of diplomat, to be in London for the next few months. So I've promised that we will have dinner with them. I am enchanted by the name! Perhaps we'll all sit around reading *Mandragola* with the most shocking consequences.

I was delighted by your description of Cyril Bruckner and the Reichians. It is not fair. Don't you think that people like Cyril should be issued with little brochures about the dangers of international conferences? I'm glad you miss me, because I miss you. I know that we don't see anything like enough of each other when we're both in the same place, but I hate it when we don't have even the opportunity of wasting our lives together. And I love you most foolishly. Things must be quite lively over there in election year. Surely they aren't going to go for Carter, are they? I've been hoping in a sentimental way for the reincarnation of Hubert Humphrey, or at least for Ed Brown – whom I know nothing about.

Please tell me what the low-down is. International doctors seem to know all the best gossip. And there must be some gossip! Or is the place sanitised beyond all reasonable hope after Watershed?

I hope you will notice that this is an inordinately long letter and – BANG. There goes the division bell. I love you, Olliphant. Take care of yourself. I'm going to Ashbridge at the weekend to see to whatever there is to see to and take my surgery, but I'll be home on Sunday evening. Only another ten days. The weather is dreadfully hot, by the way, so you'll miss the air-conditioning. I'll do my best to distract you.

Love, love, love,

R.

*

The proper lot of intellectuals is misery, which as the American professor shrewdly points out, is of interest to artists, critics and precious few others. We can't complain that we are being underpaid any more: most of us earn more in a year than a jockey's bonus. . . . At least I hope we do. (Come to think of it I don't know how much a jockey's bonus would be. Must ask Mears: it must be a staple of crossword puzzles.) Look at us, Hyperions and satyrs and all, poets, teachers, historians, lawyers, tribunes and consuls. Fit to adorn a seventh satire. And a suitable lack of philosophers, scientists, painters, sculptors – and all the other Greeks. (Mears is a philosopher turned hyper-civil servitor; and Middleton is a scientist turned pigman: so they are absolved.)

Philosophy in the Environment? What nonsense! There's far more in heaven and earth, far more!

Since we may not perish from inanition in spite of our high-mindedness, we must seek other means of being miserable. First, we cultivate conscience and having cultivated consciences we must reconcile them with self-interest.

Statius doesn't actually *mind* writing for telly, as long as everyone knows he is a serious novelist at the core. Quintilian rather enjoys his lucrative practice as long as everyone knows he's really an academic. And H. Wilson, KG, has found his niche as an expositor on the commercial waves (which is what he always wanted!) and will in due course take up as much time as the Olympic Games are about to: but not yet, Lord, not yet! So, after the cultivation of these insatiable, man-eating consciences from outer space that must devour us, we follow the triumph up by breeding another killer microbe: *we are none of us famous enough*. Yet. And the old clock's running down. While senators are turning into professors and professors into senators, I for one would not mind a chair in exile if it followed a liaison with a Vestal Virgin. (Candida Taylor would do.) Kindly note, Fortune. Other miseries: the great-hearted British public resents our noblesse and wants to go on living its cliché undisturbed. (So that revolution is inevitable in the long run.) We are no longer Great: so nobody seems to care whether we have top quality noblesse or not. You cannot buy it at Harrods, Heal's or the Army and Navy. There are too many tourists, especially Arabs, in the flower of cities all. (The area between Portland Place and Marylebone High Street is like the Qattara Depression in Wakes Week. Nevertheless this makes a rubaiyat outside a pub in New Cavendish Street salvingly appropriate.) New further miseries will be dealt with and discussed as they occur. Just thought of one. Women in public life and in their emancipated state generally.

But first, what about conscience. Let us look into aspects of Conscience, which Ingestre declares is our signal advantage over butterflies and badgers. (Thoughts about Ingestre to follow, I've no doubt. Why is consecutive thought such a problem for some of us?) The first problem relating to conscience is that it is necessary to any responsible political animal. It is *verboten* to live for the hour and one's own pleasures; it is *verbindlich* to brood upon the lot of one's fellow man, regardless of the spiritual expense (aha, hypocrite lecturer), especially those less well-endowed in any respect. And whereas self-interest is the critical juice of the hegemonies of far right and far left, conscience is the ichor of the moderate. Call Jeremy Taylor. Jeremy Taylor . . . Jeremy Taylor. . . .

You are Jeremy Taylor? Jeremy Macaulay Trevelyan Taylor, forty-eight, Managing Director, Rameses Goss & Co, publishers. Connoisseur, gourmet, bibliophile: with a delightful house in Highgate, an attractive and mature wife, two very pretty daughters. (Still harping on my daughters!) Successful and dynamic. But cursed with conscience that makes out of his natural conservative landscape a no-man's-land of radical ravagery. Oh, the cruel irony to be born an instinctive Tory in a family of Whigs. And to marry into a radical tradition. M/s Barbara Dunn (alias Mrs J. Taylor), fair Fabiola of a Fabian gens, motivated by the same tiresome conviction that to deserve is to serve. And without service, there shall be no pudding: because the proof of the pudding is in the meeting: the meeting of minds that will make of us one nation. Well, it's not a bad delusion. And I suppose Mears, Trumble and Rachel Bailey are all subscribers. Mrs Bailey has a conscience and a dazzling left hook to back it up. Sock! Pity. Married to that intense hillock of nervous vulcanicity always on the point of eruption. Can't understand it. But there aren't all that many like her in the House, certainly not of our generation. The inescapable deadly sin of politicians is Vanity. And the twin monster children of Vanity are Ambition and Self-Interest. I admit it. But when I see conscience in others, I begin to have a conscience about having so little myself. So it is natural, in such cases, to seek around for supporting evidence that this is the usual human condition. Evidence is not lacking.

Ingestre. Playing an endless master-game, defining other people's terms and watching them wriggle with pleasure or pain quite impartially. And yet. . . . Did Daphne hurt him so badly? Rampant cow and her sister a supine bitch. Alas, poor Ingestre, we have the bond of our broken marriages to the Stymphalian birds and we have both reacted predictably. You are as amoral as I am: fashionable, likable don, dropping names there, ideas here: believing what? In the validity of changing opinions. The liberal fallacy in its most advanced and terminal stage. Marie: still wanting to be a political hostess but too eager for the Tory gentledregs and too rich for the smartyarses of the living left and too quickly in bed, but oh what delicacy of touch, strictly non-party. In it for what she can get. Unkind! What she can give. Soft-spoken Simon Farrell, elfin eyes and teeth out of Enid Blyton, padding his sharp-eared way along the passages, chef of a kitchen cabinet specialising in the sauce which makes what is hard to swallow appetising. His sideways look. We are all waiters cooking flambées at the table to him: flash and presentation. No real skill. Mists of eminence.

Whoop! What a superb . . . Oh, for Christ's sake, Anthony, take yourself in hand. You don't mean that! Poofff. Women with bodies like that should not be allowed to wear such dresses. I worry about you. A plain brown silky thing and. . . . Now I have spots before my eyes.

Conscience. So. The Taylor tandem looking sweet and relatively stylish. Who else? Rachel. Surely. If she joins. But her conscience will militate against and what has she to lose but her virtue. Well, we know about that already! Most of them are in it for what we can get, not just Marie. Not just, for that matter, me. If I don't make it part of the way in this administration, then I am lost in the snowy wastes. Safe seat, bollox! Because next time. . . . Next time! If we get back at all, the Yahoos will be in the treetops.

If Apollo goes to Europe and Athene decides she's sick of it and dear old Hephaestos is tiring, it leaves only big Zeus to fend off the wild and wily alien gods. And there will be no apotheosis for Anthony. The liberal conscience, ladies and gentlemen, is no match for the revolutionary or reactionary conscience. A reactionary conscience? Discuss. Thank you, your eminence.

The revolutionary and reactionary conscience knows what it wants, knows how it proposes to get it and knows exactly how intolerant and (if necessary) ruthless it intends to be. The liberal conscience must *by definition* allow everyone to have their say, even the wildest of ethical hooligans: so it is always vulnerable to demagoguery and the profanum vulgum tearing up the terraces when their team does badly. Must then the liberal conscience be inevitably stifled; or go into a state of catatonic hysteria in which it does not feel electric shocks or branding irons? Not necessarily. What we need (identification for purposes of argument and convenience) is organisation of available intelligence and ability and resources and the humanely ruthless deployment of all these things, backed up by absolutely perfect PR. These are the facts. I daresay Ingestre could dress them up more politely. Taylor's been astute enough to get the communicators in. Trumble, Delahaye, Fulford, Sandra Beeton. . . . (That's a thought! Nice legs and not averse to flashing them.) Imagine Delahaye writing a comic novel about me. What was it? *The Dazzling Pilgrimage of Augustine Cornflour*. Anyway, I hope it's funnier than those solemn lamentations of the fifties. I don't mind being sent up, as long as I have my share of the good lines.

But we all (tolerance again rears its Gorgon head) have our hypocrisies. The centre-left is our unceasing commitment to the masses, whom most of us are quite happy to serve and whom most of us despise. Some people after all have in them the stuff of saints. Taylor is good at heart, so is Barbara. So, blast her newest knickers, is Rachel. And what? Half a dozen honourable members that the peak-viewing public has heard of? And a few more civil servants, And a few more probonopublicos in the Lords.

I look up from my premature Transylvanian grave at the bovine peasantry watching in sullen triumph above my elegant catafalque as the possessed puritan plunges the left-handed stake into my liberal rib-cage. And they line up their mallets.

Oh fuck it. I reserve my rights. I care enough for it to matter. I work for my electors. And I believe in things. Europe. The Alliance. Détente. Too much is over-simplified: the quality of news is bad not in content but in presentation: too many slick young men who can't speak the language and who cannot therefore think. What I really cannot accept is a cliché culture in which there are shorthand paradigms. Does this make me a bad democrat? Does it buggery! And the Third World will have to wait until I've sorted out my soul in this one and the next.

So. Time to go home. 'Come on, Teddy.' Jim has said he won't fix it. And that's accurate enough. The Shipbuilding and Aircraft Nationalisation Bill hath murdered sleep; but who needs it? Life, liberty and the pursuit of some enthusiastic woman who has already proved all she wants. Tomorrow the ecstatic struggle. Today the bloody Land Tax Bill. Pick up tha musket, Tribune.

*

The Dazzling Pilgrimage of Augustine Cornflour

When the Right Hon. Warrington Stokes, MP, in the middle of an otherwise undistinguished morning, announced his intention of retiring from the high office which he had adorned (with one quite short and generally regretted interlude) since 1964, some hearts fluttered, some minds missed a beat and many gazes focused in mid-clause upon a *néant* abruptly yawning outside their office windows which seemed to be impenetrable.

In an age when the counting of heads and the ensuing categorisation of taste, proclivity and utility has been dignified into an academic pursuit thought often to be examinable, the assiduous social scientist would (in time) be able to isolate and classify each separate aberration. The social historian, accustomed to a more modest canvas, is obliged to consider in this instance only those female hearts that jumped, murmured and became enchanted on behalf of Augustine Cornflour, whose career could not fail to take

34

an imminent turn for the better. They were not few: for Augustine's virtues of persuasion and tenacity had been extended generously in recent years to cover the emancipated and demure alike in the cities of London and Westminster, where he resided; in his constituency of Sprake East, which he visited; and indeed further afield, where he gladly travelled. For some years Augustine Cornflour had savoured of caviar in a baked-beans administration: not admittedly the best spawn of the Volga sturgeon, but then the baked-beans were themselves of cut-price supermarket pedigree.

Augustine heard the news himself while travelling earthwards in a lift at Broadcasting House. He had been fixing with grey-eyed irony a dainty young woman in evident high spirits and a close-fitting floral dress. At an interim stop there entered a bald producer. Augustine had wide experience of producers, knew them to be a rotten sort of fellow and was able to spot them instantly.

'Have you heard, Roddy?' said the bright-eyed young woman.

'What?'

'Warrington's resigned.'

'Fuck off!'

'True.'

'Go on! It's balls. Say it's balls. There wasn't a glimmer.'

'Listen to the headlines at twelve o'clock.'

The floral nymph left the lift at the important third floor. Augustine was obliged to travel the remaining distance with the young man who, after brief and obscene self-communion, proceeded to examine an evidently unhealthy tongue in a mirror, no doubt provided for just such a purpose. Augustine's distaste was occluded by the moment of what he had just heard. His heart was not given to fluttering or his mind to missing beats and he was a year or so away from the mid-life crisis in which any kind of *néant* gaped suddenly before him. He felt, nevertheless, cheated, Here was he, an MP of the governing party, hearing such portentous news in a mere public elevator. And not even at Television Centre! He was grateful for the mercy, however small, that he had not been recognised, as was clear from the demeanour of the bald producer, who disposed of his off-white tongue and stepped in front of Augustine to leave the lift.

Augustine Cornflour was a fastidious realist. Many members of his party viewed his fastidiousness – expressed in matters of dress, wine, choice of food, preferences in the arts – with some suspicion: but they respected his realism, his cinemascopic pragmatism. The various women who were experiencing mild agitation on his account much appreciated the same fastidiousness; but were less convinced about the virtues of realism, which some of them had tested.

Leaving the self-styled Temple of Arts and Muses, Augustine hailed a taxi at the rank situated in the wide debouchement of Portland Place. The driver saw fit, albeit recalcitrantly, to respond and the machine crawled courteously across the line of traffic towards him.

'House of Commons,' said Augustine.

'Parliament Square?' said the driver.

Augustine remembered, in time, his guise as a man of the people. And feigned laughter.

'Alas, alas!' he said.

He entered the cab, sighing as the driver ominously slid back the glass partition intended, surely, to separate him from his clients.

'You an MP, then mate?' said the taxi-man.

Augustine confessed that he was: and submitted to the inevitable treatise on social, political and economic matters, delivered with all the wit, wisdom and compassion (especially in such areas as immigration and welfare) for which taxi-drivers are renowned. In the time it took for Augustine to achieve the accolade of 'Guvnor', which seemed several hours, they reached his appointed destination.

Rubicon Tweed, whose father had been an apologist for the Julian and Augustan epochs in Roman history and who had died a disappointed man, sucked his pipe and thought about lunch. His buzzer buzzed.

'Tweed,' he said.

'It's your wife, sir.'

'Oh, of course. Sorry, Primula. Put her on, will you?'

'Darling?'

'Hello, darling.'

'Darling, guess what?'

'Tamburlaine has mumps. No. Sorry, darling. It's good news. I can tell from the inflection.'

'Warrington Stokes has resigned.'

'Is this authenticated?'

'It was on the news.'

'The "World at One"?'

'Hardly, darling. It's only half past twelve.'

'Sorry, darling. Darling, this is terrific news. It's what we've been waiting for. Can you get hold of Anaximander Split? I'll ring around a few of the ministries.'

'Well, I can try Dahlia Dackord. . . .'

'What's it got to do with her?'

'Oh, darling, you are dim! She's been having it away for weeks with Naxy Split.'

'What happened to Dackord?'

'I don't think he did.'

'Did what?'

'Oh darling!'

'Sorry, sweet. But terrific! There is a tide and so on. We must take it on the rise. Get Anaximander Split around tonight if you can; and from this moment – on!'

'Oh Rube, darling! I thought you'd be excited.'

'I am. There's only one thing that bothers me. . . .'

'Oh darling! What?'

'Why didn't anyone tell me?'

'Oh nonsense. I suppose with the Budget coming up and so on, everyone knew you'd be terribly busy counting.'

Gina Gutteridge unwrapped an exclusive package and held up the contents.

'Do you think these will turn him on?' she asked.

Mrs Naomi de Wagram enveloped herself in a screen of dense Caporal smoke in the hope that it would obscure the hectic light that must have flashed in her eyes, thick-lensed spectacles or not; but she was unable to control a sort of spasm of her thighs and so shifted position on the divan.

'From what I hear,' she said drily, 'turning him on is not exactly the problem.'

'No,' said Gina. 'But he does so like being teased. And this is perfect. It's very fine. Almost like silk. And there's absolutely no way of getting in. Feel.'

'No, thank you, darling,' said Mrs de Wagram in a somewhat shaky voice.

'It'll drive him absolutely crazy,' said Gina delightedly. 'Round the bend.'

Once again Mrs de Wagram marvelled at the meaningful coincidence that had brought her and this succulent little slut together. The sheer good fortune was almost incredible to anyone who was not of Mrs de Wagram's persuasion in metaphysics. Into her landlady's bosom had been delivered a totally amoral sensual secretary at Transport House, who had already enslaved an up-and-coming backbencher.

As she busied herself putting away her latest *frou-frous* in already well-stocked drawers, Mrs de Wagram straightened up and glanced at the evening paper which Gina had thrown idly down. The headline announced the resignation of the Prime Minister.

'My God, Gina!' said Mrs de Wagram. 'Stokes has quit.'

'Oh that!' said Gina. 'It's going to be a madhouse down there now. They say the field's wide open.'

'Don't you realise, child, that it may mean Augustine's star is already in the ascendant. You may not have to move on.'

'Oh?' said Gina, sounding perhaps a little disappointed. Gina unzipped her skirt and slipped it down over her lovely round hips before stepping gracefully out of it. Mrs de Wagram sat bolt upright and lowered her eyes to her own pelvic girdle, plump but strong and almost perceptibly quivering.

'Oooh, Naomi,' said Gina mischievously. 'I can see right up your skirt. Suppose I was Mr Wynstanley!'

Mrs de Wagram put one hand between her thighs and squeezed.

'Gina, *please*,' she said between clenched teeth. 'I have a seance at six-fifteen and I must remain *very* calm.'

Yet again in the course of one of the most delightful days of his long and extremely successful political life, the Right Hon. Warrington Stokes, MP, doubled up in irresistible laughter. The cat was among the pigeons, right enough. The fox was in the hen-roost. The sheep and the goats were standing up to be counted. And, he chuckled happily, the wolf was further than ever away from the door.

In his meticulously ordered office, exquisitely laid out and furnished, though without luxury or ostentation, Anaximander Split looked stonily at his reflection in a polished black marble cigarette box. One of the most powerful directors of the Merchant Bank, Furgusson Jungfrau, the real source of Anaximander Split's enormous influence in and out of the City, was in his huge range of contacts. His distant and aristocratic manner enabled him to effect the most useful introductions with discretion and effortless good taste. The only commission he charged was goodwill: but early intelligence of what was in the wind and the occasional handsome present enabled him to live in the manner that he chose to (away from the office), as a nineteenth-century gentleman. He had recently contrived an alliance with a girl he had known during a refugee adolescence in Paris, whose rather vulgar manner was less relevant than her circle of smart friends and her encyclopedic knowledge of fashionable gossip.

She arrived wearing an unsuitable hat.

'What is all this about?' he said pleasantly.

'I'm not sure that I know, Anaximander,' said Dahlia Dackord, who always projected when she spoke. 'But Ruth Tweed rang to ask me around for drinks and would I bring you, because Rubicon Tweed wants to talk to you urgently.'

'I know Rubicon Tweed. Why couldn't he ring me here?'

'I think that's rather the crux of it, Anaximander. I think it must be frightfully hush-hush and awfully under the rosebush. I think he wants you to meet without your actually being seen to be meeting, if you know what I mean.'

'I think I do.'

'After all, Anaximander, he's something frightfully important at the Treasury, isn't he?'

'He holds a very senior position in Her Majesty's Civil Service.'

'I wonder what he can want.'

'I have no idea. Perhaps we'd better go.'

Anaximander pressed a green button which would mean that the Mercedes he used for driving about in London would arrive outside Furgusson Jungfrau within three minutes. He had a fair idea what Rubicon Tweed might want and beneath his habitually icy calm, he was almost desperately excited by the fertilised cell of an idea. Vast as his spectrum of influence was, Anaximander Split never had succeeded in penetrating deeply the inner labyrinths of politics and government: his opportunities for exercising persuasion were superficial. Now, with the shock retirement of Warrington Stokes, a wily but incorruptible moderate, he saw his chance. And the prospect filled him with the rhapsodic sense of a grand conception. Unlike his father, Wladislaw Split, who was vociferously and obstinately Marxist in all his utterances and opinions (while continuing to enjoy the fruits of his son's financial acumen), Anaximander maintained a conservatism that was entirely in keeping with his nineteenth-century gentility. It would have come as a great surprise to old Wladislaw to know that his only and admired son was in fact an irretrievable Communist and a very important member of the KGB.

Josephine Cornflour got off the train at Paddington and was surprised to hear her name being called over the public address system. She found her way to the relevant office where she had been requested to present herself, rather worried that something must have happened to her uncle, Augustine, the Member of Parliament.

Josephine was not desperately interested in politics, as it happened, and so was blissfully unaware of the momentous events of the day and the seismic upheaval that had followed them along the various faults in the governing party's crust. She had expected her uncle to meet her and was disappointed that he hadn't. Various kind railwaymen explained that he had been overtaken by very urgent business and would she take a taxi. Since Josephine was an unusually pretty girl, the railwaymen escorted her to one in a sort of posse. She was delighted with them.

She wondered what her uncle would make of her after all these years. She remembered him as a handsome, rather roguish person when she had been little: but she supposed that his responsibilities and the dignity of his position as Member of Parliament for Sprake East must have made him a lot more serious-minded.

*

'I understand, Signorina, that you are here on what is known as a diplomatic mission,' said Alan Trumble.

'And I think, Mr Trumble, that you are taking what is known as the piss,' said Clodia Oricellari. 'Can we use first names?'

'A pleasure.'

'Mutual, I'm sure. The truth is that I am a very glorified

41

secretary, about to enjoy herself in the most civilised of cities.'

'I thought that was Paris. Last of the human . . .'

'For an Irish writer in the twenties. Not for a struggling diplomatist, and an Italian lost in the EEC at that. No. Nothing human.'

'Are you, by some happy chance, Francophobe?'

'If you promise never to reveal the source: Yes.'

'You have an empty glass.'

'Roger is heading this way with a bottle. I like what you do for the *International Tribune*. If I may say so.'

'I am flattered.'

'You're refreshingly acid.'

'Not since I had the operation, I'm afraid. Before that I was corrosive. . . . Thank you, Roger. This is especially sparkling wine.'

'I hope so. . . . Clodia, this is Simon Farrell, an economist who runs a museum, albeit a very good one. I'm quite sure that Alan will explain.'

'Why should an economist run a museum, indeed?' said Alan Trumble. 'I think Roger may have left matters in doubt: Simon is a good economist and it is a good museum.'

'Quite a small one,' said Simon Farrell.

'For all that,' said Trumble, 'he deserted a discipline which lacks the security of evidence for one that relies on it. An intellectual symptom of our times, don't you agree?'

'He talks a lot,' said Simon Farrell. 'Meaning no harm. Terrible problem in most political pundits: they don't know what is deduction and how much is inference. Sorry, I am going too fast, perhaps, am I? . . .'

'I doubt it,' said Alan Trumble. 'Your problem is one of old-fashioned liberal honesty. . . .'

'Simon!'

'Francesca,' said Simon Farrell, 'how delightful!'

'The rocks from Wales?' said Francesca. 'You got them?'

'That line is either Mosaic or Mafiosa,' said Clodia. 'What rocks, little sister?'

'Inscribed stones,' said Simon Farrell. 'A new site in Gwent. Francesca is very interested.'

'Yes. She expects us to recolonise you.'

'Only if we have the promise of Vikings,' said Francesca. 'She speaka da English so well. What's the feminine of Mosaic?'

'Don't go . . .'

'I must. I'm helping Roger.'

'Pretty girl, your sister,' said Alan Trumble.

'Terrible at languages,' said Clodia.

'But we're forgetting Simon, who spent so many years theorising at the Treasury that he fled to bones and stones and primordial toothpicks.'

'He's right,' said Farrell amiably. 'I've become weighed down by fact. Roger calls me a positivist who lost his way and Alan says I'm a throwback behaviourist. It is all very flattering that friends should bother with labels. Have you known these people long?'

'Alan I've just met. Roger and my father are friends. And so are we. Francesca and Roger and I. . . .'

'Ah, Marie,' said Alan Trumble, 'Clodia . . . this is Marie White who doesn't have to bother with labels. Clodia Oricellari.'

'Can you tell me what I am doing here?' said Marie White. 'Everyone is so clever and, in the case of the ladies, also so attractive.'

'You spent too much time in Washington, Marie. Here, you insult people: you don't flatter,' said Trumble.

'I've heard quite a lot about you from Roger,' said Marie White. 'And, of course, I've already met Francesca several times. How are you settling in? You must come around to my place and let me help because I have nothing in my life but time. Simon, you have to talk to that lonely girl with Robert Blakemore.'

'She may be enjoying it.'

'Think, Simon. Would you enjoy it if you were her age?'

'But . . .'

'Come on. You look marvellous.'

'An Earth Mother,' said Clodia Oricellari. 'I wish I could be one.'

'Curiously shrewd in fact,' Alan Trumble said. 'She takes what can only be called a vivid interest in politics.'

'What does her husband do?' said Clodia. 'I take it she must be married.'

'I think he's a successful embezzler. Anyway, it's academic. He may be a croupier. There have been several others, since the original White, whose potential she's exhausted. We had in the early sixties a period of what was called Tory misrule and she became a prominent part of it. She then went away to America and was no doubt at the heart of scandal: only to find when she returned that things were not as they used to be.'

'I think she's very attractive.'

'You are rebuking me. I am unchivalrous?'

'No. Not at all. I'm just adjusting to the protean British mood. Elsewhere things stay the same and my father says it was once so here: but not any more. Would you agree that there was a sort of political fashion among you intellectuals?'

'I'd vehemently deny being intellectual first! That is an insult to any serious British man or woman who does not appear on television in some sort of regurgitive capacity.'

'You're not serious. Any of you.'

'I'm sorry. . . .'

'You're all playing games.'

'Oh I don't think so. Do you see Bill Delahaye over there? He was once a good novelist and I think he might still be, but he cares. And Roger Ingestre cares. And this lady cares. The one coming in. Rachel Bailey. Do you know her?'

'Do *you* care, Alan Trumble?'

'Enough.'

'Can't you see what is happening in Europe?'

'I think you're teasing me.'

'It's much too serious.'

'Then why are you laughing?'

'I'm not laughing. My eyes are like that. It gets me into trouble.'

'I can imagine!' Alan Trumble said. 'But are you teasing me? About politics?'

'Do you have to ask? It's still a game for people like you in England. You clever people.'

'That sounds very scornful.'

'Politics isn't a game.'

'Nor any longer is tennis or football – as I'm sure you are aware in Italy. Not even, Roger tells me, cricket. I've always been bored by cricket....'

'I sometimes think, Alan, that you are impossible and frivolous as a people – whatever you are, Welsh, Irish, Scottish, English. As soon as you are educated, you play games. You don't know where you stand.'

'Hello....'

'Rachel! You are just in time. Rachel Bailey, Member of Parliament for Ashbridge – right?'

'Right.'

'Clodia Oricellari....'

'Yes, I know. You're starting a tour here, Signorina....'

'No, Rachel. We're all using first names.'

'I am and I'm looking forward to it. At least, at the moment we have an identification of interest.'

'As the Cinderellas of Europe?'

'I think we're the ugly sisters. The French see themselves as Cinderella.'

'Well, as long as the Commission doesn't see itself as Baron Hardup. You know the pantomime very well....'

'Yes. Fairy tales are a sort of hobby of mine. How is Parliament?'

'Very tiring. By a stroke of good fortune my husband is in America, otherwise I'd be divorced.'

'Up till all hours?' said Alan Trumble. 'Then so are we.'

'I like grumbling as much as any journalist does. It's been

45

a hell of a week: the Land Tax Bill and Cabinet leakages and the Rotherham by-election with a swing of thirteen per cent to the Tories. It's no fun being Labour.'

'It never was,' said Trumble. 'But Clodia doesn't think we're serious enough.'

'And she's bloody right!' said Rachel Bailey. 'Sorry. But you are.'

'We have neo-fascists and we have the really militant left,' Clodia Oricellari said. 'It is quite difficult and very necessary to be a democrat – any sort of democrat.'

'What can you do?' said Alan Trumble. 'Europe is sick. The body politic is sick. As democrats, we believe in treatment and what may be needed is surgery.'

'Where physicians bungle,' said Rachel Bailey,' surgeons can't put things back. They can just cut things out.'

'Transplants,' said Trumble. 'What about transplants?'

'Where the tissue won't match and won't take,' said Rachel Bailey. 'I have a nasty feeling that in this country we have relied too long on cosmetic surgery and tranquillisers.'

'Rachel,' said Roger Ingestre. 'I'm sorry to interrupt, but I'd very much like you to meet a couple of young people over here who come to me at Oxford. . . .'

'Can I ask you something personal?' said Alan Trumble.

'If you must.'

'Why are you not married?'

'I'm a Catholic. And I have never, yet, got into the habit of lying. If you've ever wondered about Francesca, she's still quite young and . . . she's still quite young. . . .'

'Signorina Oricellari. . . .'

'Good evening. . . .'

'My name is Robert Blakemore. Have we met?'

'Alan Trumble. . . .'

'Of course. I read your amusing squibs frequently. I'm sorry to interrupt, but I have heard so much of you and your family from Ingestre, Signorina, that it was irresistible. Forgive me, Trumble. . . .'

'No. You must forgive me. I . . . er . . . must have a word

46

with Lord Washbrook anyway. Excuse me, for the moment, Clodia. . . .'

'You are Robert Blakemore,' said Clodia Oricellari. 'I don't think Roger's letters are complete without a new epigram from you.'

'I am enchanted. I hope I did not interrupt a serious conversation, but since you are here on an extended visit I hope you will visit us at Oxford. Autumn is our best season because we are an autumnal people – as *you* are a springtime people.'

'In all seasons, Mr Blakemore, we are sinking into the lagoon.'

'Yes. And you have earthquakes. But you survive. I hope you do not encourage Ingestre – who believes that we are all sinking into the lagoon.'

'You don't believe it?'

'Do you?'

'I shall reserve judgement.'

'Unlike Ingestre, I do not belong to any local commando of political enterprise. I heard enough nonsense as a young man in the thirties about "the struggle" to last any normal lifetime. I believe that there are no good causes: only good men. The best survive and sometimes thrive. In the very worst of times. I happen to be a late Imperial scholar and a lawyer. Rome, I mean. It is a question of resilience. We need curators.'

'Well,' said Clodia Oricellari, 'we are perhaps all getting tired. I don't remember who said it: "Civilisation tends to rot men away, just as great cities corrupt the air." '

'How very apt,' said Blakemore. 'It was Henri Frederic Amiel. It's worth a thought, is it not?'

'Robert,' said Roger Ingestre. 'I will not have you depressing my guests.'

'I am the least depressive influence present, Ingestre. I am a sort of Samuel Smiles in a generation of Jeremiahs in this company. In this *terra dei ceneri d'inventori senza riposo*.'

'Is that Montale?' said Clodia Oricellari.

'Ungaretti,' said Robert Blakemore. 'And I have to admit I quote it out of context. Restless inventors in a European wasteland. I'm sorry. I was carried away.'

'Impressively.'

'You must believe in what you are working for. As a diplomatist.'

'Not necessarily, Mr Blakemore. It's a question of survival. When the shooting starts, diplomatists are on the whole excused. Not so academics. And historians, Roger, they execute first.'

2

Perhaps, at last, I am learning the rudimentary arts of cunning that have to compensate (in my case) for other forms of sophistication. I must admit I am pretty pleased with myself that my various tactics have worked well enough for me to almost think I have a strategy. That would be going too far! I have an objective and a talent for improvisation. The pub is nice and I have quite a pleasant room, with a view of trees and grass, which goes with the job. We eat the same lunch as the customers (very good and pleasantly varied – much better than college food) and a much more ambitious supper because Teresa, the guv'nor's wife, is interested in cooking. The said guv'nor is called Clifford. (Never Cliff.) They are both about thirty and very keen to run a good place. He seems relieved to have someone on the strength who can count and work hard. Probably because he is quite young and the clients are for the most part professional types, Clifford likes to maintain a very dignified and unsmiling presence. He wears suits and a clear-eyed, unimpressed expression. But he is extremely fair and does more than his share of the labouring and cleaning. Teresa is quite severe – especially with me. I think she expects me to make a pass at her and wants to make it quite clear that I must know my place and anyway there's nothing doing. They've got two nice little children and I ingratiate myself a bit by kicking a football about with the five-year-old and taking him and the dog for walks. All of which I quite enjoy. There is also a part-time Australian barmaid, who comes in the evenings. Even for a *preux chevalier* like me, she is quite something: so she is a great success with the general public. I'm not sure whether or not she's married. She has a fine line in sexy back-chat, but otherwise only talks about the weather (still bloody hot), trade and whatever is immediately happening.

The pub, which is called The Reeve of Brecknock, is about half a mile from Millfield Rise, where Candida lives. It's one of the ways of getting to the Heath, so when I take the dog and young Brian for walks, I go past her place. It is a nice-looking house with a garden (not particularly well kept), obviously owned by people who are well set up. I haven't set eyes on her yet. Our last meeting was after Ingestre's final tutorial of the term on the 17th (June). As described, not an unqualified success!

Ingestre himself has been most civil. I thought he would be my best chance of maintaining contact and I'd been wondering how to keep in touch without being a nuisance, or in danger of being thought pushy. So I asked if it was worth while applying for a reader's ticket at the BM. Quick as a flash, he offered to sponsor me, delighted I was showing such dedication. Was I going to be in London? Goodness gracious, then I had only to utter and books would rain in from every quarter. This has helped convince Dad that I haven't come to London because it is (still, God save us) 'swinging'. (I bet, all the same, he and Mum will be just passing through one Sunday to see the pub's 'all right'.) I haven't done any actual work yet: but once I've settled in, and got used to the routine of the job, and made some reasonable contact with Candida, I shall start properly. I have one day off per week: besides which there is a lot of time in the early morning, before Clifford starts organising the day, and also in the afternoons. Also long stretches of Sunday. Curiously, I never get much done, never have, on Sunday.

I was asked round to Ingestre's flat in Beaumont Mews, not far from Harley Street; a neat and very well-appointed place, needless to say. I had hoped that Candida might also be there so that, away from Oxford, I might present myself more like the virgin's dream of Steve McQueen. Too obvious for Candida. And is she? Anyway. She was *not* there. There was a, I suspect, deliberately placed nice and attractive secretary from the *Guardian* and a very ebullient Liberal without a seat called Ellis Fulford. It could be, of course, that the girl was intended for him, or that she was being, herself, offered a choice. It is never easy to tell, with Ingestre, watching life passing by him with amused detachment. Perhaps he is not that much aware of people. A kind of reflex generosity: if you tap him in the right place, he responds. But you have to know exactly where to tap.

It was disappointing that Candida wasn't there. Otherwise, marvellous. Good talk. The *Guardian* girl was a bit dim. (She was called Alison. A nice name: but Alison What?) Fulford belongs to the same pressure group as Ingestre and this seems to be focused around Candida's parents – placidly identified for my benefit. Pity that Candida wasn't there because they both treated me as an adult with worth-while opinions. (Ingestre is good about this at Oxford, but in the contrived teaching situation, which can seem patronizing.) Fulford shares his enthusiasm for the eighteenth century: less for the politicians but more particularly for Burke and Swift. In fact, he seemed to me to be a spiritual Tory, which Ingestre most certainly is not, so I was rather surprised that they claimed to share a political viewpoint. We had a good argument in which I think I held my own pretty well, and then a fairly comic chat about the state of the parties. As a political commentator, Fulford is obviously very much in the know. He chooses, however, to wear his knowledge lightly with a nice turn of wit. I didn't do badly, but I'm afraid it was all wasted on Alison.

Reasoning that as she was a friend of Ingestre's she might also know Candida, I thought it might be a good tactical move to ask her out for an Indian nosh when we left. Then my courage failed me. She was friendly without being obvious. I think I was afraid of a snub, because she's about five years older and I'm sure that Fleet Street secretaries have better curries to cook than bright young lads still at the University. So I had a solitary experimental supper, which nearly took the top off my head and was back in the pub at nine-thirty. I went to help behind the bar, which pleased Clifford, after a lot of piss-taking. What was the union going to say, if they found I was working on my day off? What union? The National Union of Bar Incumbents and Licensed Employees! You're a member aren't you, Samantha? Of What? NUBILE. Laughter all round and the drinks on Steve. Then we got into an argument about cricket with some of the regulars, who evidently thought (quite wrongly) that it was one way of getting to Samantha. Healthy Australian soul that she is, she prefers riding and surfing.

Conversations in the pub are interesting but amazingly banal. I don't mean that I expected the kind of self-consciously intellectual and 'serious' chat of Oxford (which is often highly artificial, at the undergraduate level at least). I did think, especially when the economic situation must be affecting the ordinary family, that there would be more interest in politics and the way the country was being run. There isn't. (After all, Dad takes a fairly informed interest in what's going on and talks about it with his chums – Hailsham Tories to a man.) Here, apart from the usual preoccupation with sex, most of them pretty straightforward, people are either moaning about someone at work or talking about horses and what's on television. Occasionally, there's an unlikely bit of grooming play. Interesting that the barman is invisible to the real dedicated seducer: I've heard two propositions in the last week that would have made Saint Anthony think again. Both from women too! The only male versions have been very unimaginative by comparison. (Fulford was talking about Juvenal and Women's Lib the other night. We were allegedly doing him at school, but not *Satire Six* which apparently is the lubricious one. Must read it.)

Apart from these diversions, the only passing reference to politics or world affairs has been about the Israeli hijack at Entebbe (a sort of super-spectacular, Frederick Forsyth job), and some kind of clever currency fiddle at Heathrow in which some enterprising characters have got away with a couple of million. This, of course, is seen at The Reeve as a terrific joke. I suppose it is what the News leads on, so it's hardly fair to blame the public for triviality. No one seems to give a damn about the Puerto Rican summit, or Rhodesia, or the Lebanon. I wonder if I'm an intellectual snob. Anyway, I suppose it's a generalisation: since I only hear the conversations near the bar and the people who stand up at the counter don't come out to seminars. I must get down to some work. This is no way to get a first.

A much more satisfactory day. I got up at six and did a good couple of hours on French and English colonial policy leading up to the Seven Years War. I think I'm in some danger of being over-interested in the eighteenth century, which is the obvious influence of Ingestre. I must be careful not to neglect the other stuff, which is more important. Then, I went for a walk on the Heath before breakfast. As usual, this summer, it was a lovely morning and pleasantly fresh before the real heat of the day. There was a girl in the garden of Candida's place who I imagine is her sister. Quite a pretty kid, pleasant-looking but (naturally enough) nothing like as poised as Candida. She was playing with a kitten.

I decided that I'd give it another day or so and then, if I failed to meet Candida naturally, I'd ring up her home and try to see her. After all, that's partly why I'm here and what all the clever planning is about. I wasn't looking forward to it, however; whereupon about half past twelve she walked in with Ingestre. Into the pub. We had a lovely 'My God!' performance from him, as though he had completely forgotten I was in London and where I was working, which did not convince Candida one jot. She was furious but determined not to show it. I was furious too, because I'd been helping Clifford in the cellar and had been too bloody idle to change my shirt, so that there were black marks on it which I don't suppose she missed. She is always so immaculate and it puts her at an enormous psychological advantage, even with smooth bastards like Lumley, in Ingestre's tutorials. Anyway, she managed to be civil. I introduced Clifford and Teresa, who were impressed that I was on such good terms with my 'professor' at Oxford. (At least I have gone up a notch or two in status and Teresa has started smiling at me. Ingestre's pupil is clearly above reproach.) Ingestre pulled out all the stops of charm: he impressed Clifford by his interest in the economics of pub management, and Teresa by gallantry. I think I profited from all this because Clifford, who likes to stand in front of the bar with the customers at lunch-time, came to serve behind, so that I was able to have the odd moment with Candida. The manner of Ingestre's contrivance was such that she couldn't show how angry she was or play the *grande dame* with me. Candida is enough of an inverted snob not to want to be cold and haughty and misunderstood by people like Clifford and Teresa, to whom she feels instinctively superior. At the same time, she would not want to present herself in this thoroughly undesirable and unadmirable guise to Ingestre (whom she obviously *does* fancy). She therefore had to be polite even to me. It's all a question of upbringing – as far as I can see the perennial obsession of the educated middle class who always want to disown what they are, without actually being anything else. Dad *claims* to be working class, but *responsible* working class.

I managed to get her to agree to see me on my next day off (Wednesday) and in the evening. I tried for the afternoon as well, but she said she was busy and I didn't press it because that might be too long and inevitably (unless there were some drastic change in our relationship) I should get on her nerves. I'll find out a bit about Chinese food and take her to one of the places in Gerrard Street. (Teresa is amazingly knowledgeable about that kind of thing and so is Clifford: anything to do with catering is a matter of intense professional pride.)

When we were washing up, Clifford asked me man-to-man if I fancied Candida. I said I did. He wished me good luck. He had noticed her around and about. He knew where she lived and offered the information that her old man sometimes came in with his friends (*not* mates) for a drink. He would point him out. Teresa told me later that my professor thought very highly of me. It's nice not only to be liked but to be approved of. I'm quite sure that Ingestre did the whole thing deliberately and thoughtfully, without being remotely interested in either Candida or me.

As it is, I am to meet her next Wednesday at six-thirty in the pub opposite the British Museum (which is a Watney's house). I had hoped I might be invited to the house, but no. When I suggested the afternoon, she said she was visiting some people in Kensington: so I said (*amour propre*, of course) that it didn't matter. I was going to the BM. So. . . . The thing now is to get down to work, forget about her till then and concentrate. CONCENTRATE. If that were possible.

I don't know why I should have expected a success but it wasn't. In fact it was a royal case of failure. I think she had made up her mind to be as nice as possible to someone who bores her rigid. (Not an inaccurate bloody description!) She looked terrific, wearing a white dress. It wasn't in any sense 'see-through' – except that white dresses often can't help it. So I could see the kind of light lacy bra she had on and the line of her pants, especially against the light. I understand what people mean when they say they almost went round the bend. Not in the sense of violence but a sort of intolerable, ceaseless desire. The dinner was all right. Clifford recommended a place called the Jasmine Garden, because there was plenty of room, good nosh and Chinese 'who weren't obviously racial'.

Naturally, she left me to order, pretending that she didn't care what she ate. I knew bloody well she would fix exactly on what was right and what was wrong. And if I'd stuck to what Teresa had told me, I'd have been all right. Instead, I decided to be daring and asked for something which turned out to be a sort of Yangtse broth, with what would otherwise have been perfectly compatible dishes. The waiter put me right kindly enough, but some Anglo-Chinese at the next table (one of whom was dazzlingly pretty) thought they were at the Palladium. The girl smiled at me, though, and annoyed Candida. (I hope!) Well, everyone had a laugh and the drinks on Steve again. No, strictly Stephen when in the company of Candida.

I kept off any talk of a) love b) passion c) Oxford d) Ingestre. There was some mileage in what it was like to work at The Reeve: funny stories about the customers, how nice Clifford and Teresa are. From there (or thence) to people's relative aspirations and what really matters. God knows what the smooth and well-dressed London Chinese Society made of this; they have this advantage of retaining inscrutability when it's called for. Effortlessly, we went on to Candida's own aspirations and Daddy's and Mummy's. Daddy is terribly hard-working and basically gentle; Mummy is brilliant and desperately sincere but a little cold. Their slightly unreal relationship has made her ask questions from quite an early age about values. She takes female independence, obviously, for granted. Fulfilment is something different, however. Candida sees herself as an intelligent, contributing partner in a marriage that is a *unit*. Of course, sex is important and children are important, just as important as ideas and careers. . . . We talked most of the evening about her. Not much about me. Which is what I wanted. She doesn't seem to like the way her parents live. Her mother uses her own name, Barbara Dunn, professionally – and this seems to annoy her. (It would annoy Dad!) She kept returning to the importance of a close understanding that was basically erotic.

Might have been prick-teasing. If so, it worked. I kept getting it up all through the noodles, which must be obvious in so many ways to a reasonably sophisticated girl. We had a fair bit to drink over the evening, as a whole; but then, we were hanging about around Leicester Square, which is pretty horrible at that time of night, waiting for a taxi.

56

Maybe if we'd got one immediately it might have worked out better. As it was, I suppose I seemed over-anxious and ineffectual.

When, at last, we got a taxi (driven by a right shit), whatever had been working had stopped. I was too nervous to touch her until around Euston, when I took her hand. I'd got around to kissing her by Camden Town. She was very stiff and rigid, but this made me more excited – so I put a very nervous hand on her right breast and she did nothing. She opened her mouth a bit, but only passively and there was no . . . I don't know . . . no response. And then I noticed her legs were slightly apart and so, bloody stupidly, I took my hand off her breast which was marvellous and tried to push it up her skirt. And she went mad! Tits, fine! But nothing else. . . . Which is bloody ridiculous.

It was like a Victorian maiden being ravished, but much nastier, and I bet the bastard taxi-driver missed nothing of it. When she started struggling, I did nothing at all, but she was going to have her scene and stop the cab. . . . So I had to plead with her and got once again the feeling that only she gives me – as if some clever torturer had got at all the nerve ends near the surface of my skin and given them all the same mild electric shock. I didn't know whether I was trembling or not. And it was bloody humiliation! *I* should have stopped the taxi and got out and left HER.

So we went the rest of the way with me whimpering apologies and her across the seat all clasped into herself and frigid, shuddering delicately. And the taxi-driver sneering, when we got out. She went into her house without saying anything. I walked down to The Reeve wanting to cry. But I didn't. When I got in, however, quietly, I was sick.

This morning, I obviously had to pretend in my nice-lad, shy way that everything was great to Clifford and Teresa, who I don't suppose were fooled for a moment. At lunchtime, Clifford pointed out her father who came in. He was reading the *Economist*, the *New Statesman* and the *Listener*, looking vigorous and alert. 'That's your bird's Dad, over there,' said

Clifford. 'Often in on a Friday, reading.' I suppose that's it. I haven't been able to do any work today, but I suppose, at least, there won't be many distractions from now on. Christ, but it does hurt!

*

Clodia seems to excite people in a way that Francesca (who is objectively more beautiful) does not. It is difficult to define how: Francesca has a certain cool confidence, as well as her rather disconcerting business flair; she dresses, walks, talks, and stands with effortless feminine grace which is there in the way she uses her eyes or touches her hair. Clodia chooses instead to be subtle, irreverent, intellectually provocative; she also wears more emphatic clothes and there is more than a hint of sensuality. Everything that Francesca does, while not impulsive, seems prompted by instinct – whether for admiration, pleasure, success or even profit; almost everything Clodia does seems to be cerebral – an exercise in the theory of admiration, pleasure, success or power. And yet she is unquestionably the more sexually assertive. Of course, Clodia is also an unusually good-looking woman in her own right. I detect in many of the people who have met her recently, even the austere and decisively married Blakemore, a particular fascination. It will be interesting to observe the relative impact of the Oricellari on some card-carrying amorist such as Connors. I imagine that any number of men speculate, as I do myself, about the erotic delights of Francesca: I wonder how many wonder about Clodia's emotional excitements.

Dimchurch is very cross about the state of the nation, which of course, for him, means our rather abysmal performance in the Tests. He has taken something of a dislike to Greig, not so much for his egregious demeanour before the spectators (which he notes) but because he looks too much like an actor. He is also (asserts Dimchurch) much too tall! Slyly, I slipped into the conversation the name of Frank Woolley. 'Ah!' said Dimchurch. 'But *he* was majestic!'

It is a depressing performance all the same: not so much that we are losing to a better side, but there is so much evident spite on the part of the fast bowlers. Dimchurch, who remembers vividly Jardine's tour of 1932 and Gregory and MacDonald before that, dismisses this as an argument, suggesting that the fault is in our stars. I don't recall, since the War, the same quality of viciousness in cricket, whoever had the fast bowlers. Crowds are becoming more noisy. Fulford and various others point out reasonably that the black minority have such an underprivileged existence that it's only natural for them to let off steam, especially when they are so much on top. This may be so, but there was an extraordinary display of ill temper at Lord's yesterday in a Sunday match between Middlesex and Surrey (which was otherwise a splendid afternoon in the bang-and-wallop class of cricket) when Featherstone was caught by a chap with his feet on the boundary rope. He was given out and hung about while there was some argument and then called back to an appalling and moronic chorus of jeering from the Mound. I like the look of Brearley as captain, though Dimchurch thinks he is far too 'busy'.

I picked up an extraordinary thriller about cricket more or less by accident, called *Testkill*, which read like an unholy synthesis of *The Rover* (as it used to be) and *Penthouse* (as I assume it usually is). If cricketers lead such priapic lives behind the screens, it is perhaps not surprising that they are drained of initiative on the (very parched) field. I think it had better be kept from Dimchurch; quite apart from his calling and natural unworldliness. Exotic knickers at Headquarters! ('I fear, Ingestre, that Blakemore is right: the barbarians are inside the fortress.')

I discover that Connors has moved into a flat a few streets away from mine and that we both use the same pub.

Fortunately, he is busy at the House in the evenings with the Conservatives putting on a lot of ostentatious and quite meaningless pressure after the 'nodding through' a few weeks ago. In fact, to be entirely fair, Connors works quite hard: so that he is in proper attendance most days, working on committees and sorting his constituency problems out. Rachel, Hay, Fulford and the others all think he is a good MP. And it's not that he is an uncongenial companion: just that I maintain my intolerably selfish preference for the society of others only when *I* want it.

My pupil, Stephen Kent, is working in a pub near Candida's home in Highgate, no doubt having chosen the site as a favourable salient. The incumbents of the pub are, as it happens, pleasant young people who think very well of Kent. I took Candida there deliberately, having established that they had not yet made contact, which may have been irresponsible. She was furious and Kent was typically confused: but at least in these circumstances she had to be polite. I don't give two hoots about her because she is obviously going to make a game of this sort of torment for years. But I remember how painful it can be and Kent wants to take a decent degree. If I can help it, I am not going to have him upset by Candida's sort of *allumeuse*. And if things can be brought to a moment of crisis: the sooner the better. I expect, however, that he will be encouraged by the people at the pub who obviously were impressed. God alone knows why: she is pretty enough, but hardly endearing.

Taylor and Barbara do not notice. In fact, I am inclined to think they notice each other less and less. Beatrice and Sidney Webb who used to be Jack and Jill. So how little is there left for the two girls? Jessica is enterprising about it and probably has a splendid time; but Candida is bored and does nothing much except think about herself and get by with the minimum of expenditure of spirit. Such boredom, as I remember, is destructive: although it has been suggested that I do not understand women.

Supper with Ellis Fulford, whose cooking is as eccentric and delightful as ever. Rachel Bailey arrived and recognized immediately an assault upon her party integrity, to which I was an absolutely innocent recruit – no, dammit, conscript! Expertly enough she told us about Oliver's adventures in New York, making them wonderfully farcical. (I doubt that Oliver sees himself quite as the Figaro of the World Health Organisation, in spite of his excellent voice.) In a thoroughly sly way, she mentioned the reappearance of swine influenza in an American army camp as a source of concern: so that Ellis, who among his numerous accomplishments is a magna cum laude hypochondriac, went pale and momentarily forgot his Highgate preoccupations. When it was all going too far, Rachel switched to a gently ironic description of Clodia (partly for my own benefit) in order to stimulate Ellis back to equanimity. She succeeded and Ellis cursed me for not having introduced them. Rachel as always is a masterly tactician and a sound strategist, fully aware of Ellis's long-term sentimental regard for her.

He began, over an astonished dish which contained very thin slices of beef, apples, bean sprouts, and mixed dried fruit in a rich and piquant sauce, to press enthusiastic Highgate points; asking me for support that, in the face of about six such inventive dishes, all different, I rather feebly attempted.

Rachel was entirely on her mettle and counter-attacked well. She asked if the gloom of the Liberal party was so impenetrable that Ellis had been driven to this edge of desperation. For the purposes of the argument I was dismissed into an enclosed order, which thinks on behalf of the rest of the world without actually participating. It was amusing. The cut at Ellis was not entirely kind, because she reminded him that her seat was relatively safe and his own parliamentary hopes were dimmer than yesterday.

At the same time there was a lot of obvious stalling. Both devils were citing the CBI survey of the early part of the week to their purpose. Rachel said that the recession was *it*self receding. (A charming example of infinite regression, surely.) Ellis wanted to know what would happen when there was an inevitable shortage of vital commodities that would corkscrew inflation again. In a flash we were back at public spending and the sort of probing that is genuinely discomforting for the Labour right. Ellis's quite sound contention was that if there was a rise in commodity prices, these cuts would be essential to the maintenance of a steady supply of funds to industry. Rachel would not allow (I think wrongly) that this rise is likely, because the Americans dispute it; she saw, too, the predictable thrust at the left of the party. Ellis's obvious proposition was that Foot and Benn must resign from the Cabinet on grounds of conscience: Rachel conducted an able theoretical defence. Unlike Tony Connors, she is alarmingly loyal in private as well as in public.

The drift, mercifully, became more frivolous. I wonder if I am not a disappointment to Ellis, who is a passionate, if sometimes sceptical Highgate, by not giving more to the shove. Rachel, however (as perhaps he should know), is stubborn and loyal. If events bring about a centre alliance *because it must be* then all is well: otherwise nothing is going to persuade her sort of politician to defect from whatever party. They distinguish between theories and ideals; and they understand practices. Neither party has much tradition of defection: even when there is no question of compromise. (If Roy Jenkins had not resigned the Deputy Leadership, he might now be Chancellor, or else Foreign Secretary: in either case with incalculably better effect upon our international status. Yet, he is still loyally in the Labour party. If Edward Heath had broken right away, he might have set up the foundations of a national coalition which in the two years since 1974 might have come into effect. He is still in the Tory party. Such loyalties are *not* trifling. God knows that Ellis himself has been an unshakable member of the Liberal party, without ever sitting in the Commons and without the prospect of a seat.)

Rachel left early to go back there, whereupon Ellis and I drank sherry and enjoyed scurrilous conversation about friends and acquaintances, not to mention public figures. He has been shown parts of Bill Delahaye's private novel, which has less an anti-hero than a proto-villain and Tony Connors as one Augustine Cornflour, incessantly tying himself in sexual knots with various women, most of whom Ellis says he can identify. It seems that I am amiably caricatured as a benign theorist called Bushchat, and Alan Trumble appears less amiably as a drunken journalist.

Jeremy Taylor has been reading Rex Warner's novel *The Professor*, published in the thirties. He is impressed. Perhaps our lives would have been fractionally less urgent if Jeremy had stuck to Physics at Oxford and had not been diverted into PPE. He is a natural measurer: and one of his perennial problems (happily abandoned) was measuring metaphysical propositions. He refuses to be defeated by moral and ethical projections and indulges his urge to quantify and categorise, perhaps excessively. If Barbara's nose had been a fraction shorter, if she had not read Economics, if she had gone to Cambridge, Marcus Antonius Taylor would have been pursuing obscure Californian quarks.

Coming rather late to the revolutionary effusions of the thirties, Taylor is inclined to brood untowardly about literary agonies that were (as most of the agonisers came to see) a passing phase in their progress towards respectability and success. He was profoundly shaken by the religious cobbler's strictures upon the professor, whose liberalism is held at fault for teaching men to see themselves as wretched, and by encouraging greed and an obsession with culture for turning them against one another. Since Taylor is an honest and self-questioning measurer, he did not find it difficult to identify with this essential liberal (the professor), or with the bourgeois bringers of light and fire of the thirties, *locum tenentes* for the as yet non-existent proletarian artists serving a working-class audience in a working-class tradition.

I did my best to set his mind at rest, and the outcome of the evening was an enthusiastic invitation to their cottage in Gloucestershire, with its four bedrooms and acre of grass, at the weekend, when I could do them the service of driving Jessica down, also Rachel Bailey if she could be persuaded to abandon her constituents for once. The prospect was pleasing enough and so I accepted.

Wisely perhaps, Rachel decided that her constituents needed her. I think she must have had enough Highgate coercion to last a normal Parliamentary session, but Candida belatedly decided to come. Barbara was driving from the North and Jeremy himself coming from some kind of publishers' gorsedd in Cardiff, if I have it right. It was a pity about Rachel: she brings out the best in Barbara, who dresses up, physically to outshine and mentally to keep up appearances, when they meet; while Jeremy is steered clear of the sloughs of solemnity that litter his *paysage moralisé*. But the food is always excellent, there are abundant books and records, a Cotswold stone house in delightful surroundings, and everyone is relaxed.

Jessica was in the Action Working Dress, generally favoured by most young people, of jeans and a sort of cotton vest which testified to her joyful bloom of not quite sixteen. Candida, by contrast, looked like a figure out of an old, elegant edition of *Vogue*. Female clothes have been very soft and pretty this summer and I suppose it is natural for someone as self-regardingly attractive to take full advantage of them. I wish I liked the girl more: but she is an exclusionist. Displaying a great deal more of her admirable legs than the dress or my car made necessary, she tried her best to cut Jessica out by talking about our tutorials of the past term. Since her enthusiasm and acumen were not as signally evident at the time, I was surprised that she had retained as much – notably of what the other people in the group had contributed. She was slighting about Kent. None of this had any effect upon Jessica, who bounced about in the back seat like a healthy young labrador, interested, startled and amused by everything.

We drove through Marlborough and I happened to mention the Avebury Ring. We were in plenty of time, so we went to look at it. Candida was eager enough until she realised that Jessica too was asking highly intelligent questions, whereupon she subsided into displeasing boredom. Jessica wanted to climb Windmill Hill.

We did. Candida complained, justifiably, that her shoes weren't suitable for quite a long pull, so we let her go back to the car to listen to the tennis final between Borg and Nastase. (It came as no surprise that Jessica wanted Borg to win and Candida found him boring and therefore supported Nastase by default.)

There isn't very much to see from the top, which is a pity, but I was delighted and rather touched by Jessica's unaffected sense of wonder and, I think, sense of identification with something that was happening so very long ago. Neither of her parents show much imagination, but here was this child asking the most penetrating questions about how and why we bother to piece together evidence of a lost and very primal culture. My answers were necessarily inadequate but I tried to respond to the freshness of enthusiasm in which there was nothing coy or self-seeking. She said: 'Funny, isn't it: all this mess and confusion, because people like them managed to survive.' I laughed in a predictable, supercilious, adult way. And she laughed as well, for which I was thankful: I should hate to thoughtlessly defile any young enthusiasm. 'It must have been bloody freezing in winter,' she said (on what must have been one of the hottest days of this or any year). 'There couldn't have been many brass monkeys.' And ran off.

Candida was unusually amiable for the rest of the journey.

At Oxford, Blakemore was entertaining a very engaging

American polymath, James Lloyd Mitchell, endowed with all the courtesy and charm of the transatlantic academic along with an extremely acute mind. Even at New College and in the company of Blakemore, his conversation was noticeably good and I suppose it is a shameful mark of my own vanity that I was surprised to find that he was a professional writer and a right-wing polemicist. Blakemore relished the opportunity of holding up social democracy in an embattled island to the light of Mitchell's scorn, only to be elegantly chided for the tepidity of his own Conservatism. As this is high Tory by all reasonable standards, there was quite a lot of hilarity. Mitchell is spending several months in England, working on a book and writing syndicated columns for an American and a European paper: I look forward very much to his impact upon some of the Highgate people.

*

Dear Olliphant,

God-speeded summer's middle, at last. And the day winding down, also at last. God can't speed either away fast enough, with the marvellous news that you will be in Geneva from the end of the month. At least with both of us somewhere in Europe, we might be able to arrange an occasional weekend, or even a week or two in Italy unless times get so bad that we sit right through the recess! Italy would be like old impecunious times, before World Health and the mother of Parliaments. What did we do with all the time? Would you agree to Lake Garda? Beautiful and not crowded if we make the end of August or early September. And near Verona and earth-treading stars.

Anyway. . . . The echo of a song at twilight at the beginning was the plaintive cry in the canyon of someone ambushed by three Celtic apaches while having a bloody-minded mary on her own. I spent the afternoon trying to convince civil (hah!) servants in four different departments that my constituents matter not because they are my constituents but because they are people living in a democracy. (For the time

66

being, it would seem!) I won't go into seething details: but when you have been talking to people who are worried sick, it is infuriating to be fobbed off. I spent the rest of the early evening chasing Ministers of varying shapes and sizes to moan and rant. This is not good for the soul. Vodka and tomato-juice are. Then along came the Celts. A persuasive Welshman at the apex, chiding me about my right-wing opinions, wanting support on what they euphemistically call 'selective imports'. My God, however little contingency planning is going on, there's a lot of contingency arguing. And this is just another economic lull. It is said, by those who always claim to know, that Jenkins (R.) is a certainty for the Presidency of the Commission. Hardly cheering. Unless, once absolved of party obligations, he speaks firmly and authoritatively about economic necessities which are being fudged. The buzz was that it was all arranged at an enthusiastic top private dinner party. (Whose finger on the buzzer?)

Meanwhile the anti-Marketeers are forcing a vote about direct elections to the Assembly and getting 109 votes. The issue, if you will believe it, is that decisions have been made in Brussels without consultation. Then the Tories began pressing for greater powers of scrutiny over the Steel Corporation and we were up until a quarter to seven. That is to say, some of us were!

Never mind: the Olympic Games will be starting in a week or so, with or without Taiwan, but *with* Princess Anne riding her horsie and for a week or two we'll be bored out of our minds on television every night, and everything else including the palsied £ will be of secondary importance. After listening to the left-wingers tonight, I am astounded at the petty Little Englander approach, which I suppose to some extent reflects an awful lot of opinion in this island. The Democratic Convention starts this week and the run-up to what is really still the most momentous event every four years in Western politics; the Germans are having an election in the autumn; the Italians are very precariously balanced – but what the hell does anyone *here* care. All the same, these three weren't

67

strident or even particularly rhetorical for left-wingers and Celtic left-wingers at that. There are so many these days, in the constituencies, on the NEC and some here in Parliament, who behave with the mentality of football hooligans on the terraces, always yelling *Foul* when their side is losing (as they've done throughout the whole European issue) and making the most absurd fuss. The danger will come when they stop just yelling and start looking round for things to smash.

I know that you will tell me that there is a lot of injustice and inequality still, especially outside the West: but I believe in democracy and in social democracy and I don't believe it can survive on a gospel of hate and envy. I don't see any chance of the World Community that we once hoped for – and I don't believe that you, for all your stubborn loyalty, can imagine that the UN has any kind of political credibility any more, however marvellous the work being done by the various agencies is. (Even so, people tell me how much fiddling and mismanagement goes on in the field and what happens when the Americans pull out, as they seem to be doing already in UNESCO?) But I do believe we can still have a decent Western alliance, based on liberal politics and Roosevelt's four freedoms, and I think it is worth fighting for: so we have to look outside ourselves. So much of our left are resentful and vengeful in a way that is long out of date; others are simply subversive and want to destroy all the existing systems and throw in with the Communists. People like Batman are dazzled by something they saw on the road to the Wigan gentleman's convenience when in dire need of a pee.

Still, enough grumbling! I had supper last week with Ellis Fulford and Roger Ingestre, both of whom were true to themselves. Ellis provided the most extraordinary dishes to date, all very delicious, but he has had North Sea gas connected since we last ate there and is having great trouble adjusting to variations in heat. As usual, we all stood around in the kitchen drinking while he cooked and it was all splendid: listening to Roger Ingestre's smooth disquisitions on this and that, with Ellis yelling at various ingredients in the brightest pots imaginable, 'Simmer, you rotten bastards! *Simmer*, I said, for Christ's sake!' I think Roger was supposed to hold me down, while Ellis did the barbarous king bit, but Roger wasn't keen to rudely force anyone. Did you know that when Eliot visited Gertrude Stein in Paris in the twenties that they had a long conversation about grammar and why she used split infinitives? Well, that sort of high-church refinement is exactly the sort of thing one gets more and more from Ingestre. I remember the days, when he and I were both rookies in the Campaign for Democratic Socialism, when he was very acute and much less amused. I think after the divorce he decided never to be hurt by anyone again and has made emotional detachment such a habit that it influences his intellectual judgement. That may sound paradoxical, but I think it has worked that way round. Ellis wanted to know if I was setting my cap for the European Assembly especially when there would be direct elections and perhaps some hope of legislative power. I decided to be evasive – more to test reaction than for any other reason. So Ellis held forth about the impossibility of any effective decision-making in a European Parliament and defined a new kind of animal called the Euroslob whom he claims to have catalogued on several trips to Brussels and Strasbourg on behalf of the Liberals. Passionate as he is about the EEC and eventual political union, he thinks that civil servants all over the Nine are uniting. They have nothing to lose but their chins!

Incidentally, I met the Oricellari lady I wrote to you about, who is quite something; and whom we are to both dine with at the earliest opportunity. She is what I imagine as a Renaissance Julia Augusta: not quite as beautiful but clever. In fact, my darling Olliphant, I admit that she is the sort of woman that I envy. Years of effortless privilege, cultivation, conversation, an assumption that power, any power, is desirable and that political intrigue is the brandy of the damned in bowges eight, nine and ten. I know I can't complain about privilege, but nice old dons do not bring up their daughters in the manner of the Princes Volupine, not that there is anything phthisic, incidentally, about this particular princess's hand. But I had an uneasy feeling on the evening that I met her that she was laughing at something that she already knew to be futile and a waste. I began to wonder if there was some genetic transmission, which might enable Italians to survive power struggles and even years of abysmal defeat patiently, in a way not given to us. But that (you will say) is my Protestant conscience speaking again, as (you will recall) it did in Assisi, when you, wretched heathen, were taking it all in like Barnum and Bailey's circus. But this can wait. You will be fascinated by these sisters, who treat each other with the coolest irony – though, again, I don't know how much of that is genuine.

I have been invited to Jeremy Taylor's on Friday evening, once again I expect as a prospective member of his group.

Quite apart from all the theorising, I am truly worried, even upset by some of the people that I see at my surgery. The word 'surgery' is an apt one, whoever first thought of it: I remember, when you were a junior doctor, the feeling of helpless compassion with which I could identify without exactly sharing. I think I now feel that sort of compassion for my people; I know that I feel pretty helpless. I sometimes wonder if I can possibly be a very good socialist: at the same time I know (for all my elitist leanings) I am a very good democrat. And I do believe that the best way to help the desperate people who come to see me is to have a government of very able, very tough, altruistic and disinterested people whom the electorate will want to go on and on and on in office. I wish you were here to talk to. Ingestre won't be serious for long – although he can be very intense about the need for constitutional reform; Ellis Fulford preaches; Simon Farrell is busy being enigmatic and Jeremy Taylor and Barbara both proselytise. In the House itself, there is a lot of good talk about issues, but on the hand to mouth basis that keeps governments in office and alliances

70

in being – at least with the votes spread as they are. Do you find it is the same? I think you used to when you worked in a hospital: you were all so involved in cases that there wasn't much time for taking an overall view. In the best of all possible worlds that shouldn't apply at the WHO, but I expect that it does.

I wish there was some gossip of the racy comic kind, but there isn't. Sorry if this is a rather dreary letter. I promise to be in Geneva, sparkling louder than the lake, when you arrive and . . . you name it! Write when you can and until then,

All my love,

R.

*

Red hair thrown back in what she no doubt thought was a haughty and contemptuous movement, putting the rest of us in the perspective of her youth and her beauty. And the lift of her breasts in the movement, high under the white shirt, the nipples pushing through – big medallions or little tender buds? – nice, manageable breasts, white in contrast to the flowing flaming hair and the (yes) little nipples starting up and firming up as her eyes become hot. But, for the moment. . . . The tapering, tiny waist, tightly belted, flat below the firm ripple of the muscles of her belly. Caressing hand slips down touching the silk knickers and pauses. Wait! Wait! Under the bright green skirt, the line of her thighs. Stockings, perhaps? Dare we hope for stockings as well? Oh Christ, I can't bear it! High, dark stockings with a good wide band and (yes, shiny) taut white suspenders and the very white, very white thighs, pressed together having to be teased and prised apart. Round knees and the full calves, the plush little centre of her hot little imagination cleaving the white silk to it. . . .

Enough, my God, enough! She saw me looking at her and under lowered, still lids, her head thrown back and her shoulders hard pressed against the high chair, held my evident lechery contemptuously. I wonder if she ever has. Emancipated kids these days with all the Heath and empty afternoon houses? Probably. More than a dewy feel against a tree-trunk or in the angle of a churchyard, these days. Oooough! Remember. . . . Imagine that delicate white hand (beautifully manicured) diffidently (upturned taut fingers) stroking (so lightly) the rampant rhino-horn under the trousers and then gripping . . . aagh . . . squeezing rrrgh and coolly unzipping, tickling, searching beneath. . . . Hey! Enough! Perhaps I've already rotted early but I hope I'll be the first to offer a wild weird fleshly thing, very tender, very yearning, very precious. . . . Curious thing for Gilbert to have written. Gilbert! Indeed, Miss Candida Taylor. Perhaps we can sneak a weekend in Jeremy's cottage and have an idyll: I'll pursue her naked through the orchard in the early dew and fuck her ecstatically on that sloping bank at the other end. I wonder would she? That look. Thank God, I've kept in shape: not an ounce of flab and stomach muscles like a juvenile lead. But I suppose the drought will have spoilt the grass and the moss. (Save it till next year.) Never tried her mother, though I can't think why. Too classy: I think I was frightened. But why of her? I do not believe Trumble, telling her in the car when he was pissed that he fancied her. She stopped the car and turned to him and said: 'Well, do something about it,' starting to unbutton her dress. I do NOT believe it. Trumble's a whisky-sodden liar. Though the lanes around their place are quiet enough.

Christ, I'd better say something intelligent. *A toute à l'heure Mademoiselle Candida.* I must agree that a refinedly dirty mind is a perpetual dinner party. There's something honestly joyous about getting the same old delightful kick in the equilibrium at my age. Not that I'm so old. Adolescent eternal. Though I should confess by now that I do not really believe that I shall fall in love this time. Conscience! Aha and again! Well, so what: if I were a Catholic, I'd go to confession, having deceived myself until the priest got pissed off. No, I know better than that. I don't even get infatuated any more. Just the moment of ecstasy, particularly after it's been given and they become compliant. . . .

Something intelligent. . . . What are they talking about?

Do I think that the Americans have really emerged as idealists without illusions? Everything that J. Taylor says sounds like a motion for debate: that this dinner table agrees that the Americans have emerged as a nation of idealists without illusions. It would be too facile to say that they have remained what they always have been, illusionists without ideals: so Jock Hay says it instead and gets a big laugh, especially from the delicious Candida. Head thrown back, pearly little teeth, tits aloft again, rustle as she does something with her legs. . . . Enough! I wonder if Sarah's in tonight. Saturday: unlikely. Or Delahaye's Lana. (What price Augustine Cornflour, now, old boy?) Marie would as ever, but I want someone young. . . .

Sigh! Look at them: J. Taylor, alert and responsible, hair like a shaving brush flattened out sideways and lean, lined face creased in awareness, matched at the other end by Barbara of the clear eyes and the economic helmet, bestower of the liberal casting vote and best grounded in tactics and strategy, not relishing the fight, but the treaty when the war is over. Perhaps some wisenheimer Poseidon was having a joke and there was old ramrod Trumble whipping round from the blazing presses only to find himself in the most ethical struggle. Glaukopis. So calm. But keep talking, Anthony. It's going well and you have got her attention. Greyish, bluish, greenish eyes attentive, no longer scornful, but just enough contempt to make it fun. . . . As I was saying: the telling pause that covers the stall in the flight of a thought almost taking off . . . (can't seem to get away from that line of imagery, dammit).

. . . need of the American national character to get out of the inquisition and back on to the psychiatrist's couch and the fine old tradition of talking oneself out of trauma. Alas, though: are there any untamed territories of the psyche for the frontiersmen to scout? Incidentally, has anyone wondered whether the top Mafiosi visit analysts? Imagine: *I was an analyst for Cosa Nostra*. What hangs up a Capo? I must say that I feel some of the crusading journalists might crusade a little in that direction. What was all that yesterday about the 'big shot crooks going free while the poor ones went to jail'? . . .

Then Marie, just along for the ride (*as* I imagine she sincerely hopes). Not the worst way of stopping the week, suspenders guaranteed. The nice thing about Marie is she seems actually to enjoy getting dressed for it. No strings: the act for its own sake. And, dear me, dear me! in her it is already a little sad, so what of . . . bloody woman knows what I'm thinking. Wicked smile and promises of that luxuriant pubic prairie to get lost in. Uafff. Well, why not? It's an arrangement as good as any other. Ingestre would advise, no doubt: *quieta non movere*.

Rather sad couple, the steerage of Barbara's conscience, junior lecturer and his pastel-shaded wife. Wonder what colour wallpaper they have? It must match one or the other. Unkind thought. Unfunctional guests for J. Taylor. Please do not do that, Candida: it is one thing to disturb an experienced libertine in politics but quite another to inflame junior lecturers in political theory. He seems to go a paler shade of grey and she knows, godammit she knows. Jock Hay was unnecessarily savage to the lad earlier and poor little pale gold Buttercup is not having much of an evening.

Ah well. Ravelled sleeves of care about the National Front's 6 per cent at Thurrock. I think I've had enough politics for one week. Let's see if I can unknit Candida, in the sitting room. Not that it isn't a serious matter. . . . But there's a busy week ahead: there'll be a row over the guillotine measures and then Healey's economic package after that, with the left in full cry and hours of argument when there is nothing to argue about. Think I've drunk too much anyway.

. . . no, the problem is relaxing. It's not that I can't think of the most enticing ways: but when you're in politics these days it's devilishly difficult to get away from them. I mean most of my friends are either in politics or are interested more than the ordinary. And casual acquaintances, even if they're only vaguely concerned, always want to know what's happening on the inside. What about you? After all this is a pretty politically minded household. . . .

A jerk of the head and the lovely flaming red hair, movement of the slender shoulders. Blasé little bitch is bored with contemporary affairs. (I'll remember that.) Much more interested in history which she is reading under the wonderful Roger Ingestre, whom I of course know as a twinn'd lamb, my dear. And such is the irony of the times that I have to listen to an account of his wit and wisdom, when all that is ignoble in me wishes to make it plain to her that all this red-haired, grey-blue-green-eyed, lithe-limbed virginity is wasted on him and any quivering she proposes to do in the amaranthine asphodel should be alongside me.

. . . actually because we had the extraordinary misfortune to marry sisters. Roger's wife was called Daphne and mine was called Rosemary. We made the mistake quite independently; unmade it respectively in the same spirit – though he more in sorrow than anger, and I the reverse. Since which time he has lived a commendably chaste and dedicated life and I have had frequent cause to commune with my conscience. I'm glad it amuses you. We seldom refer to that dark age, but we know that it is a bond between us. . . .

At least she does seem to be amused. At worst, not even Ingestre in his highest moral tone could accuse me of not being honest about my disreputable nature. Not that he would bother.

I should guess that Ingestre must be the only male in this circle who hasn't had Marie, if that is the right way of seeing it. Well, Jock Hay. . . . Perhaps even so. It is all distasteful to someone as frankly impenitent as I am. Shall I set myself up as a judge impenitent? I should do good business. Strange how the confession keeps turning up. I don't go in for fictions.

Now what? J. Taylor has been talking to Ingestre (will no one rid me of this turbulent bloody historian going around like the still centre of a doldrum) about the conscience of the thirties and Roger has said some interesting things about the changing role of the middle class in definition as well as in intention, now that a viable and indeed vivid working-class tradition has developed in the arts and . . . Oh my God! Ingestre must not make jokes about television to a publisher! This is all such crap. Never mind. Call George Orwell. Call George Orwell. George Orwell, et cetera.

. . . after all castigated the Auden gang. Did he call them that, by the way? I can't remember. He said: 'They can swallow totalitarianism *because* they have no experience of anything except liberalism.' Now, given that there was so much posturing, this is still true of kids today, except that they seem to grow out of it faster. But much more disturbing is that it's not only middle-class kids. And one of the things I wish we could remind the far left about, inside our own party as well as the ape-men beyond, that they know nothing about a society that is not liberal.

J. Taylor snaps alert. It is reassuring that his daughter looks so unlike him. She is much prettier than Barbara, who is attractive enough: but quite unlike her father. Sallow, lined, rather dry face. Seeming encouraged, he asks if it is possible to get that message across to the people. For someone with such zeal and energy, J. Taylor needs a great deal of constant encouragement. If . . . She settles across the room and sweeps one leg across the other. Not able to resist the one glance . . . but now she knows I was watching. . . . Barbara puts a record on: *Blue Champagne*. What a very un-Taylor-like sentiment and commodity. The trouble is – and I had not thought about it until a moment ago, remembering *Wigan Pier* thinking about Orwell – all the inner Highgate people, are by origin, middle class or bourgeois. And the moderate centre *has to be* working class. And the

76

price of its moderation must be prosperity and incentive. So the theoretical administration has to be centre-right, rather than centre-left. It is a problem of inertia. The majority want stability and not change. But once the mass begins to move towards change, the momentum will not be easy to control, the inert force will build up. It cannot be guided by the middle class. Disturbing to see oneself as an archaism all at once.

An unmistakable signal from Marie, who is bored . . . Oh dear, where did all that surplus lust go? Thus conscience doth make eunuchs of us all. Come, come! It's as disturbing to realise that I want *young* women as it is to understand how seriously I take Taylor and Ingestre and the others.

*

Augustine Cornflour redux

The Gothic Club in Albemarle Street enjoyed a reputation, not unduly the envy of other such establishments, of favouring members who inclined in the broad sense to heterodoxy. Some were old-fashioned bohemians, which meant, in the context of London in the seventies, that they were drunks; others were *bon ton* radicals who did fashionable jobs and belonged to unfashionable (and ineffectual) trade unions. Many members were journalists, often writers of gossip and travel columns; script editors in television, smoking ugly little cigars; *declassé* talks producers; middle executives who liked to get drunk in good suits with their peers; peers, indeed, who desired a swinging reputation and who were too old for the fashionable fairgrounds of the moment. Among these were a handful of Members of Parliament, who held, discreetly, certain social predilections that cut across party lines in the most amiable and natural way. One of these was Augustine Cornflour – at least for the moment.

As he sat in a comfortable but faintly repulsive chair listening over a stiff brandy and soda to some very loud conversation from a nearby group which quite drowned out the repartee of his immediate companions, Augustine Cornflour wondered if it was time that the Gothic and he parted company. As a bachelor he did not need a club, and while under the Stokes administration his star had been firmly anchored to an irrevocably stuck juggernaut, he felt it would be wise perhaps for a politician of the left about to enter the vestibules of power to eschew the feckless reputation of clubman and boulevardier that had been worn with such rakish charm by the Member for Sprake East, as long as he had been a mere backbencher. Since Augustine was troubled more by appearance than principle – and cheerfully acknowledged the fact at least to himself – such adjustments of his life-style were of more immediate import than the shift in attitude that might be dictated by the sort of pragmatic alliance within the party which would ensure a junior ministry. Secure in his first-class intellectual virtuosity, he knew perfectly well that he could handle anything offered to him with superficial brilliance. And now that Stokes and his clique were departed, there was no reason why he should not rise rapidly.

The conversation that had attracted his attention by its volume rather than its quality, nevertheless succeeded in holding it, at the expense of the more adjacent trade in aphorisms. Two fellow Gothics, one a commentator on Parliament, the other the presenter of a television current affairs spot and both, as it happened, profoundly inspired by some Pierian brand of whisky, were engaged in talking each other out, vying for the privilege of being most intimately in the know. They had not seen Augustine or his two companions, each of whom even these brahminical ear-benders must have recognised as that much closer to the fountainhead of rumour. The nature of their speculation was obviously the retirement of Stokes and what it portended for the Nation, the Party; who was favourite to succeed; which long knives would be thrust where and when.

As very much a Man of his Time, Augustine Cornflour was not slow to grasp the importance of allies in the mass

78

communications trade, popularly misnamed the Media in a usage which had hammered quite a few sprigs into the coffin of decent syntax. Of his two companions Jonah Suckling-Bushey was a member of the Opposition and so irrelevant: while Rupert Wray, though of his own party, was unlikely to succeed. Augustine Cornflour, alone among the political Gothic on view, was metal attractive enough for these atlas-eaters. The odd world-weary still on television, as one of the promising younger men a pace away from the escalator; the mention of his name as an energetic, intelligent campaigner backstage in a widely read (sometimes believed) column: none of these and other accruing perquisites of Gothic association would do him any harm. Conversations, interviews, brief profiles.

Abruptly he got up, emptying his brandy and soda with the purposefulness of someone who has come to a decision.

'Time we were at the House,' he said pleasantly, after indulging Suckling-Bushey's most recent epigram.

The decisive movement distracted the journalist, Fenton Tumbril, as he was swinging emphatically sideways to deny a telling argument of Brian Spink, his brother beneath the skin, who turned following the direction of his gaze.

Moving amiably past them, Augustine allowed himself to be button-holed, as it behoved a fellow Gothic. He exchanged a joking word, noncommittal and charming. They wagged knowing fingers at him. Tumbril tried to wink but was too drunk to remember how it was done. Yet contact had been established and Augustine could easily make the next tactical move. Quite suddenly, he remembered Josephine, his niece, left to her own devices and, in a prophylactic spasm, shut his eyes.

'Hoy!' Gina said.

'Errahgh. . . . What? What you want?'

'The same again. It was deelishicious.'

'What?'

'No. Exactly the same.'

'Ignorant little cow, aren't you?'

'So what? You're a greasy barber's mate from Newport. *Aren't* you? Yaaach!'

She shrieked and for a rapturously loathing moment or two their hatred was consummated.

'Welsh bastard,' she said, struggling for sound.

It was true that Lucius Spiedermann had been born in Newport, Mon. (as it had been in those days). He had even been baptized as Sidney Derwent Perkins. And he had, indeed, begun his working life in a barber's shop as an apprentice. The entrepreneurial talent is not to be stilled, however. Quickly computing the number of clients who, suitably shorn, availed themselves of the wide variety of contraceptive outfitting, haberdashery and anointment in stock at J. J. Jones, Gentlemen's Hairdressing, the young man had cultivated a clientele and opened up a business of his own. As the progressive society of the sixties established itself, his own fortunes had flourished. Endowed with the lust of his fathers and the means to deliver it, the young but maturing Perkins had at the same time soon realised that a libidinous Welshman was, to the rest of Europe, a figure of fun. He had therefore shopped around for another patrimony. He was too pleasant to be French, too sallow to be Scandinavian. Along with most of his generation he had been brought up to be superstitiously anti-German, however sneakingly regardful of their drive and organisation. Central Europe was out of the question, although the Hungarian Revolution of 1956 offered a tempting opportunity to one of Nature's refugees. His first brief experiences in London taught him not to mix with Italians except on the most fixed touristic terms. And so he decided to adopt a Jewish persona: on the grounds that he could look the part; that he would be identified with the most tolerant, humorous and ironic people he had met; that Jews were thought to have infiltrated all profitable categories of business, without (on the whole) much violence; and that they were acknowledged, however erroneously, to possess enormous business acumen. In a very short time Perkins (now Spiedermann – a name chosen for its outlandishness as unlikely to give offence) rose to be a princeling of pornography and ultimately a kingpin in his own right. His sex shops, under suitably attractive aliases, opened all over London, Paris, Rome and sundry other tributary cities. The ingenuity of the artists and craftsmen who contributed to the gadgetry in which he dealt and the concordance of erotic invention of which he was the chief compiler astonished even Lucius Spiedermann. He prospered: and thought, at last, about entering politics.

In the ordinary way of business he had met a considerable number of important and powerful people in circumstances that could only have been to his advantage, without ever once imposing on any of them. At the same time, their intelligence and initiative quotient had not impressed him unduly. He had made the pleasant discovery that a most reliable conduit to their private society, their intimate lives and professional secrets, was through their junior staff, most of whom seemed susceptible to seduction.

Soon Lucius Spiedermann had co-ordinated a huge network of influence, intelligence and intrigue. At every turn, however, he had been thwarted by the dour chauvinism of Warrington Stokes from penetrating the inner sancta of power, and a single experience of the hustings had revolted him so completely that he soon abandoned any hankerings for the actual hurly-burly of the Palace of Westminster. Representations on his behalf to Warrington Stokes in regard to a life peerage had not been successful. The recently retired Premier had objected to Lucius's pre-political career, which he did not consider wholesome. Lucius had argued (out of shot) that he had provided entertainment for thousands perhaps millions of people and it was well known that Stokes liked the people to be kept entertained. Not apparently by the kind of spectacle mounted by Lucius Spiedermann! Bitterly he reflected that a Welshman would not have been so narrow of outlook in high office.

And so a sanguine, essentially outgoing and accommodating nature was soured. By his mid-forties, Lucius Spiedermann was thoroughly disenchanted and his creative energies turned to the bad. Retaining all his surface amiability, Lucius began to plot with the zeal of an imperial Roman, but more sanely, a work of magnificent destruction that would leave British politics a wasteland.

He knew about Augustine Cornflour and had chosen him as the agent of destruction. Then, by a stroke of sheer good fortune, which suggested that the omens were in his favour, he had discovered too that Gina, one of the girls who had been started in films by Lucius himself, had reverted to a secretarial career and was in the employ of this designated angel of wrath. A mistress shared is a labour spared, had always been an axiom with Lucius. Soon he was privy to the cellarage and rumpus rooms of Cornflour's ménage. He was able to provide certain services, and, as mutual trust grew, was able to offer discreetly the assurance of financial support.

Yet once more the Right Hon. Warrington Stokes woke up in the middle of the night laughing from a dream of blissful confusion, as he realised that the confusion *he* had caused surpassed even his wildest dreams. He gurgled quietly in the dark so as not to disturb his wife and breathed, 'Oh dear me!' to himself. The fox was at the grapes, the boot was on the other foot, the geese were fancying themselves like nobody's business, and it was no longer a matter of kicking against the pricks.

'How are things at Furgusson Jungfrau?' asked Rubicon Tweed.

Anaximander Split remained silent, having cultivated the art. He did not actually smile, but he allowed a suggestion of humour to flicker in his dark eyes.

'Pretty sound from the Jungfrau end of things I imagine,' said Tweed, hopefully.

Anaximander sipped a paint-stripping sherry with stoic aplomb and gazed unblinkingly at his host for drinks. Ruth Tweed crossed her legs. Anaximander Split blinked on a rare occasion: for a woman in her early forties she was unusually shapely.

'Anaximander has been frightfully busy, haven't you, Anaximander?' said Dahlia Dackord.

Anaximander Split glanced at her: she appeared to be wearing chintz pyjamas which were even less suitable than the hat.

'It's a busy time for everyone,' he said unemotionally.

Everyone laughed.

'I don't suppose things are too bad at the Furgusson end – from what I hear, putting two and two together,' said Rubicon Tweed.

'So Stokes has resigned,' said Anaximander. 'How will that affect you at the Treasury?'

'Not intrinsically.'

'Perhaps impendingly?'

'I'd prefer to say convergently. If you get my meaning. Darling.'

'Yes, darling?'

'I'm sure,' said Tweed, 'that . . . er . . . Dahlia would like to see the new disposal unit. Of perhaps the microwave oven. . . .'

'Love to!' said Dahlia Dackord. 'I know what that means in our set, Ruth dear. It means business talk, doesn't it, Anaximander? Which, anyway, is frightfully boring.' She smiled with fixed concentration at Anaximander Split who gave her a cordial slow grin in return.

'Split,' said Rubicon Tweed, when the two ladies had departed, 'I won't beat about the bush. The opportunities at the moment are good: we must profit by them and so must England. I don't think that is pitching it too high.'

Anaximander Split moved his glass enigmatically from left to right and a little way back.

'Whoever succeeds,' said Tweed, 'now that Stokes has gone, it means that his entourage must go too. And even if Cokeoven remains Chancellor, discontinuity is assured. There must be movement at the Treasury, whether it be Elwyn Poinsettia, Barnaby Freeth or Sir Hoke Dick who moves into Number Ten.'

Anaximander watched as Rubicon Tweed arose impressively from his chair, juggling his glass lightly between two well-kept fingers and took an airy turn around his autumn-coloured sitting room, rounding with an authoritative tilt of his jaw and eyebrows that suggested imponderable knowledge.

'I am in a position to provide important Treasury advice to a consortium of talent and ability prepared to put this country back on its feet. But that cannot be done under the present lot. And the others are no better and from many points of view worse. Once Dame Letitia Cloude and her cronies are in, it will be mightily difficult to recruit from industry and the City the kind of brains and determination that we need for the cause.'

Rubicon Tweed paused dramatically.

'I am inviting you, Split, as a man of incomparable business skill and of matchless contacts, to form this consortium of conscientious drive that I have outlined. Names come to mind: Lord Steroid from industry, Mungo Starveling and his vast press empire, Reynard Tarsus from the media; men of energy, resolution, with the ruthlessness necessary to grasp this nettle power and shake it in the face of the world. If I may say so, I know you to be a patriot in the way perhaps that only someone who has learned to love this country and culture as a foster child can be: that is why I take this risk in putting this excitingly dangerous idea to you. You know what I am able to deliver. And deliver it I will to the right men.'

Anaximander Split fought with a bubble of bursting glee

84

that he had not known since the age of eight and a half. Here was a glorious opportunity to infiltrate not only the politico-economic labyrinth of the United Kingdom, now perhaps less a maze than a derelict earthworks, but to gain access to the secrets of Europe, to traffic with the mages of Washington, Tokyo and the Alpine fastnesses, at governmental level.

He nodded coolly.

'You realise that I will have to think about this,' he said.

'Of course. But time is short. We need, at the top, an important figurehead. Someone loved and respected as a symbol of our Island race.' Again Tweed paused significantly. 'And we need at the immediate level someone who will be our creature, but who will at the same time present a convincingly statesmanlike image to the mass.'

'You have someone in mind?'

'At the moment someone relatively obscure – but possessed of the shrewd intelligence which, in his case, is modified by the required mindless hedonism. His name is Augustine Cornflour.'

Of all her uncle's friends, Josephine thought that Rufus Bushchat was much the nicest. Not merely because he was quite good looking, but because he was also very clever and behaved extremely well towards her. Josephine had never doubted that she was pretty: many men had told her so and others had not bothered to waste time or words. She had all the same been more than a little surprised by the reaction of Uncle Augustine's acquaintances, some of whom must have been friends. She had been patted, frotted, stroked, paddled, pawed and even pinched by gentlemen of various status in age, accomplishment, importance and matrimony. Apart from the ones who were quite evidently otherwise inclined, only her uncle and Rufus Bushchat had refrained from actually touching her somewhere or on some pretext.

Josephine had been brought up at a school run by nuns in The Hague, which she had enjoyed. Any religious influence had been suitably countered by home life, where both her parents encouraged a healthy scepticism about all things, including faith of any kind. At the same time they held highly everything associated with fidelity, aided in this by their own compatibly rational affection for each other. This was why Josephine had always been intrigued by her devil-may-care uncle, Augustine: now so responsible and busy in Parliament. Her pleasant and uncomplicated childhood had not made of Josephine an ingenuous, much less a dis-ingenuous, young woman. She was virginal but not innocent; and her only exercise in guile was to conceal how clever she was. She spoke several languages: French, German, Italian, some Spanish (and therefore could read Portuguese), Dutch, of course, enough Swedish to get by in Norway and Den-mark as well, and Russian. But languages alone (easy enough, after all, for someone brought up by nuns in The Hague) were not the core of Josephine's intellectual surety. Her father was an international lawyer and her mother a professor of Classics, but her own flair was for aesthetics and she had been lucky enough to nourish it upon experience of many of the masterpieces of ancient, medieval and modern times.

Josephine knew that her sardonic, laughing uncle was mildly amused by Rufus Bushchat. He respected his scholar-ship (which had after all been proven on both sides of the Atlantic and in Australia), but he knew him to be (so he said) ineffectual. Josephine wondered if this simply meant that Rufus was kind, thoughtful, not a bit lecherous – if inclined to be demonstrably a little brighter and better informed than most people around him at any given time. She was interested enormously to hear about his long book (to which he referred somewhat coyly as 'the tome'). It was entitled: *Towards Apoliticism in British Politics*, and was subtitled 'A Necessary Paradox'. Altogether it was packed with ideas, adagia and lucid marginalia – or so it would seem to be from his en-thralling account of it.

As he leaned forward eagerly to explain a tricky corollary, using his hands expressively, she thought for a moment that he *too* was (in the enthusiasm of the moment) about to touch her. She was rather disappointed when he didn't, and accordingly started with quite needless guilt when her uncle suddenly opened the door.

'. . . the under-subtlety of the intellectual centre at a time of centripetal national anxieties . . .' Rufus was saying.

He leapt to his feet.

'Hello, Gustin!' he said warmly.

Josephine saw her uncle's eyes travel over her slightly disarranged dress, which she had just not been aware of, listening to Rufus. His eyes seemed to mist over a little – she hoped very much that he had not misconstrued what had been happening. He fixed Rufus Bushchat with an exceedingly ironic eye.

'Don't let me interrupt, Rufus,' he said. 'Do carry on with what . . . you were saying. . . .'

He seemed astonished when Rufus, gratified, did exactly that.

Naomi de Wagram sighed deeply inside and heaved one plump thigh over the other. The fanatic light in Mr Wynstanley's eyes behind his grubby spectacles became feverish; he licked the straggled ends of his already damp-looking moustache with the tip of his pale pink tongue. Mrs de Wagram thought shudderingly that it matched the colour of her *lingerie* of the day. It was almost distasteful but it kept Mr Wynstanley screwed to the right pitch of enthusiasm and a little vulgar display of her underclothing was not much in return for his devoted and tireless leg-work, especially since he never showed any inclination to do anything than lick his moist moustache. She consoled herself with the thought that perhaps Gina would need a massage when she came in.

'The Psychobolic Church is doing remarkably well in Bognor,' he said, in his curiously deep voice. 'That means that we have significant branches in seven towns on the

South Coast between Dover and Weymouth as well as cells in all the Home Counties. In Greater London we grow almost hourly. Bequests to the end of June amount to £357811 and 7p. It was a stroke of genius to extend psychobolics to the animal kingdom beyond, Madam. A stroke of genius. You could afford,' he looked respectfully around, 'to move into more luxurious premises. You could afford, Madam, to give up taking paying guests.'

'Wynstanley,' said Mrs de Wagram, cocking her leg a little more, 'do not meddle in these matters which are not your concern. We will invest our resources wisely. We must bend our minds to earning Dollars and Deutsche marks. We can become a not inconsiderable invisible asset. Wynstanley, I have every hope that we shall soon go into politics; I have reason to believe that the Guide will shortly offer us access to the most highly placed. I shall say no more for the moment, Wynstanley: but you must be prepared.'

'Madam, I . . .'

'Not another word, Wynstanley!' commanded Mrs de Wagram, swinging the raised leg (with some difficulty) away in generous revelation. 'Obedience is the key to Psychobolic Hyper-living. Remember that.'

She closed her eyes upon Mr Wynstanley's heated stare and quivering lip and leaned resignedly further back.

All the men wore dark, well-pressed trousers with white gaiters and well-shone service boots. Their gleaming shirts were of military cut with epaulettes and the same armband flash. One or two wore badges signifying length or distinction of service. To a harsh command they all stamped smartly, as one, to attention. At a second command, they lifted their arms in stiff salute as a slender figure stalked into the hall and wheeled to face them. She wore brilliant knee-length boots, riding breeches and a startlingly white shirt of slightly modified cut – otherwise similar in style to those of the men. Her hair was drawn back severely into a bun. In her right hand she carried a riding crop with which she returned their salute.

The men roared a guttural greeting. Her eyes blazing, Dahlia Dackord stood proudly before the East Peckham Cohort of the English Valkyrie Brigade.

Arnold Espadrille surveyed his supermarket from the glass-encased vantage-point which served as the manager's personal cubicle. His high, domed forehead was furrowed and his deep-set eyes were anxiously watchful. He was obviously a highly strung person who took his work seriously and for whom the Maple Street Fresh 'n' Freeze was a pleasure-dome of victuals, liquors and toilet requisites equal to none. But as in the case of all such men holding down responsible jobs, a casual observer, less imbued with ambition, might have asked himself if the tireless pursuit of perfection in grocery and its allied trades was worth it. Towards the end of a day, Arnold Espadrille's eyes took on a mauvish weariness, his quick movements suggested hair-trigger tension and his Napoleonic habit of standing with one hand inside the flap of his light-weight business suit might have been seen as testimony of appalling acidosis.

It was, of course, laughable. Inside, Arnold Espadrille was icy calm. Alone in his glass cubicle, above the shoppers, a quietly supercilious smile often settled complacently upon his mouth and the deep-set eyes shifted in lazy mirth. Complacent he could be: because very few people in the entire world, even in the closely knit world of espionage (where there are few secrets), knew that Arnold Espadrille ran, from the Maple Street Fresh 'n' Freeze, the deadliest and most efficient arm of British Internal Security, so tightly organised as not even to have a cipher.

At that moment, he noticed a rather shabby customer with a draggled moustache and spectacles stealthily slipping a packet of Tampax into his raincoat pocket. In a flash, Arnold Espadrille was out of the cubicle, down the steps in a bound, and jinking expertly through the shopping backs and wire trolleys, avoiding pensioners and toddlers alike in his single-minded purpose. Things must be desperate if an experienced man of the calibre of Cyril resorted to Gambit 69. His hand fell upon the greasy shoulder of the shoplifter, who immediately began to cringe and whine. With firmness but not without humanity, Arnold Espadrille led him to a private part of the store, away from the predatory curiosity of the shopping public. He told the staff he could manage; and it was only behind the bolted door, that his pale kindly face became hard and alert as he snapped:

'All right, Wynstanley, what the hell's going on?'

*

'I'm surprised that you weren't in Intelligence,' said Clodia Oricellari.

'There's a simple explanation. I volunteered in August 1939,' said Robert Blakemore. 'The immediate assumption was that I wanted to see action.'

'I think it's what I would have expected you to do.'

'Not a very difficult decision, in fact. I was twenty, fiercely patriotic and a conservative. It was an infinitely more searing predicament for the intelligent and sentimental left, who had been talking for years about a "capitalist" war.'

'Why was that?'

'They felt alienated from their intellectual peers. It's remarkable how few of those who talked about "the struggle" in the preceding years felt called upon to join it actively when it occurred. They found work of national importance.'

'Whereas for you . . . ?'

'I knew quite well that I should be commissioned, of course: but it did not matter into which regiment. I became an infantry officer.'

'Did you regret it?'

'There were times when I cursed my recklessness. But we matured quickly and I don't think, given foreknowledge, I should have opted for anything else.'

'But there were bad moments.'

'There were. At first I missed the fighting in Belgium and France, because we were posted to Palestine. Subsequently to Cairo.'

'And the desert.'

'Yes. It wasn't pleasant: but more a matter of discomfort, dirt and boredom than horror. There were, of course, moments of danger when we were very frightened: but what I remember most now is that it was dirty, sweaty, gritty and desperately tedious. I imagine you were much too young to remember what it was like in Italy.'

'I was five when the war ended there. Was that worse?'

'Very much so. I shan't bore you with campaign anecdotes, but it was difficult. At the beginning the weather was atrocious and we were advancing uphill, so to speak. The enemy took to the hills where we had to pursue them. If we'd tried moving along the valleys, they could have picked us off with the greatest of ease. It was cold, muddy and murderously hard going. Then there was Anzio.'

'I've read something of that.'

'Intended, of course, as a quick savage strike to take us neatly into Rome and avoid weeks of fighting. A month later we were bogged down in carnage. Battle is never ennobling, however well individuals behave.'

'And then, at last, you did enter Rome.'

'Which, mercifully, had been declared an Open City. I cannot describe to you the sensation of driving into Rome in a jeep, as a conqueror. I had always loved the Classics and been temperamentally more drawn to Rome than to Greece. I do not recall ever being so deeply moved, while at the same time aware of a bitter irony.'

'No feeling of triumph?'

'Absolutely none. A feeling of waste. Perhaps an intensely painful spasm of humility.'

'It's easy to forget that you were still only a little more than twenty.'

'And by that time a major. But, as I said a few minutes

ago, we matured quickly, of necessity. I'm sorry. I've digressed. What I was trying to say at the beginning was how deeply fond I am of Italy.'

'It was I who prompted the digression.'

'Did your family suffer at all?'

'I imagine my father suffered quite a lot emotionally, but he managed to keep us sheltered. I suppose that even as a child there was some sense of the humiliation that attends even a wished-for conquest.'

'Your father was not involved in politics?'

'Very deliberately not. I've sometimes wondered if this was not a form of collaboration. But, as you know, we have a long tradition of swaying before the tempests of one tyrant or another. My father was always suspect to the Fascists. Then, when the partisans took Venice before the Allies arrived, they, too, had doubts. I suppose that is why I grew up with a sense of belonging to nothing very much except the Oricellari name. I suppose we shared the usual privations, but as a child I wasn't especially aware of them.'

'You were only five.'

'Yes. And my sister, Francesca, wasn't born.'

'And none of your family were involved in the actual fighting?'

'No. My father was wounded in the First War quite badly. My brothers were too young. . . .'

'Which, alas, would not have mattered had they been German.'

'Indeed.'

'Our European resilience is really something astonishing, I think: this extraordinary capacity we have had, for two thousand years and more, to fight most savagely and then, as the occasion demands, to make treaties and behave with total if temporary amicality.'

'Ah! You are not a committed European.'

'As it happens, I am. But I'm not a sentimentalist and I see no evidence of any desire anywhere in Europe, except among the Germans perhaps and the Dutch, for any practicable unity.'

'I think there's something of the sort in Italy, but we're obviously weakened by the economic and constitutional mess we're in. I should have said, perhaps rather too bluntly, that the British and the French are the obstacles to unity: you, because your people don't want to relinquish a cosy and cherished xenophobic tradition; the French because they distrust everyone and are most blatantly interested in their own well-being, if necessary at everyone else's expense. And anyway, what about your devolution problems?'

'Pure expediency. Apart from a handful of relatively well-educated brahmins, the Welsh want nothing of the sort; and I suspect it is a fashion bred of discontent among the Scots. Given any kind of economic recovery separatism will die of natural causes. Would you care for some brandy? I do not take coffee myself, but of course you would like some.'

'Thank you. A little Cognac perhaps. Do you know what impresses me so much each time I come back to this country for any length of time?'

'It would be amusing to guess: but please tell me.'

'Quite apart from the usual clichés about tolerance and good temper against an amazingly durable class structure, all of which are true, it is the British appetite for theories.'

'Yes. Bonaparte was misinformed. We are a nation of committee-men, at all levels of society. It is why our trades unions are so over-developed.'

'Oh, I'm not making any criticism. It's better than tearing up the pavements and smashing windows, or other people. I'm simply interested in the almost universal desire to be identified with a group.'

'I suppose you're right. . . . Ah, Charles. . . . Some coffee, please. And we will both take Cognac.'

'The Remy-Martin Fine Champagne, sir?'

'Thank you. . . . Yes, I suppose you're right. Do you know the word "clubbable"?'

'It's a very good word. If I may say so, you seem much more independent than a lot of other Englishmen.'

'Do I? I think they would be rather surprised to hear it. And some would dispute it energetically. I went to a certain school, then to a particular college. I belong to my Senior Common Room quite actively. I served in a regiment and occasionally attend its functions. I am a member of one of the Inns of Court and subscribe to two learned societies. Even at this moment, I have the pleasure of entertaining you here, by virtue of a deliberate wish to associate with others of similar taste and temperament in the shelter of an exclusive institution.'

'I didn't mean that exactly. . . . Ah, thank you. What elegant silver. . . . No, I meant that you are independent-minded. Roger Ingestre says that of you.'

'I'm sure that Ingestre says all manner of things about me. He certainly does to my face! Well, I am, naturally, flattered to be thought such an individualist. But I'm inclined to think that what independence I possess is cerebral and on the whole political. As for Ingestre, apart from his connection with this band of North West frontiers-men of modern democracy, he is independent enough to be thought wilful.'

'You have reservations about his group?'

'To do him justice, I don't think it is *his*, is it? As I understand it Ingestre is senior choreographer, rather than impresario. In fact, from what I have seen of the other members, they are people of excellent conscience and quite alarming fatuity. Have you met many of them?'

'Not yet. One or two. But I am very interested in the chance of observing such a . . . what shall I call it . . . such a political phenomenon.'

'A political phantasm. Made of moonshine. But, of course, I am an old-fashioned conservative who believes in polarity rather than consensus – so that the public is offered a choice which is positive. I happen to believe in leadership as manifested in senatorial government, allowing as much freedom of enterprise as possible. I shall confess to you that I believe this, while absolutely right, to be archaic, in that it is no longer possible to denationalise. A "mixed" economy must, in the long run, fail somewhere in the treacherous shallows of collective bargaining, with the inevitable discrepancies between the private and public sectors. The long march to Marxism must inevitably arrive in Whitehall. And then, my dear lady, and only then, will individuals of courage and distinction reassert themselves.'

'I hope you're wrong. For the sake of Europe, anyway. And I think you are. You see, as an outsider, it seems to me very healthy that you have so many able people prepared to give time and energy to this sort of theorising. Roger's group is just an example and a good one, I think. It's what I meant when I said you, the English, have a talent for theorising in little groups.'

'Yes. You said: "getting into groups to examine even the tiniest symptoms of national malaise". Doesn't this suggest hypochondriasis? In any event, such groups, including even Ingestre and his friends, are fiercely exclusive. If we might borrow the metaphor from *Coriolanus*, it is as though each representative part of the body politic imagined itself to be entirely healthy while the rest was ailing and liable to infect the healthy organ. You see, I was interested in my own defensive posture when you accused me of independence of mind.'

'Well, it wasn't intended as an accusation. . . .'

'No. Of course not. . . . Some more brandy, I think. . . . I did not intend to sound churlish. . . .'

'You did not. Nor, incidentally, did you sound defensive!'

'Nevertheless, I was. I listed immediately my school, college and so on. The charmed circles inside which I felt secure. I think you have put your finger upon our extraordinary capacities in these islands to seek out opportunities for ritual. When I think about it, it is a European tendency which is satisfied variously by religious ceremonies and political rallies. Now we have no great ceremony in our churches except on those rare occasions which involve the Royal Family; and we are not much good at political rallies – so we have turned to other kinds of ritual that involve, generally, a freemasonry of shared experience and interest. Sometimes vested interest.'

'This *is* very good brandy.'

'*Touché*. Nevertheless, I shall round off my hypothesis. On great occasions of state we all get together and are complaisantly moved: the rest of the time we band together in compact units and commune inside them.'

'It's not quite what I mean, but I like the game. What were the areas you listed? School, college . . .'

'And University. Especially Oxford and Cambridge.'

'Yes. Then regiment or whatever it might be, professional or learned society, club and so on.'

'Anything where we submit to the rules and protocols of a corporate body. I'm inclined to think we take it further than you do, or the rest of modern Europe does. Look at the way our football supporters behave. I don't think that it is as ritualised in other countries, however fanatical the enthusiasm.'

'Perhaps the young share more of these rituals across the boundaries. I was on one of the Greek Islands a summer or so ago which is almost entirely taken over by very young people, living on next to nothing. Yes, certainly, there were rituals – but in no sense circumscribed by some kind of national identity.'

'Oh dear! I refuse to manifest any untoward hope in the young. I see no sign that they are any less confused than they ever have been.'

'Except of course for your own rapidly matured generation. I'm sorry. That sounds insulting now that I've said it.'

'There's no need to apologise. That generation had its own psychological problems. It was disciplined and destructive, all at once. Usually after drinking bouts. Destruction is one kind of outlet which is legitimatised by ritual.'

'Ah now. If there is one thing that the British do ritualise, it's drinking. Even more than the Germans. The "pub" is the parish church of ritual. Think of the words you use – "local", "regular", "governor" and so on. . . .'

'How very depressing! Do you know, I think the British pub is the most over-rated and uncomfortable and dirty of places, usually sauced with surly indifference. I use them as little as possible. In Italy and in France it is possible to drink, even to get drunk, in a civilised manner – without relying on privilege. Here it is not.'

'But pubs are fun.'

'There we are at a point of absolute deadlock. Would you like more coffee?'

'No. I'm afraid I must be going soon. It was very kind of you to give me lunch.'

'It was kind of you to agree to come.'

'Are you going back to Oxford?'

'In due course. I'm meeting my wife, who has been shopping. Perhaps that strikes you as odd. She very much dislikes this place. We shall be driving back later.'

'How long have you been married?'

'Twenty-nine years. After Anzio and Rome, which is more or less where we came in, I was transferred to a staff job. My wife's father was a brigadier who took a liking to me. We've had a very happy life together.'

'Do you have children?'

'Five. You look surprised. But that is my fault. I spend so much time in predictable company that I sometimes neglect the ordinary courtesies. I hope we may meet again soon. I have very much enjoyed this. . . .'

*

The summer continued to be intolerably hot. Candida was often bad-tempered and annoyed with herself for being so easily ruffled. She wished that she had agreed to go away somewhere on one of the various parties she had been asked to join. Not that any of them were especially exciting: most people of her own age were impossibly juvenile and much more suited to Jessica, now pounding about on the already brown grass after a ball at the end of a length of elastic. Graceless little cow, Candida thought.

She was always ready to admit the truth to herself: she was cross because she had made up her mind to be seduced by Roger Ingestre. Having prompted him quite subtly and discreetly, so that there was no embarrassment possible, the stupid and arrogant man had noticed nothing. *Then* he had taken her to a pub where Steve Kent had obviously taken a vac job in order to be a bloody nuisance. She had known nothing about it and it had ended in a ghastly evening when Steve had tried to grope her in a taxi. Of course, it was ridiculous to suppose that there was any kind of conspiracy between Roger and Stephen Kent: but how dare the fucking man try to interfere in her life and arrange things. The insult was so typical of the ways in which her parents' generation went about things. They were dishonest.

They were also pipe-dreamers. She listened, on and off, each day to some avid reaction to a scrap of news into which they had read the token of imminent collapse of the existing balance of idiocy: so that their musical comedy alliance with Roger, and Rachel Bailey, and so on, could take centre stage. How could supposedly intelligent adults behave so fatuously. And then her mother had been humiliatingly rude to her in Roger's earshot about reading Namier on George III. Sometimes Candida wished that she had ordinary, reasonably stupid parents who would just be pleased with what she achieved. She was sure that Stephen Kent's father, the village bobby somewhere, was absolutely delighted with him whatever he did. And Candida knew quite well that she was better than Stephen Kent. She was intelligent and no one gave her credit for intelligence: they treated her like Jessica.

Candida swore, using as many disgusting words as she could effectively string together. She went upstairs to her room and snatched *Structure and Politics at the Accession of George III* from the table. Candida had no doubt that her mother was enormously clever and had lapped it all up: but

98

it was so bloody BORING! She fell into a reverie about her parents' sex life. How on earth could two such cerebral people have produced daughters like Jessica and herself. Candida had inherited something of her mother's effortless elegance, but she knew that she was better looking, and so was Jessica in a bucolic sort of way. Candida saw her sister's over-developed boobies flopping about as she pursued the ball and shuddered. Intelligent as she was, however, Candida realised that she was nothing like as bright as either Barbara or Jeremy. And as for Jessica – she was simply thick.

Her mind drawled idly over the almost unimaginable intimacies between her parents. My God! A passionate Mummy coiling herself around a Daddy possessed by high wild animal lust! Candida giggled. In fact, it was probably all carefully timed, wonderfully efficient and expert, orga- nised along the lines of a maximum pleasure principle with every finger tip (et cetera) on the right spot at the appropriate moment. It was all a bit cruel and she felt momentarily ashamed of herself. But what the hell: they really asked for it. Barbara and Daddy both laughed a great deal but neither of them had any real sense of humour.

It was probably all over between them anyway: that side of things. Intellectual stimulation was what they wanted and got from one another and (of course) emotional support. Emotional! They were both entirely capable of deciding that sex was no longer apt on any regular basis, though still a useful cathartic. Which is how Candida saw it. She had firmly decided that it was time to stop being a virgin, but she was not going to become an easy lay and certainly not with any hobbledehoy of her own age like Steve Kent, beautiful as he was. Idly she found herself wondering whether her parents had affairs and if so with whom. Curiously enough, for the first time she coupled her mother with Roger Ingestre. It simply hadn't occurred to her before. And it was a dis- agreeable and discomposing idea. She was all too readily able to imagine a passionate Ingestre, intellectual or not. And ...

She threw her book aside. It was always the same when she was bored. Sooner or later her mind would start working on erotic lines, and as often as not the fantasy got the better of her. She stood up firmly and went to look out of the window at the blazingly hot afternoon, trying to quieten what was stirring inside her.

To her considerable surprise, she saw Roger Ingestre himself coming along the road at a brisk easy pace, wearing his permanently agreeable expression, which she supposed in some contexts might be construed as smug. Candida knew quite well that he was expected sometime in the evening, along with several other politic would-bes – but not for hours yet. He turned in at their gate.

Before she actually had time to really think about it, Candida found herself stripping off her dress. And her bra. She went to her wardrobe and reached for Daddy's witty Christmas present – an absurdly sexy dressing gown. Then she chose the old tatty one hanging behind the door and slipped it on. She knew that Roger had his own key and would let himself in, probably expecting no one to be there. Now, if stupid little Jessica would go on belting hell out of her bloody tennis-ball . . . Candida arranged the dressing gown so that it almost covered her breasts, tied it at the waist, but let it flow open below. She was wearing, as she always did, very pretty white pants.

As soon as she heard the door click, she went downstairs, calling: 'Is that you, Daddy? I didn't expect you back so soon. It's so bloody hot, I was just going to have a bath. . . . Oh,' (with a little shriek), 'Roger!'

Roger Ingestre was putting a brief-case down upon a chair. He looked up, smiling: and, with some triumph, Candida noticed, for the first time, something perceptible changed in his face. Something definitely happened. She let him look for a moment and then pulled the dressing gown tighter over her breasts in instinctive confusion, having of course to readjust it lower down a moment later, so that it fell partly away again from the top half.

'Hullo,' he said. 'You're a very pretty sight on a hot afternoon. I'm sorry to barge in. I didn't think there'd be anyone here. I was seeing someone in Hampstead for lunch and so I walked across the Heath. I didn't think it was worth going all the way home and back again. I thought I'd do a little work here. It's not inconvenient, is it?'

'Not at all. I'm sorry I'm in this state of undress. God, it's so *hot*, isn't it! I'm taking about a dozen baths a day. Can I get you a drink, or something? I made gallons of lemonade this morning.'

'Thank you.'

'Or would you like something else? We've got some Pimms, I think.'

'Lemonade will be fine. I've already had rather too much wine. Don't let me keep you hanging about, Candida. There's no rush.'

'It won't take a second.'

Candida turned quickly and swept away, so that the dressing gown swirled a little. Unlike Jessica, she always moved gracefully and made the most of it. Roger followed her into the kitchen, which she thought was probably a good sign – usually when he was not interested, it was perfectly evident. She bent to take the jug of lemonade out of the fridge, wrapping the dressing gown around her hips more tightly as she did so. It fell away a little as she reached up for a couple of glasses. She turned towards him, her eyes innocently widened. But Roger was at the window watching Jessica pounding about sweatily with her tennis racket.

'Splendid little Jess!' he said. 'Where *does* she get all her energy.'

'Shall we go back into the sitting room?' Candida said.

She was terrified that Jessica would turn around and see him, whereupon she would come lolloping in – sticky and panting – to gulp lemonade and chatter away pointlessly. Jessica would immediately notice how she was dressed and would say all the wrong things.

Roger's eyes dawdled momentarily over her partly exposed

breasts. But only momentarily. Luckily she blushed, with her hands full of the jug and glasses. There was something promisingly quizzical in his expression.

'Let me take something from you,' he said. She handed him the jug and adjusted the top of the dressing gown.

As usual he managed to lounge stylishly on the sofa. He was always so effortlessly relaxed: Candida wondered if it was a natural gift or something he had acquired. Of all the people she knew, only her mother could match him; and even then she relied on elegance of movement rather than a properly easy manner. She sat in the deep chair opposite, crossed her legs, and was careful to cover herself modestly with the tatty gown.

'I'm surprised you're both in London,' Roger said. 'Even if you don't want to rollick around Greece in the boring path of your coevals, I'd have thought you'd be at the country retreat.'

'Why?'

'Well, as much as I love London, this heat is almost too much.'

'Can you imagine what it would be like stuck down there with Jessica? Anyway, I'm trying to work. At the BM and so on.'

'Indeed.'

Candida was not quite sure that she liked the inflection.

'Anyway I hate the bloody country. It is so *boring*.'

'I enjoyed the other weekend very much.'

'Oh, so did I! It's fine when they have people to stay. That was a super weekend. I'm glad you thought so too. But even if we wanted to, Daddy's not terribly keen on our going down there alone.'

Candida made a wry and amusing face.

'I think,' she said, 'he's afraid we'd be ravished by rampaging yokels.'

Roger Ingestre's eyebrows shifted amiably.

'Terrifying prospect,' he said.

Candida changed position artfully.

'Perhaps,' she said, smiling. 'I suspect that Jessica would love it.'

Without making it especially apparent, she sensed that he was not pleased by her joke, though he looked as serene as ever.

'The association of ideas is entirely fortuitous,' he said, 'but are you seeing anything of Steve Kent?'

'No.'

'Nice chap,' said Ingestre.

Candida shrugged.

'I can't imagine what he's doing in Highgate,' she said. 'I'd have thought he was the perfect candidate for sun-baked banalities on a Mediterranean rock.'

'Really? I'd have thought you knew him better. He's a very serious young man. He's after a first. And I think he has to take a job in the vac.'

'He could always sign on at the Labour Exchange,' Candida said.

'Not the type. I've got a lot of time for young Kent.'

'What's this, Roger? Do you disapprove of Social Security? What would Daddy say?'

Ingestre chose to ignore the challenge.

'If hard work counts for as much as it should, he'll do pretty well,' he said.

'Stephen Kent?'

'Yes.'

'What about me, Roger?'

'What *about* you, Candida?'

'Will I "do well"? And shall I deserve it?'

'You've as good a chance as anyone else. In fact, there's a hell of a lot going for you.'

'Such as Daddy and his friends?'

'And your mother.'

He waved his hand vaguely around the room and the books.

'It's all here,' he said, 'if you want to use it.'

'Do you think I'm lazy?'

'I suppose I do. Yes.'

'At least you care?'

'What d'you mean by that?'

'Well, I hope you won't take this the wrong way, but you've never shown much interest in me. Academically, I mean. Of course.'

'I'm sorry.'

'Obviously you think that Stephen Kent and Lumber-knickers are worthwhile. . . .'

'My God! Are you accusing me of that whatnot that won't confess its name?'

Candida was badly flustered.

'Christ, no! I didn't mean anything. . . .'

'I was talking about male chauvinism, Candida.'

That made it worse. Candida used the moment of confusion to disarrange herself a little. Ingestre smiled gently.

'Well, you've been helping Stephen Kent quite a lot. . . .'

'I've been helping him get hold of a few books. This place is sinking into the famous London clay under the weight. And Jeremy and Barbara belong to libraries in the way that most people have cups of tea.'

He spread both arms along the back of the sofa. For an essentially cerebral man, he was very well made, almost athletic.

'So you have been seeing Steve?' he said.

'Only when we went to that horrible little pub.'

He nodded.

'Oh Roger!' she said. 'I don't mean to sound petulant, but it's not easy. Mummy and Daddy are so fucking clever that everyone expects me to sail through everything. And I quite honestly haven't a clue what I am, or how good. So much rubs off. Even Jessica sounds bright sometimes.'

He seemed not to have registered her carefully placed obscenity. No doubt deliberately.

'Do you honestly care that much about how well you do in Schools?' he said.

'Obviously.'

'Why? What do you want to be?'

'I just want to prove I'm good at something.'

'And that's all?'

'Isn't it enough?'

Candida leaned forward and gripped the arms of the chair. She actually felt angry and guessed she must look pretty startling, because the dressing gown which had already slipped away from her thighs was now drawn tightly off her bosom. What was wrong with the bloody man! He eyed her fleetingly.

'Yes,' he said. 'Of course. What can I do about it?'

'What do you suggest?'

'What are you offering as a special subject?'

'Economic policy. Peel and so on.'

'Then Heaven alone knows you live in the house of one of the best possible . . .'

'Mummy? None of you have any idea about how impatient she can be! You really haven't. You see the soignée Barbara Dunn, veteran of a hundred "Any Questions"! But I won't go on. . . . Will you really help me?'

'I'll do what I can.'

'It's constitutional documents.'

'Don't you have Miss Bradshaw?'

'Oh Christ, Roger! It's like communicating with Saturn. Look, I know you're busy and I know you're preoccupied with Daddy's group and everything else, but can I beg a little extra privilege?'

She smiled as charmingly as she knew how to. He shifted on the sofa, reaching for his lemonade.

'All right,' he said.

'I really want to prove something, if only to myself,' Candida said.

'Why only to yourself?'

She smiled.

'I think I'll be here pretty often throughout the summer. I'd be happy to help. Let me know what you're finding difficult.'

He drank the lemonade.

'Couldn't . . . Oh bugger! This sounds awful. Could I come to your flat. I mean this place is like an air terminal. And if Mummy or Daddy set eyes on you . . .'

For once on cue, Jessica came slamming and banging into the kitchen.

'See what I mean,' Candida said, laughing.

After some preliminary slurping, Jessica appeared at the door, steaming and messily eating an orange.

'Roger!' she bawled.

He seemed quite oblivious of her gooey state and allowed himself to be hugged. Candida thought that Jessica was affected and that it was high time she grew up. She was much too well developed to behave, still, like a little girl. She had stood up and rearranged her dressing gown at the first thump.

'We'll arrange something for next week,' Roger said, patting Jessica absent-mindedly on the head. 'Now then, Jess, where do you get all that energy? I thought you hated tennis.'

'I do. But I'm too fat and I want to improve my reflexes if I'm going to be a surgeon. Anyway one odalisque loafing about is enough. Why are you half-dressed like Madame Butterfly?'

'Stop being boring. Roger arrived just as I was going to have a bath. You should try it some time.'

'What? Slipping into something loose when Roger comes?'

Roger laughed as Jessica flopped into a chair, absorbing the orange again.

'Carry on,' she said. 'I'll take care of Roger.'

'Oh, don't be a nuisance, Jessica. He came here to work before tonight's meeting. Give him a moment's peace.'

'Did you make that filthy lemonade?'

'I did.'

Candida was furious but could think of no way of not being drawn into a silly, childish wrangle.

'Ugh!'

Roger laughed again. Jessica was a disingenuous little slut.

'Oh, go and have your bath, Candy, then I can have mine.'

'Do NOT call me Candy!'

Candida looked blazingly at Roger, knowing quite well that she was blazing.

'Wednesday,' she said.

'I can't wait,' he said evenly.

Candida went out of the room gracefully. Jessica yelled after her:

'I bet he'll scrub your back, if you ask him nicely.'

And stupid giggles.

3

It is almost but not absolutely impossible to think that Blakemore could be guilty of impropriety; yet it is also highly unusual for him to be plying beautiful strangers with lunch. At his club of all places. I suppose I was a little jealous when Clodia told me how civilised it had all been. The explanation must certainly be found in the unspoken sympathy which works in all European conservatives to penetrate all the photo-electric defences of national and cultural prejudice, in a way that will never be achieved by liberals, or even by the working-class movements. It has to do with the assumptions of power, rather than those of a just order on the one hand, or absolute equality on the other.

The somewhat sour note of envy about Blakemore's unassailable conservative conscience is no doubt prompted by Rachel's implied accusation that I am a dilettante, which disappoints me. It is curious that we have a propensity for being surprised when we upset, or even hurt, other people with some remark which was intended only to amuse or tease. I annoyed Rachel by suggesting that she was 'agonising' about her socialism and she in turn struck back rather painfully. This invariably happens with people we trust and admire and rely on for the scale of equilibrium against which we measure our own balance. To make matters worse Bill Delahaye, in his cups, wagged a solemn finger at me and said: 'It is good to make a jest, but not to make a trade of jesting.'

So I have been studying how I might compare myself to the other Highgate people and I find that I am as irreproachable a Social Democrat as any. I have no doubt that it is true that my interest in politics is more academic than many of the others, by virtue of my work. At the same time, apart from a modest obsession with constitutional reform, I don't see that I veer markedly away from practicalities as conceived by a moderate party of progress. Given that I am in favour of virtually all the reforms relating to the penal system, of high-quality comprehensive education, of an efficient health service dedicated to the needs of the many rather than the comfort of the few, of an effective welfare state in which people live as well as is possible but where there are incentives and rewards, of a mixed economy which allows for what is socially desirable rather than what is profitable, but which makes use of all forms of entrepreneurial energy for the ultimate general good: I am resolutely opposed to punitive taxation systems designed to bring about an entirely false redistribution of wealth which impose a further psychological tax upon the energetic and the inspired; I am resolutely opposed to any weakening of the aims of European unity and to any re-alignment in foreign affairs that is detrimental to the Western alliance; I am resolutely opposed to the extension of state monopolies and to doctrinaire nationalisation. Where in this do I differ say from Ellis Fulford or Jock Hay or indeed Rachel Bailey herself? Only in quite technical details of fiscal and economic theory. Much more markedly, in fact, on a number of constitutional issues which they seem to dismiss as virtually irrelevant. Of academic interest only.

I think, then, that I have come to see that Jeremy Taylor's enthusiasm for a powerful nerve centre for a centre party may be after all more than an intriguing intellectual toy and that it should be composed of a complexity of individual cells able to pick up, interpret and transmit an effective response to as many social and political impulses as possible.

Perhaps Rachel was right and my attitude has been much too quizzical, and indeed whimsical, all along. I did not take Taylor and Barbara seriously enough because I did not see that there was a function or an opportunity for the brand of militant liberalism that they are trying to sell. (Not that

Rachel herself is committed to them, which is what the whole 'agonising', first on her part and now on mine, is about.)

What binds us together, whatever we are by profession, is not so much a political decalogue as a set of shared ethical precepts which create a tolerant, fair (not equal), just society in which there is absolute intellectual freedom and where progress is seen to be the thoughtful and impartial examination of what exists to see if it can be improved. There may be endless argument about detail, but there is none about the essential purpose. And such argument as there is is dedicated to the means of achieving that purpose and has nothing to do with power.

Which brings me back to Blakemore and Clodia: in that Blakemore, who is a high Tory but not remotely fascist, is interested only in phantasms of power – an élitist body who provide good bread, decent circuses, civilised circumstances for labour, while yet preserving the highest standards of spiritual endeavour and material discipline. In reality, a pessimist who believes that final disaster is only some few years – five, fifteen, fifty – away. Clodia on the other hand, the 'technical assistant', perhaps more concerned with assured survival and the exercise of power that she understands and desires, is only dedicated to that maintenance of privilege as it concerns a certain prescribed group.

What is disturbing is that in spite of Hitler, Mussolini, Stalin and the rest, in this century alone, there is emerging here, as well as in the rest of Europe, beyond recognisable if irreducible manifestoes, groups who extemporise ideology to achieve power *because they want power*. They wish to dominate and to remain dominant: they will use any means of arriving and the familiar machinery of terror to establish and perpetuate themselves.

This is all very distressing but it must be salutary. Unlike Blakemore I do not believe all is already lost, so I suppose I must take my enlistment seriously.

*

It has been a great day for Francophobes and Trumble is said by Bill Delahaye to have cart-wheeled all the way from El Vino's to Ludgate Circus. Some enterprising thieves have tunnelled through a sewer into a bank at Nice and got away, it is confidently thought, with something like six million. A wit on one paper has called it the Great Drain Robbery. Since as far as I can make out the entire French nation devotes its principal energies to fiddling tax, I imagine the haul was even bigger than estimated: it is not surprising that there have been angry scenes outside the bank. I have seldom seen so much unashamed *schadenfreude*, in which I am rather sorry to say Connors and I took our part. There is something curiously exhilarating about such hyperboles of villainy – especially for conscientious taxpayers. Connors offered some assorted drinkers a neat little homily on VAT.

Candida's earnest cry for help was, it seems, simply the pursuit of some kind of fantasy happiness that she seems to imagine I can offer: in which case all seems to be fair. This is a pity: because Kent is not only eminently suitable but much too troubled about her – or so it appeared when I saw him the other day. I am not clear (nor indeed do I wish to be) about what happened between them, but I think she must have hurt him quite badly.

She looked, of course, very pretty – but, as soon as we began a preliminary chat about what her problems were, disported herself in the manner of one of Raymond Chandler's maladjusted wives. Perhaps the farcical glimpse of myself as Humphrey Bogart helped me resist a temptation that would have disturbed certain (indeed most?) of her parents' male acquaintances. I also find her fairly tiresome and so my restraint is really effortless.

I let her steer the conversation away from her new-found academic longings to her irresolution, dependence and inevitable sense of restless futility. This led to a too frank account of her sexual inhibitions, or 'hang-ups' as she put it.

I thought about interposing a word on behalf of Kent, but judged that it would be damning. This disquisition was accompanied by a further disorder of the dress that was beyond any middle-aged misconstruction. (I suppose it was the sheer banality of so much female thigh during the years of the mini-skirt that inured so many of us in offices, lecture-rooms and other battle-areas to such pleasures. There is still, however, some perverse twinge when it is a matter of display.)

How be it! There was nothing for it but brutality. I got up and walked purposefully over to the desk, saying: 'That's all very well but it does *not* get us much further with con-stitutional documents. Anyway, quite frankly, I am not the wisest counsellor in these matters.' She followed in what must be described as a silky manner, with much deliberation of the hips. Aha! But I had prepared for the event by placing on the desk a photograph of Francesca Oricellari – devastat-ingly correct in posture and demeanour, but startlingly suggestive of erotic promise. A joke, of course: suitably inscribed. It worked.

We spent the next hour discussing British colonial policy as manifest in Volume One of Keith's *Selected Speeches and Documents* (pages fifty-three to fifty-seven – as far as we made it). The explicit physical initiative that had seemed imminent was thus, at least, postponed.

Over the subsequent civil sherry, she returned to the immediate and began quizzing me about her parents' friends. All a great success. I pointed out that almost every one of them, except her mother, aspired to some other kind of fulfilment, elaborating tactfully on the basis of our associa-tion as a quasi-political group. Somewhat to my surprise this prompted from Candida a virulent but rather clever attack on Marie White (who is harmlessly over-sexed and very nice) and Sandra Beeton (who is admittedly a tireless Freudian, but otherwise house-trained). In Candida's view, Marie White has too much money, time and opportunity and is a phantom from Trollope in the too, too solid flesh. That television series has a lot to answer for. Sandra Beeton is a repressed maniac, obsessed with sex, as is everyone in television when they are not arrogantly patronising patient merit out of sight. Dear me!

I was required to tell her quite frankly how promiscuous we all were and abruptly to reveal whether I loved the beautiful girl in the photograph. (This in the course of my very moderate answer to her first point.) Quite truthfully I said that I did not, realising immediately the appalling error that I had made. (I wonder, fearfully, what Sandra La Freudienne would make of that.) Alas, this brightened Candida up considerably, she having jumped to a false interpretation of the facts.

Assuring herself of next week's visit, she left without any further complications and I repaired exhausted to the Palace of Westminster, as promised, to support Citizen Connors (debonair as ever) through a long night of guillotines. I felt uncomfortably like a *tricoteuse*. We sipped Buck's Fizz looking over the Thames, which was running softly and commendably sweetly on another very hot evening. I happened to mention Candida's visit and uncorked a djin of ebullient lust. Because of our tenuously sympathetic alliance after Daphne and Rosemary, Connors has always favoured me with his confidences and his most intimate desires. (I have a curious idea that if he had married Daphne and I had married Rosemary things might have worked out better – but that is conjecture based partly on hearsay.) It now seems that he has conceived and nurtured an enormous craving for Candida! Incautiously, I said that he might bring me much relief. Which he offered with alacrity!

We are doing abysmally in the Olympic Games: but as a result of an act of almost unimaginable folly by a Russian fencer (or surely swordsman?), they have been disqualified from the Modern Pentathlon and we look as though we shall win a gold medal. Dimchurch, convalescing after our progress in the Test matches so far this season, finds it in his heart to be sorry for this very unfortunate man. The Headingley Test began yesterday and Dimchurch must relapse. Why, he reasonably asks, should an established and much respected officer in the Soviet army, who has already benefited considerably from his prowess and dedication, risk not only personal disgrace but the sort of hideous obloquy that the Russians will call down upon his head now that he has been discovered cheating? Since he has also been watching girl gymnasts performing in the recent weeks (a source of much wonder it would seem to the British public as a whole) and claims to have witnessed intolerable strain in these very young people, Dimchurch has been reflecting on the horror of competition in almost all modern games or sports, even cricket.

He had looked out the 1946 *Wisden,* recalling an article by Keith Johnson, who managed the Australian Services team in 1945, in which he wrote: 'There was something about the games of last season, something carefree and refreshing, which I hope has come to stay. I would liken it to a mixture of Lord's, Old Trafford, Trent Bridge, Bramall Lane and the village green; it was certainly a good mixture. . . .'

He mourned the passing of this attitude and I reminded him, with perhaps a little too much prompt asperity, that it had already passed by the winter of the same year when traditionally hostile relationships had been resumed between England and Australia under Hammond and Bradman. 'You are too young to know anything about it,' said Dimchurch. He surprised me by allowing me to borrow the copy of *Wisden,* a narrow but fascinating edition, which is curiously moving – in some way more indicative of lost and gentler days than many other more serious and ambitious books written just after the war.

After a chat with Kent, I found myself reflecting gloomily that the same thing was happening in the academic world: too much pressure, too many strains, not enough hard work for its own richly pleasurable sake – a generation of over-stretched young people competing rather than learning and developing. When I was Kent's age, you were very good if you wanted to be, given some talent to begin with: but at Oxford, at least, you were allowed to be very bad in spite of it. In fact, they were all rather serious when I first went up and my own was perhaps the only frivolous generation between the ex-servicemen and the politically obsessed. The present lot are serious again and dedicated to success and competition for its own sake, which can hardly be healthy. And yet, I must confess that I am interested in success when it is accompanied by obvious intelligence and the evidence of intelligent effort outside the confines of learning. This does not include success brought about by physical beauty which can be paid for, and certainly not the meretricious success afforded to anyone who appears regularly on television. I am interested in clever people who are not in the slightest bit impressed by their own cleverness and who really do not give much of a damn about what they do and would prefer to do something else – though not less well: and there's the rub. (Into this category, it would be difficult to fit most actors, athletes or academics and virtually no public idols.)

Steve Kent is trying to bury himself in work, trying to become part of that rather pleasant pub; and he is inescapably obsessed by Candida who is by comparison fatuous. I don't care whether Kent gets a first because it will not alter my opinion of his worth: but I should hate to see him crack up and perform well below his capacities – which is always possible – and then go to pieces. It has been known.

It seems that Candida refuses to see him or have anything to do with him. He tries to make light of it but it hurts. I considered a number of possible devices – even behaving so bloodily to Candida that she must fly back to him for solace, but I'm afraid that I am not up to that kind of Restoration sophistication. Pity Jessica is not a few years older. I am almost inclined to act as Pandar for Connors, which would serve Candida right – except that, with my deft assistance in these things, it must bring about a lasting and blissfully happy union.

For the moment I'll content myself with dropping in at the pub and keeping an eye on him, perhaps introducing him to real women like Clodia or Rachel or Francesca or (for that matter) Marie White. No. *Not* Francesca.

Ellis Fulford arrived at the pub which Connors and I use and immediately had a row with the bar staff. He succeeded at last in getting them to serve him, grumbling morosely that it was not really their fault. He claims that he exudes a subliminal odour that repels barmaids and attracts wasps. 'While I have yet to be served in my due turn in any reasonably peopled bar from Acton to Zank, I have yet to sit outside any place of refreshment from Nome to Tongatapu without clouds of these foul insects descending upon me, my bargains and my well-won lunch.' He was in rare form and even in this pub, which has more than its share of interesting clients, as my own bad habits of comic fantasising bear witness, was very soon tethering the horses of his imagination to cathedral heights. One group, lapping half pints and eating really huge plates of steaming hash, had a single pint-drinker who stared obsessively at his companions' plates, gazing at them with concentrated ghoulish attention. Fulford classified him as a reformed cannibal, fighting against his nature, who watched the feeding of other humans with the greedy anticipation of a professional animal-breeder with shares and precedence at the local abattoir. In a second group he detected a case of incest between a pipe-smoking man of immaculate executive manner and a rather pale, rumpled girl with excellent tightly twined legs. 'And that chap is her husband Stanislaus Hunding, a Marylebone bucolic who does not understand the fascination of this urbane Mafioso of Madison Avenue. None of them perceive the flicker of sunlight reflected off the chrome that lights the hilt of a sword faintly gleaming. Look how enraptured she is: only a sister looks like that, take it from: *O lass in Nähe zu dir mich neigen, dass hell ich schae den hehren Schein.*'

It takes a great deal to embarrass Connors but Fulford singing in a pub where he is known appears to be beyond it. He departed in some haste, encouraging Fulford in the belief that he once had a bad time with his sister.

Whereupon we began to talk serious, complicated and very earnest politics and Fulford looked as though he had never in his life smiled or imagined anything other than an incomes policy based upon a minimum wage and index-taxed awards beyond an agreed figure, within a phased policy of participation and profit-sharing.

I asked him to define the corporate state and he accused me of not knowing which way to look, 'like a tit-freak visiting in a maternity ward'. I wonder if Connors has an idea why he appeared.

Marie White gave a splendid party, to which, without my knowing, she invited both Clodia and Francesca. Their impact upon the assembled Highgates (and many others less pre-ordained) was most interesting. Trumble, Rachel, Simon Farrell and one or two others had already met both: but the effect upon male and female was by no means alike and very diverting. Connors was not there; nor was Candida, which was something of a pity because it would have done her good. Understandably she gets a great deal of attention at most of these gatherings and she is one person for whom competition would be a very good thing. I do not know whether her antipathy for Marie White is mutual and she was not asked. Marie is a generous woman and would certainly not have excluded her because she is young and good-looking: on the other hand, I imagine that she regards Candida as a child and therefore irritating. Connors has a similar attitude to young men. Perforce in my job, this would make life much too difficult and so we all cultivate tolerance.

It was diverting to see which sister attracted which of

Marie's friends. Trumble is already a dedicated Clodian and as might be expected Jock Hay showed a preference for her, as perhaps presenting a less insidious sexual challenge. So predictably enough did Jeremy Taylor and that kind of married man, Stanley Mears and his like. The Benedicts, however, enslaved but still sprightly – such as Hugh Middleton and Farrell – homed upon Francesca, as did an absurdly gallant Fulford. Bill Delahaye talked to people he knew well already and eyed them *both* with insatiable longing.

Francesca was particularly flattering to me and otherwise spent as much time as she could possibly manage talking about fashions with as many women as were interested. In consequence, she was much more warmly received than Clodia, who wore a very sleek and expensive plain brown dress. If I am any judge, it made her look more voluptuous than she is, whereas Francesca was floral, diaphanous and unemphatically feminine.

Clodia must be really very bored by any more conversations about the European ideal and the European experience, but obviously in this company there are more cavemen who draw than hunt and she has to recline and enjoy it. Happily, she met a very charming professor of Italian who talked to her about Montale and Ungaretti – at least that was his story when I hoved upon them. Nevertheless, I think she was taken back to the Embassy by Trumble. Francesca and I left (most chastely) in a taxi.

After a thoroughly unproductive morning at the BM, it was a particular pleasure to see Blakemore's American friend, James Lloyd Mitchell, who gave me lunch at the Connaught, displaying not only the high civilisation of his kind, but an amazing generosity and a high tolerance for alcohol. Part of his charm is a cool cynicism which he brings to bear upon everything, including himself. It's a quality I have noticed in witty and urbane Americans of the left and the right. Mitchell, himself, claims to be somewhere to the west of

William F. Buckley, looking south. I hazard a guess that beneath the tough make-up and droll smile, there is a sincere, somewhat uncomplicated man in moral discomfort. (It occurs to me that if the right of the political spectrum is ultra, does that make the left infra?)

Unlike Blakemore, James Mitchell is not a pessimist. He will not open his veins in a bath. (Nor will Blakemore, who is much too rational.) He believes in large federations made up of small units, some of which will be very badly governed while others will be exemplary. The large alliance will maintain security and the people themselves will be actively interested in redressing the wrongs they are suffering (in the bad enclaves), or maintaining what is so noble (in the good). Very bad government on a small scale, he claims, is finite, citing the Rule of the Thirty. It is only strong, almost impregnably strong, in enormous centralised unions: such as the Soviet state or greater Nazi Germany which was destroyed (according to Mitchell) because of Hitler's military fantasies. With Aristotle, he argues for the compact small state and, as might be expected, has an accordingly senti-mental attitude to Welsh, Scots, Cornish, Breton, Basque, Catalonian and Corsican separatism. The whole argument was acceptably frivolous and so we were able to indulge in a great deal of nonsense about pocket rivalry. When, at length, we turned to Africa (where the pockets are so much bigger) we were obliged to become serious again. As Clodia says, Europe is so old she can conceive of nothing new. I am resolved that Mitchell and Clodia must meet. It should be a formidable confrontation. Tomorrow, I suppose, I shall be back to Walpole and Fleury. Ah well!

*

Dear Olliphant,

I find myself in what I imagine to be a purgatorial state, in which a sense of baleful emptiness is relieved and naturally made worse by remembered bliss. I am bitterly sorry we had so little time together at Geneva – but it was marvellous.

Really wonderful. It was also nice to see you again and to talk!

Things are even more hectic than last week with the guillotine rows and Healey's latest economy measures which had the left howling in full cry after the troika. Last night we had the third reading of the Aircraft and Shipbuilding Nationalisation Bill which got through by a majority of three. The guillotine caused a lot of genuine ill feeling and, with the Tories still refusing to pair, it meant that four of our people who were pretty ill had to come in to be 'nodded through'. Kauffman had to make the final speech in a terrific racket and I found myself wondering whether it was worth it and whether I should not be better fulfilled travelling with you. I'm a little tired, I suppose, and at the moment missing you more than somewhat.

I don't think I envy the trip to Africa all the same and, foolish as it will no doubt seem to you, I am worried about you. If it means that the proposals you put to them in Geneva are accepted, then I imagine it's important: though in a world where travel and communications are so bloody instant I don't really see that there's any infallible way of preventing some outbreak of a disease which sooner or later will be serious. Apart from our periodical scare about rabies, which seems to happen every other summer only to be forgotten again in the winter, there's a certain amount of panic at the moment about Lassa fever, since one or two people either have it or are suspected of having it after contact with someone who flew from Nigeria. (I suppose you know all about this, since it is in your diocese.) I had never heard of it until the other day (nor indeed of that ghastly thing you told me about which is killing off people in the southern Sudan). Please take care, Olliphant. I know it is a fatuous thing to say, but when you are interested you're impetuous and being a *grass* widow is bad enough.

Not that there's much grass left. The hot spell is now being called a drought and might even be serious. Some parts of Wales (of all places) are running out of water – which

Rhydderch tells me is the result of English lack of foresight in building and siting new towns. I remembered wryly our holiday in a tent during which nothing was ever properly dry. It's one more thing for the wireless to gloom about in the mornings: I wonder how many citizens slip softly into their bathwater and drown.

I sometimes feel desperate about the way the world is going. Or perhaps despairing is more accurate. It was once quite easy to be an optimist, but I can no longer see the slightest hope that decent democratic institutions can prevail and some kind of eventual global war seems to be more rather than less likely, Helsinki or not. This probably irritates you because you are *still* an optimist and I know what absolute contempt you have for the Club of Rome hypotheses. I think the prospect of a really horrible war in Southern Africa is fairly imminent and that may well be far more dangerous than the troubles in the Middle East and God knows they're bad enough. For some reason, which I'm not able to explain, the whole vast problem of Rhodesia and Southern Africa generally doesn't seem to bother people. Quite genuinely, we all (myself included) seem to think that it's all so far away and I'm quite sure a substantial part of the decent and compassionate electorate thought about Angola that they were all only blacks anyway and what did it matter. Rhodesia would of course be different because of the kith and kin argument, which the right-wing Tories have never let flag. Not that there is anything that they could do. I can find it in myself to feel sorry for the Afrikaners too – even if they have only themselves to blame. They have nowhere to go and surely now it is only a matter of time. How can the West in any circumstances do anything for them, unless we have an all-out war for old-fashioned economic-territorial reasons: and that (unless it happens as a ghastly accident) is surely out of the question. I know little enough about defence (which may be just as well), but when I think about our weakness and indeed the weakness of the West in the face of the continuing Russian build-up of arms and manpower in all three services, I have a nasty cold feeling. Then suppose there is a Soviet-Chinese rapprochement. I can all too readily imagine the desolation which would be called a Pax Sovietica.

I think it is for reasons that relate almost entirely to foreign policy – NATO, the Atlantic alliance, Europe, a pragmatic attitude to the Arabs and to Africa – that I've decided (cautiously) to be associated with Jeremy Taylor's group. The party is speaking more and more frequently in public with two heads and two voices and it is almost a matter of course, on any number of issues, that the BBC and the Independent people have a Tory, a moderate and a left-winger. The poor Liberals are having an awful time at the moment after the frightful treatment Thorpe got from the press. Well, I have doubts and problems when it comes to any number of domestic matters: but I have no doubt where I stand internationally and although no one significant is at all likely to resign from a top job and be the first to stand and be counted as a centre democrat (Taverne did and for the moment at least is making straight in the desert a highway, no doubt, but without much encouragement), it must happen. Connors is quite outspoken, at the moment, in favour of a vigorous pressure-group, but that could easily change if he were offered even a fairly junior job in actual government. The chances aren't high. Jock Hay is keen and thinks there is a lot of discontent on the left of the Tory party at the moment, which could lead to considerable defection. I doubt it very much. Their discipline is better than ours and always has been. And Captain Marryat is by no means the emotional equivalent of Batman. In fact, however much he may still be seen to be sulking, his authority and integrity are more impressive than they ever were in office. Ingestre says it is one of the ironies of British public life.

I went to a party of Marie White's, which is the only time I have been on the tiles since coming back, only to find that it was a delightfully organised Highgate venture. Marie herself seems to have given up protracted affairs and settled amiably for whatever turns up – as long as it is clean, civilised and uncomplicated. It's a pity because she is an attractive woman, reconciled to being wasted, now wanting only to be somewhere near things as they happen. If she had been less highly sexed and had less money, without the contribution from the American hooded terror, she would be having a more useful and (I think) happier life. The point is that she is a really committed liberal, spends a lot of money on very worthwhile causes and would honestly like to *do* something. Barbara Dunn and the Highgates all regard her as something of a joke and, up to a point, use her – some of them quite literally. If she takes to drink, of which fortunately there is no sign, she could end up as an unhappy and pathetic figure.

She had invited Roger Ingestre's Italian friends: the Oricellari! I described the elder sister to you in some detail, but this was my first meeting with the younger one who is making a fortune in low couture. She is unusually good-looking and appears to be absolutely indifferent to it. I don't suppose it fooled a single woman present, including those of us who are sometimes less than immaculate. (Oh dear! I wish I was a bit less intellectual, and a lot more astute.) Be that as it may, she charmed an awful lot of people. If ever I saw an effortless declaration of feminine independence and liberation, here it was. I should not have said that the Highgates (excepting Marie and allowing for the odd flurry in unguarded moments) were a particularly sex-conscious crowd. (Sorry, I was also forgetting Connors, but that isn't difficult as far as I'm concerned and he really is a joke in such matters.) The Oricellari are changing all that. Roger Ingestre is playing some intricately disingenuous hand: apparently unconcerned and amused. Both the sisters play up to him and he has an elaborate conversational ritual with Clodia: but I guess that he desires Francesca (the younger one). As you know, it is very difficult to guess whether Roger desires anyone or anything most of the time. Nevertheless, I caught him following this particular woman around with his eyes.

There wasn't a moment when he did not know where she was and who she was with. I don't think you knew his wife, who was called Daphne and was absolutely unsuited to him: you know the kind of cut-price Aphrodite that sometimes emerges out of the minor aristocracy. She couldn't get anywhere near him intellectually and he couldn't match her sexually, as he freely admits.

Ellis Fulford had been watching *Spartacus the Gladiator* on television and so, for quite a lot of the evening, was playing Charles Laughton as Gracchus. This fooled everyone, however, since the imitation more resembled James Durante as Augustus, He quite upset Jeremy Taylor by accusing him of 'a bad attack of dignity', which it appears occurs in the script. The situation was saved by Trumble doing a marvellous version of George Saunders as Fabius Maximus Cunctator from some film which I did not catch the name of. They sang various songs lustily and exchanged crazy dialogue such as 'Politics is a practical profession: how are the geese?' et cetera. Then they cast Ted Heath as Gracchus and Madame Thatcher as Crassus, playing all the parts – Ellis still inescapably Durante. Then there was quite an argument about who Spartacus should be. I think the best suggestion was Woodrow Wyatt.

Ingestre asked me if he could bring an American friend to the House next week when something exciting is going on. That's not difficult at the moment. I'm not quite clear who the American is, except that he has impressed Roger formidably. I think he is a writer of some kind who is over here observing the failure to rise of the European dough. Apparently, he is well to the right of Goldwater and Reagan, but charming. The imagination totters helplessly.

I think that Northern Ireland is still the single most depressing feature of a pretty bleak landscape: simply because it seems to emphasise the original savagery, mindless and soulless, of men. And it is too easy to mumble excuses about Irish history. It is happening on our doorstep and in our society. Looked at closely, it is evidence that we are just as hypocritical as most.

I'm beginning to sermonize so perhaps I should stop. I hope you have a good journey to Africa and that you'll look after yourself. Write when you can and keep away from mystery viruses in Philadelphia for heaven's sake: because

I love you,

R.

＊

Big Ben has stopped and if that doesn't give us all pause we are not worthy of the omens that the gods provide. What we need in this place is a lot more healthy superstition, a touch of decent awe and considerably less cool pragmatism. The impressive discipline of the Chinese in Peking, though: moving in an orderly way into the centres of the street to await the next earthquake. Also frightening, of course. Is it that they really have more sense of purpose? Especially looking around this other Eden. That too is an uneasy feeling. Is that, after all, the answer. Is all personal freedom illusory and very much less important than the general well-being?

Oh come on, Anthony. It is a bright sunny morning and the girls are delicious in their pretty frocks and cotton T-shirts. Think of all the ratmen just waiting to people a secret police. Could it be that cowardice makes for conscience? The fear that it might happen here and to us: and is well on the way to happening. If so, then my laziness and insouciance are criminally inexcusable. And ambition should be made of sterner stuff. And I don't have it. Opportunism to a tolerable degree, but not ambition. How is it possible to be ruthless and liberal at the same time? Aha! The 'R' factor. It is *always* possible to rationalise.

Why Russia thinks she could *win* a nuclear war. That was Chalfont the other day and here are the reverberations. Weakness of tolerant societies. We idle along. Idle is the good word for it. So: strong conscientious government. Carter/

Ford/Reagan, who does not seem to frighten people in the way that Goldwater did. But if he gets the nomination what will happen on the far left in Italy and France? And think too about the leverage on the 'soft left' here. From the Tribunites. I wonder if I am justified in just hanging on in the party. Conscience, again. If there were the remotest possibility of office, I doubt that I should be thinking like this. And it's not simply a question of honesty and idealism. The Highgate lot are all in their way idealist and some are indifferent honest. Rachel, Barbara, very much honest . . . I . . .

Candida. Must remember to telephone. Flowers? No. Would attract attention and I doubt Barbara would be pleased. Taylor? Probably some Freudian condition that covers what he would feel. Must ask Sandra Beeton. Who could blame him? What on earth can it feel like to have a woman like that around and be her father? Pah! Probably never thinks of it. My God, though: she is so lovely. I could not believe . . . Nothing virginal in the subsequent . . . No. Ripe for the plucking and a fine natural flair. Can't remember quite such excitement even with experts like Marie. I wonder if . . . Well, she learned very fast and if I play it cleverly a very sensual recess is promised. Take her away. Somewhere. Why not? Somewhere I can show off my gift of tongues. Yes. . . . Must certainly get her some sort of present that no one will specially notice, but she'll like. Though how much do they notice anyway? Christ, I'd better stop thinking of her stretched out there on Ingestre's carpet. . . .

Ingestre! Yes. Now then. I don't suppose he would have expected things to go so far so soon. Wonder why he dislikes her so much. Must do. 'Coming here later this afternoon, if you want to stay and see her. I have to go out and I may not be back at the time we arranged, so you could let her in.' Very detached. But my suggestion after all, initially. Can't think why, if she was eager, he didn't take full advantage. . . . Could be that it was *he* who was trying to make the running and *she* wouldn't. Hardly! Not Roger. Shouldn't think he's very highly sexed. And she was dressed for it. Those knickers. Turn again Saint Anthony: better saints would have fallen, except that they wouldn't necessarily have got to seeing her knickers. And those lovely long legs. Enough! I say. Down . . .

Suppose, after all, she doesn't come tomorrow. Must telephone. Ah well, then she will have to be wooed and that could be quite fun. Highgate meeting on Saturday. Yes: the problem is that sooner or later Mummy and Daddy are going to have to know. Pittheus Ingestre already does. (Thank God, he didn't get back at *quite* the wrong moment.) And she carried it off very easily. He'd been delayed by Rachel, late after a meeting indeed! It won't be the first time a girl of nineteen had an affair with what you might call a fully mature man. Would you, indeed? Forty-six next birthday. Emancipated days, progressive parents. It's wonderful, though, how *unprogressive* people can get when it's their own daughter and a friend of the family: too close to incest. Seen it happen.

No, the problem will be Ingestre's delayed conscience. Already a little acid I should guess. And he will certainly see it as conniving. In what turned out to be the defloration of someone who is more than just a pretty pupil. Not that he would know *that*, of course. In fact, I'm quite sure he'd be as surprised as I was. As soon as his mind adjusts to it, he'll start fretting about being dishonourable: but then the famous detachment will lay hold. Life is a faintly amusing dream for Ingestre. Anyway, it's done. Curious though the way that he and I are thrown together in amatory comedies. Farces, indeed. Our marriages. One thing I'm glad about: I didn't take Daphne when she wanted to. Do I flatter myself? No, I think it would have mattered to him when the others were somehow not important. And I was her sister's husband too. Odd. I never wanted her and I always *did* want Rosemary so much. And she. . . . Daphne was always more sexy and a splendid voluptuous body. That was it: there was something secret about Rosemary. Or so it seemed. In fact, of course, nothing. Amazing she was able to hide that total revulsion for such a long time. Ingestre to confide in. I must never forget that. Gentle with her and properly detached when he was going through a bad time himself. Tactful with me. And ultimately Daphne wasn't even bothering to dissemble. The scent of Messalina, as the poet has it. No: not forget that. Ingestre's mocking self-preserving kindness. But he'll not feel easy about Candida once he knows for *sure*. . . .

Unusually good cup of coffee? Same old jar. Oh yawn. Bloody devolution. Going to be the biggest bore in the history of constitutional government. Good speech of Anderson's though. Constitutional castles in the air.

Soweto: looks nasty. Worrying. Another gap when Kissinger goes, if he goes. Must do. Rusk one of Carter's advisers. Good man, but no Henry Kissinger. God, it looks bad. Russians already in Angola, richest of all potentially; Mozambique. And they'll push up towards the Red Sea if they can: Somalia, Ethiopia. Arabs won't like that any more than we will. We have to back Kaunda and Nyerere. What a balls we made of Africa!

Roy Thomson dead. Canadians and newspapers. Much more amiable image than the Beaverbrook always. . . .

Powell again. What now? North Sea Oil is a curse (and the wicked Europeans were going to siphon it away from us for their own benefit, I thought, the other day). Which is it to be, Father Enoch? Ah, a curse: because its promises of wealth are sapping our natural enterprise and they are exaggerated. Yach.

Tomney will split the vote in Hammersmith if they reject him. Good! As Parliamentary Labour candidate. That's interesting. Nice little row in that. But good for him. We'll all have to make a stand. I've got my own little band of Joseph's brethren who would like to consign me to the pit. But Albert has everything in marvellous control. Must ring him too, later. Strong personality. Deserves something rather better than me in his constituency. Still there can't be many complaints from the electors. And I might just have made it. Albert always thought I might. No, I'm not bitter about it. But I'm bright enough to be *somewhere*. Europe. Oh yes: but the pace is murderous. Direct elections, maybe. If they ever happen. After Harold, I had hoped, but . . . I've been over it often enough and it's quite profitless. I could get bitter without realising it: good thing I'm not a drinker. Doesn't do to be too intelligent in Parliament. Still Thorpe and Grimond have put up with it for a long time. Is that part of the problem: neither quite serious enough? Inclined to savour a joke against themselves from time to time. And enjoy themselves hugely theorising. A party politician cannot bear too much humour. Or have too much reality.

Costa Del Dole! That's funny. Yes, I like that. Come up today. I can hear Varley telling us how exaggerated it all is. Frogs and the holy Germans think we're all scroungers. Still a healthier, happier society than France. How many people would work if they did not have to. Take the Highgates. Well, not a particularly random sample. Taylor, Barbara, Fulford, Delahaye, Rachel all would. All natural busybodies in one way or another. (Wonder how Delahaye's book is going? Why doesn't he like me and why doesn't he admit it? God knows what he'd make of this thing with Candida. Wonder if any of the others have tried their luck?) Yes, so what about the others: Trumble, Ingestre, Farrell, Mears, Jock Hay, Sandra, Marie, Middleton, me. . . . Not a bad list. None of us would do a stroke if we could live pleasantly enough without working. Chatter, puzzles, fantasies, gossip, loafing about. We've all, as it happens, opted for something relatively interesting that suits us. If Trumble was not, and hadn't been, so bone idle, he could have been right at the top. Don't suppose he's done all that badly. He was going on at length about Ingestre's Italian lady, whom I've not met. (Hardly being sheltered from me, is she?) Anyway, who can cast the first stone when it comes to laziness? None of them would admit it. Marie and I are the only out-and-out, declared and avowing hedonists. Marie . . . Marie. . . . Quite the most inventive I've ever met. . . .

Right then. Burt's answer to Chalfont on the Soviet

threat. Strategic superiority not to be exaggerated. Perhaps. But dangerous to minimise any likely threat. Surely. I should say. . . . Oh bugger! The telephone already.

. . . Hullo? Anthony Connors. (Candida) Candida! How marvellous of you to call. . . . It is most decidedly still on, my darling. . . . Oh I shouldn't care if I were whipped all round the Square and along the Embankment. . . . Well, I'm not sure that I could tell you over the telephone. . . . I can't promise you a carpet quite as elegant as Roger's, but in other ways it's a comfortable little flat. . . . True. . . . Yes. . . . My love, I don't know whether in the wonderful confusion of the moment I said what I wanted to about . . . Well, I'm glad there's no need to. Thank you, darling. Thank you. You are quite enchanting. Bye.

Dear me! That girl has quite an effect at long distance. *Du calme*, Anthony. Deep breaths and think about the Tribune group. A detumescent lot if ever there was one.

Dammit, I *shall* take her away. During the recess. Italy? Yes. I know my way around, speak the language, it's beautiful and romantic. And I also could look in on Viazzani and Landi. Taylor and Barbara tend to go to their country place, a lowering bloody height if ever there was one: so I doubt that she'd know it too well already. In fact, as far as I remember they sometimes went with the kids to some educational cottage in the Dordogne, or on some outcrop of the Massif Central, when they were younger. And we will. . . . (Wonder how many erections, or pseudo-erections, I get in a day: suédeau erections of a suédeau innerlecshual. Perhaps a politician has crypto-erections.) Nothing good or bad but . . . After all. She'll pretty certainly want to come and there's absolutely nothing to stop us. And I will cogitate about Taylor and Barbara.

I wonder, in fact quite seriously, about family sanctions. The ice-cold upper-class climate in which the entrance of a slightly odd friend was just a part of growing peculiarly up is certainly not one that Taylor and Barbara would understand. And we are none of us especially earthy. No: good

Arnold Bennett Country Matters and Morals. Best to keep quiet for the moment and persuade her to. Already there is Ingestre foreboding. And when Rachel hears of it, there is certain contempt.

Yet: put such seductions in a play (with a few laughs) and they would all be twittering merrily enough over the slim-lines. The taboo is inside a given charmed circle, whereupon a commonplace affair is almost as bad as the molestation of a child, given an age differential. That thought lurks indeed and is sickening. After all, I did know her as a little girl. Rubbish! She is now a fully grown, reasonably intelligent young woman.

There is this to consider. Oh God! once again the spectre of pragmatism. Never mind. Spirit of health or goblin damned, angels and ministers of grace are all around. Let us just suppose that this year or next, Delahaye's prognoses are almost right and we have an election, a Labour defeat, a strong Tory element in a hungish Parliament, or else an outright temporary runaway. Will not Taylor's thinking infra-structure for a new centre party come to mean some-thing? Jenkins away in Europe for at least four years. Who will follow? (Where, in fact, he was ever reluctant to lead.) Though I would have to take my turn, I have seen the various checks and balances and brakes that may be, and are, applied to the careers of those who transgress. And, in the Taylor book, fucking pretty but inexperienced daughters is most emphatically transgression. I think my blood-sugar must be down or whatever it is. Anyway, time to telephone Albert.

Expect there will be the usual clicking and humming nothing. No, by heaven: this must be one of the good days!
. . . Albert? Tony Connors. How are you? . . . This week-end. I'm hoping to get away reasonably on Friday afternoon and be with you in the early evening. . . . I'd like that: it would be very nice. . . . Who? . . . Ah well, then! And very useful too. Good then, Albert. I'll take a surgery on Saturday for as long as it lasts. . . . Yes, that's all right. Yes, I can do

131

that. . . . Not very keen: but I'll see them on Sunday if I must. And I also have to go to church, if you remember. Then we can talk with the others in the afternoon. . . . Well, if it runs into the evening, I'll get an early train on Monday. Good. . . . Bloody hot: what's it like with you. . . . Look forward to seeing Rita. You tell her that, won't you? . . . What? . . . I'll sue you, you devil. Give her my love. . . . Yes. . . . Yes. . . . Goodbye.

Oh dear! So much for the good constituency MP!

*

The Dazzling Pilgrimage continued

Across the polished desk and gleaming woodwork of the historic desk, in the burnished ambience of his personal study, Augustine Cornflour contemplated with respectful calm the polished and gleaming face of the Right Honourable Sir Hoke Dick, who had succeeded Warrington Stokes to the premiership of the United Kingdom of Great Britain and (reluctantly) Northern Ireland, and the First Lordship of the Treasury.

'Augustine,' said Sir Hoke Dick, massively. 'We need new blood and young blood and it is my opinion that you have served in the sidelines for too long and waited for patient reward with a most uncontumelious and meritable spirit. You know, of course, that this high and arduous office to which Her Majesty has behoved me to hitch my star allows me to flex the spurs of an old ambition.'

Sir Hoke's kindly face strengthened and stiffened in pride and resolve, while Augustine fixed him with unwaveringly blue sincerity, controlling a little postpabulary flatulence.

'I am at last able to institute a Department of Morale and Public Decency,' said Sir Hoke. 'I need optimists, Augustine. And I know that you are one. It is too soon, my boy, to offer you the leadership of this important new Ministry which will bring back to our people the heroic impulse that will find us again winging to the bright skylands of the West, blithe and limber for the fray. That task goes to my faithful colleague in thick and thin times, Gregor Valdes de Chambourcy, who has grown grey in the service of the working men and women of this fertile Atlantic rock. But I am offering you the challenge, Augustine, of being his Minister of State and helping to restore the faltering spirits of an island race who still have much to contribute to a less happy world.'

'Prime Minister,' said Augustine. 'I am honoured and proud to accept. I hope that I shall justify your confidence.'

Sir Hoke Dick rose like an Alp in charcoal worsted and advanced around his desk to impulsively grip Augustine's hand. The benign and rubicund face seemed to gleam even more resolutely at this forging of a new loyalty.

'Today Morale,' he said in his unfaltering, pragmatic way. 'Tomorrow – who knows? The Environment. Or – and I speak now in the strictest confidence, Augustine – my cherished projected Ministry of Cosmic Resources.'

Even Augustine's calm was shaken.

'To your portfolio!' said Sir Hoke, stirringly.

Augustine walked from Downing Street to the House, keenly appreciative of the lovely summer morning but (for once) too preoccupied with a wild flight of ambitious dreaming to notice the many lovely women in pretty dresses who normally decorate Parliament Square and Great and Little George Street. Morale and Public Decency was not what he would have ideally wished for himself; and Gregor Valdes de Chambourcy was not the most dynamic of possible senior ministers under whom to serve: but he was an intimate friend of Sir Hoke Dick, whose cherished project this new department was. And Cosmic Resources! It might sound a bit wild at the moment, with vaunted resources in oil and coal all there for the taking, but Sir Hoke was well known for his conservationist fervour and a profound environmental angst that matched well the open sincerity of his character.

In the course of a routine morning in and around the lobbies, Augustine tasted the vintage champagne of serious attention from customarily insouciant journalists. Barnaby Freeth, who had held on to the Chancellorship with the change in administration, clapped him bluffly between the shoulders. The startlingly elegant Elwyn Poinsettia dropped a discreetly congratulatory word in his ear as he passed. And even that fierce and articulate scimitar of the left, Tertius Barebones, glowered at him, smiled and said something witty and wry. Only Bert Flexion (once upon a time Ethelbert Francis Sheraton-Flexion) looked straight through him in his notorious, piercing way. It could not be bad, Augustine thought, it could not be bad.

'Morale and Public Decency,' chuckled Warrington Stokes, irrepressibly. 'And they say he's thinking of a Ministry of Cosmic Resources. Oh Winnifred, I think I shall rupture something laughing.'

'Yes, dear,' said Mrs Stokes, placidly.

She enjoyed hearing her husband chuckling: it was a pleasant, peaceful sound, suggesting that he was contented, and Mrs Stokes liked people to be contented, especially Warrington. Her knitting needles clicked intricately.

Oho, thought her husband, many hands will soon be making pretty heavy work of it and there would be too many cooks in the garden wanting their cake and eating it while birds of many a different feather would be flocking to the water and refusing to drink. Oho.

Anaximander Split presided over a crystal-laden, candlelit table, gazing with lambent eyes at Ruth Tweed (while his father expatiated on the iron logic of Lenin and his own youthful days in the Red Army before Stalin). Sheer pounding logic ... iron will ... poor presence ... the implacable revolutionary spirit. Anaximander Split had heard it all before, but it would impress Rubicon Tweed who belonged to the sub-section of British intelligentsia which regarded Stalin as a shit and Lenin as the good earth. That, in Anaximander Split's view, was the trouble with the British intelligentsia.

The Chinese understood the significance of shit, applied in the right place at the right time.

'Why have you not eaten your green cabbage, Anaximander?' said his mother quietly. 'Very good for you.'

He ignored it. Dahlia Dackord was listening to his chimpanzee father waving his arms about with shining eyes. 'God!' thought Anaximander Split, 'what fools these liberals be!'

In a moment the old idiot would start talking about black bastards everywhere, so until then Anaximander Split took a few moments' respite from KGB priorities and contemplated a baroque weekend with Mrs Tweed, sketchily painted if eminently desirable. As long as he aroused himself in time to divert the attack on Jews, which was high upon his father's list of folk-prejudice (and for whom most Western Europeans retained a somewhat sentimental perspective) he might indulge himself.

When Dahlia Dackord laughed, he listened again. She was always inclined to encourage the wrong sort of excess in his father's natural xenophobia, because she thought it amusing. He rang for the servants.

It was all going well. His spectacular capitalism and irreproachable Toryism might now be seen in the context of eccentric socialism that was always comforting to a Britisher. The steel will that Rubicon Tweed, Lord Steroid, Mungo Starveling, Reynard Tarsus and the rest wished to impose upon their compatriots was still tempered by the famous sense of cricket and fair play. Although Tweed cared little for games, Steroid, Starveling and Tarsus, like Anaximander Split himself, were all members of the MCC. Each spoke up loudly for co-existence.

'You know, after all this time, it really is the most extraordinary coincidence,' said Ruth Tweed.

'And a pleasant one, I hope. We seem to have taken up quite naturally where I think we left off,' said Augustine

Cornflour. 'My God, let me look at you! You are quite magnificent.'

'Don't. It makes me embarrassed. I've had three children since we last did this.'

'And you still wear stockings!'

'I can't bear tights. They're so hot and expensive.'

'Champagne?'

'You know you've always had a sort of style, Augustine. In all sorts of ways. Oh, I *did* enjoy it. What an extraordinary coincidence, though. Haven't I read that you're something very important in Parliament, or whatever?'

Mrs de Wagram opened *The Times*, the *Telegraph*, the *Mail* and the *Express* at the appropriate page. It was a beautifully framed ad. The International Psychobolic Church declared itself in favour of:

1. Spiritual resumption on all planes of being, with those passed on and those yet to be.
2. Love on all planes and in all manifestations, worldly and otherworldly.
3. Communion with all life, all souls and the spirits of our natural kindred in the animal kingdom.
4. The preservation of God's green creation, the precious rind of consciousness.
5. The development of Cosmic Enterprise, the deployment of natural and surnatural waves and impulses to which only now are those with open minds becoming sensitive.

It was a strange moment. Mrs de Wagram had never been mystical though frequently psychic: now all at once she felt a presence that disturbed her with an elevating vista of glory and perfection where she had an exalted place in a white robe. Not for the first time, she felt ashamed of her own insistent sexual desires, and her pragmatic accommodation (over the years) of men. Not cynical now, she was able to imagine rather than contemplate release. Blessed release from the mortal coil of grubby lust: never again would she display her knickers to Mr Wynstanley; never again would she want to experience Gina's . . . In all sincerity, Mrs de Wagram could not admit *that* yet.

'Oh, Guide,' she said, 'it is a beastly world and we *have to* get the better of it before it gets the better of us.'

As long as she could remember, Mrs de Wagram had wanted to be undefiled, or beyond defilement.

Lucius Spiedermann accepted smoothly a telephone call from Milan. He was not in the best of spirits, but he seldom allowed spirits to interfere with the diurnal acumen that would make England great again and anyone else who wasn't stupid enough to get devolved.

'Lucius Spiedermann,' he said, with lovely modulation.

'Catherine Borgedici,' said a cool, contralto voice.

It was an effort not to drop the receiver.

'Catherine! Cara!' he said. 'How are things?'

'Bloody awful,' said the Tuscan aristocrat. 'The lira is doing even worse than the pound, though we live in hopes. You look like you are ripe for collapse, Spiderboy. I want to meet eight important people by Friday. Got it?'

'But you're in Milano.'

'Look behind you.'

The unfortunate Spiedermann swished around in his air-sprung chair. There was Lucrezia Borgedici, beautiful in wild mink and emeralds and probably nothing else, holding a toy Walther.

'We're ataking over,' she said.

'Me?' said Spiedermann.

'Buckingham Castle, St Paul's Abbey, Oxford and Cambridge,' she said. 'You name it. The works, bambino, the works.'

*

'The thirst for liberty,' said Roger Ingestre, 'is the thirst for power.'

'Did you make that up?' said Clodia Oricellari.

'No. I adapted it from Hobbes.'

'I thought he was a saintly cricket-player.'

'You are impossible. At all events, I intend to use it in our defence.'

'But what is the *point*, Roger? You all sit earnestly around in that nice, untidy house with the trees and the grass and the civilised company. But what impact are you having on the housing estates and in the tenements and the slums that are slums before they get to be slums?'

'After all, we're trying to do something new.'

'Yes and I wish you luck for wanting to try.'

'And we are hoping, not entirely foolishly, in so doing, to cut right across existing party frontiers.'

'Do you still claim to be a Socialist?'

'A Social Democrat.'

'You used to say Socialist.'

'Hugh Gaitskell used to lead the Labour party. Tony Connors, whom I don't think you've met, who's an MP, reminded me the other day how very much things have changed since we first joined.'

'But anyway, apart from the people that you have already, Rachel and the others, do you think you have any hope of attracting MPs from all three parties in big enough numbers to give you real political clout?'

'I don't see why not. The right of the Labour Party has been seriously depleted by Roy Jenkins going to Europe and taking one or two others with him, and a lot of the people left have been hearing their pips squeaking recently.'

'What a horrible image!'

'You know the phrase, don't you? Squeeze till . . .'

'Yes, of course I do. So go on. That's a few politicians who share your own disillusion.'

'The Liberals, at least the mainstream of the party, have been keen on a centre alliance for some time. Grimond was talking about a re-alignment of the left almost twenty years ago. And I think there'd be fairly solid support there.'

'But aren't they in a terrible mess?'

'Well . . . I don't think there'll be an election for some time – certainly not before the autumn of '77. And they may recover a little ground by then. Not that I think they have a hope of doing as well as they did in '74. It was then or never.'

'Yes? And the Conservatives?'

'Your guess is as good as mine. There was quite a bit of disaffection after Heath and I think that there are still some able people more or less out in the cold: but it's always difficult. And I think most people would agree things look better and better for them.'

'And you don't get defectors from a successful party.'

'No. But I think they'll move steadily to the right and so our centre party would attract quite a few people who are on the left of the Tory vote.'

'And what if there is a full-scale economic disaster: not just a crisis, a disaster?'

'There's almost certain to be another crisis. In spite of which restraint, which was supposed to be the cure-all, things still get worse. I've no idea, Clodia. Anything might happen.'

'Even here? In stable tolerant England? Or should I say Britain?'

'That's another rub. Should you, indeed? You might well ask. Yes, I'm afraid so, I think the unions are too strong for there to be much danger from the right, but you never know, do you? One of the thirties writers says something about the strength of the fascists was they gave people a minority to hate.'

'It's frightening. Suppose *we* were to collapse and things broke down here, France would not be long in following. And in France and at home there are massively organised Communist parties.'

'I'm not sure that that isn't an advantage. Like it or not

there are Communists in both countries of quite considerable ability. Any revolution here would be less disciplined and the really wild terrorists would have much more scope.'

'At least you're not shooting each other at the moment.'

'Give or take six counties.'

'Sorry!'

'That's the trouble. It's so easy to forget.'

'But in Italy, everything seems to be a pretext for violence: abortion, relations with the Vatican, any kind of election.'

'One of my friends at Oxford, a German called Willi Bechmann, is worried about neo-Nazi resurgence in West Germany being ignored by radio, television and the papers, in the vague hope that it will go away. We did exactly the same thing with the Catholic discontent in Northern Ireland before 1968.'

'It's a time-honoured way for anarchy and terrorism to take hold in a complacently civilised society.'

'That dreadful phrase "learning to live with it". Which is exactly what we have done with this new brand of urban baboon.'

'We're going to have to learn to live with a lot more. But I don't know. I suppose I can take comfort from the last of the Chinese emperors working happily as a public gardener.'

'Perhaps. But not from Jorge Luis Borges being made an inspector of chickens.'

'Was he?'

'By Péron in the forties.'

'I suppose it's all carved in the blue stone, if we knew how to interpret it. I'm told my kind always last.'

'Aristocrat or diplomat?'

'What on earth is an aristocrat, Roger?'

'I sincerely hope that you last. Who is it makes these comforting predictions?'

'Someone at that nice party of Marie White's. I like your friends. Perhaps it sounded as though I was being a little dismissive.'

'Not at all. You ask perfectly pertinent questions which

we should always be asking ourselves. I'm rather fond of Marie.'

'She seems a generous sort of woman.'

'She is. In many ways. And without an ounce of malice. I think her only ambition is to be a successful hostess. One of her husbands gave her a taste for politics and she enjoys being in the know and having things going on at her house: a little scandal, a little intrigue. Trollope has a lot to answer for. I think Trumble said Marie's idea of bliss would be to hear an exquisite confidence over a perfect martini after a really spectacular lay. He didn't mean it unkindly.'

'Have you been to bed with her?'

'No. I must admit I've never been invited. I don't think I am quite her type.'

'He seems to be a very clever man – Alan Trumble, I mean.'

'Perhaps too clever.'

'Oh? That sounds as if you don't like him.'

'Quite the contrary. What I meant was less that he was too clever for his own good than for his own well-being.'

'Is that why he drinks heavily?'

'You noticed? It doesn't show particularly.'

'Not in any unpleasant way. What's the trouble? Does he think he's wasting his time, working on a newspaper?'

'I'm sure he does *not*! There may be some lurking resentment, a disappointment he doesn't talk about. I'm sure it's not because he wanted a career in politics. He has never tried to get into Parliament. I should say he was a moderately influential political journalist. As Bill Delahaye is. Except that he is a leader writer. Not as well known.'

'The rather nervous man with the stammer?'

'That's right.'

'Yes. Very shy.'

'I'm afraid so. I've often noticed him looking rather hungrily at certain women, without daring to approach.'

'I don't imagine that's very typical in your group. Although you are, personally, a model of decorum.'

'Am I?'

'Ask Francesca.'

'Good heavens! Does Francesca think I'm shy?'

'Pity that girl never bothered to learn good English. Trumble told me he thought that you were all, himself included, playing an elaborate game, which you hoped would never be for real.'

'I don't think so. I doubt that he does. Barbara Dunn has an international reputation as an academic; Jeremy is a successful publisher with important contacts all over the world; most of the politicians and civil servants are pretty serious people. Though, as it happens, our best ideologue is Bill Delahaye.'

'Really?'

'He has a gifted political imagination. I suppose it's because he used to write fiction. He is splendid at working out political scenarios and various forms of antidote strategy.'

'For you of the moderate left.'

'I have an idea that I am being mocked. At all events, we are uniformly philistine and do not go to the opera.'

'While the rest of the country wastes? I've annoyed you.'

'Not in the least. I must be sensitive about our effectiveness. Perhaps that, too, is a symptom of despair.'

'Francesca tells me that I am patronising. I don't mean to be. But, you see, I have this unusual opportunity for meeting the civilised in one country after another. . . .'

'You have wide experience of the liberal left and we are a rotten lot of fellows.'

'Oh, you are a buffoon sometimes! No. The opposite. You are what I said: civilised. And kind and worried and serious.'

'And doomed.'

'We shall see. Anyway, I hope that you don't think that I am patronising. Trumble does.'

'That's unlike him. To be so direct.'

'I think it was to annoy a Freudian television producer. . . .'

'Sandra! Yes, it would be. They are working out some

terrible ancient blood-feud. Alan Trumble detests psycho-analysis. I think he prefers the idea of sin.'

'The situation was saved, though. By that nice man, Ellis.'

'Oh dear! What an evening you had! Ellis is a guinea a minute. Given inflation, perhaps three or four these days.'

'He berated me about Italian children and a game called "conkers".'

'Conkers!'

'Yes. A game with horse-chestnuts . . . you know, those brown shiny things that fall from trees. . . .'

'Clodia, for God's sake, I know all about conkers.'

'Well, Ellis Fullet . . .'

'Fulford. . . .'

'Thank you. . . . He'd been walking in Treviso, which is a town he has the good sense to like, on the ramparts during last autumn. And there were these small philistine Italian boys racing toy motor-cars, of which they each had hundreds in plastic bags. While they were knee-deep in conkers! The consequences for European unity he says are dire. Insensitivity to the environment has never been more blatant. He says he became a Liberal because of a conker-deprived childhood in Islington.'

'And you've been commissioned to see it. Ellis is an Italophile almost in my own league. Don't be taken in, by the way. He is really a serious man. If he'd been in either of the other parties, he might be quite near the top. . . .'

'Roger, my dear. Isn't that true of a number of your friends in that "group"? A lot of talent and some reason for not quite exploiting it.'

'A very simple reason. The liberal conscience. I think many of them would be disappointed if they were thought not to have made a success.'

'I didn't say that.'

'But you implied not quite the success, which is to say *fame*, that they might have enjoyed. Fame is the respect of

143

the people you respect, for some. Would you care about the esteem of television-watchers?'

'No. But that is the last (literally the last) intellectual snobbery.'

'Not in the least. It demands high professional humility. It is the determination to live up to a modest reputation, regardless of adulation or money. And it is rare. At the same time, none of us want to be happy gardeners, inspectors of chickens, or spreading sewage on the Good Earth.'

'None of your Highgate Group.'

'That's a convenient name. Nothing more. It amounts to a number of quite disparate people who would like to preserve a system where we choose our own level of participation, reserve the right to be judged by those we respect and decide for ourselves how we will contribute to the general good.'

'In a word: élitism.'

'No! Because we do not seek to perpetuate ourselves.'

'So avoiding the Platonic fallacy.'

'I've never heard of the Platonic fallacy. I hope that's not official.'

'It's not. I just thought of it. Anyway, it's only a fallacy if liberals are citing it to their purpose. Plato was *quite* certain about guardians.'

'I see myself more as a slave. Like ...'

'Like ...?'

'All right, you win again. Like Epictetus.'

'Who was of course spiritually a Social Democrat.'

'He was quite irreproachable. Morally, I doubt whether any of us can match his example. Bill Delahaye is said by Ellis to be writing a wicked fiction based on our shortcomings.'

'Is he a novelist?'

'Yes. Which is to say he's written several fairly serious novels. But not for some time. He seems to have lost the impetus. I've got them all somewhere, if you're interested.'

'What's he doing now?'

'Ellis says he writes to amuse himself. This particular thing is a satire built around Tony Connors, who is the ex-husband of my ex-wife's sister and something of a philanderer. In fact, I have a confession to make and I've been looking for a suitable confessor.'

'Then look no further. I adore confessions. I shall go behind that trellis, if you like.'

'No, that would be too much of a spectacle. The trouble is that I have connived at a seduction.'

'Involving the aforesaid Connors?'

'Precisely. I'm not sure that this is going to sound very edifying. Candida, the elder Taylor daughter, was temporarily coming to me for tutorials. Of course, I've known her for years. . . . And in the course of these seems to have conceived some kind of minor infatuation for me. . . .'

'Perfectly understandable.'

'You're very kind. But a bloody nuisance. She asked me for a little extra tuition and came to my flat with all sorts of other things in mind.'

'Which you nobly resisted?'

'Yes.'

'Well?'

'Then Connors declared an interest and I happened to tell him she was expected later the same afternoon and that I had an earlier appointment, so he could let her in. I thought I should be back well before any drastic action, but then Rachel Bailey was delayed and I was much later than I'd expected to be.'

'During which time Connors had his way with her?'

'I'm very much inclined to think so.'

'I think it's funny. After all she's well over the age of consent. Why does it worry you?'

'Oh, I don't really know. Obviously I expected to be only a few minutes late or I'd have made some other arrangement with her. And it was convenient to have her let in. And then when Rachel was late, I knew that she'd have somewhere comfortable to wait. . . .'

'And someone agreeable to wait with.'

'That's where I was a little Byzantine. For my own convenience. I know quite well that young people these days are much better able to look after themselves emotionally than I was at their age: but there's a nice lad called Kent who's genuinely rather fond of her, though I think she'd be very bad for him and his work. I should hate the idea of being the agent whereby the girl was hurt.'

'It happens to most of us at one time or another.'

'I suppose so.'

'I honestly should not let it worry you. There is an Anglo-Saxon tendency always to make a scandal out of nothing, quite unimportant sexual peccadillos that would pass unnoticed anywhere else.'

'Well, we've had some whoppers in the last fifteen or so years.'

'No more so than, say, the United States. And you have *not* had the financial and industrial frauds on anything like the same scale as they've had; or, for that matter, the rest of Europe. Take this Lockheed business: America, Japan, quite naturally at home with us in Italy, and even Holland.'

'Where it is especially embarrassing. Ellis says "a Dutch arse of a problem".'

'Very appropriate.'

'One thing about the Americans, though, Clodia: they do not spare themselves a second's agony when they find something wrong. Seen in a historical perspective, one could certainly argue that Watergate was good for American democracy and therefore not bad for Western democracy as a whole. After all, abuses in a healthy society can be corrected and eliminated.'

'I suppose so. What did you think of Ford getting the nomination.'

'Oh, I think he deserved to. And I certainly prefer him to Reagan.'

'I don't think I do. Reagan is a very shrewd man. I've heard him talk at various diplomatic functions and he thinks

146

fast on his feet. I suppose there's nothing to stop Jimmy Carter.'

'I must confess he worries me. I should still prefer Hubert Humphrey who's the nearest thing they have to a Social Democrat, if you allow for Eugene McCarthy. I can't see any challenge from anyone else. If you have this regard for Reagan, I must introduce James Lloyd Mitchell, who's a friend of Blakemore, incidentally. He's well to the right.'

'I'd like to meet him. I enjoy comparing notes with other aliens. Not that I find Americans abroad all that endearing. As a veteran of a hundred Harry's Bars.'

'We Europeans are not kind enough. I've met as many gentle and courteous people in art galleries as I've met boors in the Burlington Arcade. In fact, very many more: since I go infrequently to the Burlington Arcade.'

'Wait until the pound sinks further. We have longer experience of the secondary phenomena attendant upon weak currency. We were a cheap-holiday nation when you still had an Empire.'

'A glum prospect.'

'Yes. I recall a conversation at a restaurant in Florence. Quite a young woman, expensively turned out, with a geriatric husband and one of those cloying, sycophantic voices. She wanted him to teach her to use their perfectly simple camera so that she could photograph him next to Michelangelo's *David* at the Academia. "You two would look *so* great!" That morose, decaying old man.'

'It has a certain tragic irony.'

'Oh yes. All round. I think it's very tiring being European.'

*

If anything it was cooler in Bologna than it had been in London, but perhaps this was because the wonderful high colonnades of the main streets offered shade even on the most sweltering days. Candida loved the town with its wide squares, high buildings and crazily leaning towers: it was altogether on a much larger scale than she had expected, especially after landing at the small and very tatty airport. She knew sufficiently little about the Renaissance to indulge in effusively Romantic dreams about the past, but she was delighted to find that Tony knew a surprising amount about the inter-city rivalries in the thirteenth and fourteenth centuries.

In fact almost everything about Tony delighted her or excited her. She had been taken completely by surprise when he had proposed an Italian holiday between the recess and the party conference, and still took a rather childish pleasure in all the conspiratorial deceptions they had made in order to keep it absolutely secret. He had been anxious that, for the moment at least, her parents and their friends should not know about their affair, which suited Candida who thought that one way or another people would have found ways of being boring. She did not suppose that Jeremy and Barbara would actually care that she was going to bed with Tony Connors, whatever the discrepancy in age: he was a decidedly civilised and elegant man. (What *they* knew of him!) But she guessed that parents could suddenly, for no good reason, become very tiresome about that sort of thing and then there would be Roger Ingestre and his detached, supercilious amusement. (God! what an escape she had had there, if she had but known it. Candida was absolutely astonished that she could have changed so much from a girl with a stupid crush into a fully awakened woman, whose sexual appetites were now so real and defined, in such a very short time.) She looked affectionately at Tony, slim and elegantly casual, sipping his wine. That was also an important part of it: as well as the marvellous sex, there was so much affection.

It was much better that no one else should know. When she had suddenly told her mother that some friends from Oxford had invited her to a farmhouse they had taken in Tuscany for a few weeks, she had shown very little interest and it had all been achieved easily. Daddy had given her quite a lot of money, which, since Tony naturally insisted on paying for everything, she spent on some really beautiful clothes and accessories. She knew that she had never looked more lovely.

She was, of course, sorry that it was soon to end – the holiday. Obviously the affair was going to go on and on. After a few days at Bologna, Tony had hired a car and they had driven to Florence and then south to Siena, Perugia and Assisi and back to Bologna (which Candida had liked best) via Ravenna. It had all been wonderful. They had made love – sometimes passionate, sometimes slowly sensual, sometimes violent – several times on almost every day; they had visited the most elegant restaurants and some of the most jolly and riotous little places; they had seen thousands of pictures and probably hundreds of churches and galleries. Tony was the most expert and unobtrusive guide, who knew an enormous amount, but who wore his learning very lightly.

But it was not the grand sites and the great works of art that had impressed Candida so much; these had been marvellous to see at last and sometimes deeply moving: more important, though, had been the people, and perhaps most of all, the magical moments of peace and pleasure and sometimes comedy. The sun setting over Florence, seen from La Loggia in the Piazzale Michelangelo, with the lights beginning to twinkle in the dusk on the opposite hillside of Fiesole; or nuns wolfing spaghetti at incredible speed in a packed restaurant opposite the Chiesa della Santa Clara in Assisi; or a row of very daring knickers on a clothes line in the cloisters of St Apollinaris in Ravenna, which she somehow remembered more clearly than the mosaics; and in Bologna the endless street meetings taking place between groups of men all arguing and gesticulating – whose wives (according to Tony) all went in large buses to Assisi to eat, drink and be holy while their men were committed and harangued each other around the Palazzo Communale.

Candida felt vaguely resentful that her parents had not taken them abroad more often. She had been with her school to Paris and to Rome and on a ski-ing holiday, but, apart from one August in the Dordogne about five years previously, Jeremy and Barbara had always been too busy, for foreign travel. Both had too many commitments: lectures, seminars, summer schools, publishers' conferences, book fairs – quite apart from their own already hectic professional lives. And neither of them really liked going abroad, preferring by far their place in the country, where they could relax and read and go on the most boring walks imaginable.

Still, if she had been better travelled and more sophisticated, she would not have had this enormous pleasure of discovering things with Tony, who was so much more urbane and witty than either of her parents. Throughout the holiday she had been convulsed by his quietly ironic asides; and she had sometimes made him laugh. Candida knew that she was not particularly clever in conversation (and not a natural buffoon like Jessica who seemed to have everyone in fits of laughter all the time by saying the most banal things): but Tony made her feel that she was. And, so encouraged, she knew that she talked intelligently, and really quite well, when she was with him. And their love – because it was love at its gentlest and most tender – made her more aware of others, sometimes unhappily of the sadnesses of others. Candida thought of an American couple in a bar somewhere (Florence, she thought): a handsome man with a finely chiselled face staring coldly and completely without love at his wife who must once have been beautiful, and who was still attractive, but whose face had become embittered, presumably by years of this blank indifference. She watched the woman try to talk over the martinis, to be answered only in monosyllables, and watched her eyes becoming poisoned and her good lips beginning to curl. The fine academic man just stared at her, absolutely untouchable. It was because Candida, holding Tony's hand at the time, felt so happy that she became desperately sorry for these two, especially for the woman. She thought that Roger Ingestre must have behaved in that sort of way to his wife: small wonder that

150

their marriage had broken up. She had said something about the American couple to Tony, who had laughed gently and kissed her hair. No one seemed to notice the difference between their ages. They looked well together. She thought that he was pleased and flattered when other men looked admiringly at her and perhaps enviously at him. And she herself was terribly happy to be with a man of such easy grace of manner, such authority and confidence.

She was also impressed by his diligence in keeping up with events. He read five papers in the course of each day – *The Times* and any other English paper he could lay hands on, *La Stampa, Corriere della Sera* and the *International Herald Tribune*. Obviously, Candida read the English language papers as well and they talked over various items of news: she liked the way Tony listened to her and treated her intelligently without the slightest patronising. Very unlike, say, her mother. Or Ingestre.

The news, of course, was seldom very good or cheerful, but Candida admired Tony's optimism as much as his high seriousness. She knew that her parents and their friends thought of him as a very brilliant man, who was perhaps a little frivolous and lazy in the application of his talents politically. How very superficially they knew him! Candida was increasingly angry at their dismissive ways. They had pigeon-hole minds, all too eager to categorise, catalogue and file away. Why take the trouble to get to know people? Of course, her opportunity of getting to understand Tony was rather special: but quite apart from the fun they had in bed and everywhere else, she had time to appreciate the keenness of his analytical mind and also the skill with which he was able to explain things to someone less well informed.

'You're very thoughtful, darling,' he said.

'No. I'm just very happy,' Candida said. 'I'm just very happy. And still amazed at being so lucky. It's crazy. That chance meeting at Roger Ingestre's flat.'

'Well, I'm sorry about the constitutional documents. . . .'

'F– constitutional documents!' said Candida.

Not out of coyness, but she liked to keep such words for precisely intimate moments and a particular kind of erotic situation which she was very pleased to have guessed. The first time she had whispered something into his ear of that sort, she had been amazed at the effect.

He laughed.

'I'd much rather not,' he said. 'Have some more wine.'

'Thank you. Anything startling in the paper?'

'I'm afraid that it's all much too startling. This business in Seveso looks bad. Naturally, the Italian press is preoccupied with that.'

'Those poor children.'

'Yes. The implications are worrying. Quite apart from the human considerations, which are most important, there's the point that it was a foreign company and that raises issues about international industrial concerns. And if this kind of thing happens in that sort of works, think of what *could* happen in a place like Windscale.'

Candida was not absolutely certain about what went on at Windscale, but she guessed that it must be something to do with nuclear energy.

'And there was Flixborough,' she said. 'Which was ghastly.'

Tony was, as usual, unsentimental and clear-headed.

'Absolutely ghastly,' he said. 'But what the environmentalists always fail to do is to balance the occasional horror against the immensely beneficial results of urgently needed sources of energy.'

'Of course.'

Candida nodded her head slowly.

'Anyway,' he said, 'we're being much too serious for six o'clock on a lovely day.'

'We are,' she said. 'I'm sorry. My fault. But you are so *interesting* when you talk about things that matter to you. This is my favourite bar in the whole world.'

'It is rather special, I agree.'

'What's it called?'

'Zanarini, I think. Yes. Look.'

'Do you know, I'm surprised that this town is so elegant. I mean it's been Communist for years, hasn't it? And it's so splendid and so rich.'

'It's said to have the best cuisine in Italy.'

'I'm quite sure it has! But doesn't it surprise you?'

'Nothing surprises me about Italy. Or for that matter the Italian Communist Party. I admire Signor Berlinguer quite a lot. After all, Candida, they have a pretty good tradition intellectually.'

'But not for you?'

'Oh no. Not for me. I didn't grow up under Mussolini.'

'No,' said Candida. 'But there are still Social Democrats here who did.'

She was pleased to see him glance towards her with the sort of half-amused, half-surprised smile that indicated that his intelligence had been properly engaged.

'This is where I say *touché*,' he said.

'Only if you mean it.'

She enjoyed seeing the change in his eyes. Quite abruptly, from being clear and sardonic, they became blurred and dull with desire. She wished she knew what happened in her own at such moments. In due course she thought she would find out, as their relationship matured and developed.

'Shall we go back to the hotel?' he said.

'Wouldn't you like some more wine?'

He signalled to the waiter. And made a funny face at her. She laughed and crossed her legs elaborately.

There was a Radical Party meeting in the huge square in front of the Basilica San Petronio demanding the right of abortion for Italian women. The people conducting the meeting looked amazingly serious and political, with yet that same rather determinedly farouche look of feminist-centred demonstrators even in London. There was a great deal of passion in the speeches, listened to with some evident mirth by the largely male concourse in the Piazza Maggiore at that time (or indeed, as far as Candida could see, at any other) of day. She listened hard and followed what was being said pretty well.

'A bit "vecchio cappo", isn't it?' she said to Tony.

'I think, in their mood, they'd settle for that,' he said seriously.

They went back to the hotel. She could sense his urgency as a reflection of her own rising excitement, wondering if she would ever get used to this vibrating lust for him that so easily possessed her. (And in so short a time! She still had difficulty getting it into any kind of perspective.) In such a short time, however, she had found out what pleased him: he called himself a 'stocking freak'. So Candida wore stockings and the pretty lace-trimmed accessories that went with them. Not particularly comfortable, but then only loose silk clothes were really that. She wondered whether he would want to be dominant or not. It had taken her a little time to get used to the idea that sometimes he wanted her to be. But she would know very soon, once they entered their room and closed the door.

*

The hideous irony of it all is that having conned everyone that I was taking a job in London to work in the BM and so on, I'm getting so much of it done! After that disaster of an evening, Candida has resolutely refused to come out with me again or even to see me, and has now disappeared. Apparently she has gone to stay in Italy with Oxford friends: but Ingestre does not know who these friends are and they are not Sue Devlin or Jane Scott, whom I've always understood to be Candida's closest friends at LMH, because they were both at home when I rang. I can't very well telephone her home again and ask who she's gone with: I've made quite a big enough fool of myself already, but I have this nasty certainty that she's gone with some other man and I spend far too much time feeling sorry for myself.

Clifford and Teresa are both being tactfully sympathetic,

to the extent of providing alternative distractions in the very pleasant shape of a couple of girls who are friends of the family. They were both extremely nice and apparently quite eager and uninhibited: but I can't really bring myself to having it away casually with someone I know I don't give a damn about right at the outset. It seems too cynical by half: and anyway it would be bad politics as far as relations with the pub are concerned, where they have been extremely kind to me.

So has Roger Ingestre. He calls in at The Reeve when he's in Highgate and has invited me round to his flat a couple of times. Rather surprisingly, he asked me directly about how things were going with Candida and so, sparing him the more exquisite details, I told him. He seemed embarrassed about it all, but for some reason almost obliged to talk about her. In a decidedly guarded way. I think he was trying to put me off her. He said that he thought she was wayward and conceited, or showed a tendency in that direction. Of course, he admitted, she is very pretty and poised. I wondered in fact whether at last she had actually succeeded in seducing him, which I'm quite sure she would like to, and whether he was feeling guilty. But, obviously, this is an absurd notion – since she would hardly have gone off to Italy in the middle of a successful affair. Perhaps it has been unsuccessful. . . . Ridiculous! Why suppose that a civilised and mature man with a wide circle of female friends of his own age should be bothering his head about Candida? The answer is that I am so obsessed with her myself that I assume everyone else must be.

Not only was there that delicious Italian girl he brought to the dance at Oxford, but he called in at The Reeve the other day with a very attractive and intelligent MP, called Rachel Bailey, who also belongs to his political group. They seemed to be on very easy terms, which of course does not necessarily mean that they go to bed together. I liked her very much and we had a very lively conversation in which I think I must have done pretty well. She made quite a speech about

155

how impressed she is by the stability and sense of responsibility of the present generation of young people and
Ingestre agreed with her, though he wondered incidentally
if, after the professional protesters of the late sixties, anything
different would not be a relief. They had both been up at
Oxford in the fifties and, according to Ingestre, it had been
for him Arcadia. It was a transitional and blissful period (he
said) between privilege and protest. Rachel agreed with him,
but thought that those years had been curiously frivolous and
naive. Ingestre preferred to call them innocent. (Since both
of them got comfortable firsts, I think their frivolity couldn't
have been all that remarkable. I wonder if they think that I
am too earnest.)

Rachel wanted to know what I was going to do and I had
to admit that I didn't know, but I supposed that I was
vaguely hoping for an academic career of some sort, perhaps
a year or two in the States. She asked if I'd ever thought
about politics. This took me by surprise, since in fact I have
never thought about it for a second. 'Pay no attention to me,'
she said. 'I shall really have to make some quite spectacular
retribution, Roger, like doing a strip in the lobby or something. The trouble is that whenever I see anyone who is sane
and promising, I want to sign him up for democracy. It's
like some people who enjoy writing so much, they're always
trying to persuade others to try it.' Anyway, I was flattered
that she thought I was sane and promising and mildly
excited by the thought of her doing a strip in the lobby, or
anywhere else. We, then, had a really fascinating conversation about the latest Cabinet reshuffle and it was most
interesting to hear the inside view of things. Clifford was
delighted, which takes the form in his case of a very dignified
and grave look and little murmurs to the regulars.

I began to think a lot more about politics at odd moments
after this chat, which was a change at least from thinking
about Candida and what some bastard might be doing to her.
They went on to their meeting at her house, after Rachel
very kindly invited me to call in on her at the House of

Commons some time during the next session, if I was interested. This is obviously something to do: although I don't think that I have the real dedication or commitment to go in for politics. Apart from the fact that they obviously work enormously hard, I think they have to really care deeply about the various ideological issues and a vague liberalism isn't quite enough. I suppose I'm about left of centre in attitude. (Certainly a lot left of Dad!) But I realise in, fact, that whereas I know what's going on in the world and I react with this or that opinion, my ideas aren't coherent. Of course, that also means they are not wild and following some noisy fashion: but I don't think deeply enough. I work hard and read and listen to what others think, but I don't think enough for myself. This meeting with Rachel Bailey, who impressed me a lot, made me see that.

On Sunday Dad 'happened to be passing through' and so they both called at the pub, where they took very much to Clifford. (Very dignified.) He lost no time at all in telling Dad how much my 'professor' thought of me and how he often dropped in with politicians and that. He gave the distinct impression that the class of client had gone up quite a lot since I had started working at The Reeve. Dad wanted to know who the politicians were and commented: 'All Socialists, I see.' It then transpired that he and Clifford shared pretty nearly identical views in spite of their difference in age, the corner-stone of which was the fact that the world had been a better place when what is now called the Third World had been the Empire. 'These foreigners,' said Dad, 'always preaching at us. And where would they be without us? What ideas would they have on their own?' 'It stands to reason,' said Clifford. 'All ideas come from Europe, don't they?' 'And we spread them,' said Dad. 'We also exploited people,' I said. 'That's as may be, lad. But where would they have been without us. Look what happens once we get out: democracy lasts for half an hour and all this aid goes into someone's back pocket and they're in an economic mess.'

The line-up around the bar was Dad, Clifford and seven

regulars against me. Mum neutral, on the grounds that politics are boring. Teresa keeping wise counsel. And the lovely Samantha supporting the Queen who does such a marvellous job keeping us all united. (Incidentally, Mum and Dad were both glancing speculatively at Samantha, as who would not with her figure and glowing smile, but at least she was a royalist! I thought it would do them good; but Teresa, who is very canny in such matters, dropped it into the conversation that Samantha lived out and asked after someone called Malcolm.)

After they had gone and we closed, I went out for a walk on my own. It was a lovely clear night again, still very warm. I found myself thinking about the different assumptions people make about their lives and what they expect. And how things change and how they do not. Until he told me differently, I'd always assumed that Ingestre had gone to Oxford from a public school and from an upper middle class family, because his manner and confidence seem to have been inherited. I can't imagine him as gauche and inept as I sometimes feel and sometimes am. Perhaps this is why he told me. But if we take the tutorial group last term, the assumptions of Lumley and Candida are so different from my own and Sheila's. It *is* a class thing but one that does not involve resentment: I assume that I have the right to anything I work for; Candida assumes certain privileges because she has never known anything else. And they *are* privileges: good conversation, intellectual ambience, acquaintances in demanding but interesting jobs; a taste for wine and good food; certain rituals of taste and behaviour. It has never occurred to me to be ashamed of my parents and I really do not think that I am: but I am embarrassed by them. Suppose Dad had been sharing his political opinions with Ingestre, or with Rachel Bailey, rather than with Clifford and Teresa? Well, would it have mattered? I suppose not at all. Ingestre would have accepted Dad for what he is, a good honest Tory yeoman, not very sophisticated but thoroughly deserving of his vote. Rachel would have argued on Dad's own terms. And so what does that make me? A snob. I don't see that I can dodge it. And I don't suppose that Candida has ever for a moment been embarrassed by her parents, let alone ashamed of them. A top publisher and a lecturer in economics. How could it be?

Not that I feel any real sense of grievance. I've been reading a couple of books by Goronwy Rees about his early years and Oxford in the twenties and thirties. Then, I doubt whether I would have survived there, when privilege was so absolute: and it was interesting to hear Ingestre and Rachel talking about the fifties and the interval between privilege and protest.

This all occurred to me, somewhat fancifully, as a new form of the pragmatic sanctions that Ingestre is so fascinated by. Strictly as they apply to the splendid Maria Theresa of course. But as her father arranged the supportive sanctions for her by alliances with the other European powers, so people like Candida have their futures guaranteed by knowing the right people at the right time: not in any sense of jobs for the girls (in this case), though it is noticeable how many second generation successes there are, but because she has already so much valuable experience, so much contact with people whose assurance is more or less complete, so much going for her. All things that I have to work for. And then I have the advantage of Oxford. And Ingestre. And Ingestre's goodwill.

There must be all kinds of sanctions (pragmatic or not!) that people impose on each other inside families and, for that matter, in ordinary friendships. The way, I suppose, we use other people as levers in a relationship. And are used. I see it sometimes here in The Reeve, where already Clifford and Teresa are working on the kids because they have certain ambitions for them. And then, even, the alliances around the bar, here. Inevitably Clifford must fancy Samantha sometimes, as I do – in a certain dress, or caught in a particular movement. We don't do anything about it. But Teresa always knows, I think. As she knows when I fancy her. Christ, what does that make us all but normal! Nevertheless, it is extraordinary the little tensions that can occur. I was never aware of these at home: I suppose because I didn't want to be. I don't want to think about my parents in sexual situations and I'm bloody sure they wouldn't want me to. *But*, here we are again. Does this apply to Candida and her family, with their high sophistication? I can't imagine Ingestre or Rachel Bailey worrying about it.

After all this, this morning a nice chap called Ted White came into the bar. About my age, perhaps a bit older and we fell into conversation because it was very quiet. Bank Holiday and the first day of rain since the Lord's Test. (Ingestre was so fed up about that, it's stuck in my memory. Perhaps it's because the Sikhs praying for rain in Southall have succeeded.) He thought I was a professional barman; perhaps this means I'm getting good at it. I'm ashamed to say I let him think so – because I thought he looked like a professional student. He turns out to be a teacher in a polytechnic with a passion for the Spanish language and Latin American literature. He teaches maths and can't stand his family and their friends. He is the first person I've met who calls himself an intellectual drop-in; and clearly believes his own standards to be infinitely superior to anything else he has come across. It's refreshing after so much self-doubt.

At the same time, 'at the end of the day', as the wireless has it each morning, where does that leave me and Candida. God rot her! (Not really, God.) (Just a bit.)

4

Dear Roger,

Thank you very much for your very entertaining letter and the 'Highgate' stuff about Europe. I must say it's something of a relief to have been shifted to the European group from the Economics coven. In my brasher moments, I think I know quite a lot about economics, but half an hour with Barbara Dunn makes me feel that I learned them out of *The Story of Ginger and Pickles*. (Come to think of it, that's not a bad introduction to economics. There have been quite a few parallels to some of those characters around Number Eleven and the Treasury!) In all seriousness, though, I am hoping to do something in Strasbourg in the future. I'm not sure that I'm ever likely to be considered for any senior job in government with the party the way it is at the moment. And so my clear spirit isn't spurred to that kind of fame any longer. If I had known how much time Oliver would have to spend away from home when he took on the WHO job, I think I might have put myself forward for nomination some time ago. Even so, it is a murderous schedule what with commuting to Strasbourg and Luxembourg, putting in appearances at the House in the normal course of things and doing one's duty by the constituency. Anyway, I shall look forward to working with you, however theoretically it may all turn out to be. The last time we all met at Jeremy's, I'm afraid I was still not convinced that the group has enough muscle and it seems to me that there are serious policy deficiencies with regard to Northern Ireland, Africa and immigration. All right, none of them easy matters: but it's in such clumps of nettles that we have to go gathering flowers if we are to be convincing. Having said that, however, I think the draft material for the economics pamphlet and this preliminary stuff on Europe and détente is very good. I've been seeing the British papers and so I've noticed some steady stuff in what must be Bill Delahaye's leaders. Trumble also did a brilliant piece for the *International Tribune*.

I'm enjoying being here very much. Quite apart from being with Oliver, whom I miss more than somewhat in London, I like New York and I don't find it particularly frightening, although I've met a surprising number of people who have been mugged. Even Oliver, who used to view such things as if it was still just a matter of playing for St Mary's Hospital against the Metropolitan Police, is quite amenable to taking taxis after dark. But we've walked about quite a lot during the day and it is all so alive and exciting and *funny*, as well as being impatient and violent just below the surface. What really does scare me is the latent hostility that you notice in the working-class blacks from the moment you land at Kennedy. Thank God, we have nothing quite like it yet in England and so it was deeply depressing to read about what happened at Notting Hill during the carnival. The papers made it sound very ugly.

We spent a few days in Connecticut with Bob and Milly Krantz, who send their warm regards, and we went down (or up, or over) to Princeton where David Willow is teaching creative writing, somewhat bemusedly, in the next couple of semesters. He has taken enthusiastically to American usage and to bourbon.

It was, of course, great fun to be here for the end of the Republican convention which most people think was, for once, more interesting than the Democratic equivalent. I was delighted that Ford got the nomination. I don't care how pedestrian he is and how many cruel stories there are about his intellectual wattage, he is so patently a decent and honest man. So is Reagan, of course. But I can't think of a more difficult and thankless task than Ford's after that agonising triumph of a democratic system of government that brought down Nixon, Agnew and the rest. There is something of a lull at the moment before the campaigns start in earnest and, at the moment, it looks as though Carter is well ahead. I must say I feel uneasy about him. Folksy determination makes my funny-bones ache in that nasty way they do when Batman talks of the working people and some of the top Tribunites spout about democratic processes. I remembered a phrase of Adlai Stevenson: 'Your public servants serve you right.' And began to regret, I suppose for the 927th time, that he had never been President. It is almost dispiriting to think of all the really able and good men who have missed the top in English and American politics: add to Stevenson, Rockefeller and Gaitskell and Butler and Roy Jenkins. I suppose in Gaitskell's case it was an untimely death that deprived him: but not so with the others. And I cannot help wondering how different it might all have been if Stevenson had been leader of the Western world in the fifties and Gaitskell had been Prime Minister from 1964 to 1970. I can see you smiling across the Atlantic, Mr Ingestre. Don't be patronising! Academic historians need to be regularly scandalised.

It will be interesting to see what happens at the party conference at the end of the month. I think we can expect all kinds of tag-wrestling, Siamese boxing and genuine karate. I imagine that you too are asking yourself who is going to take over Roy Jenkins's mantle. There's obviously Shirley Williams: but whatever may happen to her in the future (and the Deputy Leadership's coming up soon) it isn't happening at the moment. I have a long-standing regard for Crosland, although his style and manner isn't exactly proletarian enough for many others in the party. And it's too easy to forget that fifteen years or so ago, he was one of the leading ideologues for Democratic Socialism at a time when you and I were both rookies. I don't suppose you have forgotten, anyway. I think if he cared to, he could certainly be the focus of a lot of rightist support and (because he has taken an independent line on so many issues, as did Jim Callaghan for so long, without rocking the boat) he may have earned (if that's the right word) the esteem of the conservative middle-ground. (Do you know I think that is the problem: who are more conservative than the skilled working class, more jealous of their differentials, more worried about the lowering of their expectations and standards, more frightened of immigrant or foreign competition in whatever form? They are all there in the Midlands and the North West and South Yorks ready for the Tory apple barrel.) Anyway, it remains to be seen. He is a good and loyal party man and, as everybody knows, is most amazingly eager to be Chancellor. This is the point, Roger, about centre pressure groups: short of revolution, how are they going to attract the Croslands and Healeys and Heaths and Howes? At any event, it should all be very exciting. I don't suppose you'll be there, but I daresay we might have shared the odd laugh.

And so to gossip. I was, naturally, agog to hear of your suspicions about Connors and Candida Taylor. I can't think why, off hand: because I don't like Connors and hardly know the girl. I'm sure that Sandra Beeton could give me a sound Freudian explanation in four longish sentences. I suppose, however high-minded we pretend to be, there is something lubricious in us all and a vague stirring in the pool of old emotions. I don't understand, though, why you should feel responsible, whatever is going on: Candida is above the age of consent and quite well aware of the way she disposes herself. (I always had a private idea that she was hoping you might be interested.) Also, the mere fact that Connors was once married to your sister-in-law, and that you find him tolerable company, does not make you his moral tutor and I'm sure you are not hers. I fear, dear Roger, that we have never, however much we have tried, tuned into the sexual VHF of the young. However much I am tempted, and I sometimes am of course, I cannot easily (in fact, don't at all!) enter into passionate affairs: because I love Oliver and want to go on loving him and am afraid of the risk of spoiling something and losing him. Or, indeed, losing myself. Of course, I remember what you went through with Daphne; and I remind you of it now not to be cruel but in order to suggest gently and affectionately that it is possible to take these things too seriously, too sensitively. Connors is not like that. And I'd guess – in view of what you told me about that very nice boy Stephen Kent – nor is Candida Taylor. Perhaps I'm not the best consultant: try the lovely Marie White. Or ask your beautiful Italians! Unlike Oliver, about whose personal associations I have never asked, but in whom I have absolute trust, you are a family man who does not have a family. Forgive me. That is perhaps impertinent.

Bob Krantz and I had a ferocious argument, while remaining the best of friends, about my Protestant conscience. Oliver was vastly amused and told lots of funny stories about me in Assisi, which I hope, if we ever *both* get to meet Clodia, he will spare me in her presence. I'm never really convinced that Catholics have a truly sound work ethic and I seldom read a Catholic novelist without a nasty flesh-crawling feeling of moral equivocation at the back of my neck. (Quite different, incidentally, from the pain in my political funny-bones!) To a Jew like Bob Krantz or Ellis Fulford or an atheist like Oliver this is of course hilarious. Are you really still C of E?

Oliver is flourishing. He looks amazingly well, quite genuinely as though he could play rugby for Surrey again tomorrow. And he is working hard. As usual, he is exasperated by the delays of any international organisation trying to achieve something and enraged by the cases of corruption and misdirection of funds that occur: but he is working hard and happily. With any luck, he will move to Geneva either later this year or early next: so we might be able to meet that much more easily, especially if my miasmal hopes for some kind of meaningful place in the European parliament materialise. As always, he has gathered the most extraordinary set of friends: cadaverously grim, trollishly sardonic, Fitzgerald suavites and an astonishing, glossy hostess (much richer and infinitely more cellophane-packaged than Marie) who really does say Sinclair Lewis-like things as: 'Harry orders the best meal in Paris.' She has travelled everywhere outside the Iron Curtain and is called Ariadne. Ariadne DeMott!

This is a very long letter. And I have not, as I intended to, made one or two points about the 'Highgate' notes. Can I say that the argument for economic union looks convincing and there are strong points made about the way the French are isolating themselves without any help? I think we should make a much stronger case for agricultural policies that conform because we are otherwise going to find *all* the other eight against us. We can ask for stay of execution (which is what it will seem to the housewife!) but sooner or later we must make big concessions. (Burn this letter!) I think we should morally make our goal of ultimate political unity quite explicit and, to this end, we should indicate where compromises and concessions are necessary and argue much more extensively the case for a strong independent Europe. You are well equipped to be *advocatus diaboli*: it's very necessary that someone should play the part.

A word about France and Giscard's possible problems: presumably he too will have read *Henry V* and realised that the best way to distract attention from discontents at home (even today) is to look for trouble abroad. Now think of the mess that Italy is in. Much worse than we are, in spite of the plunging pound. (It is noticeable here, especially: though fortunately Oliver is paid in dollars and so I am not yet a candidate for international rehabilitation.) And then ask yourself how long the Germans are going to pick up the tab? What I am really saying is that *all* these points (including likely Communist participation in the governments of France and Italy) must be faced and answered squarely in any policy document about Europe, whether issued by an official party office or by an *ad hoc* and self-appointed group such as 'Highgate'.

I'm returning next Tuesday and, given an hour or so to recover, hope that we can have a drink or something before I pack my bags for Blackpool, a place which I loathe. The seamen's settlement seems to have driven a juggernaut lorry through the pay policy and I notice that the car workers and the miners are already making the wrong kind of noise. And the pound is down again. If you will be in London, I'll try telephoning next week. I'm sure Oliver wants to send warm wishes, but he has to attend some special seminar today (as hot as London was when I left but much more humid and louring). So I took the opportunity of writing.

Looking forward to seeing you,

Ever,

Rachel.

*

Who was it had the bright thought that democracy substitutes election by the incompetent many for appointment by the corrupt few? Shaw, I think. Yes, it must have been Shaw. (How far does that apply in local government? Ah! Thereby hangs a councillor. Would an it were so, my liege. Silken, insinuating jacks in and out of office.)

Anyway it is this kind of incompetence that brings the worshipful Communist MacGahey to represent the miners at a *Labour* conference. And looking around, he is far from alone. This is an eclectic junket. I suppose it has to be for me to be asked on the one hand and Les Budge on the other.

It's been a rancorous business from the start. I fear we have deciphered here more rancorous spite, more furious raging broils than yet had been imagined or supposed. Different play. Something like that, though. Can't remember which. My memory isn't as good. Nor my concentration: yet . . . We seem to have become the party of envy and spite. It's a long way back to 1945. 'We are the masters now,' forsooth! God these things are a bore.

. . . Hullo, George. Very stimulating day, wouldn't you say?

Benn set out to stir it up before Conference actually started. All very well for Rachel to say that's the way he sees politics – endless debate and argument. To me it savours of cultural revolution. Never-ending turmoil. No consolidation. Change for change's sake. And whatever Benn intends, totalitarian change at that. The absolute conviction of being left! Most of them have it: all the non-Moscow Marxists. Idealists are more dangerous than the actual subversives. The anger of men without opinions. . . . Ah, got that one. Chesterton.

. . . Alan. Nice to see a discontented face. What do you think of it so far? I couldn't agree more.

Trumble wears his prematurely autumn face. The drink that does it so they say. A dramatic week for a columnist, yes. Prentice castigating the left at the weekend and Grandad Archer speaking firmly to him. We're a family, Reg: and a family sticks together. It's what made Ambridge what it is. Am I perhaps guilty of thwarted ambition? A slight case of paranoia?

. . . I dislike the parties more than the sessions. Still I suppose it's less a waste of time than all the years since Gaitskell. There is, at least, a real difference about issues. We were once two parties: now we're at least three or four.

Trumble worried about the sheer venom some of the left have shown. Not only Trumble! Grandad is worried about it too, which accounts for the plain statement about banks and nationalisation and the good speech on Tuesday. Press have come away with an overriding impression of hatred and envy. And so have many of the electorate. But good for centre re-alignment surely.

. . . All to your purpose, Alan. Perhaps I should say the purpose. The rethinking we must have in British politics?

He hopes so. And so do I. I think I probably *am* a hypocrite: but I've declared myself openly enough on this one and there are enough people in any group including the Highgate hagiocracy to make sure the rumour gets around. Oh Gawd! Candida. I'd better telephone after this. Thank Christ I persuaded her not to come to this annual wayzgoose. A different sort of open declaration. I should have known she'd get too serious. But when she switched so smoothly to me from Ingestre . . . Then, she was a virgin and that should have warned me. She must . . . There must be some suitably endowed Bellerophon in the bushes of Norham Gardens waiting to pounce. I'll have to turn on the gentle disenchantment. It's worked before. . . . Concentrate, you bloody fool. Listen to Trumble. . . .

. . . I agree, Alan. Roosevelt said we'd always known that heedless self-interest was bad morals and now we could see it was also bad economics. Ironic that the situation's been reversed and it's no longer big business but the unions who are guilty of heedless self-interest. Isn't it? And we've started to pay the price already. I can see us going down to one dollar fifty yet. Look at it: seamen threaten a strike, an appeasement settlement; all this talk of nationalisation of the banks; Atkinson made party treasurer. And the pound plummets.

Perfectly legitimate for him to ask why I stay in the party. Same reasons that I'm staying on at this one. There's nowhere else particular to go at the moment. Trumble knows quite well that I must be a disappointed man who disguises it fairly easily. I've admitted, at last, what the latest reshuffle did for my slenderish hopes. Too many enemies on the prompt side. My own fault: but when I was first elected I was genuine mainstream Labour. Trumble wants to know about Heffer's answer to the leadership. . . .

. . . It's all very well for the blander commentators to say that no Labour conference is complete without loud and fierce disagreements on policy, Alan; but you know as well as I do that this year has been unusually acrid. The NEC have just about got through a very left programme. And Jim's speech on Tuesday, good as it was, has done nothing much to stop it. The big unions saw him through on the social contract but then look what happened on cuts in government expenditure, just as Healey is about to go cap in hand to the IMF for two thousand three hundred million! I suppose it suits you. The Highgate lot must be hugging themselves.

Oh yes. It suits me too. Except that any centre alliance

must be an election or so away from office and in any coalition there will be a good many ahead of Anthony in the pecking order. I doubt if I have the moral stamina any longer. Or indeed the quality of conscience needed to see it through. Ah. Rachel, looking especially attractive. Trumble getting a worried and glazed look. Not because of Rachel. We're a long way from the bar and the Transport and General brother with the tray hasn't been around our way for ten minutes.

. . . Yes, I suppose so. Well, see you around in Highgate, or the lobby, or somewhere, in due course, I've no doubt.

God! Look at it. The comradely conniving and hob-nobbing. The brotherly clubbability of it all. Surprising how many smooth, stretched, waxen smiles there are among the rough-hewn countenances of the shop-floormen and the yeomen constituency workers. How much bespoke suiting among the High Street superfine worsteds. And the senior ministers manoeuvring suavely like destroyers among the little ships. What a peculiarly, jarringly apt image, Anthony. What does that make the union bosses? Tramps, coalers, dirty British coasters. Quiet, Connors, you're not human tonight. Some of these people must get so monumentally pissed. All that earnest fretting and colluding in little local caucuses and then the great boot-filling blow-out. Of course, the Tories get just as pissed, but in a slightly more stylised way. I suppose there is a certain raw humanity in all this. I wonder if we can match them in the other department: the sad fact is, given one or two exceptions and notable unsolved liaisons, they have generally more attractive women. Who was it – Bert Gregg – who always wanted to pleasure (as he sincerely believed it would) upper-class women from sixteen to sixty? 'By God, Tony lad, if I get in a room with them I'm like a bloody ramrod in seconds. They give off a sort of scent under all that perfume and powder.' And here Bert was as safe and as certain a pillar of rectitude as a column in a Methodist church. Rest in peace, old Bert! We could use a few of you now. I wonder if we have had our great days already, as the Liberals had theirs and the Whigs had theirs. Only the Tories go on and on and on. And will so do come hell, high-water or revolution. Everyone is having a great time. The squabbles of the session all forgotten in the bonhomie. Jenkinses of every shade and refinement easily adapting to every nuance and timbre of Jones and Williams and so on. Not just squabbles. Storms. The gaggle and cackle of conviviality drowning the crow and whimper and snarl. Heavy hand closing upon fleshy silk upper arm, broad palm clamping upon flinching shoulder. Backslap and rib-dig. Friendly pulled punch into the lower gut. Smile and keep the Capone eyes level and menacing. Oratorical hand flowing adjacent to a nicely presented tit. Quiet arse-pass, mischievous and lip-smiling.Wink and eyebrow. And through it all those slick destroyers making their way with the minimum use of the hooter. Out of this retreat will grow the Phoenix unity that will fly ahead upon the path to Victory. But what Victory and whose? Teetotal and near teetotal and a few still susceptible destroyers and frigates. The capital ships. Calm, bland with an alarmingly slow blink-rate: the smug and sufficient look cultivated for an age of violence and sensation. The noise rises and ebbs and fades and swirls. What is it? Eight-fifteen. I could leave quietly and have dinner quietly alone. Then what? Ring Candida. . . . I suppose I should look for some loyal party workers and . . . I'm tired. I'm . . .

. . . Hello, Rachel. . . .

Christ! What have I done to deserve this?

. . . Yes it is. Very pleasant. Considering the hosts. In truth, I don't really mean a word of it. But you look (if I may say so with no possibility of being misconstrued) particularly charming and blooming.

She has been in America. Oliver. She had a splendid time. Exciting place, New York. Oliver. Republican convention: Ford, Reagan, Jimmy Carter, the union vote, the Black vote, the Jewish vote, the Central European vote. Oliver. Oliver. Oliver. The WHO. The UN. And what do I make of all this? I make Oliver and why anyone as intelligent, as charming, should want to be a foothill to some pompous medical volcano erupting to order, when it was suitably dramatic or politic, I shall never know.

. . . I think it's been a very bad conference. And the only consolation is that it could have been worse. If the pound had not been in such a mess, we might have had a runaway avalanche of the left's idiocies. As it is Jim and Denis have been playing Cassandra and Laocoon as though the heavyweight championship of doom was in contention. Think of it: 'If our policies do not succeed, dictatorship is on the cards. . . .'; 'If we don't stop the sterling slide, the alternative will be economic policies so savage that there will be riots in the streets.' What were we this morning? One dollar sixty-six. God alone knows what's happened since.

She is depressed. Well, I'm not sorry to hear it. It might take her mind off Oliver. And of course she is, as not infrequently, right: the NEC have given in grudgingly and people like Mikardo haven't been slow to link the whole sterling débâcle with capitalism and a mixed economy.

. . . Full loyalty and support to resist any conditions for international loans which would impose spending cuts and increase unemployment! That is loyalty?

And so where do we stand? She and I? I might have known it was not for my body but for my *beau ideal* that she desired me. In fact, she dislikes me quite a lot. It's a bad sign: there are fewer and fewer of us. If I think about it fairly, she has fared worse than I have: because she is able and much more committed (still) to the party. She might reasonably have expected something. She is not as clever as I am, but she is truly loyal.

. . . I give warning, Rachel. I'm about to quote Burke. Five, four, three, two, one, zero. Right: *Your representative owes you not his industry only, but his judgement; and he betrays instead of serving you if he sacrifices it to your opinion . . . authoritative instructions arise from a fundamental mistake of the whole order and tenor of our constitution.*

Parliament is not a congress of ambassadors from different and hostile interests . . . it is a deliberative assembly of one nation, with one interest, that of the whole. . . . You choose a member indeed; but when you have chosen him, he is not a member of Bristol, but he is a member of Parliament. Isn't that marvellous and the answer to all this rubbish about members being delegates? I can't see how they can get through that kind of double-think and still present themselves as democrats – Benn and Jack Jones and Heffer and all the others.

As it happens, *I don't* have a particularly good memory. . . . No, I *don't*. I came across it the other day and since it was apt, I learned it by heart. As they say. I had intended to use it, tellingly, in a speech: so you've had a preview. Or pre-audit or whatever it may be.

Looking as sprightly as she does, she is obviously deeply fed up. By contrast, about the room the triumphant, well-fed face of the NCOs of the left gleams and the new generation shake their gory locks and smirk the same dreary clichés. What does it matter, the red-faced and loyal cohorts from the constituencies are having their well-deserved spree. Evening, Sam. Hullo, Maggie. There you are, Emrys. Rachel wants to talk seriously to me about the Highgate Group. Then she will have dinner with me and we can talk at length. No! Ah, not *that* urgent, evidently. She is very tired and has to telephone Oliver. (What times does he get up, for Christ's sake, in New York?) And her agent at Ashbridge and . . . All right, sweetie. It was worth the try. Work out proper ideas. Face up to *all* the issues: so that when the time comes to talk and negotiate, we know we are on firm ground. If we decide to join.

She moves off in a flowered dress that is a little old-fashioned. Perhaps a little broad across the hips now, but distinctly trim and desirable. The nice thing about her is the intelligence and the fun in her eyes. Even when she doesn't like you. She's quite small: but it's never noticeable. Who needs protection? Oh! Bloody Candida. . . . It's becoming a nuisance. It would be quite pleasant to have her along now.

For the ride! Male chauvinist laureate, Anthony Connors, was accepting a fresh drink at a conference party at Blackpool. When I think about her in *that* way, I'm reluctant to end it all. But it has to be done. *Gradually!* Oagh! She does so like playing the whore. . . . I can see her now in those long black stockings, kneeling. . . . That wonderful red hair. . . . And drawing on long silk gloves. . . . Enough! There won't be any of that tonight. Get your mind off it.

It simply isn't fair. Not remotely fair. Oh all right, she can look after herself: but she's nineteen. And I'm sure that if Taylor and Barbara . . . If it turned out wrong. Well, it won't. There's no reason why it should. Somehow though there is a tinge of self-disgust every time, however orthodox it is. . . . It's one short step to something vicious, or bordering on the vicious. And yet. She has an appetite for it, damn her!

. . . Evening, Terry. No, not bad, I suppose. I can't pretend it's gone the way I'd have liked it to, as you know. But then what we have to have is some kind of cohesion, particularly with the pound in the state that it is. Jim obviously wants absolutely no disruption and it couldn't have come at a worse time. Nor could this Ford nonsense at Dagenham on Tuesday.

A dozen or so hooligans. Yes, of course. Slight, unmeritable man come to homilise. Sly hints of the unrest in the constituencies among party members who really want socialism and socialism that works. Stupid man. The backbone of the party. Not left. Not right. The bigot who has no opinions. Someone was saying the other day that the constitution of the party is geared entirely to opposition, which is why the conference is thought to be significant and why the NEC has any kind of muscle.

. . . Oh yes, Terry. Quite so. I think you're absolutely right. . . .

I think I've had enough. . . . Dear me! Sir Harold, no less. Wonder how long he's been here. Got his seat on the platform, after all. And how absurd it would have been if he hadn't: but I'm sure I wasn't the only one to experience a delightful tingle of *schadenfreude* about all the honours list *embarras*. And Ron Hayward didn't know what all the fuss was about! Someone trying to wash dirty linen in public when the public wasn't interested in muddy water, no doubt! I wonder if things are as bad, really as bad.

. . . Yes, he does look well. Power is ageing. Terry, if you'll excuse me a moment, I want a word with Delahaye. You know him? That nervous-looking chap. Keeps his ear very close to the ground.

Big wink. Poor Bill, twitching almost audibly. Rachel must have missed him: she is unfailingly kind. I suppose it's why Bill could never make it in the lobby. And so he is condemned to the leader page. But he wasn't always so nervous. *Not* neurotic. Sheer nerves: unless he's talking to people he knows, and knows respect him. He should have gone for some peaceful job in the BBC. Good conscientious talks programmes. . . .

. . . Bill! What a pleasure to see a friendly, if worried, face! Come, let me get you another glass.

The stammer is getting worse.

. . . Tell you what, Bill, unless you want to hang on here for any devious journalistic purpose, let's go back to the bar at my hotel and have a chat. Perhaps a spot of supper.

The devious journalistic purpose indeed! Bill begins a disquisition on the helplessness of the press and the stammer subsides. Only certain consonants. Ellis Fulford reckons one broken marriage in anyone's life is enough. All very well for Ellis, who's almost as indifferent as Ingestre whether he has a woman or not. Not for Bill. Bill has too many hang-ups. Pity. A clever man, who has lost all faith in himself. And not a drinker like Trumble, who is admittedly cleverer and who has just decided to waste what's left of his life. I suppose the alcoholic level for most of us is well above the Plimsoll line. Yes. . . . The proof of the distillation. . . . I wonder why he dislikes me so much.

. . . What about those days, Bill, when Cecil King used to

hector all and sundry from the columns of the *Mirror*? I suppose those were the growls of the last Titans when he and Robens and a few others thought they could run the country under Mountbatten. Isn't that the story?

No. Not quite the story. Of course Bill will know. And it's a much better story, which will one day come out. Bill is anti-Titan, by instinct and after reflection. In fact, Bill, met alone, is a sombre and undefeated person who isn't going to give in easily to anyone except himself. And that he has already done.

... We're here, Bill.

Not to be deterred, Bill, who has a nose for these things, swerves back to the press and their tribulations. Do I remember Benn's speech as retiring Labour chairman in 1973 when he looked to the day when the liftmen in newspaper offices ultimately have a say in editorial policy? He starts to stammer again, looking f-f-forward to the day when surgery is interrupted by the hospital porter and monoglot P-p-portuguese cleaners who've come to have a say in the operation! He is furious.

... Two large whiskies, please. Ice, Bill?

No ice. The interesting thing is that the fury is an entirely nervous, superficial phenomenon: beneath it all he is quite calm, watchful, reflective, even calculating. It is only when he is obliged to communicate orally that he becomes tense and tortured and, even then, among the Taylor group, he can be authoritative and fluent when it is *his* floor. Candida! I wonder what he would make of her. And this comic novel he is writing about me. ... Augustine Cornflour. ... Surely this isn't some invention of Ellis's. Ellis isn't malicious. No stirrer up of strife. So. ... Bill now doesn't seem to bear me any special malice. And yet, what I've heard suggests a kind of slow-burning dislike, if not hatred. About the book. Not apparent at the moment. He is talking seriously. ... And quite suddenly. Quite suddenly. ...

... I haven't thought much about them as a family, as a matter of fact, Bill. They're certainly both very pretty girls.

I think the younger one is going to grow to be quite something.

So that's what it's all about. Yes, well it was sure to happen.

. . . Yes, as a matter of fact you probably did. Candida said she wanted to see the show and someone happened to offer me a couple of tickets. So I took her along. It was a very pleasant evening. She's a very charming girl. Rather staid, as you might expect from a daughter of Jeremy and Barbara. I loathed the musical. Whatever happened to articulate lyrics?

A beautiful girl. Well so she is, William. And you can have no idea how beautiful in certain moods and poses. That red hair, those clear eyes, perfect limbs and . . . This must stop and I must remember to telephone.

. . . Yes. She is, I suppose. Thanks I will. The same. How are things on the paper?

Things are never very wonderful on the paper. Bill thinks it is all getting much too frivolous and there is a power-mad features editor called Natalie Bliss who is determined to become the first woman editor in Fleet Street. Think I've met her at a party: rather pleasant. Jewish, attractive. Plump. Nice, misty brown eyes.

. . . We all have our crosses, don't we?

The stammer has more or less disappeared and he can be acidly funny, especially about the press generally. Admires Deedes and Harry Evans, strangely enough for a natural radical. Independence and guts. Well. So be it. Reflections on leadership and firm direction. . . . I'm beginning to regret suggesting supper. That was rash. I like Bill well enough, but I'm sure it's not reciprocal and we haven't all that much in common. Somehow, we have got on to Bill's secretary who drives him up the wall. This is unusual for Bill, surely. Doesn't usually go in for confessionals. Pretty clothes girls are wearing now and that girl bends down in one of these close-fitting slit skirts or. . . . Dear me. . . . *Ah!* That's it, is it, you cunning bastard! Back to Candida. . . . A clever contrast: his sexy secretary and Candida's fresh English . . .

fresh English what? *Perfection!* Yes, well. . . . Thank God! Sandra Beeton. It will mean a mini-analysis, but Bill will disappear like a nervous marmot.

. . . Hullo, Sandra! Come over and join us for a drink. I didn't know you were staying here.

Very elegant in a navy-blue suit and a sort of frilly blouse. Documentary film about scenes behind the scenes at the conference. I can imagine the kind of thing: ironic juxta-positions achieved by clever cutting, beaming faces and vitriolic voice-overs, facile and savage and snide. Bill's stammer returns and he begins to shuffle his arse on the bar-stool. Sandra takes one, hoists herself up and crosses her legs. Spectacular legs. Bill's eyes home hungrily in at once. Must be torture for him. Well, William (she says), stretching her back, what's going to happen in Rhodesia. Bill stammers. She turns on me: I see your absolutely true-to-form National Executive has this very day rejected the only hopeful mum-blings to come out of that country since UDI.

. . . Emphatically not *my* National Executive, Sandra. And I think that was most unkind. Anyway, this constitutional conference idea is doomed. Apart from Smith, let them get the blacks to agree with one another for five consecutive minutes. . . .

Agreed there's no point in stalling and the Rhodesia Front cannot ultimately win, but there's an awful blacks-to-the-wall stubbornness. It is profoundly depressing and is going to be nasty and dangerous. Ah, what the hell (Sandra says), I've had enough politics. God knows. Bill begins shuffling again. Sandra swings on the bar-stool, nicely composed, and fixes him: Well, Bill, how's Natalie. . . . Deliberately wicked. Whatever he says is going to be taken to the Freudian cleaners. L-l-look, Sandra, if you're tired of politics, I'm f-f-f-fed to the back b-b-bloody teeth with F-f-f-freud. . . . She sees an immediate chance, but Bill won't let her. . . . W-wh-why can't you take up w-w-women's lib or something wh-wh-wholesome. It has the . . . er . . . desired effect, however. Poor Bill! Decides to take flight. Thanks me for the drink and, never entirely without a counter-punch, says he is to meet Trumble and various others. And perhaps they will all come back to join us. Sandra stiffens. Trumble can always reduce her to incoherent shivering obscenities and even tears, well near enough. If you bring that man back here (she says), I shall take off my bra, burn it in the foyer and start laying about with gelding shears.

Bill grins and goes and Sandra wants to know why I am looking like *that*! Suitably roused.

. . . I'm sorry. Just for the moment you conjured up the enchanting image of you taking off your bra, which was rather disquieting for a middle-ageing, mildly libidinous hetero-sexual at this time of day.

Uncertain for a moment. Whether or not she is being put on, in some way. Then she smiles. Promising. And even (Sandra!) blushes. And shifts one leg silkily higher along the other. Lovely. Still smiling.

. . . And please don't explain to me how I got to be like that. I'm quite happy about it.

Didn't think she was going to. Wonder how we pick these signals up? ESP. Rubbish! Asks if I am making a pass. And why haven't I tried before. *Very* promising.

. . . I was about to ask you if you were free to have dinner with me. That was all. But since the subject has come up, may I say that you are looking especially pretty–even for you.

The leg moves a little higher. The barman turning further down the room lifts his eyes along the caryatids to the gilt cupidons in silent supplication. Who can blame him?

Sandra tells me I am in luck. Very frankly. She came in in a randy mood and what she really needs is a man. But first, yes, dinner.

Exciting. Another drink first. No wish to rush things. Savour the pleasures to come. Yes. She says. Exciting. Convenient. Expedient. Exquisite. And she does have a lovely smile. And the most heavenly legs. . . .

*

179

More of *The Dazzling Pilgrimage*

In her elegant penthouse office overlooking the City of London, Katerina Borgedici sat writing in a forcible Italian hand which, without being impetuous, was expressive of a certain fire and panache. She wore a close-fitting dark brown dress of pure silk, with a high collar and short sleeves. It was a favourite colour because it was unobtrusive and showed to advantage, by its undecorated austerity, her excellent figure; it also matched her chestnut hair and greyish-green eyes and set off the effortless hauteur of her presence. She looked up as her younger sister came into the room, furnished comfortably but unceremoniously with office fittings from an exclusive West End firm whose discretion was a byword.

'Good morning,' she said.

'*Ciao*, Katerina.'

'Catherine, please,' she said with a little asperity: of the sort that an elder sister might legitimately show to a slightly feckless junior. 'We must remember our image. It is all very well for you to be delightfully Florentine. Not for me.'

'Anyway, we are afrom Venezia . . .'

'Don't be obtuse, *cara*. It is your role to be temperately exotic: it is mine to be internationally apt. Since I speak perfectly English, French and German, "Catherine" is obviously more suitable and draws less attention to our country of origin.'

Her sister shrugged and fitted a short cigarette into a long holder, betraying the influence of a hundred television commercials for vermouth and underwear.

'I'm aproud to be Italian,' she said. 'And anyway, why are we aspeaking da English.'

'Because we are in England. You know what they say. . . .'

Lucrezia Borgedici sighed wearily.

'Something about Roma,' she said. 'It's aboring.'

'What have you to report?'

'I have adone the aleg work,' said Lucrezia.

As she said this, she crossed her own elegant limbs, right arm over left and left leg over right simultaneously in an ineffably graceful movement. Catherine, in spite of herself, admired her sister's absolute control of her beautiful body. For an unintelligent creature, she learned remarkably quickly: persuaded out of egregious garments that overemphasised her tendency to voluptuosity, she now wore black and white or blue and white with aristocratic femininity that must have been almost irresistible. It was a pity she retained the basic tastes of the Neapolitan back streets from which they both hailed.

For the truth was that the glamorous and severally endowed sisters were not, as they claimed, daughters of a Venetian aristocrat. They were part of an admittedly devoted family which had started off poor, but by the initiative, business verve and ruthlessness of their father, his seventeen brothers and their own siblings (who numbered a modest nine), had established itself in a respected (not to say feared) place in local society. As was customary in decent Catholic gangster families, the girls were protected from the sort of scandalous intimacy with vice and crime that the daughters of other less chosen parents were expected to adapt to almost carelessly. Cesare Alessandro Cosimo Giulio Borgedici had, in fact, made the rudimentary mistake of sending his oldest daughter (Katerina) to schools in England and Switzerland. She had returned incurably independent and ambitious, fired with all kinds of feminist dreams that were upsetting to her parents.

Possessing her father's own quickly calculating brain, his cunning, and several advantages of her own, inherited from her now rather plump mother, Catherine (as she chose to be called) went to Rome and set up in very exclusive business. Her clients were either rich or powerful, sometimes both, ranging from church dignitaries, always plentiful in Rome, to diplomats and senior service officers. There were regrettably few financiers, who found little to move them in Italy. First, Catherine sent for her sister, Lucrezia; then one by one for the other three. There was little that her father and brothers could do save rant in a peculiarly Neapolitan way made fashionable by certain films. As soon as she was sure that Lucrezia was capable of taking charge in Rome, Catherine moved personally to Geneva. There she met lots of financiers and established in a very short time her enterprise on a sound capital footing.

As soon as their operation expanded sufficiently she withdrew her sisters from active participation in business, uneasily suspecting that two of them were more than reluctant, and appointed them to administrative posts. Acquiring some surplus arms from an American general, who had been a valued client, and the gift of an Apennine estate from an old Viscount, impoverished in everything except lust, she advertised in the right places for a certain type of instructor. Fortune blessed her astuteness by sending as applicants, among many who were unsuitable for various reasons, a confirmed homosexual and a former Mafioso from Pittsburgh who had held quite high office but who had suffered the most unfortunate accident during an internecine dispute which had made him quite safe with young women. As soon as she had earned their loyalty, these two instructors quickly rendered her chosen force of female soldiers into an efficient and versatile unit. Women are, as Catherine already knew, more courageous than men, often more devious and infinitely less vain. It was not malice that had made her move first against her father's organisation in Naples: it was simply good business sense. She knew how it operated and where to strike. Surprise was invaluable. Thereafter, she acquired neighbouring interests and, in due course, became powerful enough to treat with some of the most illustrious names in Italian crime, almost as an equal. She promised to confine her activities – with a view to expansion abroad – and showed herself to be well beyond accusation of chauvinism by giving employment at a relatively menial level to men.

Things, however, were not good in Italy, so she had looked for other opportunities rather sooner than she would have wished: but, once again playing to her strength, which was surprise, and a knowledge of her victim's organisation, she had chosen to begin in England with the pornographic empire of a sometime visitor, Lucius Spiedermann. And suddenly she felt like a lady Ali Baba, as she became aware of the richness of opportunity for a businesswoman in that stable but precarious land.

'I've aseen Spiedermann and he's aput me in touch with seven aproper Lords, eight alife peers, six afunctionaries, two ajudges and has agiven me the names of atwo hundred and forty-three aMPs of aboth sexes. He's avery bitter, because the Queen of England has not agiven him any honour.'

'Have you made a list, *cara*?'

'Here.'

'Perfect. The junior Minister for Morale and Public Decency. What more could we ask? Come, we must go to church. I've found a nice Italian priest who will hear our confessions.'

'But it's aSunday....!'

'Lucrezia! You forget what Sunday is for? Have you strayed so far from the things you were taught as a child? Come. Then, after church, I have a lot of work to do.'

After The Gothic, Elwyn Poinsettia's club, The Royal Hyperborean was for Augustine Cornflour like moving from his grammar school wicket to the square at Lord's, or from Sprake Covered Market to Fortnum and Mason's. The one was rough, homely, with its own scents and peculiarities – all rather endearing – which you learned to manoeuvre: the other was distinguished, elegant, exact, where any vagary of behaviour was a matter of immediate consternation and even alarm. He drew contentedly, with his effortlessly debonair manner, at a splendid cigar, reproaching himself for not listening more carefully to an anecdote being told by his senior Minister, Gregor Valdes de Chambourcy, whose lifelong experience in the socialist movement and educated society had made him rich as a raconteur; but, realising that Elwyn Poinsettia himself and Barnaby Freeth and furthermore that very bright young rising star Doctor Simeon Sidestreet were also not listening, he felt less badly about it.

The Royal Hyperborean, densely carpeted and thickly wall-papered, dignified without being sombre, was perhaps, after The Parthenon, the most desirable club to belong to for those who cared for such things. And Augustine cared for them. So far, it had evaded the embarrassment of admitting women members by the device of long and pains-taking debate about how best they might be accommodated and served, thus deferring the admirably agreed principle of their admission. Elwyn Poinsettia adapted to his surroundings there like a skilfully wrought portrait to its background and indeed frame, a benevolent and contented portrait, that of an altruist of stern wit but quick conscience. Few would have guessed, though almost everybody *knew* (since Elwyn Poinsettia was not in the least shy about it), that here was the son of a Salford bricklayer, a skilled man, who had married a Welsh girl, from the impoverished North of the principality who had pushed east from Liverpool into domestic service in Manchester. Poinsetta was thus availed of the lyric oratory tinged with melancholy of one race, and the passion-ate intensity tinged with gaiety of the other. It was an enviable admixture. As host, he excelled – whether at his club in a heartily, almost aggressively normal male gathering, or at his Hampstead home where the female guests were as exquisite and intelligent as might be found in this half of the twentieth century.

Such was the nature and style of The Hyperborean that it also boasted as members, distinguished figures on the Opposition Front Bench, such as Sir Hamilton Flare (whom some thought to be ineffectual) and Raphael Wintergreen (dashingly handsome, whom some thought to be rash). Both happened to be in the club on that occasion and there could have been no better testimony of the shared bonds among those to whom the management of the nation befell than the cordiality of waves and gestures exchanged between them and the senior Ministers with whom Augustine was spending the evening.

As the conversation broke up, Augustine found himself chatting amiably with Elwyn Poinsettia, both of them relaxing in the warm, deep armchairs for which The Hyperborean was envied.

'I hear,' said Poinsettia with that undefinable lilt that was neither Italian (nor Spanish) nor Welsh, 'that you're making quite a fist of the job at Morale and Public Decency. Well done, Augustine. A lot of people have their eye on you, you know. And there must be changes. It's no secret that Barnaby's had enough of the Treasury and I'm raring to have a go, which means the Home Office is going for whoever's there upon the hour. And if Hoke decides to move Tertius to Industry and Llewellyn to the FO when Gerald moves upstairs, then Hal can't stay long at Environment and Deborah must go to Social Services. So there will be opportunities. And I must say, Augustine, although I obviously can promise nothing, I'd like you somewhere in my team.'

'I'm very flattered,' said Augustine, judging accurately the right tone of deference tempered by charm and natural ease. 'I hope that if the chance occurs, I shan't disappoint: but I must say I find the new department absolutely fascinating.'

'Morale and Public Decency?'

'Yes.'

'Very important at a time like this. But the Treasury (which I really am itching to have my shot at) is the big stuff. And if the call comes . . .'

'Oh, I shall be there, Elwyn. Thank you.'

They basked a moment in each other's smiles. Then Augustine asked out of sheer curiosity.

'You didn't mention Bert Flexion,' he said.

'Astute fellow,' said Elwyn Poinsettia, suddenly grim. 'Flexion will stay where he is, Augustine. If at all.'

Anticipating whatever call might come, however, that very evening, in The Royal Hyperborean, Gregor Valdes de Chambourcy was moved to recount a particularly rumbustious anecdote, which called for some vigorous imitations and one or two other effects. In the course of it, he was stricken by a severe thrombosis (not immediately diagnosed by his companions, who thought it was part of the anecdote) and a few moments later succumbed. Augustine Cornflour undertook his duties during the brief period which embraced the obsequies to this dedicated socialist and public servant and subsequently was offered by Sir Hoke Dick the actual portfolio. Such was the euphoria of the moment that he did not reflect at all upon the irony that Morale and Public Decency was held in his own frail hands.

As the weeks passed, the mirth of Warrington Stokes became less irrepressible, though it was still likely to overtake him unexpectedly and sometimes inconveniently. A sudden reckless gust of merriment almost overcame him at the memorial service for Gregor Valdes de Chambourcy, the old socialist warhorse who had staggered in the traces of Morale and Public Decency.

It was not caused by lack of respect for his former colleague, but by the sight of old Hoke and Poinsettia and Barnaby Freeth and Tertius Barebones and Bert Flexion all in inky cloaks and customary suits of solemn black (except for Flexion, who wore a solemn brown, as a token of his radicalism) all having to put on a semblance. Oho! Warrington Stokes gasped and clutched at Winnifred, alarming one or two bystanders and disappointing an alert press photographer who misconstrued the symptoms. It was the old Welsh wizard, Lloyd George himself, who had said it was impossible for the top five men in the Cabinet to be friends. And how right the old devil had been! Warrington Stokes wheezed, just inside control.

'Oh, Warrington!' said his wife, in kind exasperation.

Now they knew. *Now* they knew! That the grass wasn't so much greener and sheep may not graze all that safely while the big bad wolf was in grandmother's clothing huffing and puffing and you couldn't see the wood for the avenues which everyone was so busy exploring.

'Amen,' said Warrington Stokes.

The full-length mirror reflected a truly charismatic figure: Dahlia Dackord was not vulgarly built but she was excellently proportioned and the gleaming white shirt, the black riding-breeches, the highly polished boots and the little whip emphasised her trim authority. Her hair was again drawn severely back into an immaculate bun.

There was a tap on the door.

'Come!' said Dahlia Dackord imperiously.

The door opened smartly and four senior members of the South London Legion of the English Valkyrie Brigade stepped keenly into the room. As one man they saluted.

'Live Albion?' they cried.

'Albion!' returned Dahlia Dackord.

The four men waited for her to seat herself at the head of the plain whitewood table, before taking chairs themselves. They were a disparate group: a senior lecturer in mechanical engineering, the third son of an earl who had some years before left his regiment obscurely and now dealt in second-hand cars, a post office clerk and a hospital porter who had once been a major in a mercenary army which had fought in central Africa, all proud men contributing to an idle, decadent, cringing and wasteful society, which they despised for the charters it afforded to scroungers, loafers and aliens, until the wrathful dawn of Anglo-Saxon awakening when they would each assume their rightful place in the leadership of Phoenix Albion or Britannia Rediviva – although they had no great hopes of the Celts.

She spoke rapidly and efficiently to them, explaining,

without divulging too much, that she had reason to suppose a certain consortium was planning to exert a stranglehold upon the nation's economy, combining massive industrial resources with the wealth of the City and the administrative expertise of certain top civil servants. With the country drifting sluggishly towards the vortex of ruin, these bold men would make public their intentions alongside certain scandals, putting out an incentive-based programme that would encourage all those who *made* things. The social weaklings, undesirables and degenerates would all go to the wall: work-shy wasters, pensioners, sickly parasites, vampire immigrants, artists, journalists, the entire BBC and ITA companies, Members of Parliament, 98 per cent of University teachers and 50 per cent of all other teachers, who would be selectively replaced.

Dahlia Dackord's lieutenants looked at each other in some consternation: this programme, apart from no mention of blood and enforcement and smashing things, was not all that far from their own. Surely they were not to be pre-empted. (None of them phrased their fear as succinctly to himself, but it was what they felt.)

'What they lack,' said Dahlia Dackord, 'is of course a para-military arm. At the moment – and I am often in a position to know – they will rely upon the thoroughly unreliable support of an already subverted police force and the etiolated and lamentably led armed forces. Encouraged by Communist agitators, the dispossessed will no doubt take to the streets. It is then, Praetors, that we will come into our own. And gradually, when they realise they cannot exist without us, we shall take over – assured of immense financial backing.'

Her voice, she knew, was thrilling. They gasped in admiration.

'We lack one thing,' she said.

They looked expectant.

'A Father Coughlin,' she said.

None of them had heard of Father Coughlin, but she

quickly explained to them the value, in a rejuvenated nation with totally reorganised networks of information and entertainment, of a propagandist who was also a delegate of Supreme Authority.

'We must set about finding such a man in the discontented cellarage of the decaying religious establishments: a man gifted in oratory and persuasion, suitably receptive to a new theology.'

It was really quite exciting for Josephine to visit her uncle Augustine at the new Ministry for Morale and Public Decency, where he was now (after the sad passing of Mr Valdes de Chambourcy) in absolute charge. The offices were housed in a building in Northumberland Avenue previously tenanted by the Department of Committees and Enquiries, instituted by Warrington Stokes, but dismantled by the bluff Sir Hoke Dick, who had no time for rigmarole and was less susceptible to affront.

If a little disappointed by the shabbiness of the building inside, with scuffed and stained walls and rather scruffy carpeting, Josephine was quickly reassured when she entered the Minister's outer office where there were three desks. One was empty, one held a severe-looking lady in her fifties who was addressing a typewriter, the third was occupied by a pretty blonde girl with an extraordinary figure and rather too much make-up, also typing but with less address. They both stopped.

'Miss Cornflour,' the older woman said. 'A pleasure to meet you. The Minister has asked me to beg your forgiveness but he has had to pop along to Number Ten rather urgently to discuss the New Morale with Sir Hoke himself: but he does not expect to be detained long as the PM has a luncheon appointment with the Caliph of Fqwat. And we all know what that means, these days, don't we?'

Josephine smiled.

'I'm just off to lunch,' said the woman, 'but I'm sure that

you'd like to make yourself comfortable in the Minister's own sanctum sanctorum.'

Another brilliant smile which reached the points of her decorated spectacle frames. She opened the door to reveal a richly carpeted office containing a splendid desk with a high-backed leather chair, several other comfortable arm-chairs, bookshelves, several beautiful cabinets and what looked like a psychiatrist's couch.

'Please sit down,' said the severely smiling person bene-volently. 'I don't know that there is anything for you to look at. The Minister works frightfully hard and I expect it's all dry as dust. Goodbye, Miss Cornflour.'

She left, closing the heavy door firmly. Josephine walked around the room, looked at her pretty reflection in the mirror, touched her red hair and felt pleased that she wore just the right amount of lipstick and eye-shadow. The books were what one might expect a busy and serious Minister to have on his shelves. Reference books, companions and manuals to this and that, Erskine May, a few directories, Roget, Fowler as revised by Sir Ernest Gowers, Hansards, White and Green Papers, Reports; and, in respect of the specialist task of the Ministry, a selection of works on broadcasting, the press, propaganda and morality.

Josephine wandered over to a chair and idly shuffled a stack of magazines and HMSO publications. Again they were what might be expected: the *Listener*, the *New Statesman*, *New Society*, *New Scientist*, and so on. Then buried some-where in the heap of coarse-grain, off-white newsprint, she caught a glimpse of glossy colour. She thought it would be *Time* or *Newsweek* or perhaps *Paris Match*, all of which she enjoyed reading. Instead, to her surprise, it turned out to be a magazine called *Seraglio*, and the cover-picture showed an opulent girl with rather wild hair wearing around her shoul-ders a lace stole which revealed entirely her well-developed bust but which she had clutched conveniently to her pubis, though with taut, splayed fingers in a manner that Josephine thought suggestive. Somewhat taken aback she opened the magazine, which rejoiced in contributions from sundry intellectual household names, to find the same girl with the same stole now flicked aside to reveal a rich *crinière*, et cetera. In subsequent poses, some of which were more lewd than artistic, the girl displayed herself even more frankly.

Josephine had obviously noticed such magazines on various news-stands, as who could fail to, and she supposed that she must have imagined that they might contain this kind of photograph: but she had never before opened one and felt her cheeks burning, she was not quite sure with what emotion. She quickly leafed through the other pages and found other similar sequences in which the girls were either fully naked or partly clothed. These seemed to be particularly lubricious. She put the paper down, only for her eye to fall on a second such journal, entitled *Deb's Desire*. This had less text and fewer stalwarts of western culture among its contributors, though there were one or two names associated usually with literary journalism. The girls were uniformly naked and had been made up to look sophisticated in a sort of late thirties way; they assumed expressions which were a curious blend of haughtiness and lust. And they were, in almost all cases, equipped with props – which could only be for one conceivable purpose. Josephine's heart was pounding hard enough for her to be able to see the palpitation of her left breast under her dress. When she found two other magazines called *Sneaker* and *Raunch*, the covers of which were so unequivocal as to be alarming, she could not summon up the moral courage to open them. Starting guiltily, she looked up to see the younger secretary at the door watching her.

'Hullo,' she said. 'I came to see if you'd like a drink. It looks as though your uncle's going to be late. My name's Gina. Mrs Broadbent's just gone. She never introduces people.'

'I'm Josephine Cornflour.'

'Yes. Would you like something? He keeps a beautiful bar.'

'I think I would. Gin and tonic, if there is some.'

'Nothing easier, love.'

Gina walked across to the largest of the splendid cabinets. She was wearing a very tight brown skirt with a generous slit up the back which revealed a lot of shapely thigh, and an almost transparent white blouse under which the filigree pattern of a lace bra was to be discerned in every detail. She was remarkably pleasant but perhaps a little obvious. And this impression must only be reinforced by the way she walked and the way she moved her body. She squatted down at the cocktail cabinet to look at the bottles and Josephine, who had never once at school been tempted by any unorthodox feelings, was uncomfortably aware of the girl's unusual roundness. In a mild state of shock, undoubtedly, from the magazines, she wondered how heterosexual men, such as her uncle unmistakably was, could work in close proximity with girls of this type. Josephine was ashamed of herself and confused.

Her uncle's junior secretary poured out a generous glass of gin, opened a mini-refrigerator for ice and a slice of pre-conditioned lemon and uncapped a bottle of tonic. She brought glass and bottle across, undulating and smiling.

'Say when,' she said.

'Thank you,' said Josephine. 'Aren't you having one?'

'I'd better not. He mightn't object: but then on the other hand he might. He's wonderfully unpredictable. I expect you're wondering about them . . . those magazines,' she said.

'Er . . . magazines . . .' said Josephine.

'Yes. He has to look at a selection every week you know,' said Gina. 'In the line of duty. I don't suppose he enjoys it much. But he has to keep his finger on the pulse of public decency, hasn't he? I mean it's part of the brief for his portfolio.'

'Of course,' said Josephine, trying not to sound too overtly reassured. 'I'm sure my uncle wouldn't mind if you had a drink yourself. Aren't I keeping you from lunch?'

'No, love. I never eat it. Perhaps I will then. He's very

nice, your uncle. Not a bit stuffy. But, of course, now he's a Minister, he has to observe certain decorums.'

'You've known him for some time.'

'Oh yes, I used to work at Transport House, and I first met him there when he was on a project. I'm just a short-hand-typist really, but I hope I might get on like Mrs Broadbent.'

'I'm sure you will,' said Josephine, fearing that perhaps she sounded a trifle patronising.

Gina ambled wantonly back to the cocktail cabinet and poured herself some gin. She added ice but didn't bother about tonic.

'You all right?' she said, indicating Josephine's glass.

'Fine, thanks.'

The young secretary perched on the edge of the sort of psychiatrist's couch, not exactly sitting but resting her bottom against the black leather cushion.

'What are you going to do?' Gina asked. 'Just a holiday, is it? Or are you going to University?'

'Just a holiday,' Josephine said. 'I have a place at Oxford, but I'm not sure that I'll take it up.'

The secretary, who could not have been more than a year or two older than Josephine, shook her head and smiled sadly. Then, remembering something, she put down the glass and came over to the table.

'Better straighten these up,' she said, tidying the maga-zines. 'He might get upset if he thinks you've seen them. Embarrassing for him.'

Almost uncomfortably close, Josephine could smell Gina's perfume, which was something expensive, unquestionably expensive. Gina stood up and looked down at her and Joseph-ine, normally entirely composed and self-possessed, once again felt seriously troubled and disturbed. Then Gina went back to her drink and her perch against the couch.

'Nothing much wrong with you, love, is there?' she said.

'I beg your pardon. . . .'

'Staying long with your uncle?'

'A week or so. He's become so busy. The original idea was that he'd show me something of London. I rather thought I might take a job rather than waste all that time at University.'

'Yes,' Gina said. 'That may be. But I wouldn't be in too much of a hurry if I were you.'

Josephine thought that, under the heavy make-up, the young, pretty face looked strangely tired, much older than that of a girl of twenty or twenty-one.

'Don't suppose you get no guarantees, though, even at Oxford,' Gina said.

She swallowed her gin. And moved back to the cocktail cabinet.

'Want some more?'

'No thank you.'

'I've been working since I was sixteen,' she said. 'You know those pictures in those magazines?'

'I ... er ... well I saw them. ...'

'Know how much you can get for that? And what goes along with it? No. Why should you? You've been protected. But believe me, love, you're pretty enough to find out soon enough. The propositions you get! From everyone.'

Gina stood up and with an easy little gesture of her hand down her own body indicated its splendours.

'Don't I know it!' she said. 'But I daresay you're a lot more sophisticated than I was.'

'I doubt it!' said Josephine with feeling.

Gina looked thoughtful.

'Has he ...' She paused.

'Yes?'

'Oh it's none of my business, really. I wondered if he ... the Minister, that is, had advised you. He's a man of the world. He'd know what would be best for you.'

'No. He's told me I can stay as long as I like until I make up my own mind. He has a very refreshing outlook, quite unlike my parents. But they're always so busy.'

'Yes. Very refreshing. That's why it's such a good thing

194

that he's in this department. You don't want anyone too puritan, after all.'

That seemed to be very sensible.

'It must be interesting work,' Josephine said.

'Oh, it is very. Especially the Public Decency side of things.' Gina looked thoughtful. 'I wish *I* could have gone to Oxford, though,' she said. 'It would have been . . . different.'

She sounded very wistful and forlorn.

'But what are we going to *do*, Minister?' asked the private secretary. 'I'm sure Sir Hoke will want our high-minded ideals, for no one in politics, however bluntly affable his manner may be, enjoys a spot of high-mindedness more: but he will expect us to back them up with proposals.'

'Don't worry Hilary,' said Augustine Cornflour. 'I have unlimited proposals a) for the uplifting of Morale and b) for the upholding of Public Decency. First of all: Morale. What is it that depresses you most in any day?'

'Quite honestly, Minister, my office and the antiquated lavatories on the third floor. . . .'

'Hilary, please look a little beyond the more banal discomforts. We are talking about Morale and Public Decency. Think.'

'I suppose travelling on the Underground.'

'Good point, Hilary! I don't have to do that, so I hadn't thought about it.'

He made a quick note in his neat, tiny handwriting. 'Jolly up public transport,' it read.

'I'll tell you what I was thinking of,' he said, perhaps giving up hope that the private secretary would arrive there on his own behalf. 'The wireless in the morning. Gloom and facetiae. One of the first things this ministry will do is provide at least two first-class cheerful items per bulletin and provide an instant happy gloss on all items of news which are domestic to counterbalance agencies at home and abroad

195

who are selling Britain short. We will also dig up as much depressing news as we can about other nations, especially France, West Germany, Australia and the United States in that order and present it in as virulent a way as may be compatible with our great broadcasting tradition. We shall co-operate at all levels and absolutely with the BBC and the Independent lot. Television doesn't matter as much as radio because people are usually making tea or fetching their evening Guinness; otherwise they are speculating on the sexuality of the announcer. When it comes to the Soviet Union or China, we shall be careful to monitor any remark pejorative to a British personality or institution and report it in the worst possible form of words, so that latent patriotic feelings are aroused.'

'Minister, this savours dangerously of propaganda!'

'Propaganda is what the enemy make use of, Hilary. When we do it, it is information to encourage morale. You are too young to remember the great days of the War, when morale was so wonderful here.'

Augustine Cornflour glowed with the inspiration of those desperate years.

'Next,' he said, 'we must have far less depressing material on television and many more jolly programmes – comedies and family buffoonery. We need more of it.'

'That, with respect, would be difficult, Minister.'

'Difficult? Why?'

'Well, Minister, you lead such a busy life that it would obviously be unusual for you to view much television: but there is an awful lot of what you have just prescribed already.'

'Then let us have more. Keep the people laughing. We need far fewer of those gloomy and allegedly satirical pseudo-examinations in depth by producers such as Linda Wood-chuck.'

'Linda Woodchuck, Minister?'

'A sex-mad subversive. In fact, Hilary, we need less satire all round unless it is thoroughly nihilistic. The British public have never understood nihilism and think it is simply comic material written by graduates of Oxford and Cambridge.'

'Yes, Minister,' said the private secretary, who had once been a member of the illustrious Footlights Society during its glittering period.

'It often is,' said Augustine Cornflour. 'I have two further immediate proposals with regard to the encouragement of morale: I propose to co-opt a special advisory body to include Lepidus Pounce, the man of letters, and Branston Simcox, the television master.'

'Lepidus Pounce,' repeated the private secretary, slightly dazed by the rapid flow of ideas.

'Even you must have heard of Lepidus Pounce, Hilary,' said Augustine, almost irritated. 'He is on several Arts Council committees, he is an editor and a critic and a reviewer, as well as being a poet in his own right and author of a little book about modern poets, based on his lectures to the Esquimaux under the aegis of the British Council. Pounce is a wholesome family man who will keep art buoyant and be watchful for the *graffito* element, if you follow me. Simcox was only begetter of the series *It Warms the Cockles*, which he edited, produced and often presented: the most cheerful thing in reporting since the death of Beaverbrook and the departure of Arthur Christiansen.'

'I see you have thought it through, Minister,' said the private secretary.

'Now, then, Hilary,' said Augustine Cornflour, with his instant grasp closing upon a new idea like a talon upon a lambkin. 'This thing about brightening up transport presents us with a certain dilemma. What, for the sake of argument, would you suggest?'

The private secretary's eye strayed to a copy of *Bellegravia* on the nearby table, the cover of which depicted an absolutely splendid woman in a hat with a veil and a fur-scarf and long shiny stockings, looking superbly contemptuous.

'Aha!' said Augustine, wagging a worldly finger at her. 'All very well for you and me, Hilary: but what about public decency. Often the things that will go furthest to boosting morale are in fairly direct contradiction to the maintenance of public decency. *Et venerem et proelia destinat: frustra* . . . as Horace puts it in one of the odes in Book Three, I think. Yes, Book Three. That might be our motto in the Department, Hilary. One horn for battle and the other for love. If you follow me. So you see that we cannot put *that* kind of thing . . .' he gestured contemptuously at the arrogant woman on the magazine cover '. . . on the walls of our commuter trains. *Frustra*, Hilary. "In vain." At the same time, there is no reason why we should not, in conjunction with the Department of Trade and several commercial interests which are *good for Britain*, encourage the return of the miniskirt and those concomitant aids to public chastity, tights.

'This may seem to you a smidgeon unpractical,' went on Augustine Cornflour, aware of his brilliance. 'But let me leave two thoughts with you to ponder over: extra VAT on all such magazines as that, so that only the decadent rich or the truly obsessed will spend hard-earned cash upon them. And, indeed, on other pornographic products. That's one thought. The other is a very high tax on all male cosmetics. What do you think of that?'

'Masterly,' said the private secretary.

'Meanwhile, I know just the man to advise us on the whole area of public decency,' said Augustine Cornflour. 'A chap who's had some dubious connections in the past, admittedly, but who has profited from them. When you go out, ask Mrs Broadbent or Gina to get me Lucius Spiedermann.'

Lucius Spiedermann, not only an atheist and a cynic but a disillusioned atheist and cynic, could not believe his telephone receiver: but couldn't think of any close acquaintance intelligent enough to play such a joke.

After a very trying day Neville Chamberlain Wynstanley, a Bad-Godesberg baby, sat down at his desk. The telephone rang. Wynstanley clenched his forearms in the way many would clench their fists, and his moustache worked involuntarily. He knew it would be Arnold Espadrille. And it was.

'Wynstanley? Espadrille . . .' said that calm terse voice. 'I want you to look into someone called Bushchat, who has been behaving strangely in Fresh 'n' Freeze today. He bought eleven packets of white blancmange. What do you make of that?'

'He might be inordinately fond of blancmange, X.'

'Please, Wynstanley, when we are unscrambled, call me by my name. It does not do to draw attention. No. The fact is that there is throughout London a run on white blancmange. It is being used in a process of quasi-sculpture whereby under copies of our Elgin marbles, vital formulae are being *cheaply* transferred behind the curtain. Tell me, Wynstanley, what do you notice about Bushchat?'

'I have not had the pleasure of meeting him.'

'Shch! Shch, Wynstanley!'

'I'm sorry, sir. I said nothing. Nothing at all. . . .'

'The Russian consonant "shch". Whoever heard of a decent citizen of the English-speaking world with such an adjacent of liquid sibilants. He needs watching. I want you to enrol as a washer-up at the Rushlight School of Iconography tomorrow. It's all arranged. Look scruffy and go early to that place in Mortimer Street. They are expecting you. Good night.'

After a few seconds' justifiable rage, Neville Chamberlain Wynstanley was able to relax at last. He unlocked his desk and drew out a plain buff but bulging folder. He looked at it softly for a moment, without opening it. Then, his fingers almost trembling, he lifted the cover. Strings swirled into his tired brain with gentle trombones throbbing Uwha Uwhawha beneath.

Permesso (he read)
Just a smile and an espresso
And two strangers in a Renaissance town
Long after the sun was down . . .

(Uha Uwhawha . . .)

There, weariness and the day's disappointment had made his inspiration falter briefly and he had put the lyric away. Tonight, he had hoped for something. . . . But then the ghastly stateless Espadrille had interrupted just as his creative fibres were screwing themselves to the exact pitch. If it were not for these moments of peace with his hobby, Neville Chamberlain Wynstanley doubted that he would have kept sane. The humiliation of simulating lust for that dreadful medium, of grubbing about in old mackintoshes in disreputable quarters, of shoplifting in Espadrille's super-market, of enrolling in crass mysticisms, would have been unsupportable without his modest Muse. Hopeless! All gone! He was too tired. Then, miraculously, the strings started again. . . . Uwha Uwhawha. . . .

Va bene?

he wrote, and ecstatically chewed his pen, waiting for the rhyme.

*

'I'm having a marvellous time,' said Clodia Oricellari. 'The work is interesting, I'm incurably Anglophile and I am continually being taken out by charming men. How about you?'

'Oh, I love it,' said James Lloyd Mitchell. 'I shan't describe myself as Anglophile in bicentennial year, but London (*not* Paris) is the last of the civilised cities. I just wonder how long they can hold on to it.'

'The civilisation?'

'Democracy. It adds up to the same thing.'

'I'm afraid that "adding up" is all too near the mark.'

'It's not that I go along with all these facile comparisons with Weimar, which seem to be naive in the extreme. What bothers me is the way the British, who had the gift of courtesy without a hint of servility, have become surly and apathetic.'

'I think it's because of the Arabs. In spite of the T. E. Lawrence romance, they've always rather despised the Arabs. And now this extraordinary collection of people, with vast funds and no manners, seem to be taking over. I was telling Roger Ingestre not long ago that rich aliens are very bad for the native population.'

'I think it goes deeper. They're getting more and more used to compliance with rules and it's sapping enterprise. They're losing their old pride and spirit. In other ways, I should say, compared to the French, their xenophobia-rating was quite low. It's a reluctance to serve: their own people as much as the aliens.'

'Have you spent much time in Germany?'

'I visited there.'

'There you will find reluctance to serve!'

'Possibly. I'll be going back later in the year. What impresses me is the energy of the Germans. The determination to survive. They think of themselves as a poor country and so they have a thriving economy. The only people I know who match them are the Israelis.'

'And how do you account for it?'

'I'd say that however bust the British are, they have a vast balance of confidence to draw on. Quite unjustifiably. The Germans have to keep banking confidence. To build up reserves. And that does wonders for productivity.'

'Spoken like a true conservative, sir.'

'Always a pleasure in the company of a beautiful woman.'

'It's an ironic match: the Germans and the Israelis.'

'A question of different kinds of guilt: the Israelis have to atone for the failure to resist, when resistance might have been possible against the Nazis.'

'Over-simplification. I'm sorry. That's an American point

of view. Resistance to totalitarian government and an absolutely efficient, absolutely brutal secret police is impossible, especially when it is backed by latent hostility. Anti-semitism was rife in central Europe. The Americans and the British don't know how virulent it can be.'

'Wouldn't it still be better to die in a square or a public park, fighting, than to go to a gas chamber?'

'People cling to life. And how were the victims to know about gas chambers?'

'After the 1938 pogroms, they could only have expected humiliation. And, indeed, torture. Anyway, my point is that the shame has been lived down. Israel is a proud nation.'

'I agree. I was there two years ago. So have you no hope for the rest of us in Europe?'

'France was recovering until de Gaulle departed. He was a truly dynamic conservative, which is the point about real conservatism. It has very little to do with a class system. And I'd say the French were a lot closer to us in that respect than they are to you and the British and the Germans. England breeds a received conservatism, as it once refused to breed slaves. The welfare state acted upon an imperial tradition to make the newly affluent expect things as of right. Did anyone ever suggest as an electoral gambit: "You never *earned* it so good"?'

'So you're saying the mixed economy doesn't work?'

'Patently. I'm even saying it cannot work.'

'So do the Marxists.'

'All right! But their interpretation of society is more practicable than the liberal one. And I am implacably opposed to it.'

'Why?'

'An egalitarian society is static: there's no progress.'

'Ah? But what's progress?'

'We must mean the same thing: justice, opportunity. I'll tell you what progress is: higher standards of the commonplace in all respects. Intellectually and morally as well as materially. The great twentieth-century fallacy is that this is the prerogative of liberal politics. *And* the equation of equality with justice is a Marxist perversion of truth.'

'Must I conclude that you hold little hope for France?'

'It's my opinion that France is a fragmented nation that won't admit it and believes in its cooked books as it once believed in its cuisine. De Gaulle was a dynamic conservative, love or loathe him, who made people proud to be French.'

'I tremble to think of what you predict for Italy.'

'I know too little, as yet. Except as tourist.'

'Veteran of a thousand Harry's Bars. . . .'

'What was that? Yes . . . I guess I am.'

'I didn't mean to be rude. Surely we, too, have residual guilt?'

'Why? Mussolini never had it all his own way. You are skilled at biding time.'

'And have been since Tiberius.'

'Since the Tarquins.'

'And I suspect that we are not politically significant.'

'You've always had a strong Communist tradition: but independent of Moscow.'

'Nevertheless, we have now the first Communist-supported mayor of Rome. What about the soft underbelly of Europe? Greece, Spain, Portugal. And then France.'

'A house of cards.'

'Is it?'

'I thought that was the point you were making.'

'No. I was trying to establish your own conservative premise. Which I suspect is Fortress America: with certain regrets about Germany. After all, Scandinavia is beyond recall.'

'We started off talking about the British.'

'Well?'

'Their problem is not material as much as moral. They have caught an everlasting accidie. Isn't that so?'

'I doubt it. They are intellectually restless and there are too many professional rebels who care nothing for their personal gesture of rebellion.'

'Have I annoyed you, Clodia?'

'Of course not. I'm a diplomatist.'

'So where does a Communist take-over in Italy leave *you*?'

'Exactly where I am, I hope. If the Communists take part in government, or even a dominant part, I am a technician.'

'Without political anchorage.'

'That's a very strange phrase. I am a confirmed European. In some ways I don't care much whether it is a capitalist or socialist Europe, as long as it is not subservient to the USA or the USSR. I believe in certain social assumptions; I have certain ideological preferences. I do my job.'

'And I'm put in my place.'

'I doubt very much that you are ever put anywhere you did not wish to be.'

'It may seem naive to someone of your long tradition, but isn't it all about power?'

'I had a similar conversation with Roger Ingestre not long ago. And I confess I was asking that question.'

'A case in point! I was allowed to attend a meeting of their discussion group, the other evening. It was fine! Civilised. Sincere. And not a damn thing decided in four hours! Nothing emerged. Nobody could have asked for a more fluent commentary on the way things are, but as for practical policies...'

'Did you tell him?'

'No. I thought he might resent it. After all, I am a foreigner. And Roger has certain fixed notions about moral influence in politics. He has also a talent for procatelepsis. So whatever I was going to say, he'd have anticipated in his careless Oxford way and set up some clever counter-ploy.'

'Did he, in fact?'

'He asked me if so much earnest talk had not sounded to a galvanic right-winger like myself like the flapping of so many luminous wings.'

'And you said?'

'Something appropriately galvanising. He wasn't shocked. He is, incidentally, a very . . . ah . . . charming man.'

'Very.'

'I don't know how you'll take this: but may I be permitted to ask if you and he enjoy any "special relationship"?'

'We are old and close friends. There is perhaps a remote and pleasing sexual interest in both of us, which is strictly vestigial. I think he perhaps admires Francesca.'

'She's very pretty. I hope you didn't mind the question.'

'Not at all. They all have a lot of charm. Even if they are ineffectual as a group, they are serious and they work hard.'

'Yes. But, in so doing, they underline the essential weakness of all liberalism, especially the English brand. Tolerance, scepticism and intelligence all combining to create amused enervation. The well-bred shrug.'

'Which is where it can be misleading. Networks of influence still obtain in England. And no longer based on schools and universities. Mass communications are a sort of binding fluid for successful people: they meet and chat and have a civilised drink here and there, and there is extensive contact across the professions. The catalysts are the journalists and commentators and presenters who make the introductions. Roger and his kind don't want *power*. They want influence.'

'Influence is the liberal escape-hatch.'

'Are there no longer any significant liberals in America?'

'Of Ingestre's kind, thousands. Even tens of thousands. But not in the old Kennedy illusory image. Johnson was a personal holocaust. Humphrey didn't make it and would talk himself out of anything. McGovern was Santa Claus's personal contribution to Republicanism and McCarthy is an elegant polemicist.'

'And Jimmy Carter?'

'A pragmatist. The first Mr Niceguy in the White House since Professor Niceguy, who had a stroke round about 1919. Of course, we all recognise the moratorium from 1952–60 when we had General Niceguy.'

'When it might have been Adlai Stevenson. I wonder what that might have meant.'

'I shudder to think. Suppose it had been Goldwater in 1964?'

'I reserve the same rights.'

'Maybe. But we'd have won the war in Vietnam. We'd have had a sound economy to treat with the Arabs and OPEC. There would have been no recession.'

'And no talk of an energy crisis.'

'That's not fair. I didn't say that. And, anyway, that has still to be resolved.'

'Tell me: you accuse the Ingestre circle of ineffectuality. Why are you not in politics? Why just write about them?'

'Aha! Why are you a diplomat? Have you read Conor Cruise O'Brien's essay on Machiavelli? He says he told the truth about power: if you can't stand the heat, keep out of the torture chamber.'

*

All at once Oxford seemed to be terribly provincial. She found it difficult to conceive of the state of pleasure and excitement that she had been in, only two years before, when she had first taken up her scholarship. Even then, by comparison with most of her contemporaries, she had been pretty sophisticated: she had read a lot more widely, if less deeply, than almost everyone; she already knew a fair selection of London people, some of whom were famous, all of whom were established in desirable careers. Yet, Oxford had meant something new and very attractive and exhilarating, quite different from the allegedly stimulating atmosphere of home, which her friends seemed to envy. She did not think that Jeremy and Barbara were really sophisticated; merely blasé: that was the reason that she had expected so much of the place, so much intellectual stimulation, such a personal awakening. Of course, she had been disappointed: Oxford, she thought, could seldom live up to the anticipation of most of its new undergraduates. But it would not have been fair to say that she had not enjoyed herself variously and thoroughly in an adolescent way. Now Tony had shown her what life was all about, and on the first day of a new term Oxford was already stale and flat and incredibly immature. She must do her best to make it, at least, profitable.

It wasn't just the sex, which had quickly become something profound in itself and out of which she had started to love him. Of course it made a difference: she realised how completely a woman she now was and felt distantly ashamed of her (concealed) condescension to some of her acquaintances whose careless promiscuity, in past terms, she had listened to enviously, though with an air of enigmatic detachment (borrowed from Roger Ingestre). It was laughable: and even then she had known that some detail, or vividly recounted exploit, had betrayed to any really trained eyes her fundamental innocence. Fortunately, the people telling such intimacies were so entirely self-absorbed, for the most part, as not to notice. Now Candida listened to accounts of frantic 'fantastic' couplings in various parts of Western Europe, and one notable event in Prague, with a lazy indifference. What could they possibly know about it? She felt enormously grateful that Tony was the first man she had actually had. Memories of breathless petting and fumbling were almost hilarious. But she thought in the circumstances that she could afford to be kind to Steve Kent. Back at Oxford, she saw him in its perspective. And of course there were many others who had not had any sort of adventures and had gone home and worked, part of the time to earn some pocket-money, most of the time for Schools. Nice, serious, quite plain girls, on the whole, to whom she did not feel in the least bit patronising. In fact, she thought more of them than the feckless idiots who had fucked their way across Cos or Morocco or Benelux. Or so they claimed. Most of them were about as juvenile as Jessica. . . . Candida shuddered as she remembered the two or three grotesque little scenes that she had been dragged into at home (after the wonderful holiday with Tony, of all things) when Daddy and Barbara had decided that Jessica was having precocious sex. She did not remember them worrying as much about her. In late, and defiant, nasty little details about clothing, evasions. Daddy, worried and earnest and wire-haired, saying: *Just be frank with us, Jess: and whatever it is we love you. Don't do anything silly.* And Barbara elaborately not losing her cool: *The point is, Jessica, that we are not mid-Victorian bourgeoisie. We aren't easily shocked. It's just a matter of seeing this rationally.* And the ghastly little creature had tried to turn it all against her: *What about Candy? I bet she's been laid under every bush on the Heath by your precious chums. Except the one she wants.* Candy!

She hated the name more than anything. And her hateful sister always used it whenever she might dare. The only person in the world that Candida wanted to physically hurt. . . . Other than Tony in certain transcendent moments of passion. Big, bouncy breasts and bottom, ridiculously over-developed. Now the addiction to silly games had become a sex obsession. The trouble was she was stupid and opinionated and had this disastrous facility for making people laugh at her, which seemed to be the panacea of all her faults of omission and commission. Half-listening to the conversation in Jenny Scrubb's room, drinking foul chicory-substitute coffee, Candida thought that some of these girls were no more adult than horrible little Jessica. A giggle and a tumble and (oh God!) a 'trip', and the idea of a good time some overcrowded cellar and loud, endlessly repetitive music and goodwill. Wine, leisurely brandy, silence: looking at him . . . and he at her. . . . Then, the long deliberate silky preparation for the eventual mutual seduction and love-making; the excitement of wondering how it would be that night.

She smiled obscurely at them. . . . And fought down, and fought down the agonising, dissolving spasm of quite meaningless jealousy that sometimes possessed her. . . . They were becoming rather more frequent and often she was tortured for hours on end by quite precise imaginings of Tony with some other woman and she sometimes wondered if the discretion he insisted on was not to keep their relationship unspoilt but to keep it secret from another mistress . . . or other mistresses. And inevitably perhaps from her mother. But while she had (how absurdly) worried about Roger Ingestre and Barbara intertwined in some rarefied form of physical passion, she could not for a moment imagine Tony rampantly eager over her trembling, waiting. . . . And yet she herself was often described as cool, poised, unruffled: how different from the exuberant, sweating and panting Jessica. And she knew very well what Tony had awakened in her. So might he not do as much and more for her mother. At these moments her hatred of his experience and his languid expertise, delicacy and brutishness, the exigencies of his need to submit and to violate, reached a pitch of unreason. Could a man that she had decided she loved be that corrupt: to have a mother and daughter as mistresses at the same time? There was something corrupt about him: something cruelly opportunist. After all, the accidental meeting at Roger Ingestre's flat, when she had gone there determined to . . . How long ago that seemed in that very hot summer. And he had taken the opportunity and her, without hesitation. It had been so easy for him. How often in the life of a handsome Member of Parliament, in his mid forties, did these opportunities occur: there must be secretaries, journalists, researchers, party workers as well as all the people he met socially. . . . There were people like Rachel Bailey whose husband was at the other end of the world, there were people like Roger Ingestre's friend, Francesca. . . . And God! given the choice between Roger Ingestre and Tony! Candida did not think she could compete on anything like equal terms with Francesca – *unless she was really, honestly loved.*

On the occasions when they had been in the same room together, she had (from a distance that was always discreet) watched him, painfully, as he put an arm around Marie White or clasped Sandra Beeton's hand. (Sandra Beeton! A

psychological freak, as she could *see* in her saner moments.)
He was cautious with Rachel Bailey, which probably signi-
fied most, since neither would be anxious to draw too much
attention to any lust shared. . . . And there were wives:
Mears's dusty, faded blonde and Farrell's rather tarty
mistress who passed for a wife and Middleton's. All probably
aching for a real man like Tony. She remembered, and it
made her feel cold and sick still, the time when she had
shown she was jealous, watching him eyeing a girl at another
table in a restaurant. First she had sulked, then she had lost
her temper rather deliberately. He had laughed at her. Quite
kindly: but hurtfully, whether or not that was his intention.
*Darling, I'm a normal, reasonably matured man. Speculative
admiration doesn't even imply desire, let alone intention. Wait
until you're a little older. It's exactly the same for a woman.* She
had felt obliged to laugh, otherwise she might have looked
silly and young and naive: but she had resented the implication of worldly superiority. Who were these women with
lecherous, predatory eyes. Marie White – very likely.
Rachel Bailey – hardly: much too intense. Sandra Beeton –
given the remotest chance. Her mother. . . . Who could
honestly tell? Sometimes, obscurely and remotely, she felt
sorry for her father. Gentle, earnest, misdirected, a success
in spite of himself, playing almost against his own character.
And she detested the way that Barbara played down to him
in public, when she dominated so ruthlessly in private. It was
not loyalty, it was politics. And that was another thing about
Tony. He was a politician by instinct and by inclination, as
he had revealed to her when they had (seriously) discussed
the big issues in the best moments of the summer (when not
actually making love), when he had made her feel so quick
and acute. Always, he saw the realities which might mean
submission, retreat, compromise, accommodation, partial or
total assertion; always he took a pragmatic view of which
should obtain in a given case, weighing up an alternative
play, not discarding other possible tactics. And she had
learned, too, how quickly he latched on to the sanctions of

defeat and compromise as they were imposed on the defeated and the half-determined; and how effectively he defined those of the strong. It was not impossible that he lived his whole life in this cold, calculating way, distracted only by his satyr's need for women. . . . And yet he was so passionate, so emotional, so vulnerable. . . .

She had been quiet for a long time and one of the others asked her if she was all right. She smiled knowingly and told them that she had been listening with amazement and admiration, but that now she was tired and going to bed. Susan said that she had not told them anything about her vac. And that Steve Kent had rung her up looking for her. The stupid oaf! *That* kind of thing Candida could do without. So where had she been. In Italy. Yes, with friends of her family who had a nice old farmhouse in Tuscany: very peaceful, working for Schools. She gave them her most brilliantly deceiving smile. They wished she hadn't reminded them of Schools: she was a bitch and a prig and several other things.

Candida swung off the table where she had been reclining and left them. Her room was cold and bare and silly. In other years she had tried to make the place where she lived pretty and uniquely hers: now she thought she wouldn't bother. It would be a cell in which she lived until the whole nonsense was over and she could be in London with Tony. In the meantime, she would spend as much time there as possible, she would work hard for a good degree in order to prove herself to him as intellectually worth-while, and she would stop being an adolescent. She would grow up. She would not be jealous or allow herself to think of what he might be doing. She would concentrate on the hours when she was with him and the rest of the time work.

She had undressed without thinking, but now went to look at herself in a long mirror: not with any vanity or desire to stimulate herself. Critically and calmly. Then she put on a nightdress and went to bed.

She fell asleep quickly, but during the night dreamed

uneasily. She was on one of the conveyor-belt moving pavements that she had used in international airports, but she was not herself: she was a footnote to what she had been that same day looking for the real self to deliver the note to and aware that all the time she was being switched back on the black rubber causeway, meeting again the same landmark scuffs and scratches, the same adverts, even some faces going in the opposite direction. If only she could get to the Candida waiting for the note.

She awoke uneasily, long enough to register the dream and lay awake or half awake, anxious and unhappy. She thought deliberately about Tony in the most erotic situations, but when she fell asleep again dreamed about Stephen Kent standing in front of her with a huge erection, which led to a terrible family row in which her mother and Jessica were both humiliating her father with savage, bitter and nasty accusations of cowardice, selfishness and all manner of horrible personal things. She entered the scene to defend him. (He was weeping, by this time.) She moved towards her mother in order to slap her face – for she was obviously hysterical. Instead she clawed her and drew three or four lines of blood across that fine-boned, well made-up cheek. She ran for the door but it would not open.

She woke up very cold and shivering. There was a dim white light through the curtain. Candida lay very still and frightened for a moment until she was absolutely sure that it had been a dream, then she looked at her travelling clock. It was only six-fifteen, but she did not want to go to sleep again.

She turned on the bedside light, but the last images of dreaming were still too closely with her, though she could not understand why they should be so upsetting. She knew that she didn't like her mother and it was reasonable enough that latent resentment might be translated in dreams into actual blood-drawing violence: but why was she so horrified. And why (suddenly) remembering that brief tableau with Stephen Kent and an enormous phallus, should she feel excited in that specifically sexual way. She despised Steve Kent. She loved Tony Connors and wanted no other satisfaction or whatever the word was than he provided.

To stay the rush of impressions swirling about in the emptying bowl of sleep, Candida got up to make some tea. As soon as she had put on a dressing gown and fiddled with the electric kettle, focused on her books and what remained to be tidied after unpacking, she was reasonably secure again. But she was trembling and she felt a little sick. She concentrated on the day ahead and things to be done.

There was a meeting with Miss Bradshaw for all third-year pupils at ten-thirty and another with Mrs Wellbeck at eleven-thirty – purely routine, to fix up tutorial times and classes, with a few wry remarks about it being Schools year for them and one or two acidulous asides about one or two of the moderators. Candida felt no pang at all about not going any more to Roger Ingestre, which she would not have believed had it been put to her at the beginning of the summer. As much as she had laughed at them in the past, the dry, scholarly and remote Miss Bradshaw and the sharp-tongued, quick-brained Mrs Wellbeck would be rather agreeable again after Ingestre's faintly rococo style of teaching; certainly neither of them could match his conceit.

Then there was Stephen Kent. There had been the inevitable note in her pigeon-hole waiting for her, in his neat, small, cramped handwriting. And she had opened it with a sigh: could he please see her and talk to her? The new policy was to be nice to him, so she had gone around to his college and left a reply arranging to meet him in the King's Arms at lunchtime. She proposed to explain the situation, without mentioning Tony's name. She would have to make it clear that it wasn't Roger Ingestre, but there was no need to say any more – since Tony still wanted it kept secret. . . . The familiar stab of doubt and anxiety and jealousy. She must control it. Must . . . must. . . . And Stephen Kent might do something silly. Probably not. Rather a stolid boy. Not neurotic. She also intended to offer him a strictly platonic friendship, if he wanted it. He might not, of course: but she thought he would because he was tenacious and stubborn and wouldn't give up hope. It would be useful in fending off other young men, and there was nothing dishonest about it if she made it clear that she was in love with the very much older man with whom she was . . . having an affair.

The very phrase hurt her and once again there was the numbing and yet painful feeling that spread through her body as she thought of him with other women and she thought of the tenderness and intimacy and the straightforward raw and fierce sex. . . . She could not bear the thought of these things between him and anyone else. He had said he loved her, said it often. . . . She asked for reassurance perhaps too often. And often she managed to believe him, sometimes she was even certain. And yet she could not trust him. She must get him to come to Oxford. . . . It would prove something. If not, she would go to London as often as possible, especially when the House was sitting again. . . . But she must get him to come to her and she must persuade him. . . . What was he afraid of, after all? It must be her mother and it must be for sexual reasons. Her father was not forceful enough to worry him and was not in a position to do him the slightest harm. . . . And anyway what was so shameful or undesirable about a heterosexual relationship between two attractive people? The nagging worries clanked around in her mind like a treadmill.

She finished her tea and picked up her towel and sponge-bag for her bath, feeling unhappy and depressed and wondering whether she should go down from Oxford without taking Schools. She could take a secretarial course in London and she would be there with him. . . . No, that was silly. It was the lingering and lowering aftermath of a restless night and unpleasant, menacing dreams.

As she turned, she knocked a copy of *Hard Times* off the table. She had been reading it on the way down, identifying (humorously at the time) with Louisa Gradgrind. It did not seem as humorous now. The Gradgrind marriage she saw in reversed roles when compared to her own parents: it was

Barbara who was the iron-minded, dogmatic worshipper of fact and Daddy was the rather passive, overwhelmed disciple out of loyalty and admiration and perhaps a little intellectual fear. Certainly Tony was no Josiah Bounderby. . . . That at least was still funny. Of course she did not hate Barbara and she loved her father, although she wished he was more assertive and wished that he loved her as much as Jessica. . . . How could all those others who were quite forceful each in his or her own way, even people like Roger Ingestre, accept Daddy as the leader? She supposed he must have some kind of moral fervour that they all recognized that she was too close to and Barbara let him appear to be the moving force, when all the ideas were hers, because it suited her. . . . And Jessica, whom he still almost played with. She didn't hate Jessica, but she disliked her; always had disliked her from the age of about eight when she had been a noisy, irritating nuisance and a show-off whom everyone seemed to want to cuddle and whom, she knew, they always compared favourably to her. Oh God! Candida thought, how I wish I could have had nice, dim, unambitious parents who didn't want to *do* things! And who would have been just a little proud of me for what *I* could do!

She went to the bathrooms at the end of the corridor. There weren't many people about that early, just the college servants and to them she was as pleasant as usual. Quite suddenly, she remembered that dream about Steve Kent again with the same stir of excitement and could not fathom it out at all. She understood a little of the way she had made him feel, but she felt nothing else for him – except sorry.

*

I don't think I needed the reassurance that Candida's lover was not Ingestre. (I hadn't even asked: because I never for a moment imagined that she had got to first base with him.) I wonder, all the same, who it could be: unmarried and much older. And in love! I daresay she is, but I wonder if it's reciprocal. Probably no one that I know. There is no

215

eason why I shouldn't go along with this Platonic rubbish, although I suspect that she's using it as a convenience. As I see it, however, there is no point in being proud. If I can bring her round, it will all be (in the end) worthwhile. It's not a question of winning, or proving anything or getting her into bed. That's easy enough with girls who are just as pretty. It's a matter of loving her and of making her want to love me. If it's not about that, it is nothing and worthless. Perhaps, if I can show her that I am patient and decent and I'm not again going to shove my stupid hand up her skirt and that it is something essentially quiet and serious and something good as well, perhaps she will start to think of me differently. Obviously a girl with her contacts and background will be superficially attracted to an experienced older man (as she was, I thought, to Ingestre: but he wasn't interested); the important point is that it will not necessarily last. I don't want a virgin, anyway. (Even if she was.) The only problem is, now, if this character is really expert and she learns from him, will I be able to live up to it. We can learn together, I suppose: and that should be fun! I don't think I'm so bad, but I can't be sure.

I wish I had the confidence of Ted White, who is certainly the most integrated man I've met in a long time. The London summer wasn't wasted: I met a lot of interesting people like Rachel and Ellis Fulford and some of Ingestre's other friends; I had a solid and worthwhile relationship with Clifford and Teresa, and with Samantha too, and that was good – nothing special but decent people getting on well and working together without any nonsense. (I think I begin to appreciate some of Dad's attitudes; not that I'm going to be reckless about it!) At least I learned you could work alongside people you fancied quite a lot and still behave rationally, which must be the way of the world: and the other opportunities made me quite sure that I was dead serious about Candida. And, not least, I got quite a bit of work done.

In all this, Ted White was perhaps the most exhilarating

event of the summer, perhaps because he and his mother both know Candida and her family and were charitably jokey about her. Marie White more than Ted, who says that he has no time for her. They have themselves an enviably uncomplicated relationship in thought and word and, I should imagine, deed. Ted's mother obviously has a great deal of money and lives in a splendid house on Windmill Hill, which isn't a depressed area of Hampstead at the worst of times. She seems to be an amiable cosy woman, still attractive in a ripened sort of way, and has no reservations – as far as may be seen – about Ted turning up with various girl-friends, whether for the night, the weekend or whatever. He has a cheerfully promiscuous attitude and I've no doubt that he shook me out of a mood of intense self-pity, when I needed some kind of rough therapy. And his mother helped too. He calls her The Wife of Bath: and it isn't all that far out. They both have a direct earthy approach which is what I needed, rather than the shy sympathies of Ingestre.

And then there was also meeting Rachel, who made me take a proper interest in politics for the first time – by that casual, cast-off suggestion. I don't think it was meant to be patronising. It's made me read History more perceptively, I think. It is a nonsense that at twenty years of age, this is the first time I've related events to the lives of people and to works of art and to discoveries and to thought. That is the problem! I'm a conservative policeman's son and we all go by the book, whatever the book's about and whoever wrote it. Dad never asked any questions which weren't in the line of duty. And at school in Ashbridge, all of them, Jenks and Harko and Boris Omsk, good and sincere as they were, wanted you to go for the safe thing: the good A-level grade, the S-level chance. At least, Jenks made me go for Oxford too. Funny Welsh thing of wanting prestige and security all at once, manifested in cautious rhetoric that, at the time, I did not recognize. It's difficult not to envy people like Candida for the opportunity to relate ideas and events and everything else. It takes time and there are so many clever

217

buggers in this place who are playing at it. What is so salutary about Ted White is that one year at UCL was enough and he knew it. There was the added advantage that his mother could put up the necessary advance: but he did find his own way around. And she let him. I can imagine what Dad would have said if I'd thrown up everything to go to Mexico. Anyway, I am not Ted White and I could not, for whatever reason, have given up Oxford.

There's a lot of sentimental rubbish about the place and Rachel Bailey is probably right when she says it's best forgotten unless you intend to make a career of it. (Was that an oblique jibe at Ingestre?) And yet it is so beautiful now, in the autumn, and the air seems to be fresh after London, and it is all that much slower and kinder. I remember what it was like when I first came up and can imagine what it must be like to people from the deep country or small villages.

I don't think that I'm in bad shape emotionally and spiritually, after all: when once I expected to be. I think, for the moment at least, that I can accept Candida on her terms and we don't have to meet at tutorials any more. I think I can wait until things start going my way. And back here, in spite of Clifford and Teresa and all that was pleasant about being in London, I am more myself. Going to tutorials with just Michael Lumley should mean that we both get much more out of them: Candida and the other girl were a distraction in many ways, not least because of the quality of their work.

I notice from the Labour Club publicity that there is a joint session early in the term with the Conservatives and Liberals about the future of a European Parliament in which Rachel Bailey is taking part. I'll certainly go along to that and try to have a word with her, which will be preferable to writing. I'm sure she would not mind and was quite genuine when she invited me along to the House of Commons, but a sort of 'chance' meeting of this kind will remind her who I am and of the connection with Ingestre who is obviously a close mate. It won't do my prestige any harm if she recognises me either. Perhaps it might be a good idea to take Candida along to the symposium: then again, perhaps it might not.

I've taken to reading the *Statesman, New Society, Time* and *Newsweek* and *L'Express* regularly, as well as glancing at the dailies, and I think that I am gradually deciding that I should like to be a political journalist. Obviously this means starting on a paper as a reporter somewhere in the provinces, and then with luck moving on to a national: and I foresee trouble with Dad, whatever happens in Schools, who has a traditional policeman's attitude to the press at any level. 'I don't understand you, Stephen: all that effort and expense to put you through Oxford – and the hard work you've put in yourself – just to be a bloody newspaper-man: when you could really make something of yourself. It beats me. . . .'

Ah well, I shall have to sort that one out when the time comes. That's a long enough raid on the inarticulate for one session.

I am really enjoying this term so far. Candida has graciously allowed me to take her to the pictures three times and once to the theatre. It's an interesting experience sitting there next to her with all kinds of full frontal thrashing about going on on the screen without daring to glance and see how it's going down. My reward so far for all this monastic self-control has been a little tiptoe peck on the cheek and some husky murmuring about being so gentle and kind. I don't think she is very happy: she disappeared the other weekend, presumably to spend it with the middle-ageing lover. I felt miserable for a few hours, but then Ted White and his mother appeared by chance. She was driving down to Banbury to spend the weekend with some friends and Ted cadged a lift, ostensibly to lavish scorn on the University, the town and me for being a bourgeois caterpillar. We had a hilarious and drunken lunch with Ted waspish and Marie as relaxed and easy-going as ever. She never seems to have anything malicious to say about anyone at all, quite unlike her son – though she came out with a memorable piece of invective directed at a couple of loud-mouthed idiots standing in the open doorway of the pub and cawing at each other in the usual way about the clientele: 'Darling, while you are making your exquisite decision whether or not to favour this thoroughly unworthy hovel the honour of your custom, perhaps you wouldn't mind shutting the fucking door!' Since this was delivered in impeccable Hampstead with the most generous of smiles by someone wearing a cream-coloured cavalry-twill trouser suit (obviously expensive), a dark brown silk shirt and carrying a Gucci handbag, they looked as though the room had suddenly depressurised several thousand feet up.

Ted and I saw her off at closing time. I was slightly worried about whether she was fit to drive, with visions of Dad's horror at the sort of people I'd started to consort with in London (he'd known all along no good could come of it), but I kept them to myself, until she'd gone. Ted wasn't in the least worried and said she had a head like a rock. 'My first stepfather was a South African alcoholic; and my second a New York entreprennewer who had worked his way from Flatbush to Park Avenue in six easy tramplings: she can take care of herself potation-wise.'

Marie asked me to give her love to Ingestre, which interested Ted. 'Waste of a good intelligence,' he said. 'That's what you've got to watch out for, Steve, my son: faffing about over trivialities in some academic attic like this place. And they'll want to store you away with the rest of the learned lumber, if you get your first.' I told him I wanted to be a journalist. That was funny too, but served to prompt an extempore lecture on crusading and investigative journalists: the ones Ted admired were the ones who went to the wars and the famines and dictatorships and told it and photographed it as it was. Not letting him have it all his own way, I asked him why he wasn't working somewhere in the deprived world. He became very serious: 'I teach where I do, my son, because that's where I can have most influence. Any talking head can do it in the kind of complacent conformity of Oxford or Cambridge, where occasionally a few naughty children who think they're rebels begin to question the syllabus. In a polytechnic you have to shift great granite lumps of ideas from point A to point B and back again. You have to break down every kind of prejudice and received opinion and solid, unimaginative doggedness. You aren't treating with bright middle-class or very bright working-class infants, but with much less able adults who've already gathered a bit of experience. And you have to tell them there's a real world out there where things happen and people starve and are tortured and enslaved. Not your Roger Ingestre's world of ideas and diaphanous nightmares and clever little footnotes, but Amin's Uganda and Pinochet's Chile and Vorster's South Africa and the Khmer Rouge in Cambodia.' I said that, to be fair, Ingestre was as well aware of these things as he was. 'Ingestre, my son, is still pretending to be Tarzan in an intellectual adventure playground: that's all these things mean to him.'

We had reached the towpath by this time and he was watching with an expression of marvellous scorn an eight skimming under Folly Bridge. It was a beautiful sight on a sunny October afternoon with a washed blue-and-white sky and the trees in Christ Church Meadows beginning to shed their leaves. He said nothing, just flung out his arm in a gesture which he seemed to think needed no words. 'No system is sacred, no regime is right, inalienably unchallengeable,' he said. 'Everything can always be improved.'

As always, abruptly, he changed the subject. 'Are you still pursuing that Taylor girl,' he said. I said I was seeing her again, but not much more. He said quite kindly: 'I wouldn't bother, Steve. She's a fatuous little bitch. And if you try to thump me, I'll put you in the river. Or we'll both go in. And Blessed Marie of the Purple Daybed tells me she's having it away with some decrepit pal of hers.' I told him I knew that and asked if he knew the man's name. 'Wasn't interested enough to ask,' he said. 'But I'd forget it if I was you.'

We turned back and I think, by his own standards, he thought that he had overstepped the mark, because he was curiously silent. I was slowly getting more and more angry: but then he started being funny again and actually said he was sorry. We had a couple of pints when the pubs opened and he decided to hitch back to London. It was something of a relief; but it's made me see the relationship with Candida in a new perspective and I don't feel quite as helpless somehow. I'm not quite sure why.

Rachel Bailey did come to the European Parliament symposium and recognised me immediately. She waved from the dais and when it was over came over to talk to me, which impressed one or two aspiring politicos quite a bit. Then Ingestre came up and after a few civil words, they went off together. I was slightly disappointed not to be invited along, but I can't expect to tag on every time someone I met, when he was being kind to me in London, turns up. Anyway, I was able to remind her of the invitation to the Commons and she repeated it very warmly.

I read a bloody good essay in the tutorial this week and Lumley was for once riding shot-gun. Work is going well and I am actually quite looking forward to Schools.

*

It seems these days that a news story lasts for three days and there an end, whatever it is, however relatively important or trite. During that time the papers and the broadcasters give it space and a certain amount of background detail is provided, though much less on radio and less still on television: then it stops. There is another scandal, crime, swindle, crash, crisis, obituary, disaster. So that even the death of Mao in September only received attention for a few days and just over a month later no one seems to know or care what is happening in China.

Even the more alert undergraduates, who have a reasonably good idea of what is going on in the Soviet Union and Europe and even in Africa, are pretty vague about China. Perhaps it is ignorance that has bathed the dead Chairman in a kind of antiseptic radiance as far as a lot of people in the West are concerned. There was certainly no guarded admiration for Hitler or Stalin: and Mao was just as ruthless in his determination to be dominant at home and just as hostile abroad. Many of the self-styled Maoists here have no idea what Maoism is really (perhaps one should say 'was really') about and how the rigorous questionings of the cultural revolution were simply a technique for undermining opposition in the party and the army. Perhaps we should learn the lesson that the cultural revolution was *really* about culture and the use of art and propaganda to get through to the masses in a positive, if cynical, way. The Nazis had a glimmer of the same idea.

In the SCR after dinner, Farnaby was complaining that the trouble with the present generation of undergraduates was that they had no real understanding of tragedy. Rather glibly I quoted Samuel Hynes's remark in the book, *The Auden Generation*, that 'tragedy and revolution are surely incompatible'. This, somewhat to my surprise, started several people going. I explained that he had made the remark in the context of a discussion of the Marxist view that historical reversals were inevitable parts of the dialectical process to be assimilated and learned from. Farnaby eagerly joined issue on this, advancing the perfectly tenable thesis that tragedy was not a collective experience anyway and this led to a discussion of the hero, inevitably. Farnaby is a voluble scholar, with a very nicely turned wit. But he met his match on this occasion in a small, rather shy woman called Bridget Ross, a political scientist, clearly incensed by some of our assumptions, but admirably in control of her moral indignation. At one point she stopped us all in our tracks with the ironic and bitter aside: 'Of course tragedy never happens to the working class!' She may very well be right, at that! Aeroplane crashes, the Gresford pit accident, Aberfan, earthquakes – such disasters are communal events, while tragedy is a personal, individual matter in which there is an essential element of self-destruction. But is it not barren and pedantic to deny that word to, say, a hundred families after a mining catastrophe? And was Bridget Ross right in diagnosing (so scornfully) that Farnaby and I should have such assumptions? Disturbingly, she was perhaps hinting at just such academic aridity.

Another eccentric supper at Ellis Fulford's which was, in its customarily strange way, excellent. Ellis has been appointed to two more advisory committees, one to do with energy and the other with industrial relations and dismisses both as a 'bloody shoemakers' holiday' because he has never come across a bigger coach-load of cobblers. He is also thoroughly depressed about the state of the Liberal party, in so far as it is possible for him to be depressed, and so thinks it more important than ever that an effective centre party is recruited and developed. He has prepared a list of some fifty or sixty names of people he thinks should be approached to extend Jeremy Taylor's Highgate Group and augment its impact. The analysis he offered was quite acute: we have the support of about a dozen MPs, but we have failed to net any of the more recognised mavericks; we have in people like Mears and Middleton senior civil servants who have quite a lot of power in their quiet way – but are naturally and properly bound by their professional responsibilities; we have three first-class economists who miraculously more or less agree; there are a number of interesting theorists among whom he numbers Farrell and myself; and we are particularly strong on the communications side with Trumble, Bill Delahaye and Warner from Fleet Street, Sandra Beeton and Brian Templar from television and Harry Joseph from radio talks, with Jeremy Taylor's own influence in publishing. He ran through a few of the other regular attenders, assessing their value. 'What we clearly need, though,' he said, 'is someone in real authority in every aspect of political activity: people who have served on commissions, advisory bodies and so on.' I asked would we not be likely to weigh it down with academics? He thought not. 'It's obviously particularly important to attract moderate trade unionists – though there isn't a chance, of course, of getting a really big name.'

Another thing he wants to get to work on is a detailed summary of policies and suggests that Farrell, he and I prepare a draft for the approval and comment of the group as a whole. I agree that this is important because it means that we must square up to those issues where Jeremy and Barbara have seemed to be deliberately vague, the ones in fact that Rachel is always returning to – including Africa and Ireland. I wondered if Bill Delahaye, who has an imaginative eye, shouldn't be included in the inner cadre, but Ellis was doubtful because Bill is sometimes carried away by his own analyses and behaves as though they must happen. Ellis is perhaps slightly disillusioned that, where a number of Bill's prognostications have been accurate, the government has always managed to muddle through.

This shifted the conversation to Bill's novel, which Ellis has been allowed to read. It is apparently scurrilous and now includes a sketch of me and of the Oricellari sisters. Bill's venom is apparently reserved for Connors and people on his newspaper. 'I know,' (Ellis says) 'that Baudelaire said that the more a man cultivates the arts, the less he fornicates, but in Bill's case he's missing the fornication. It would make a lot of difference if he worked up the nerve to screw his secretary. Which, I might add, is not an ignoble ambition.' I explained that I had not had the privilege of meeting her. 'It's getting suspiciously melancholy, though,' said Ellis, 'and Bill is at his most equilibrious when he's being funny. The portrait of you is harmless enough and your Italian ladies are a crazy pair of feminist gangsters. Bill is very wary of

Italians: he regards them all as descendants of the Julian emperors or of the Renaissance princes tutored by Machiavelli (whom he is determined to misunderstand), who make their living these days as gangsters or waiters. And since neither of your friends is a waiter, they must be gangsters.'

There is once again a great deal of talk about coalition with Sir H. Wilson, Heath and the Liberals all putting in a word. Not surprisingly the Liberals are the most ardent for it. And now the still splendid Macmillan has appeared in an authoritative toga advocating, in the dire economic circumstances, a Government of National Emergency.

This at a time when Hugh Cudlipp has revealed that the unbelievable Cecil Harmsworth King had approached Mountbatten, Sir S. Zuckerman and various others with this in mind in 1968. Understandably the noble Earl and Sir Solly were curtly lacking in enthusiasm and without doubt Macmillan's proposal is more soundly based on constitutional principles!

I should have thought that there is not very much in it for the Conservatives at the moment. If the Labour conference depressed a lot of moderates by being almost corrosively left, the Tory conference seemed to me to be arrogantly right. There was a good speech by Heath ('the crunch *has* come') but it was overshadowed by Heseltine waving a broadsword and putting every anvil in sight in peril. Mrs T. was accused of trying to talk over the heads of the party. If this criticism implied that she was doing so intellectually, it suggests a depressing assessment of Conservative intelligence.

It is a rather gloomy autumn with all the to-ing and fro-ing of the IMF investigators and much loaded talk of 'our masters', an ex-governor of the Bank of England forecasting food-rationing before very long and Callaghan castigating the decline in educational standards (how true, O Lord!) and calling for a Great National Debate. (All very well in theory: but it will turn into a Great National Flatulence, rumbling its bellyfull and signifying nothing – which is what is depressing.)

One of the few light notes came from Alistair Cooke reporting that after the television debates between Ford and Carter the American public fear that one of them will win the presidential election!

A note from Rachel this morning who seemed to be rather out of spirits when last I saw her when she was here for a symposium on the European Parliament, which is going to revive the caterwauling of the left when it comes up for consideration in the new year. In spite of the referendum they will not admit defeat. (That would, no doubt, be undemocratic.) They are making a jigsaw and hacking each individual piece to fit without any regard for the pattern or the eventual overall picture.

I've seen too little of her in London, since we haven't coincided at the Highgate meetings because she has been busy at her constituency and now that I've reorganised my teaching programme and commitments, I spend the middle of the week in the flat and the weekends from Friday to Tuesday afternoon here.

It was again rather a depressed letter, noticeable perhaps because Rachel is normally a positive and cheerful woman. I think she misses Oliver quite a lot and may be a little afraid that he does not miss her as much. This is the problem which, after all, she must be aware of among many people we both know where both husband and wife have demanding jobs and are ambitious. There have been quite a few casualties – Connors, myself, Trumble, Ellis, Sandra and Marie White. And some of the other marriages are brittle. Jeremy and Barbara survive better than most with a sort of dispassionate pragmatism. It was an invitation to her place for supper because she says she needs to build up her morale before a new session of Parliament. I shall look forward to it and feel rather flattered.

Tutorials have settled down again and it is something of a relief not to have Candida as a distraction, however resistible. Kent and Lumley come for tutorials together and they seem to be doing each other a lot of good. They complement each other usefully because Lumley has all the intellectual sophistication of his old school, but Kent works more thoroughly and systematically: so Lumley is learning the virtues of attention to detail and Kent is learning to be a little more daring. With any luck, they will both get firsts, which is just as well since I have no exaggerated hopes for any of the others. There is one very nice girl in the second year, quite alarmingly pretty, who is everything that Candida should be and is the daughter of a steel-worker. Four clever freshmen and several more of amiable demeanour.

Connors has been rather efficiently avoiding me since my deplorable act of pandarism: I do not know whether out of becoming discretion, shame, or because his intentions are as disreputable as I fear them to be. Reluctant as I am to do so, I feel that I must look into it. I met Kent and Candida in the street, by chance. She treated me with ostensible disdain from which I shall recover without difficulty, but I was disturbed by the asinine look of delight on Kent's face. It is a delicate situation because he must obviously resent any prying into his private life on my part, but I wonder if she has told him about Connors. Not many of her acquaintances (or his) in London suspect because they have chosen, mercifully, to be circumspect and my own part in the affair, which is hardly a source of self-admiration, has meant that I have not advertised it.

At the moment, Kent's manner and the quality of his work suggest that all is well with him; but if Candida, whom I believe (perhaps unjustly) to have a vividly destructive streak in her, is deliberately playing him along, it might prove damaging. He is a solid, dependable sort of lad who seems to be very calm and steady: but he is also sensitive and I should guess emotionally vulnerable.

A visit from Francesca, unexpected but delightful, who is in Oxford to arrange a fashion show of some kind. She is always very good for my image in the college, is entirely aware of it, and endearingly plays up to what others expect of her. I must confess that when we make fairly rudimentary physical contact I become decidedly aroused. I have sometimes thought of trying to make love to her and I do not think she would be resistant: but she is younger than I am, very beautiful and, I have no doubt, has a wide selection of aspirants. I am afraid that I should fall most foolishly in love with her and then not be able to keep her. I have not, after all, been a conspicuous success in the past. So caution prevails.

It would be much easier with Clodia whom I find also attractive and whose declared approach would be empirical. Both sisters have the uncomfortable knack of talking about the other in a way that suggests the most refined promiscuity, and from Francesca's delicate hints Clodia is causing havoc among my London friends. I don't believe that it is true or I should undoubtedly have been the victim of at least six, out of a possible eleven, confessions.

My book is going badly: largely because it is at that stage where I usually lose enthusiasm and confidence. It is then a matter of struggling on, however badly and unevenly, until the old original pleasure in the task reasserts itself. It gave me the advantage of having something, on my behalf, when I must often seem unbearably complacent, to moan about to Rachel, in case she was really fed up.

As it turned out, she wasn't and it was an extremely happy evening, with just the two of us. I suppose it is to be wondered at that neither of us makes any kind of sexual advance and while the thought may have crossed her mind and has fleetingly passed through mine, it would not occur to either of us to pursue it. She is happily married and I value her friendship. I also quite like Oliver.

She encouraged me about the book and we talked most of the time about America, or about music. There was an inevitable *andante* passage about politics. She thinks that a split in the Labour Party is inevitably only a matter of time and is not at all delighted about it. The leading left-wingers, such as Atkinson, have made it quite clear that they wish to drastically change the attitudes and image of the party, using Conference and the NEC to do so. Rachel, of course, did not need to have the paradox of Cabinet Ministers on the NEC supporting left initiatives, when both Wilson and Callaghan had insisted on their primary loyalty to the government. Most alarming she found the talk which has been intermittent throughout the summer of making the Prime Minister the elected choice of the NEC as representative of the whole party, an obvious attempt by the left to make sure that the Prime Minister, whoever he is, has to take more notice of them, if not be their creature.

Rachel says that Connors has given up and is looking fairly avidly around for some attractive job which will take him out of Parliament and politics.

The distressing news arrived on Saturday of the death of Dimchurch, whom I shall miss with real sadness. Blakemore and I went together to the funeral. So the poor old chap will miss the Centenary Test and I had not returned the *Wisden* I borrowed. I don't know why I should think 'poor old chap': Dimchurch was a deeply contented man who had a pleasant and happy life and who died with an unshaken Christian faith – unless in the very last moments of life something was revealed to change it. A particularly bleak thought, but my own sense of grief was accentuated by an unusually melancholy Blakemore, whose mind, sternly unreligious as ever, was focused upon mortality.

Dimchurch always acknowledged that his had been a life of privilege: a comfortable upbringing in a cathedral town, happy schooldays during which his academic and athletic abilities distinguished him, and a lasting love affair with Oxford. Not in any way ambitious, he settled for quiet scholarship, a gentle chaplaincy and the pursuit of cricket, as a relatively young man: but in later life sometimes reproached himself for not having participated more in the lives of people. He had worked for a short time in an industrial parish and later in a church in one of the grimier London boroughs, where he had adopted liberal politics and some views which were distinctly radical: but in both places he had found that his approach was too cerebral for people who needed religion as an emotional solace and he lacked the gift, however gentle, of being able to be one of his parishioners, without a sense of phoniness. And so he retreated to Oxford, but often felt that he should have tried harder.

I said something of this to Blakemore who dismissed it. 'There are dozens of dedicated young men to do the other kind of work among people who have a variety of emotional counsel at their disposal. Dimchurch was a respectable scholar and admirably suited to minister to young men, often immature, often foolish, who also have their problems, which he understood. I have reason to be grateful to him and so have very many others, even though I was not a co-religionist. One of the weaknesses of the Anglican church has often seemed to me that, unlike the Roman Catholic church and indeed some of the non-conformist sects, it fails to recruit enough clergy from the working class: and so there is often this uneasy sense of condescension and false bon-homie, because of the very nature of the job. I'm grateful that in the academic and legal professions, which I have followed, such dissimulation isn't necessary.'

Blakemore was deeply distressed about the death of Dimchurch; but much more depressed by the suicide of another friend, Guy Walker. I had heard of him as an influential figure in the literary and artistic world; as a gifted administrator: much more notable than Dimchurch was among clerical academics. He encouraged a great many people in his time: editor, executive, and director. Among these, many years ago, was Blakemore – who had subsequently lost touch with him. He had heard of the suicide from Morgan Rice, another friend.

Perhaps because Blakemore is clear-headed and sometimes cold, I was taken aback by his incoherent sadness about the death of Walker. Admittedly, for a man to cut his own wrists is an appalling thing to imagine: but I had always expected Blakemore to hold a stern view of despair. Rice, whom I have met, is anxious to mark the death of Guy Walker and has contacted Blakemore and various others who knew him. Among these is Henry Hasset who is in New York or Washington, wasting his diplomatic sweetness upon academic air. Guy Walker's generosity was obviously extended to a great many disparate people. Rice is a cruel satirist, Blakemore an austere academic and Henry is as serene and baffled as it is possible to be at one moment.

I was sorry to turn down Blakemore's invitation to dine with him. For once, he needed someone's company. I had promised to be at a Highgate meeting in which I was consigned to an active part. Blakemore was unusually harsh: 'I sometimes wonder, Ingestre, that on a day when you must have concentrated at least part of the time upon final things, you can return with such appetite to your political frivolities.'

I refused to take offence.

5

It would be the most splendid opportunity at the right time: a complete and more than welcome change. I'm admirably qualified and, now that I've started thinking about it, I'd enjoy that kind of free-wheeling academic ambience thoroughly. Chance to make of it what I want and to do some writing.

Sandra takes the seat opposite and crosses elaborately those wonderful legs. Oh dear, that hint of a smile at me. Why are women so boring about it always? There has to be the little intimate well-well-I-know, and I-could-and-if-I-would, and if-I-list-to speak. . . . Not boring in bed, though, Sandra. My God, no! It was also refreshing to be told not to expect to make a regular thing of it. (Perhaps I didn't meet her expectations entirely. I don't know. She seemed to be ecstatic.) And she said: as and when the mood takes us. Yet now delicate *oeillades* that signify. . . .

Ingestre to serve from the Royal Box end. Everyone more or less cock-a-hoop because of the reception of the first three pamphlets, especially J. Taylor who says they are even selling well. That is surprising; must be more thinking liberals about than anyone guessed. Taylor and Barbara on 'Today' as the William Powell and Myrna Loy of progressive reaction; then Barbara on 'PM' and on LBC. Now talk of a late-night television interview with both of them. (Sandra full of professional integrity and televisory importance: 'Of course I know them all on "Tonight" and "Panorama", Jeremy, but I have no influence. And I couldn't use it even if I had, if you get me. That's not what it's about, is it?' 'Absolutely not.' Wonder what it *is* about then. I should have thought precisely that sort of thing.) Best of all though the pamphlets were mentioned on a programme about Parliament by a couple of respected backbenchers in a highly complimentary exchange, both of whom have nothing to do with the Highgate Group. Taylor's amplitudo has taken a great turn for the better. Still I must not take the piss in case he might notice. And he is on the board of trustees setting up this appointment at Lamberhurst. And . . . yes. And he is also Candida's Daddy. That must be resolved in as gentle and benign a way as possible. But the girl. . . . I don't know: the tiny streak of the whore is becoming dominant and possessing. Worrying. . . .

Ah me, as they say! Arguments for and against written constitution. Hailsham the other day. Ingestre urbane and acute. Conscientiously radical and quite amusing. Draft of the Highgate position. Sigh. Deep, bloody sigh. I must be careful of him and his conscience though, because he could put the word about and if I don't keep Candida happy (as indeed she deserves to be), she might go running to him. Then all his sub-Round-Table instincts would come walloping to the surface and . . . Well spoken, Roger. Hear, hear.

It is too good a chance to miss. The money is good and lots of spare time for the other perks that would certainly accrue: American tours, lectures, obviously all over the Community itself. Bit of well-judged punditry. Sandra would be useful there. And so would Templar though we are not exactly blood-brothers. And Harry Joseph in radio talks.

Wink at Sandra. Ah good. The old black-nylon thigh reflex. Thank you, Delicious.

I have all the credentials for it after all. Fluent French, German and Italian, some Spanish and Russian; teaching experience at school and university here and in three different campuses in America; excellent record over Europe (where I have friends and a reliable reputation); political skill. Other trustees? Three British altogether. Taylor, I suppose, because of years of work on educational advisory councils and of course an impeccable European. . . .

Oh, get on with it, Roger! Bloody constitutional reform! Make haste while there's still a constitution to mess about with; of the kind we know and love, that is.

I have had quite enough of it. Though it was probably not wise to confess as much. Rachel Bailey looks pale but is always interesting. Tired I should think. Always appreciative of Ingestre's little ironies; always appreciative of Ingestre. I wonder. Surely not. If Daphne ever spoke the truth in her tarty life. . . . Barbara in a black dress more elegant even than usual. Little tilt of the perfect mouth. Agh! I am bored out of my mind with it all. The whole political fan-dance that conceals a raddled, diseased body. Old bitch gone in the teeth, all right.

Primary topics for argument . . . all premises based upon the survival of the monarchy . . . written constitution and the involvement of the public in debate . . . electoral reform and preferred systems, public education. . . . (If a centre party is ever formed will electoral reform be to its advantage. Moral principle must obtain! Well spoken, Roger, hear, hear!) Direct elections to European Parliament, obviously we favour some form of proportional representation. . . . (Winning absent-minded smile from Marie White; long distance, opaque. Ah, the old tempting spread and crooning voice. . . . No.) House of Lords. . . . Sacrosanctity of Parliamentary parties. Representatives not delegates. Good old Burke. . . . Tell it to our National Executive, Roger. . . . Fulford points out that the National Front could expect a few seats under PR. . . . Obvious, but a frisson. . . .

NEC came out against expenditure cuts and Big Jim said to have stalked out of meeting. Rachel worried but didn't know what had happened. Immediate effect on £. Of course, they've argued that the *Sunday Times* piece about an international agreement that it should settle at one dollar fifty did the damage. Always these days we speak with two voices: Castle and Mackintosh last Saturday on Westminster spot. No question of two Tories. To balance. No need for them. We've already got the factional delegate floating in the air.

235

Ingestre says we must distinguish between political issues and constitutional arguments. Preconcerted consideration. Trumble in leathery voice suggests political argument is the blood and guts of constitutional issues. Constitution and the unions. Zowee! Taylor doesn't drink very much and Barbara hardly at all: but always a generous supply. Tennis-court heads as the argument flicks up and down the room. No, badminton. Huge effort to make the shuttlecock travel at all. And all to what purpose? Oh yawn. (Stifled.) Trumble and Burke, the old music-hall team: abstract liberty, like other abstractions, is not to be found. Laughter and wagging of heads. Sandra claps her hands and reshuffles the admirable limbs. Ingestre looks youthfully rueful. Where's Delahaye? Very wary of Delahaye. Suspects about Candida and me, at the very least and I think if he could catch me on the hip would do so. Wants her himself, perhaps. And ineffectual. Would make the sort of snide innuendo that might cause trouble. Better to tell Taylor myself. But what about the high moral performance in such a job. Hey, Anthony! It's time you made a contribution. Can feel Delahaye's unfriendly mind on the back of my neck; his eyes surely well up Sandra Beeton. Telepathy works! Thank you, Sandra, again. I remember. Flicker of a smile.

I wish life was as simple as the ancient and charming intricacies of the transferable vote and Middleton (trust a bloody scientist!) obfuscates the entire issue by bringing up the alternative vote. That is a clear mind at work! Who says there's such a thing as scientific method? Oh Gawd. . . . No the trouble is it's not simple and is never going to be simple. . . . *I'd call it love if love/didn't take so many years/but lust too is a jewel.* . . . Where did I hear that? Except that it's not: because we haven't shaken off the idea that people of sensibility need to love before they can enjoy a therapeutic fuck. Marie knows something of what it's about and most of these people think she's unhappy: and Sandra, well there's a lot to be said for Sandra – however much is left enigmatic. . . . I suppose I've always cherished some adolescent and imbecile

236

daydream of some really young girl like Candida, as beautiful and as randy, can be simply that without any emotional guarantees. Is that so cynical? Well, by Taylor's standards it would be. Catching, suddenly, Barbara's eye . . . she smiles. I can never tell about her. . . . And that ridiculous story of Trumble and tearing open her blouse or whatever the hell it was. . . . She was probably smiling about some constitutional irony that I omitted to hear. No, she would not be amused about Candida, and 'Daddy' in his rational way would be furious.

Can't help wondering where she found so much inspiration: and so *much* noise which is exciting. (I'm not sure why it should be.) Warwick was a good idea, with a car: anything away from Oxford, or here, when the weekend was to be consecrated to the one true end. (Don't think that's quite right.) I wish, though, that she would not try to be intelligent about politics. She's quite bright and very dim all at the same time. The real worry is this determination that it must last. . . . No. No help from Ingestre: certainly not after the initial deception, for which he has not forgiven me or himself. Was he so *terrified* of her? Surely not: not with that Italian Venus in the brown dress I saw. Fff. . . . The bliss of those hips. 'Who the hell is *that*? 'An old friend of mine: well, the daughter of a friend. . . .' And I suspect, like Daphne, the kind of woman who has a spidermate attraction for Ingestre: and who frightens me. Haven't been introduced, so it's academic. Though I gather several of the Highgate mob know her. . . . I wonder how much of what one hears is fantasy from either Ellis or Delahaye (sick). Not entirely. . . . Some scraps from Marie and Sandra. Dismissive. Naturally. Errr. . . .

. . . Yes, Jeremy, I agree that it is best deferred until we've discussed Roger's third point about the Lords.

Oh Christ, all the ancient argument and de Tocqueville: who would create an aristocracy? And the Bryce Report on Second Chamber Reform from *Nineteen Eighteen* said as much and more. All the old points of non-partisan wisdom

237

and experience fully represented for purposes of reviewing and critically examining the real legislation in the Commons – with no right of revision. *Unless* elected. Mind, Heffer and his Magnificent Seven and Five-Eighths are looking into Lords reform out of which will emerge a matter of quite automatic socialist conscience. Then who and how, etc. Who is to do all this superfine electing and how is it to be done? Once again, the traditional liberal solution to the cricket-ball in the nettle-bed. Make it a matter for public debate: are the members of the second chamber to be nominated by the first and then elected by the public; or elected by the first chamber, thus reflecting support for the existing majority in the lower house; or nominated in some other way – so many from the Church, the Arts, Science and Industry, the Unions, the City, the Academic world, the Legal and Medical professions, the Media (Ugh! Festering bloody word, again!) and so on; or shall we just cast bones and ponder over the entrails of pigeons in Trafalgar Square?

. . . Before we discuss the whole complicated business of obligation to conscience or conference, Jeremy, should we not perhaps glance at devolution. I know it's a vexed question and that probably none of us here feel deeply about it, but it *is* a constitutional issue. And as Roger has pointed out this other matter is probably more political.

Of course. The inevitable 'of course'. I should have known and would have known if I had been at the last meeting (or read the summary) that the Highgate cardinals were going to emit the appropriate colour smoke on devolution in a separate bull, in the light of what emerged in Parliamentary discussion and in the national debate.

So the evil hour will not be averted. Well, it is in my own interest to impress Jeremy and Barbara, and indeed Ingestre, by sincerity and keenness, so let's take the cue from Edmund Burke (and neutralise Trumble). And let Rachel go evasively first.

It's all much too late. *Forms* (de Tocqueville said) *become more necessary as the government becomes more active and*

powerful and private persons become more indolent and feeble.
By their nature, democratic nations stand more in need of forms
than other nations and respect them less. The leaden bureaucracy is already socketed in to leathern arse-holders. (Wait,
ghost of de Tqv., and see what Abu Benn Stansgate and his
increasing tribe can dream up out of their wilderness. Red
ties only at the Sahara Hilton (nationalised). All too late. We
are printing forms like bank notes and the IMF inspectors,
an uncompromising-looking *équipe*, are at the door. The
central clearing banks cannot hold.

Oh this is a wilderness. But I can't clearly, in all conscience,
stay in office – if that's what it is. Servant, delegate, representative, public conscience approaching everything with
his mouth always open; politician. Indolent, too, yes. It
is surely human to want moments of pure indulgence which
harm no one and suggest the *futility* of pain, without denying
its existence. And I think I could serve in the Europa
College, Lamberhurst, Kent, England: Principal – Anthony
Connors. . . .

Must listen to what Rachel is saying because she is smiling
winningly at me. It'll come off the top of my head, as usual:
but there aren't many complaints. I haven't let the constituents down. For what it was worth! Oh, Sandra: not
now. . . . Women have a ridiculous sense of humour. . . .

*

The Dazzling Pilgrimage again

As Mrs de Wagram waited in the hospitality room of the
television studios for the luminaries of 'Soul Search' to
arrive, she felt mildly subservient to perspiration. This was,
after all, one of the most controversial think-programmes on
any network and its sales in the United States, Canada and
Australia testified to its influence throughout the world upon
Anglophone intelligence.

This hormonic overproduction was natural in anyone at
such a great moment in a lifetime's crusade: there was a
little anxiety and perhaps a little doubt. Mrs de Wagram did

not enjoy perspiration or waiting, but it was a great opportunity. Psychobolism was about to take off: and not in any vulgar sense.

A golden-haired child of eighteen or so came back from intense communion with the producer of the programme, Branston Simcox, to offer her another drink. '*We*,' said the little (in fact quite substantial) angel, 'will be ready for you soon. It's just that Branston has to put a Belfast Confucianist through his paces. . . . Not of course that we are going to put *you* through any paces, Mrs de Wagram. But you will appreciate how awkward the Irish are these days.'

'Brandy, thanks,' said Mrs de Wagram.

'*You*,' said the angel, 'will be interviewed by Linda Woodchuck, as we promised in our letter.'

Mrs de Wagram had received no such promise in a letter but accepted another large brandy in recompense without giving away the tactical point. She thought, a little sadly, that she was now too old to really enjoy the whole confidence trick, at just the moment when it was catching on. The spiritual swamp of the sixties was drying out under the merciless cosmic glare of the seventies. And thirst was dawning in the parched souls of a new generation. Was it after all a trick? Mrs de Wagram had never been spiritually moved. She had been entered by a certain number of men, sometimes simulating pleasure; she had enjoyed a few unreliable women. She had always been exploited remorselessly until she had discovered, in desperation, a means of exercising power over others. Then the unusual Gina had come along and allowed Mrs de Wagram's power-fantasies a glimpse of realisation. Still vague dreams and silky embraces: until Gina said unexpectedly:

'You know that man that does spiritual things on the telly that are controversial?'

'I'm sure that there are many who arrogate a form of spirituality: in word games and Rugby League, for example,' said Mrs de Wagram.

'No; don't be silly! Branston Simcox, who does "Soul

Search", a fearless glimpse into the nation's spiritual health and that. He's a friend of my friend Lucius Spiedermann, the popular publisher. . . .'

'I thought we had agreed you were devoting yourself to the almost Right Honourable Cornflour. . . .'

'Ooooh Christ! I knew I'd forgotten something. He *is* Right Honourable, as from today. They've had a sort of piss-up.'

'Am I to understand by that phrase a "celebration"?'

'No! A fuck-up, then. If it makes it plainer. People resigning and shouting at the Prime Minister. Augustine is promoted and recommended for the Privy Council. . . .'

'Gina. . . .!'

'Don't interrupt. I was talking about getting the Church on telly. My friend Lucius can interest his friend Branston Simcox, for whom he has performed certain past favours, in *our* spiritual pilgrimage.'

And so here Mrs de Wagram was, sitting beside a pretty though obvious heterosexual, sweating and asking herself if she could possibly any longer perpetuate the long and sometimes bitter deception. Swing-doors flung open and Linda Woodchuck was dominantly before them. The golden little girl faded discreetly towards a patent clip-board, as Linda Woodchuck sat down, crossing the long elegant legs that had made her a sex symbol for thinking actors and bank clerks up and down the British Isles.

'This is an amazing spiritual progress that you have to recount, Mrs de Wagram,' she said with blazing teeth.

'It's unusual,' said Mrs de Wagram, cautiously.

'I can understand that you will be wary of the brash and insensitive approach, Mrs de Wagram,' said Linda Woodchuck. 'But Branston will not tolerate that on "Soul Search". You can relax with us. When did you first realise you were Psychobolic? Of course you know that for the public we'll already have a little bit of film with me in voice-over explaining what Psychobolism is. Incidentally is it Psycho*bol*ism or Psy*cho*bolism?'

241

'We've always called it the Psychobolic Church,' said Mrs de Wagram.

Linda Woodchuck and the pretty little girl both wrote it down. The interview proceeded in the same atmosphere of calmly credulous unbelief, for which Mrs de Wagram could not blame her inquisitioner. All the deceptions of her elaborate and successful religious masquerade, the mockery and folly that she had nourished and indeed engendered, the poor old lonely souls that she had duped, with the aid of out-of-work free-lances and unfrocked clergymen, came before her, as phantoms before Richard of Gloucester towards the end of Shakespeare's play. And Mrs de Wagram doubted herself. Yet at that moment of doubt, the Psychobolic Church was being offered (perhaps by a hand, a will, a purpose: unseen, unknown, unimagined) an impetus that would alert and inspire so many viewers at home switched on to the relevant channel. A light euphoria gripped Mrs de Wagram for the first time in many years. Was it possible that she had been right after all?

She was led to the studio, spoken to out of darkness by the voice of Branston Simcox, whom she never met, but whom she saw, on transmission, piercingly peering from the screen in her living room. 'Soul Search' presented the Psychobolic Church with merciless scepticism. Mrs de Wagram went to bed and cried herself to sleep, realising that her private sham was now public knowledge. Would it want its money back?

By the middle of the next day the telegrams and telephone calls started coming in; followed in the course of the week by a deluge of mail. Bereft, desperate. Lucrative. Mrs de Wagram's head began to ache badly. Gina had already moved.

'I thought it wise to meet here,' said Lepidus Pounce. 'Nobody would expect to see either of us in the central YMCA, at the same time, swimming.'

'I'm sorry,' said Branston Simcox. 'I didn't recognise you.'

'The moustache and dark glasses,' said Pounce.

'No. . . . You're taller than I remember.'

'Aha!' said Pounce, with the fierce wicked grin that had terrified so many literary dinner tables. 'Lifts! I have had lifts built into my swimshoes. It's detail that matters in our business.' He glared brilliantly. 'You've heard from Cornflour?' he snapped.

'I have,' said Simcox tersely. 'His new responsibilities for aesthetic probity within the same department have brought him a seat in the Cabinet and more power to our respective elbows.'

Lepidus Pounce smiled, wickedly.

'We need only an expert on the visual arts with similar ideas to our own and we can begin to lay plans.'

'Have you anyone in mind?'

'Archibald Locust, who has also a forceful presence.'

'I agree we need expertise in that area, before we can make effective moves against the art establishment as well as the Arts Council and the BBC.'

'Moves in relation to,' said Pounce subtly, 'never against. That would suggest personal animus. What about the independent television companies?'

'Cornflour thinks that "Celebrity Squares" and "Sale of the Century" do an enormous amount for Morale and there is a high level of public decency on all the commercial channels. Anyway, Pounce, it isn't what really bothers *us*, is it? We are inclining to serious aesthetic pollution, as I see it.'

'Things written outside the English tradition,' said Pounce.

'Portentous and personality-cult journalism in the Media,' said Simcox. 'Stuff that is reflective rather than crusading.'

'Experimental literature,' said Pounce.

'Anything too successful outside certain precise limits.'

'We'll start making a list of names and institutions, as soon as I've contacted Locust,' Pounce rapped.

'One thing, Pounce. What about music. How do we move against . . . in relation to the musical hierarchy?'

'Difficult,' said Pounce. 'It's difficult to prove moral subversion and the undermining of public decency in simple terms of noise. Anyway,' he said as he plunged, smiling fiendishly, into the pool, 'I'm tone deaf.'

Lucius Spiedermann brooded morosely over the labyrinthine journey that had taken him to the nerve centre of public decency, without too much concern for the irony of the situation. Phrases such as 'When in Rome . . .', 'Render unto Caesar . . .' and the one about poachers and gamekeepers drifted to the surface of his mind. He was keenly aware of the hypocrisy of Cornflour, whom he must acknowledge as his lord and master and who had once been a client. Now the roles were reversed and if Lucius Spiedermann had ever heard of Juvenal, he would have found solace in the great satirist's resentment of the client's status throughout the history of our Western civilisation. As it was, he could only comfort himself with the revival of his almost extinct hopes of a peerage.

But the poison cloud of gloom that had settled over him was a distillation from the cruel sea which had swept him, just at the moment when his odyssey seemed to be ending happily, into the Scylla-and-Charybdis territory of the Borgedici sisters. Lucius was profoundly sorry that he had ever set eyes on the bloody sirens and used their Roman network with such open-minded trust and condescension. He had even helped them set up Orgies International Inc. And this was the thanks he got. That was the trouble with foreigners: always fighting and using violence. Lucius Spiedermann had aimed for the top by the use of guile and subtlety, playing only upon the latent frailties in human nature and not attempting to coerce or menace anyone into feudal submission. Lucius Spiedermann's Welsh background made him implacably anti-feudal, though he had never been tempted by that particular brand of garrulous fraternity favoured in the valleys.

Ambition was not of itself wicked, he thought. He had hurt no one who had not wished to hurt himself, or exploited anyone who had not *wanted* to mortgage her physical charms in return for a little security and something extra. How many politicians, newspaper executives, business tycoons, top administrators could say that in the capitalist countries? And it had all been honest and above board: not for Lucius Spiedermann back-handers for this or that favour, or concession, or contract. Lucius had never wheeled or dealed: he had simply recognised a basic human demand and supplied what was wanted. When he thought of what it took to get to the top in Russia, or for that matter in the United States, let alone in the Mafia, Lucius didn't see himself as a very serious sinner and wondered why the gods had been so bloody Greek with their gifts.

The renowned frown of the fearless old radical hoplite, Tertius Barebones, drove a crevasse of discontent between his eyes that caused his spectacles to slip and somehow intensify the great glare of concentrated outrage.

'Hoke has gone too far,' he said. 'Industrially, culturally and economically. The sale of the Royal Parks to the Caliph of Fqwat is in itself a betrayal not of the prochronistic impediment that is the Monarchy, but of the workers' own legitimate heritage; now this new concept of a wage-glacier that will consolidate as it flows, but is always there to tap, is so much economic day-dreaming. And all in return for a reduction in the VAT on all do-it-yourself kits, reclaimable on the production of a certificate issued by government officials who have ascertained that *it* was, even so, personally done! As for WAMCO, the Workers and Managers Congress of Optimism: it is simply the Corporate State in disguise. And the restoration of *Workers' Playtime, Music While You Work* and *Workers' Merry-go-Round* is an endorsement of opiate pap which is the lotus fruit of capitalist exploitation. I have resigned!'

'What about Bert Flexion?' asked his wife.

'Bert Flexion has not resigned. He is staying in the Cabinet to represent the conscience of the left and to be a thorn in Hoke's side.'

'Is he!' said Mrs Barebones with something of an ironic sigh.

'Yes. I can only feel free to tell the workers of this country the truth outside the Cabinet,' said Tertius Barebones. 'The truth of the terms which have delivered this land of Shakespeare, Turner and Edward Elgar into the hands of international computing machines. I will tell the workers that they have been consigned to a state of permanent enphytotic debt.'

'Oh dear,' said his wife.

Griff Crabbe of the powerful FCSAKE union (The Federated Consolidation of Static and Kinetic Employees) stirred more sour cream into his borsch thoughtfully. He had presented a draft of the latest conditions agreed by union chiefs, if there was to be another phase of the Patriotic Covenant. In his quiet-spoken, blunt way he considered it a masterpiece of bargaining with its terms of absolute equality between Static and Kinetic workers; compensation with bonus pay for loss of earnings during strike action; payment of workers' fares to and from the holiday resort of their choice, or compensation in lieu; a controlling voice for workers on the content of all newspapers, television and radio schedules et cetera – 51 per cent of such workers to be drawn from manual grades; all hospital and education boards to consist of 51 per cent manual workers; tax concessions for blue-collar workers only.

Griff was too much of a realist, after his upbringing in the hard school, his roasting in the capitalist crucible as he liked to put it, to expect to get away with all these conditions: they were merely ground for negotiation that he had thus promulgated: but he knew that Hoke Dick was in no position to be high-handed and, with resignations and defections from his Cabinet, needed very badly to prove to the people that his Patriotic Covenant had the backing of the great unions.

A dark blue Rolls drew up outside Elwyn Poinsettia's Hampstead villa. He slipped into it almost surreptitiously. The liveried chauffeur closed the door with an expensive click. He spoke over the intercom:

'Drinks are in the compartment on the left, sir. Mr Split instructed me to prepare champagne cocktails. The compartment is refrigerated, of course. There is a selection of cassette films – of various genres – in the right-hand cabinet.'

As they purred almost soundlessly to the Fergusson Jungfrau building in the City of London, Elwyn Poinsettia sipped a delicious cocktail and watched a short erotic movie, purely out of curiosity. He found it amusing.

They drew up at a concealed entrance to the great Financial and Industral Empire and he proceeded in a succession of luxurious and silent lifts, which seemed not to be moving, to the office of Anaximander Split.

By the time he was in the tycoon's dark and enigmatic presence, even the suave Elwyn Poinsettia was apprehensive, though not discomposed. He could hardly believe his ears as the calm, rather flat voice described to him the already constructed apparatus for taking over the affairs of the nation, the consortium of powerful men of destiny which included Lord Steroid, Mungo Starveling and Reynard Tarsus, not to mention Split himself and the support of key civil servants in the most significant departments.

He gathered that he was being offered a place in this elite compact, dedicated to the salvation of the country and of civilisation as we knew it. He understood, too, that the price of his inclusion was resignation from the administration of Sir Hoke Dick which must inevitably precipitate the fall of the government. Elwyn Poinsettia was flattered at this estimation of his own importance within the Cabinet. He asked for time to consider.

'If they think that I am going to run away from the blood and sand of the fight, when the going is heavy, then they must think again, my boy,' said Sir Hoke Dick. 'When the scent of battle is in my nostrils, Augustine, my sinews are stiffened for action and greyhound-like I await the imminence of the deadly breach through which I shall lead my faithful cohorts, bloody, unbowed, rejoicing in the ablest of officers who lead from the vanguard.'

Sir Hoke rose from his desk and impressively clapped a hand upon Augustine Cornflour's shoulder.'

'After the treachery of Poinsettia,' he said, 'I am obliged to reshuffle my Ministers. It gives me the opportunity to advance you, my boy. And I rejoice at it. Your enterprise, flair and loyalty has impressed me at Morale and Public Decency: I am moving you to the new Department of the Interior which incorporates the old Home Office, Social Services and your own portfolio.'

'Prime Minister,' said Augustine, 'I feel very proud and very humble.'

Sometimes Ruth Tweed wished that the Napoleonic propensities that she always believed to be latent in her husband had remained untapped. The masterful energy of recent weeks (since the Stokes resignation) was, as far as she was concerned, an essay in received exhaustion: she had not expected to find herself on a political helter-skelter of such gigantic size and it was a little breathtaking. Having always regarded Rubicon Tweed as a considerable success, Ruth was now reconciling herself to his grander dreams and expectations. There was no difficulty at all in managing the hostess side of things and she was admirably able to keep guests interested in the off-moments, when Rubicon was pressing home an advantage.

She was looking at herself in a mirror as she reflected on these things and saw there a very attractive woman who had once been a very attractive girl: a little heavier now after child-bearing, the waist a little thickened: but still a good figure and legs that seemed (she could never think why) to make a lot of men quite foolish. As an undergraduate, Ruth had had a few affairs and then, working in London, one big one with Augustine Cornflour. Once she had married Rubicon, she had been entirely faithful and had forgotten her good second to become the mother of his children. She hadn't cared at all whether he was to be successful: but was of course pleased, year by year, as he achieved more and more. Then success had started to matter to both of them and she had been eager for it. Now she wondered what might have happened if she had chosen, as well she might in the present climate, to pursue her own career with the dedication that she had given to supporting his. Probably not as much: but it would have been hers. Ruth was still recovering from the shock of meeting Augustine Cornflour again at her own dinner-table and from the ease and the apparent inevitability of what had followed. She did not think that Rubicon would suspect, but she was resolved not to go on with it, however much it restored a kind of youthful excitement to her. And now Augustine, then a schoolmaster in South London, was also a success. Very much a success and a politician on whom Rubicon and Naxy Split seemed to pin enormous hopes.

After ten or so years of increasingly important people, Ruth wondered if she was simply deceiving herself in imagining that she would have been happy in comfortable, sensibly paid obscurity: the wife of a teacher, or a GP, or any of the thousands of decent, peaceable men who did the hidden work that people thought was interesting enough not to deserve sympathy. She was unashamedly middle class. Given such a husband, she might have modestly taken up a fairly interesting job of her own, without ever having to give up the marvellous sense of satisfaction in a husband and family.

This was not disloyal to Rubicon. No: she had now merely been unfaithful to him. And she did not even know whether he would care. There had been years ago a gentle, rather humorous boy with whom she had played tennis, called Tom. He had become a clergyman: very serious and sincere. And even *he* was now a bishop. . . .

Catherine Borgedici and Nicolo Machiavelli looked at each other with the same unwavering feline wariness, showing no nervousness.

'Messire,' she said to him. 'There is surely no point in taking by force what can be won by guile and confidence.'

She spoke in Italian, using that wonderful voice-over technique much favoured by the imaginative cinema which affords enviable opportunities for face-acting. Machiavelli's portrait stared back, the enigmatic smile not flickering an inch. It was almost absurd that she expected the eyes to shift and the lips to waver.

'I've studied since I've been here three London syndicates, Messire,' Catherine said, barely able to keep the sneer out of her voice. 'They are pathetic! I've even been down to Soho and looked at the organisation of our fellow Italians. It would make you weep. Now, tell me: should I bring in my people and just take what is up for grabs? Or am I right in playing for the political stakes? Suppose I set Lucrezia on this Cornflour? With her technique, we have almost already a voice in the European summits!'

Unmoved, the great Machiavelli returned her passionate glance with his eternally canny diplomacy. The trance fell upon her.

'Child,' she heard the dry voice clearly across the time-space interval, 'even now there are arguments between historians and historians and philosophers and philosophers

and historians and philosophers about what I am communicating to mankind. All I want to say to you is this: sometimes
a cultural degenerate blooms into a genuine revolutionary.
Marx and Engels were dreamers from the North, *bambina*.
They knew it was important to relate: but they forgot
about connecting. Be eclectic, Katerina: learn even from
democracy.'

The dry voice faded, once more, into eternity. Catherine
Borgedici sank back into her swivel-chair, her lips parted,
clutching her own shoulders, her thighs wanton. Within
seconds she was sleeping deeply.

'I didn't know you were a painter,' said Josephine Cornflour
to Rufus Bushchat. 'I thought you were a thinker's thinker.
At least that's what Uncle Gustin says you are. That is quite
beautiful. What is it?'

'I only do it for a hobby. It's nice of Gustin to call me a
thinker. I'd say I was a theoretician's theoretician: but it's
pleasant to be dignified in that way. Please thank him for me.
It's called *Susannah without Elders*. As you can see the
central figure is merely sketched in a cool, evening background
of innocence where there are hidden forces of desecrative
vigour that she isn't aware of. Yet.'

'How consistent you are, Rufus. It's a bit like apolitical
politics, isn't it?'

'You're terribly acute, you know?'

'Thank you.' Josephine paused. 'Why is Susannah only
sketched in?'

'You might say that she has been painted out. I cannot
arrive at the perfect female form. I have to do it from memory,
of course, and it's years since I attended a Polytechnic life
class.'

'I don't think my hair's quite long enough,' said Josephine,
studying the painting at close range, 'but I'd be happy to pose
for you. I think it's a really inspired conception.'

It was not exactly a surprise that he was nervous about

accepting her offer; and on the first occasion, when she took off her wrap, he caused her to compose herself from a distance and talked, while sketching, of political abstractions. When he had grown more accustomed to her nakedness, however, he approached closer, discoursing more about aesthetics (owing much to Santayana). Eventually he touched her and became bold enough to adjust her body with his own hands. That was all.

On the day that *Susannah without Elders* was finished, Josephine was delighted by the delicate representation of herself bathing which he had caught. There was that hint in the luxuriance of the garden shrubbery of lust and menace: but her own innocence was irreproachable. She was standing admiring the picture when to her amazement Rufus began a hymn to her bosom, sinking to his knees and begging to be allowed to mould it. His creative fervour was turning to sculpture, he told her. Josephine stroked his thick hair.

It was only because he knew the purpose of his purchase that Rufus Bushchat felt uncomfortable as he entered the Maple Street Fresh 'n' Freeze to buy twelve pounds of the pinkest possible jelly. He had thought of blancmange, but doubted that it would hold as well. The technical problems of dissolving the substance into the mould were considerable: but Rufus Bushchat, his busy mind for the moment empty of political theory, was concerned only with the absurd business of putting down package after package of jelly before the unsmiling Oriental woman at the check-out. He was able to pick off the shelf thirty-nine packets of strawberry flavour: but was obliged to make up the quota with raspberry. It might lend a richer flush to the finished article and it occurred to him that if it began to lose its exquisite form, he might (in the circumstances of the necessary intimacy that had gone into the making) ask Josephine for one of her brassieres. She had been wonderfully co-operative and had never once assumed that he might be making sexual advances.

He began to think about a full torso, after the manner of the fifth-century example in the Louvre. . . .

As he was laying down his packages of jelly at the appropriate till, however, he became aware of a devastatingly calm man with a high pale forehead, receding hair and sunken, sardonic eyes watching him from an elevated central *caisse* with grim humour.

Rufus Bushchat was allowed to pay and pass out of the Fresh 'n' Freeze precincts, only to find himself suddenly among four large men. One of them, the most senior, proffered a black folder with an identification card.

'Walcott, sir,' he said. 'Special Branch. Would you mind coming along of us to help us with a few enquiries in the national interest, sir?'

He nodded to the calm man at his perch above them: but he had, mysteriously, already vanished.

'Wynstanley?' said Arnold Espadrille. 'You needn't concentrate any more on Bushshchchat.'

He emphasised the sound.

'I've had him taken in,' he explained. 'By Special Branch. He will be transferred to us later. Do you know he was buying inordinate quantities of pink jelly . . .'?

Poinsettia gone, Barebones unthrilled to the marrow, desperate amalgamations of ministries and the untowardly rapid promotion of young whizz-kids, which would never have happened in his day? Warrington Stokes spluttered while lighting his pipe. But it was serious really.

Oh my goodness: the walls were a-tumbling down and poor old Hoke was seeing everything come about his ears in tatters and towers were falling all over Gaza and mere anarchy was ending with a whimper, for tomorrow the struggle and few friends and many books.

*

'Perhaps,' said Stanley Mears, 'we could pursue the conversation over lunch one day.'

'That would be very pleasant,' said Clodia Oricellari. 'I should be interested to hear what your wife thinks.'

'Oh . . . ah. Ellen finds it rather difficult to get away in the middle of the day, unless something very unusual has occurred. We live in Wimbledon and she has to collect the children at various times from school, so it becomes a little awkward for her to pop up and down to London . . .'

'But isn't Wimbledon in London?'

'Oh yes. It's a London postal district but . . . I'm sorry, it's just a manner of speaking. I think quite a few people who once lived near the centre, and who've moved out into one of the suburbs, talk about "going up to London".'

'Perhaps we could have dinner in that case. Or do you have trouble finding baby-sitters?'

'They *are* a bit of a problem. But I'm often at the Ministry quite late: in fact when things are hectic I sometimes stay the night. If there's a major debate which involves the Minister, or something of that sort. It occurs to me: does your work ever take you to Brussels?'

'Not often. But I think it will from time to time.'

'Much the same in my case. It would be rather pleasant if we coincided.'

'It's always reassuring to meet people one knows in other . . . embassages.'

'I'm afraid that's too grand a word to describe our little lot. Perhaps we could arrange something, then?'

'If the opportunity presents himself, I've no doubt we could.'

'I have a late night next week, in fact. On Wednesday . . .'

'The Ambassador has a formal dinner party, I'm afraid.'

'No. Wait a second. I am an idiot. It's Thursday. Of course, Thursday.'

'And on Thursday I've arranged to go to the theatre.'

'What a shame. I suppose it's rather short notice.'

'Ah, here's Roger. We were talking, *caro*, about the way marriage is portrayed in Italian films. . . .'

'I'm so glad you could come tonight,' said Hugh Middleton.

'It was kind of you to ask me,' said Clodia Oricellari. 'Your wife is a remarkable cook.'

'Oh, *cordon bleu*! She's very keen.'

'She must be extremely well organised in order to look after a family, run a medical practice and still have time for such demanding hobbies.'

'Well, it's not a general practice. She works in a hospital. But you're quite right. I don't know how she fits it all in. I find my job at the Ministry of Defence quite enough. Of course, the disadvantage is we have very little time together.'

'That's a great pity.'

'Yes: but it's a standard problem in modern marriages, isn't it? When both partners work, I mean. God forbid I should be one of these Victorian throwbacks who expected my wife to throw up a perfectly good career in order to minister to me and the brats. We go very much our own ways. I think marriage these days has to be a partnership rather than a mystic union, don't you? With a lot of give and take. That's the way we run ours.'

'Obviously very successfully since she cooks so well for you. I'm *sorry*! Was that your leg?'

'No . . . ah . . . must have been the table. I don't suppose you have very much free time, do you, Clodia? It must be pretty exacting.'

'Only in the sense that a diplomatist is always expected to be polite.'

'God, yes. I'd hate that. I'm afraid that we rough scientists are not much good at politeness. I imagine the actual business of negotiating must be fun, though, isn't it?'

'It's largely empirical. Something a scientist would understand. Sensible, rational experiment. Trial – and error.'

'Or a really efficient seduction.'

'That's rather a cold approach to something that should be passionate, isn't it? Forgive me, it's my hot Latin temperament showing provocatively.'

'Well, I can tell you one thing. It is certainly *that*! Er . . . Clare's going to a weekend medical thing next Friday. I er . . .'

'So you'll have to look after the children. Are you good at that?'

'That isn't exactly what I had in mind. They stay with my in-laws on these occasions. I . . .'

'That must be a relief. I have the delightful prospect of a weekend at Oxford as Roger Ingestre's guest, and I'm to dine at New College with his friend Robert Blakemore. Do you know him?'

'It's a very interesting museum,' said Clodia Oricellari. 'I suppose you must be an absolutely authentic example of a polymath, Simon.'

'I'm sure I should like to think so,' said Simon Farrell, 'but I think it would be pitching it a little high. I'm lucky enough to have an aptitude for maths as well as for the Classics, I suppose: which is as good a launching pad as one could wish for.'

'It is enviable.'

'Well, you obviously have this command of languages.'

'I owe that to my father. French and English, that is. I speak very bad German because he wouldn't teach it to us.'

'But you speak far more fluent English than your sister. I mean, you're virtually bilingual.'

'It's kind of you to say so. The truth is that Francesca has discovered the charm of not being fluent and finds it technically useful not to understand, sometimes.'

'That's very good!'

'Well, thank you. I've learned a great deal about the Bronze Age Beaker pottery and, what was the other thing . . . ?

'Peterborough ware. So called. That's an interesting

256

model isn't it? Particularly the cross-section that shows the various stratifications. It's a pity the site itself has been allowed to degenerate after the original excavations.'

'It's fascinating. Curiously moving.'

'Shall we go back to my office for a glass of sherry, or something?'

'Thank you.'

'In what sense moving?'

'In the sense that civilisation began because of people banding together on those sites, as you were explaining. I don't know: I wonder what the fragments that remain will tell people about our culture. If there are still people.'

'My goodness, that's a depressing thought. I didn't mean to have *that* effect. Sherry? Gin? Whisky, if you like.'

'Sherry, please.'

'Yes. I'll have some too. There we are.'

'Thank you. That's very good.'

'Good.'

'How do you . . . Simon! This is all very sudden. . . .'

'Oh, Clodia. . . . For Jesus Christ's sake. . . .'

'There. . . . Now is that better? No, please. No more. Let's drink our sherry in a calm and civilised way, shall we? This is hardly an appropriate place and you've taken me very much by surprise.'

'Surely it must have been obvious. That I've fallen very badly in love with you.'

'I'm extremely touched. But I think we must look at this quite calmly. . . .'

'If you knew what that meant. To touch you and hold you like that . . . God! . . .'

'Yes. Well, as I've said already you have surprised me – and I'm a little breathless.'

'Look, Clodia,' said Alan Trumble, 'I don't suppose it's any good beating about the bush. Will you come to bed with me?'

'At least there is nothing sly about your approach, Alan.'

'Or subtle, I suppose. Sorry. It's not intended to be boorish. I just thought it would be better to be honest about it. Well? If you say no, I won't be a nuisance.'

'I didn't think you would be, for a moment. And I am tempted to say yes.'

'But you are going to say no.'

'That is correct.'

'Can I ask why?'

'Because it wouldn't last and I should hurt you. I don't want to do that.'

'Yes. I suppose you're right. And at the moment you think I've just got the drinking in control. Is that it? No, don't answer. That was not a fair question. Thank you, anyway, for almost being tempted. And that's that. Good, then: let's go and have oysters and champagne.'

'Yes. But *I* am taking *you* out. . . . Please?'

'What!' said Roger Ingestre. 'Even Jeremy? My God!'

'That really astonished me, Roger. You will believe that?'

'Good gracious me! You have set them all alight and no mistake. Not that I'm in any way puzzled about that. That must make just about everyone except Alan Trumble. . . . You haven't mentioned him.'

'That's right. I *like* Alan very much. He's excellent company.'

'Drinks too much. But he's a good chap. Is that why you like him: because he hasn't made a pass . . . ?'

'I just find him charming and very quick. Intelligent.'

'My God! I can't get over Jeremy. I'm not asking you to be indiscreet, and anyway I know you well enough to realise it wouldn't be the slightest use: but I'd have given a lot to be behind the arras. . . .'

'Hush! Ellis is coming back.'

'As a good Englishman,' Ellis Fulford said, sitting down, 'I sometimes feel that Life itself is refereed by small balding

Welshmen, who don't seem to care a hoot who wins as long as I don't. That barman is a living and breathing pillar of moral squalor who served two Americans, five Japs and innumerable Teutons in *my* turn. Good health.'

'Cheers,' said Clodia Oricellari. 'It's nice to see you again, Ellis.'

'It is always nice to see you. In fact it is much more than nice, it is a profound spiritual experience, contaminated at the moment only by the intrusive Oxford nonchalance of Ingestre. What do they pay you for in that hotel of invalids, Ingestre? You're never there and you never seem to do any work. When are you going to write another of those spiffing historical thrillers about the Austrian succession? This is a pleasant pub.'

'Your attempts at dalliance, Ellis,' Ingestre said, 'are damn nearly pre-Raphaelite. And Clodia is already exhausted fending off lascivious Highgate Groupers.'

'Ha! I'd never thought of us quite like that before. Moral Disarmament! Somebody must have made that joke before. If so, I'm sorry.'

'How are things in the Liberal Party?'

'Dyspeptic. But a few honest men are better than numbers, as the Lord Protector would have it, warts and all.'

'Did you stay up for the American election?' Ingestre asked.

'My God, did I stay up!' said Clodia. 'I went to three different all-night parties.'

'It's a hard life, the Diplomatic,' said Fulford. 'I have grave forebodings about that gentleman: I get the impression that he enjoys being popular far too much. Poor Ford was absolutely shattered, wasn't he? Did you see that: his wife reading out the statement...?'

'I thought it was rather moving,' said Ingestre. 'I agree, Ellis: Carter seems a lot too folksy and I fear we are going to see and hear far too much of that Lernaean family.'

'What struck me,' said Clodia, 'on British television, was the appearance side by side of Edward Heath and Roy

259

Jenkins. It's ironical, don't you think, that two of the most able men in British politics are relegated to the role of commentator.'

'I thought they both did it pretty well,' said Ingestre. 'There was for once an air of confident authority in a television studio, tempered by civilised tolerance.'

'You know, Roger,' said Fulford. 'Elitism drops from you like the gentle rain from heaven on a Test match. You were born to be the Bilderberg archivist. I thought it was all much too temperate and mandarin. What's happened to the good old knock-about artists like Hailsham Hogg in his prime and Ernie Marples. Or George Brown, indeed! An *auguste* for the people, if ever there was one.'

'I deny the charge of elitism. I disapprove strongly of the principle of Bilderberg. I believe in an open society,' said Ingestre.

'I don't,' said Clodia. 'It seems to me only intelligent that some of the most able and influential men in the Western world should get together every so often to compare notes.'

'The test is,' said Fulford, 'would you like to be one of them?'

'I'm not sure about that. Yes, I think so – with the right kind of experience,' said Clodia.

'Well, I honestly would *not*,' said Fulford. 'And to be fair to Ingestre here, I think All Souls is thin enough air for him. But you couldn't say that for many others of the High-gate mob. Under all those liberal smocks lurk the spirits of Grade-A shuttle togati. Taylor, Farrell, Connors. You've met them all, Clodia, haven't you?'

'Indeed! I don't know Connors . . .'

'Yes, I think you do,' said Ingestre. 'Handsome, well-built man; dark hair greying; world-weary smile.'

'I know the one. He dresses very elegantly.'

'And quickly!' said Fulford. 'Do you mean he is *not* one of the ones you've had to fend off?'

'Not once. Has he that reputation? Dear me: he's always been rather distant as far as I am concerned.'

'He has that reputation, hasn't he, Roger?'

'Yes. What's this about him wanting to leave Parliament to be the Principal of the latest Utopian academy?'

'It's true, as far as I know. A new European College to be set up in some country estate in Kent. Not a bad idea in fact: for bright kids from all over Europe – but essentially the Nine. A kind of much more intellectual Atlantic College. All over sixteen. They do their normal courses of study, but they live together and a sizable part of the curriculum is devoted to various European themes.'

'It sounds to me, Ellis, suspiciously like a sort of prep school for Bilderberg!' said Ingestre.

'Not if it's run on the right lines. I don't think Connors would be too bad. He's got all the right sort of experience; he's intelligent, charming. He gets on very well with young people,' said Fulford.

'So I understand,' said Ingestre.

'Wouldn't that sort of thing appeal to you, Roger?' asked Clodia.

'He's much too comfortable down among the lost causes,' said Fulford. 'Aren't you?'

'I think, as it's often put, I'm too set in my ways to change now. There will be some stiff competition, I should think, won't there?'

'Sure to be. But Jeremy Taylor's one of the trustees – so that's something in Connors's favour.'

'Is that so?' said Ingestre.

'What about someone like Simon Farrell?' Clodia said.

'I shouldn't think it would appeal to him,' said Ingestre.

'No,' said Fulford. 'He's one of nature's cardinals, a maker of other people's policies. He's waiting for the right man in Downing Street and a comfortable shelf in the kitchen Cabinet. He has a lot of quite powerful friends who are taken in by all that remote archaeological guff. And behind it there is a sharp and dogmatic economic brain.'

'Am I right in guessing that you don't like him, Ellis?'

'Too calculating. He's one of the few people I know who chews beer.'

'It's known as having a ruminative pint,' said Ingestre. 'Are you having the same, Ellis?'

'Thanks.'

'Clodia?'

'Yes. Thank you, Roger.'

'Can I take advantage of Ingestre's beneficence to issue my quarterly reminder?'

'By all means.'

'Still no?'

'Still no.'

'Well, unless I hear from you, you're safe until the next quarter. You're not going to do anything treacherous like going back to Italy, are you?'

'Not for a considerable time.'

'Good. . . . Well, say what you like I think we're going to miss Henry Kissinger. . . . That was smooth operating, Roger. I always thought you had a vaguely Silurian look, taken off guard.'

'I think you're right,' said Clodia. '. . . Thank you, Roger. About Kissinger. All this Carter confusion about Yugoslavia. It's very dangerous talk. The Russians might get quite the wrong idea.'

'Happily,' said Ingestre, 'he's modified the original statement.'

'Yes, but Clodia's right. That he should make it in the first place is bad enough,' said Fulford. 'But what's all this about the Russians? I thought you were a mere technician and you didn't have politics. Hasn't she told *you* that sort of thing, Roger?'

'Frequently.'

'It's not a political viewpoint: it's an historical analysis,' Clodia said. 'James Mitchell pointed it out to me.'

'That American journalist?' said Fulford.

'Yes.'

'Somewhere to the right of Coriolanus. What did he say?'

'Just that he could imagine in the perspective of the future, when we emerge out of what he describes as the present dark age, he can imagine Renaissance scholars wondering why the West did not fix the Soviets in 1946. Stalin was always perfidious in all his dealings. And then there was still time to un-Yaltarise Europe. Russia has always acted out of self-interest and has always been imperialist: that is why Communism as a creed sits so easily upon the Russian character: because it is voraciously colonialist and discovers conscience only when attacked....'

'Is this Mitchell still? Or you?' asked Ingestre.

'Essentially Mitchell. I don't agree, obviously, with all of it. But it's almost a truism about Russian imperialism, wouldn't you say so?'

'A preventative war,' said Fulford, 'when we had all the power and they were still in the divisive aftermath of partial occupation! Does it shock *you*, Roger?'

'Not in any sensational way. It must be something a lot of people have thought about in passing. But I find the idea shocking. Yes.'

'So do I,' said Fulford solemnly. 'Because if Western democracy is to mean anything, it cannot be cynical or amoral or pre-emptive. And if it is *not* any of those things, I find myself wondering increasingly how it can possibly survive. Ah well. I suppose that's the traditional cue for someone to say "Drink up!" It's my shout.'

*

It was getting more difficult to concentrate. . . . Not that it especially mattered. Sometimes she thought that if she got a first, it would impress Tony and make him take her more seriously again – because he had once taken her seriously when they first met and had laughed even at her political jokes which after all must have seemed unsophisticated to him. But there was no guarantee . . . silly word . . . there could be no promise. . . . That was part of the trouble: Tony made no promises so there were never any to break and when she was disappointed it was her own fault for expecting too much. Then she had a right to expect something because she gave herself, had given herself, completely and not in any stupid old-fashioned virgin-with-one-precious-gift way she thought he must give something back to her and something more than conversation and elegant laughter and occasional wild erotic pleasure. She missed this so much sometimes she could hardly believe that she was any longer the same woman. Since Tony and all the seemingly endless variety of love and fucking, she was sometimes so taut and stretched with sheer physical need that she could no longer think or register any sensation that wasn't sexual. . . . It wasn't so bad when there were other people except that she became irritated or bored by the conversation of the girls she knew, and apart from Steve Kent she didn't want to be even remotely involved with any men. And God! she had even been tempted to let Steve Kent take her one afternoon when she had wanted so badly not so much to be loved as to be violently screwed and humiliated even as Tony sometimes teased and hurt her. Fortunately she had just at the last managed to hold out and she did not think he had noticed how close he had been to having what he wanted. But then it would not have been fair because he loved her and that was partly the trouble because he was being so pure and noble that the stupid boy couldn't read her reckless passionate mood. She was still able to laugh at herself as she recalled her own eyes fixed on his thighs and the contours of his balls in rather tight jeans, almost hysterically giggling as she wondered what would happen if she did anything provocative. But she had stopped herself.

Tony would *not* quarrel. However angry she was, however wayward. She tried to have rows with him, but he treated her with the same calm maddeningly patronising confidence as though he was of such infinitely superior intelligence and if she said vicious things that would have and should have hurt him he laughed. It was no good pretending to be frigid because it never worked: he was artful and she wanted him always too much. And it would have been absurd to try to make him think that he was an unsatisfying or incompetent lover because he knew only too well how inexperienced she was and even better how much he had pleased and excited her in the past and what she would do for him and with him and what she wanted from him. . . . What she wanted was love and an acknowledged love and an irrationally shared passion that was blindly ignorant of Barbara and Daddy and everybody else. . . . That ghastly weekend when she had gone to look for him in London and found he was in Brussels visiting friends at the Commission and Daddy had been so bloody clever and whimsical about it so that the implication was obviously that he had gone off with a woman. And she hadn't dared ask too many questions in case bloody Barbara would suspect something. At least it was not with *her*; or with the fat white sloven Marie or with brisk and efficient Rachel Bailey whose sincere and technically sound approach as she imagined it she could not see having any attraction for Tony and the little elaborations that turned him on. Then poisonous little Jessica wanting shriekingly to know why she was so interested in Tony Connors though neither Daddy nor Barbara were listening. Oh that little alley-cat as she was turning surely into, with great gangling pimply oafs panting like smelly young goats all over the house and already on the sitting-room floor with one of them sprawled all over her and his grubby fingers stuck up her knickers. Christ alone knew what happened out on the Heath or when Barbara and Daddy were out. She felt a little ashamed for watching for so long. . . . Not really, just a few minutes and feeling so not exactly excited but a little stirred herself. . . . Before stalking in and sitting calmly down with some suitably acid remark and the foul-mouthed little pig swearing at her though the boy's embarrassment was huge! and red and stammering and it was quite funny really stumbling up and falling over the coffee-table while Jessica just lay there defiantly as she unconcernedly ignored them both and pretended to read Barbara's *Economist*. The two lumpish kids slouched out of the room but Jessica couldn't let it go at that which was surely enough and turned at the door and said that vile thing about not only being a supergrade bitch but not really normal, her face salmon-coloured and tears in her cowlike eyes and her rubbery lips trembling. Although it was obviously a defensive slash it had nevertheless hurt and the sting spread as though along nerve tracks. She hadn't intended to actually read the bloody *Economist* in the first place but the words blurred as the pain of the sting throbbed and she felt frightened that it might perhaps be true and ... Frightened! Because of the infantile jibe of an over-sexed virtually subnormal hoyden, it was ridiculous. . . . But there were her own obsessions and she had watched them wriggling on the floor until she feared ... yes, that was the word, feared ... that disgust was turning into a hideous vicarious excitement that was near a kind of pleasure and there were her own fantasies as these terrible bouts of extreme sexual desire that seemed to be less focused upon one man Tony whom she loved than a need for excitement from anyone and sooner or later she would give in to it and then ... And there was what she did with Tony which wasn't ordinary straight sex, all the titillation and dressing up that she herself enjoyed and the variations and rituals of submission and domination. She felt most bitterly about the row that had followed when she had suggested to Barbara that they had better keep an eye on Jessica or make sure that she was on the pill because Barbara had suddenly become desperately intense and nothing like the bored progressive parent she usually affected to be and in a moment or so there was Daddy lined and with the greyish look which came around and under his eyes when he was upset which he wasn't all that often. The first comprehensive family row ever with filthy little Jessica in tears and trying to play everyone off and Barbara icily sarcastic and Daddy harsh, during which she had realised that no one had ever seemed to care when she was starting to go with boys what happened – oh there had been clever witty caveats and implied reassurance but no one had *cared*

266

if she was being fucked from Highgate to Kentish Town or by whom and now because it was *Jessica* there was all the drama.

By the time that she had got back to Oxford she had been very low and had almost confided it all in Steve Kent except that she was too proud now to let him see that she was sometimes vulnerable and she had after all sometimes treated him badly. There was that time for example in the taxi when he had so artlessly shoved his hand along her thighs and she had pretended to be much more furious than she was and had tried to make him miserable. God! that had been innocent enough compared to the games with Tony. . . . Instead of asking her what she was doing later in the week, Steve Kent then said he was going to London because Rachel Bailey had invited him to the House of Commons and he thought it was going to be a *terrific* experience (at such moments she remembered how very ingenuous he could be) and since he was rather hoping to go into serious journalism it would be too splendid an opportunity to miss. She wondered what Rachel Bailey might be up to – perhaps with Olly the Ebullient away she liked the look of a muscular young man like Steve. No, unfair: Rachel Bailey was a do-gooder quite sincerely and always kind and sunny whoever it was, but this newly achieved greatness probably accounted for Steve's relaxed rather less eager manner with her not as solicitous wound up. She tried not to sound condescending when she said she was sure he would enjoy it and something pleasant about Rachel and how kind she always was and he said that he thought Rachel Bailey was a very attractive woman as well which she found vaguely annoying. So there he would be in London having a party at the House now and . . . She felt lonely and miserable and there was this longing coming over her again for some kind of positive physical release. . . .

Completely out of the blue, Tony telephoned on the following Tuesday after a wretched weekend at Oxford in which her futile, miserable mood had persisted and she had tried in vain to work it off. Candida immediately felt ridiculously happy and entirely forgot about her intention to ask him who it was he had taken to Brussels, or to reproach him for a whole week during which she had been unable to contact him and he had failed to get in touch with her, in spite of anxious messages left at the House switchboard. Anyway, he explained himself without being asked: he had been dreadfully busy and there was an exciting opportunity coming up for which he wanted to be suitably prepared.

He said that he would tell her about it at the weekend – if she was free to come with him to Paris. He proposed that they should fly out on Friday evening and back on Sunday. Apart from a little business on Saturday which might involve lunch, they could have all the time to themselves. Candida felt ecstatic. She had been to Paris a few times but did not know it well, while to Tony (who had studied at the École Normale) it was as familiar as London. She anticipated the sophisticated charm of it all with perhaps too much pleasure, fearing that she might be disappointed.

She was not. They stayed at a pleasant, unostentatious hotel off the Rue de Rivoli where they made love for a long time: but gently and beautifully, and although Candida had worn stockings and the sort of silky, sexy undies he liked, he hadn't paid the usual attention after undressing her. He had a wonderfully firm body for a man in his forties, strong and well-muscled with no hint of a paunch. She was very happy.

He told her about the new college to be founded at Lamberhurst and of his high hopes of being appointed its first Warden. It was in connection with this that he was seeing a French acquaintance the next day and he was afraid it would mean having lunch with the man. Candida was not in the least upset about that and was delighted at the new prospect for him. He had obviously been disillusioned recently about politics and it was quite understandable – since a man of his intelligence and abilities might reasonably have expected minor office at this stage of his career and the imminence of much greater responsibility in the not distant future. Furthermore, Candida saw opportunities for consolidating their own relationship, now that she had recovered again from her hysterical jealousy. Not because Daddy was one of the trustees appointed to set up the college (which explained all the wise smiles and non-committal discretion about Tony's visit to Brussels), but because Candida thought that, with a decent degree, she might get a teaching job there herself. For the moment, however, she said nothing about it to Tony because it was premature.

They got up early and on a lovely autumn morning walked past Notre Dame de Lorette and through the Place St Georges up to Montmartre and had coffee and croissants in the Place Blanche, which Tony said was his favourite place for breakfast in the world. Candida said she envied him all the places he had visited and knew, and looked forward to seeing them with him. He gave her a slow warm smile that did not need any words. Candida loved the Boulevard Clichy with its colour and vulgarity and gaudiness and all the interesting types whom Tony classified in the *argot*, which he seemed to know well. He taught Candida a selection of words and phrases, some of which were very dirty indeed but usually extremely funny. It was all delightful.

They walked towards the Place Clichy past the porn shops and sex boutiques and laughed together at various items on sale. Candida said that she thought a certain outfit cut imaginatively around and within lace-trimmed satin would become her and was mischievously pleased to see that certain intense look come into Tony's eye. For a moment she felt more like his wife than his mistress; then soon dismissed the thought as foolishly sentimental. They walked slowly back to the centre by another route. Tony left her at eleven-thirty for his appointment, after showing her all the most interesting shopping streets and she whiled away the hours until they were to meet at the Café de la Paix aimlessly but very happily. Five rather good-looking men tried (separately)

269

to pick her up and she thought she turned them down very sweetly, wondering a little uneasily whether in her mood of only the last weekend she would not have been looking for . . . well no, that was hardly it, not looking for . . . whether she would have submitted to some sexual adventure.

It was still a lovely day: so, when they met again, they walked along the river to the Place St Michel and he took her to the cafés that he had used when he was a student in Paris and talked about those days not long after the War when things had been much less prosperous, *very* much cheaper for even a moderately indigent Englishman, and in *some* ways (he smiled at her kindly as he said it) more exciting. He pointed out the places used by Sartre and Picasso, and took her the length of the Boul' Miche' to the Boulevard de Montparnasse, talking of Hemingway and Joyce and Gertrude Stein and Scott Fitzgerald and dozens of others, with anecdotes and bits of novels and little phrases. It was enthralling. Candida was very tired when they went back to their hotel to change, but not too tired to make love.

Over dinner, in a beautiful restaurant in the Place des Vosges where the food and wine were delicious, he talked about his plans and what he would do if he became Warden of the proposed European College. She thought that she glimpsed something of the idealism and intellectual passion that he must have had when he had first gone into politics. She was accustomed to the bored cynicism, whether genuine or affected, of her parents' circle in which Tony had sometimes seemed to be the most blasé and cynical of them all. Now, as he described something that had really caught his imagination, she saw the young Tony Connors and almost wished that she had known him then. But no. . . . She knew herself well enough to realize that, if they had been of similar ages, she would probably not have been interested: let alone as deeply in love. He asked her what she was smiling at and she said herself. He left it at that.

More love, still tender, with only that moment of violence at the climax of one or two of the wonderful times when their bodies joined in such ecstasy. And another golden relaxed day, walking, laughing together, chatting easily and without a moment of strain as jealousy and fear and resentment were all forgotten and seen by Candida to be so very silly and unnecessary.

They flew back to London in the early evening and Candida returned to Oxford very much at peace with herself and ready to work hard again. She felt that she was now sure of him, that she was at long last growing up.

To her surprise she found a note from Ingestre waiting for her, inviting her round to his rooms for drinks. She had seen him no more than half a dozen times since that fateful afternoon when she had accidentally run into Tony Connors at his flat. She was much too honest to forget her intentions on that particular day and the memory made her feel hot and prickly. How much Roger Ingestre himself had guessed she did not know, inevitably something: but she was profoundly grateful that no one else had known about her schoolgirlish infatuation and her truly absurd behaviour. Apart from one occasion, when she had been with Steve Kent, she had not met him at Oxford in the current term and she wondered why he should suddenly ask her around. That, of course, was silly too. She was ascribing some sort of motive to him when he was probably being donnishly courteous in entertaining a sometime pupil and the daughter of friends. She wondered whether or not she would accept. It might be amusing; but the lingering embarrassment she felt was still quite uncomfortable and she thought not. It would probably be full of undergraduates being brilliant and she didn't think she could be doing with that.

She had quite forgotten that Barbara was coming to Oxford as the guest of some very earnest little group until she telephoned to suggest lunch. As always, Barbara had arranged her day with the maximum efficiency so that she saw half a dozen necessary people, to talk of relevant matters, before

271

dining and talking to the undergraduate group. But she had managed to fit in an hour and a half to talk to her daughter, while eating. It was rather a bitter little thought and not entirely fair. She decided that she would behave well: particularly since their last meeting had been the occasion of that filthy row, started by Jessica, when she had felt so miserable and cried. And their reaction still smarted a bit. . . .

Barbara came to the college to see one or two old acquaintances, and Candida had to admit that she had every reason to be pleased with her mother's marvellously elegant image – in dress and manner. Some of her friends were almost openly envious. The irony impressed her since some of these people had charming, less obvious parents whom she had liked enormously when she had met them.

It was a pleasant morning: but Barbara did not want to walk through the Parks in her high-heeled fragile shoes, so they took a taxi to the Sorbonne where they had sherry and a half-bottle of very expensive wine. Used to Tony's drinking habits, she would have preferred something a little less refined and more of it. As it happened, they got on well. It wasn't that they often failed to 'get on': but Barbara was always remote and cerebral – except with Jessica whom she regarded as a troublesome but funny animal. Apart, of course, from that recent rankling evening.

She found herself talking to her mother easily and they even laughed at each other's little witticisms. (Hardly jokes!) She wondered, after one or two successful little asides at the expense of some of the Highgate friends, whether she had an unrealised talent for acid humour.

'I'm rather fond of Roger Ingestre,' Barbara said. 'I must say I once thought that you were. Not that it's any of my business.'

'Roger!' she said, in mock surprise.

'It doesn't seem to be *that* extraordinary,' said Barbara. 'He's really quite an attractive man. But I suppose you are not short of admirers. Young men today are very much more tempting than they were when I was up. I think they all wash a lot more. In my day the well-scrubbed were usually either dim or queer. And their clothes are much pleasanter.'

Barbara waited for some response. Candida guessed shrewdly that they had perhaps been talking about her after that Sunday outburst: she could imagine it. Daddy furrowed and concentrating; Barbara maternally intelligent, unsentimental. Was she happy? Were there perhaps problems? Why did she seem not to have boy friends? Was she, possibly, because everything must be taken into consideration, inhibited or even sexually inverted? Suddenly she resented all this. (When she had not long before bitterly resented their apparent indifference!) The weekend in Paris had really made all the difference. . . . God! If only they knew! And then she thought that there was no reason why they should not. Unless . . . That old fear about Barbara and Tony. But she could not bear the condescension and all the other assumptions she thought they had made.

'Mummy,' she said, seriously, 'I think perhaps it's time that I told you. I don't know how you're going to take it or how Daddy will and I hope neither of you is going to make a fuss. I've been having, and am still having, a serious affair with Tony Connors. It started last July and I spent last weekend in Paris with him.'

The fork faltered barely perceptibly in her mother's hand on its way to her small pretty mouth. She chewed daintily, looked at her daughter and put it down calmly.

'Well,' she said, 'I can't say that I'm delighted and it *is* slightly surprising news.'

'I thought it best that you should know, one way or another.'

'Indeed. For my own part, I don't in the least mind. I think that Jeremy may be a little put out. We both have the highest opinion of Tony Connors's intellect, but he is not – as I'm sure you must have gathered – the most chaste of people. In fact, quite the opposite.'

'I had heard a lot of rather childish jokes.'

273

'Are you in love with him?'

'Yes.'

'And what about him? Do you think he is in love with you?'

'Yes,' she said, stung by the implication.

'Dare I say, darling, that you don't sound quite as sure about that? He really is something of a . . . what shall I call it . . . a philanderer, you know.'

'Yes, of course I know. I know it's what people say.'

'And the discrepancy between your ages doesn't worry either of you?'

'Why should it?'

Barbara shrugged.

'The point is, Mummy: *you* don't mind?'

'I think it's a little late, darling, for me to start behaving like one of Trollope's matrons, even if it was in character. I'll break it to Jeremy as gently as possible: but men can be rather sensitive about their female children.'

There was quite a long silence during which they looked at each other blankly, it seemed. Then Barbara recovered her quizzical smile.

'It seems to have put a stop to conversation,' she said lightly. 'Did I tell you that I'm going to Kenya next month?'

*

Something certainly happened during the last long vac which has drastically changed things between Candida and me. In spite of the fact that we are playing according to her platonic rules, and she might well have taken the initiative by telling me about the attractive older man with whom it is impossible for me to compete, I have now certainly an impression that I am the more dominant. And last term, before London, it was never at all like that! It was very much *de haut en bas* with me *bas*. The advantage is that I feel comfortable and fairly relaxed with her and so I'm less apologetic all the time, less anxious to please, and I make her laugh more because I'm more myself. I daresay that's not to be compared with whoever the smooth rival is, because I wouldn't describe myself as a candidate for the Algonquin Round Table – but I have certain things in my favour.

The trouble now is that I'm not sure about Candida's own state of mind. She was always fairly predictably unpredictable in the old days – usually in the same kind of bored, irritable mood, as far as I was concerned. Now she can be anything from wildly euphoric to listless to snappy to nervous and twitching: and, apart from the moods of listlessness and lethargy, which are quite stultifying, she can switch out of one mood and into another in a matter of seconds.

One time I thought I was picking up quite distinct sexual waves. Probably wishful thinking because she was sitting across the room at quite a distance and very demure with her legs curled under her in a long green skirt: but for a moment I thought there was something and she was, as ever, looking so terrific that I started stirring uncomfortably which would have soon been obvious, so I started talking about Mill and Engels. She laughed and listened for a while and then changed the subject. Then she said abruptly that she had to go: and so my audience was over.

The listless sessions are very difficult to deal with and she seems to be looking out on the ultimate dust-bowl of the universe when they come on. The last one of these, before I went up to London, worried me enough to speak to Ingestre. I asked him if he had seen much of her recently and he said very little, since she stopped going to him for tutorials. I described to him some of the ways in which she had slightly bothered me and he looked quite concerned. He wanted to know if I had found out the causes of such variable moods and I confessed that I hadn't been bold enough to ask. I didn't like to say anything about the affair with the older man because that was very much a confidence and Candida would be very angry if she thought I had betrayed it to Ingestre – or indeed if she thought that we had been discussing her at all. Ingestre asked a few discreet questions around and about my relationship with her: but he

275

obviously didn't want to go too far and I didn't want to turn it into a confession and comfort session for my personal benefit. He said he would have a word with her. It was probably the strain of Schools coming up.

My trip to London as Rachel's guest at the House was completely successful and made me forget all about Candida (which is shameful perhaps, but rather a good symptom of recovery) and even, for the moment, about work. Jenks used to tell me at school that I was a bit short on imagination, which I think was fair enough, and I certainly don't over-react: but Parliament was different. The whole atmosphere got to me straight away: the sense of dignity and history, the laconic police (God! so quintessentially British – I even felt proud of Dad, who would have loved it!), the crowd of people in the lobby waiting for someone, or just there to watch, the famous faces stopping for a word and a chat with others I couldn't recognise. Rachel appeared from the Chamber, looking particularly charming even for her, in a dark green suit which was just right for her figure – not obvious in any way but beautifully proportioned. I thought she looked younger than when I first met her and she has such a delightful smile. It is quite ridiculous, of course, but I think I'm just a little bit in love with her in the nicest possible way. (It would have to be!)

There was, of course, a lot of excitement and considering the pressure they are all under, it was extraordinarily good of Rachel to have me there at all. After the various bills being thrown out by the Lords and then the serious reverses of the Warrington and Walsall by-elections and the shockingly low poll at Newcastle Central, the government are really battling and there is quite a lot of high feeling between the wings of the Labour party. (Rachel is on the right but loyal.) Both Reg Prentice and the Chancellor blamed the antics of the left recently for Labour's poor showing. No one seemed particularly surprised about the Walsall result because of the Stonehouse business, but Warrington is absolute bedrock and very worrying for them.

276

The afternoon, when I watched proceedings from the Visitors' Gallery, was absolutely absorbing: particularly since it led to two government defeats later in the day on the Docks Bill and two other very close calls when they had to rely on the Speaker's casting vote. Unfortunately, I'd had to leave before the divisions, obviously: but it was fascinating to be in such a privileged position when there was so much going on. With all the rumours and the air of purpose and excitement which the MPs themselves seem to take for granted and which at the same time seems to buoy them along: it was intoxicating. And if I had been vague about my intentions before, they are now absolutely dedicated. In some way I want to be a part of that.

True to her promise, Rachel took me in the early evening to the Press Bar to meet Alan Trumble, whom I read regularly. He was very friendly and splendidly cynical about it all, which I'm sure was partly for my entertainment. Rachel had to go away to deal with something so Alan Trumble gave me a very funny glossary of Whitehallese, especially as it relates to the press ('Speculative' = 'Dead right', etc.). He then told me quite seriously what the work was all about, the longeurs and the pitfalls, as well as its fascinating, even crusading, aspects. One of the pitfalls he mentioned was drink and I've seldom seen anyone take in so much whisky, with so little apparent effect, in a comparatively short time.

After warning me that she would have to dash off if there was any sudden urgency or a division, Rachel took me to the Members' dining room, which was another really great experience. We were joined by a very charming and urbane MP called Anthony Connors, who talked most engagingly about political realignment. Connors sits for a Northern constituency with an enormous majority, but would be very few people's idea of a Labour MP. And, in fact, I'd guess he was having doubts. He was, I should have said, either unusually outspoken, or he really doesn't care much about his political position. It was his opinion that the by-election setbacks were very bad not for the Labour party as such, but for the possible emergence of a centrist party with credible recruitment across all party lines. In spite of the early left reactions from the usual people to the accusations levelled against them, such reverses might bring them into line and the Tories, similarly, assured of some kind of victory at least in the short run, would be able to restrain any of their leftish defectors and coalitionists.

It was odd to hear a Labour Member actively desiring a split in his party and I don't think that Rachel was very pleased (nor, in fact, do I think that she likes Connors very much).

Delightful as all this was for me, I decided not to outstay my welcome, because Rachel was clearly very busy and it looked as though there was a long night ahead for everybody. There seemed to be general agreement that Brian Walden and John Mackintosh would carry out their declared threat of abstaining during the votes on the Docks Bill amendments and the tensions were building up.

They did: and the next day Trumble was among various others talking about it on the early morning programmes. I stayed with Ted White and his mother in her splendid house. He was contemptuous about the whole reason for my visit and about almost every aspect of politics that came up, but I learned a lot about who was worth reading in Portuguese.

I took up Trumble's invitation to visit his paper (a brief, epigrammatic tour) and the pubs of Fleet Street (more protracted and anecdotal) on Friday morning. He thought that the Walden–Mackintosh abstentions had stirred things up quite considerably and that we could look forward to some loud left reaction over the weekend. Otherwise, when I put to him some of the points that Connors had made about the difficulties of a centrist re-alignment, he said that he agreed it would have to be considerably deferred, possibly until after Labour had decisively lost the next election. Since Enoch Powell, in the course of the week, had said that the government should not be under threat of dismissal for some time and defended it from the point of view of 'what was good for Ulster', Trumble saw some short-term security. And he believed that, in due course, if there was *no question* of a fairly imminent centrist alliance, the Liberals – out of sheer electoral necessity – would have to make some pact with Labour to prolong the existing Parliament and postpone what would be for them a disastrous election.

After leaving Trumble, I went to Highgate to see Clifford and Teresa where I was again warmly welcomed. Teresa, now that I am no longer in immediate proximity behind the bar, was a little flirtatious. Ted White joined me later in the evening and we met a colleague of his from his Polytechnic called Maddox, a very embittered character who was stimulatingly savage. Clifford did not know what to make of him at all and Teresa didn't like him. Unlike Trumble's somewhat positive cynicism, this man's attitude seemed to me to be entirely and unremittingly negative.

The next day one of Ted's girl-friends, a terrific-looking Eurasian, or perhaps full Chinese, turned up and since he virtually started undressing her before my very eyes in the kitchen (which looks like Mission Control at Houston), I decided to start making my way gently back to Oxford and a spot of neglected work.

True enough, this last weekend there were the repercussions in the Sundays to the Walden and Mackintosh decisions to abstain, and reactions from Eric Heffer and Jack Jones. I listened and read as neutrally as I could. (Ingestre's Law of Critical Detachment.) But I've come to the conclusion that I am (quite apart from the marvellous Rachel Bailey) a Social Democrat in my own right. Now, for the first time, I've heard of a 'soft left' in the Labour party, which has aligned with the real and unmistakable left in demanding changes in economic policy, with no more public expenditure cuts, IMF conditions or no.

I put this to Ingestre, having the good luck to see him on my own for a tutorial because Lumley had flu. It was a terrific session from my point of view: although we were talking about Mill, Engels, Carlyle, Marx and so on, he was quite happy to apply or relate certain theories to immediate events, which I feel at the moment are especially meaningful for me.

We went out to the pub together after a long tutorial and fell to chatting generally. I told him about my visit to Parliament and he was pleasantly unpatronising about it, but I think quite amused by my obvious admiration for Rachel.

I should not have thought that Ingestre would have found as much to sympathise with in a firmly anti-coalition attitude. A moment or two before he had been showing guarded approval for Steele's open letter to Shirley Williams about the necessity of centre re-alignment. (Alan Trumble said this would be the last throw in the crap game before the Liberals had to think about putting down markers!) I said as much to Ingestre who was spot on with Machiavelli and a homily on the difference between a re-aligned *new* party and coalition. It went something like: 'His advice to d'Amboise, who, Steve, he assured his mentors, listened to him *patiently*, was that the King of France ought to adopt the practice of all sovereigns who wish to establish and safeguard power in a foreign country. Weaken the powerful, conciliate the conquered, sustain friends and *beware of associates* – which is to say all who desire an equal share in power. Regard the "foreign country" as a democratic electorate and apply that argument to coalition. Look at ourselves, at France, at the United States. Practical politics is not, as Henry Adams said, a matter of ignoring the facts but of admitting the truisms – one of which is that coalitions are impracticable and treacherous.'

I then was advised to attend lectures by Professor Taylor, Mr Williams, Dr Siedentop and Christ knows who else: better still, to read PPE (if I was so inspired!) rather than do post-graduate work in History, *if if if* I get a first. I don't think I want to do either: in my present frame of mind, which is admittedly a shade over-excited, I want to get to London as soon as possible – which means working my way through a provincial newspaper. There are no short-cuts and I shouldn't want any. (That would please Dad, at least.)

It is getting late and I've let this run on but I think I'll enjoy it in ten or fifteen years when I've learned to live with my *faux pas*. As I've learned to live with Candida. I saw her, by chance, today outside Schools, looking radiant. We had a short chat and I told her about the visit to London the other week. Rachel said to Connors, in passing, that I knew Candida. (He said she was a charming girl – not surprising since both her parents were such delightful people.) Candida thought this was very funny, though her laughter wasn't harsh and angry, as it sometimes has been lately. I think the problem may be that she does not get on with her parents. Well, that isn't exactly unusual. I must write to mine about Parliament. I'll bet they say: you should be sticking at your work and not gadding about in London until you've got something solid behind you!

*

With no small strategic skill, Jeremy Taylor has pre-empted criticism of the Highgate Group and the amazingly well-received pamphlets by saying on television that if the group is to be taken seriously it must present a coherent programme of principles. Barbara, looking rather like one of the aristo-cratic, slender fashion models of the early fifties, explained that such a programme was in no sense a manifesto because the group was not bidding for power. Taylor, vigorous and sincere, defines us as a congeries of independent centre democrats exploring the possibility of coming together as a political force with broad appeal to an essentially fair-minded and liberal electorate, dedicated to a long tradition of free speech, if only recently benefiting from a similar economic freedom. Small smile from Barbara. (I should like very much to have heard Ellis Fulford's comments if he was watching!) He pointed out that the existing major parties were bound together more by motives of expectation or survival than principle and that members of all three (even the Liberals) had more in common with other right-thinking men and women across the party lines than they had with many whom they accompanied into the lobbies. Barbara told the world – or at least that part of the world that was not watching *I, Claudius* or a late-night horror film – that this Outline of Principles was on its way. So we can all look out! The story was taken up by a couple of editorials, not unsympathetically, and dismissed as woolly academic nonsense in a couple of others. Trumble declared an interest and wrote a nice, acerbic piece about party conscience. There were encouraging noises from echoey quarters.

Cleverly anticipating the clarion call that must surely follow all this televised delphism echoing through the shires to Oxford and Gloucester and so on, it occurred to me to jot down what I understood to be our policies in several broad categories: I. The Economy; II. Europe and the Community, NATO and defence alliances, the Commonwealth, the Third World, Africa – *especially* Southern Africa and Rhodesia but with an eye upon the expansion of Soviet influence in central Africa; III. Energy; IV. Education (comprehensive and independent schools and colleges, universities and polytechnics – with reference to vocational graduates), the Environment, Local Government, the Law, Crime, Immigration; V. Housing; VI. Northern Ireland; VII. Industrial relations, investment and deployment of labour covering unemployment and re-training schemes.

This produced an amiably consistent pattern, in that it appeared that our ideas were consistently based upon a firm European commitment with aspirations towards real political and economic unity. Most of our economic ideas, especially those relating to trade, are closely linked with the strengthening of our position and participation in the Community: but our ideas on incomes and worker participation owe a lot to this same Europeanism. In this respect, as in our firm membership of the Atlantic Alliance, we might in the future be embarrassed by a Communist component in certain European governments, which is going to be far less

282

easy to deal with than some of the group think. In the same way attitudes to the Commonwealth and the Third World generally are more or less guided by the broad European policies on development and aid, but when we come to Africa there is a problem and a gap. The problem is that in our resolute anti-racist stance, we have to make up our minds about South Africa, assuming that Rhodesia must (at some time after the endless to-ing and fro-ing that is going on at present) fairly soon, peacefully or otherwise, have a black government which *may* be Marxist. That is the problem.

I'm not sure that we would not represent ourselves more fairly if we described ourselves as The European Party rather than a Centrist Alliance.

And that leaves us with immigration, colour problems generally. And Northern Ireland. Neither is in any sense a European problem, although the French have their racial problems with their Arab population. On both of these issues we are at our woolliest and most myopic. What possible civilised attitude can there be than the ideal of an integrated society, achieved through adequate housing, satisfactory employment levels and patient education? And yet what is the use of high liberal sentence when none of us have to contend on a day-to-day basis with the problems of integration in crowded conditions? And what about the attitudes of the immigrants themselves? The National Front vote in the recent by-elections was alarmingly on the upturn and there are enough Weimarish features about our present society to make the threat to liberal culture from the right much more than phantasmal.

I notice that I had made no note of an approach to Science and Technology, where we have an abundance of views; or of the Arts and Leisure, which we take for granted.

There has been offered over the last few weeks a gratuitously bloody television version of Graves's *I, Claudius* with some quite brilliant performances from the actors and some gross distortions of Graves's purpose, including a truly revolting invention of the television producers, whereby Caligula disembowels his pregnant sister and eats the foetus she is carrying!

The Messalina bits have been quite wittily handled, though once again the temptation to include explicit lewdness was too much for the television people. There was one nice touch where Messalina refused to breast-feed because it interfered with matters of state. At the same time a young and attractive Member of Parliament who has just had a baby is demanding facilities in the House so that she can perform this admirable maternal function and at the same time cast her very crucial vote for the government. I should like to think this is an epitome of how far we have progressed since the days of Imperial Rome. At the same time, the television version rather exaggerates the deficiency of just men. I received a letter from the executors of Dimchurch's estate. He has left me in his will his entire collection of *Wisden*s and his other books about cricket. It had never crossed my mind that he might and I was very deeply moved.

Kent's concern for the psychological well-being of Candida Taylor seems to have been, happily, superfluous. She answered my invitation very late, but came for drinks, looking extremely pretty and well. I had taken the precaution of not asking Kent or anyone else she might know and she behaved rather pleasantly. Blakemore came; so did Ellen Hart from St Hilda's and the articulate if shy Briget Ross, ensuring the right degree of competition. There were also a couple of clever young chaps from the college who are quite well known generally; one of whom had just picked up the Chancellor's Essay Prize, which was the excuse for the occasion since he had asked me for criticisms.

In the course of a fairly usual conversation about heroes, someone asked me whom I most admired in my own time.

Choosing to be flippant, I said T. S. Eliot, Bradman and Fred Astaire. I am not sure that I desired any particular effect, but it certainly elicited merry reaction. Blakemore agreed with me about Bradman and Fred Astaire, but could not accept Eliot's 'metaphysical inconsistencies'. Candida showed most surprise, having less imagination than the other two younger people in the particular group. I explained that these two heroes had already been middle-aged when I was a young man, but that their standards of excellence were virtually unmatched in exacting physical arts. This led to some generalisations about the nature of excellence. Blake-more suggested that I was showing signs of the nostalgia of middle age. 'Admiration is always best excited at a distance and so a privilege of youth: it is always a mistake to seek acquaintance with those one admires.' This in his most highly authoritative manner.

It gave me the opportunity to ask Candida obliquely if she did not admire people in middle age, or was she a victim of the generation gap. She answered obliquely but gave me a sharp little glance. Candida does not believe that there is a generation gap – at least not between her generation and her parents' – because relationships (she says) have evolved. Fulford on the other hand is all in favour of preserving as wide a gap as possible between Candida's generation and ours. (He usually refers to her as Tinkertits, for some reason best known to himself.) He resents deeply the tendency of the women to dress provocatively with see-through blouses and slit skirts and then to sigh and fret and grumble when they receive impurely passive attention from passing Ful-fords. Furthermore he claims that when he has been insulted by anyone abroad, it is usually by semi-educated children of this type. (Fulford was once accused in Rimini by some student of wanting feesh and cheeps and bears it hard.)

The small party worked quite well and I satisfied myself that all was well with Candida, whatever the state of play between her and Connors. I still feel naggingly responsible, but I cannot think of a way of finding out something definite without undue embarrassment for both of us.

With the IMF deciding to stay on for another week's talk and investigation and Callaghan underlining the importance of further pay restraint, the miners have chosen to run a ballot on whether to support their claims for early retirement with industrial action. When their case is seen alongside conditions of miners in Germany and France, it is pretty reasonable: but they do have this habit of bargaining at the most inconvenient moments. I suppose they might reasonably argue that this is all part of the industrial tradition.

An interesting interlude in the Highgate meeting during the preliminary gins was an untypical flash of anger from Connors at Ellis Fulford who was expatiating about the variety and power of Elizabethan verse and recommended Barnabe Barnes's *Sestina* as 'one of the finest fucks in English literature. Just your bag, Tony.' Obviously Connors wishes to impress Jeremy Taylor (as a trustee of the European College) with his immaculate character. What will happen if they find out about Candida?

Something Clodia said about accusations of tyranny and oligarchy being always made by those displeased with the existing government, whatever it may be, took me back cursorily to Hobbes, who is always entertaining – even if the entertainment is a matter of refuting and jeering. I became, because of a recent conversation with Blakemore about honour, very interested in Hobbes's ideas which immediately present such an obvious contrast to those of Machiavelli. The political implications of both conceptions of honour are fascinating and I suggested to Taylor on the telephone that we should start Highgate seminars on such intriguing political themes. He took me seriously! I should have learned not to joke with Jeremy, when he cannot see my face and so discern what is going on.

Jack Blythe, one of my most pleasant ex-pupils, now in ITN, called when passing through Oxford. He had not been back for several years and commented on the number of changes in shops and streets, in the market and in the geography of the pubs. He thought these changes reflected changing times and I suppose they obviously do, however much residents take them for granted. It is strange that revisiting a place which we once knew well, we become aware of things which we do not notice (although they are happening) in our immediate familiar goat-tracks. Things have changed enormously at Oxford in the small details of the place since I was an undergraduate, in the late forties and early fifties, and since Blythe was, some ten years later. Tat shops and campus coffee shops and a certain loss of individuality in the pubs which conform to a bland municipal formula. I made some extremely pompous remark about the archaeology of every-day life, as we were walking along the High; he seized upon it quite eagerly and said something much more intelligent: 'Archaeology is a belated catalogue of domestic accidents, but seen in this light it is a running catalogue of cultural contingencies.'

This interested me considerably and at odd moments I've been brooding pleasantly about relationships between archaeology, history, fiction and reportage. I think one of the things that emerges from the Latin American novelists is that history is a matter of words describing events. Our interpretation of the past largely depends upon words already written: so that the events become the account we read of the events. So that the past is a series of impressions or interpretations obviously much influenced by the prejudices and predilections of the author, and therefore fictions. It is implicit in Borges's *Tigers* that no writing tells the absolute truth but makes its own kind of truth. Even the most banal reportage is coloured, even a filmed documentary has a viewpoint: so the most objective truth occurs in municipal records, street maps, electoral lists. And how potent a list of shop names can be in something like Dylan Thomas's *Return Journey*!

There we have Macaulay's New Zealander at his desolate sketching and what does he make of the ruins, how faulty is the scholarship that defines the function, the erstwhile function, of the destroyed edifice. Digging up London after such a holocaust, the New Zealand archaeologist might find artefacts from an African art and curio shop, make a set of wrong deductions and evolve theories that were wholly false. But in some vast eternal perspective, would they *be* false? The hoax skulls, later shown to be fake, suggested to anthropologists that Man was much older than they had thought. And the evidence now is ascertainable that man *is* older than anthropologists once thought; and it is surely arguable that the hoax prompted a sequence of theories which were provable and so established a hitherto unrealised truth. So the archaeologist travels to look at otherwise ignorable evidence because of a wrong assumption, or indeed because of a fake.

It is all an extremely hazardous business: as when I use stepping stones and find one that is insecure on which I very nearly slip. I throw the stone away without replacing it with another (poised now upon a secure one) for fear that some stranger who follows may break bones on the dangerous stone. This stranger may fall in anyway and break bones on his own initiative, but I have contributed mightily to his chances.

I shall enjoy examining this with some of my pupils. There is nothing so salutary for young people, at their stage of development, as to be reminded how very precarious the study and pursuit of history is!

Unlike Blakemore, who has bought fine hemlock for his

cellar from one of Christie's King Street auctions, I shall have to rely on an end-of-bin and oddments sale. I don't usually share his pessimism, but, of late, shades of the charnel-house have fallen across my path ever more frequently. I came across Eliot's solemnisation of the last edition of the *Criterion* the other day with its assertion that culture will be kept alive by 'obscure papers hardly read by anyone but their own contributors'. The hideous truth dawned upon me that this has already happened and that the liberal culture which underpins liberal democratic civilisation is already dead.

*

Dear Olliphant,

Thank you for your letter which I hope left you as it found me – in a state of mildly miserable fidelity. It would be foolish as well as disingenuous to pretend that it hadn't worried me, although I am fully aware that the few lines in question are no more than the sort of merry kite-flying that you enjoy after you've had a few drinks in the sanctity of your own jug-and-bottle. Unless you are trying to tell me something, or indeed preparing the graveyard for something, which I don't think I shall be able to shrug off as casually. Oh dear! That sounds much more cross and threatening than I intended it to be, but I'll leave it because it says something honestly about what I feel.

Obviously, I know that you are not Tony Connors, or a number of others that we could name, but that only makes me slightly more alarmed by your ultra-rational reflections on casual affairs. As I think I have made clear, I find the strain of separation and enforced abstention from sex tiresome and annoying, but I think I miss the rest of you as much: the jokes, the sense of having someone who is basically on my side, however difficult and misguided I may be, and whose side I am always on as far as the rest of the world goes; and the little meaningless private codes and the unconsidered kindnesses. So there's a lot more that I value about us than the fact that I like being in bed with you (and I hope that the dreary little phrase doesn't diminish the pleasure and happiness you have given me by implication). If you are telling me that you are having an affair, then I don't think I'm going to throw fits, paper-knives, or babies out with the bathwater. There is too much that I want from you and too much that I love to be quite that stupid. But I cannot agree that 'sleeping with someone these days for most people is about as exciting as other people's martinis when you have Napoleon VSOP at home. You take the martinis because they're there and they are attractively offered: but you don't savour them and they don't make you drunk.' It's funny, in its way, Olliphant, and if you were here I'd either laugh, or we'd have a short therapeutic row: and someone would say they were sorry within the hour. Though please don't think I'm silly for worrying.

As you already know I 'slept' (if that's to be the required rational word) with two people before I met you. With no once since, except you. I could not avoid becoming emotionally as well as physically involved then, and I don't think I could now. It is impossible not to say the gentler words that go with sex, as well as the other sort. And it would be demeaning to both people concerned if it were the mere relief of an itch. I once read an effective poem about it somewhere (I can't remember whose) about the pulling of the clothes aside to get it done as quickly as possible. That's not as charming as the way you put it, but it represents my own ugly gloss on the truth. I'm truly, deeply sorry if I'm making a fuss and this hurts you in any way. I think I'm a bit run down (time-of-the-month as well as the very long hours), and without a few moments snatched with you, at some time during any day, I feel half myself. Sorry. I am not asking to be told things that were best kept secret, which is in itself an impossible thing to have written. All I want is to make my own position clear. It's often very difficult to say I love you, even from the next room.

I'm glad you enjoy the gossip. After the above, I feel slightly ashamed of having mongered it (in the past) quite as assiduously. I think, in future, I am going to try to say nice things about everyone: however difficult. Connors is a reformed character, it would appear, although the rumours about him and Candida Taylor persist. He wants to leave politics for an attractive new job as Warden of a European College for very able kids, pre-university, to be set up in Kent and, since J. Taylor, among other worthy people, is a trustee, is out to demonstrate integrity. The source of rumour about him and the Taylor daughter (the pretty, pretentious, elder one – if you recall) is Bill Delahaye, who Ellis Fulford says is the first recorded example of a split libido. I don't think it means anything, but it made me laugh. Ellis, incidentally, says he is disqualified from the Wardenship described because he proposed to Jeremy Taylor a book on the Commonwealth entitled *Pillars and Caterpillars* and had to explain that he wasn't serious. Roger Ingestre remains as aloof and sane as ever: but is actually directing people's attention towards significant flaws in the general Highgate projection – after the very good reception of the first public pamphlets. It's only when I write to you that I realise how seriously I take them. With a guilty start, because I can imagine your scorn. But it's no longer the party we joined, Olliphant: things are sometimes very bitter and others, some quite senior, have doubts.

There has been a little local difficulty (as the phrase increasingly occurs) about a new Labour Youth Organiser called Andy Bevan who is a self-declared Trotskyist and has been a major thorn in Reg Prentice's crown in Newham. Jim Callaghan has personally deprecated the appointment, but it looks as though it will go through. It has still to be confirmed by the NEC. There is a lot of disquiet among old and wise heads about what is happening in the party and much more talk about 'entryism', including a serious warning from Harold Wilson. Furthermore Transport House has told Huddersfield East to think again about its shortlist of candidates when Jack Mallalieu retires at the next election. A Scottish Tory has counted ten MPs who are active propounders of Marxist and Communist principles. I'd got about as far as the index finger on my left hand when up popped the Democratic Socialists (who would bring back your old dyspepsia) with the news that there were at least thirty such! I think it is serious and quite different from the old arguments that used to tear us apart. Batman swooped in today with a defence of Marxists inside the party, but Transport House refused to issue the text. Make of that what you will.

I imagine you have been following with the same sense of gloom and exasperation all the Rhodesian farce at Geneva. Ivor Richard is the man I envy least in the world: it must be torture having to be patient day after day while first one lot and then another go through their statutory tantrums. And the whole furious sounding off signifies absolutely nothing. They'll hang on for another week or so and then it will be all over.

The negotiations with the IMF are due to finish pretty soon and the price is a mini-budget which I think will do little for our popularity, but Callaghan and Healey have promised tax relief next year if everyone is very good and sits quietly. If they expect any kind of union agreement on a further phase of wage restraint, I don't see that there is any other alternative. I remember this was one of Bill Delahaye's predictions last June at one of the first Highgate meetings, but so far our leadership is showing a high talent for improvisation and I see no likelihood of any major defections which would make the atmosphere favourable for a centre party for a long time yet. An idealist might be excused for asking whether improvisation is enough.

The appointment of Vance seems to be a very good one although I don't suppose he will have the impact of his astonishing predecessor. Perhaps that's not a bad thing: too much power concentrated in one man who was nominated but not elected. Anyway, it's reminded me of the splendid joke in an Irish paper, worthy of Myles na Gopaleen himself: I wonder who's Kissinger now? At last we know.

I hope you will write soon. I'm not asking for reassurance and you are obviously desperately busy: but your letters are warm and funny and full of you and your confidence and I am very silly to fret about the odd sentence, because they make me feel as I used to sometimes on Sunday mornings when we had a little time together and it didn't matter whether we were in the same room or not. I'd better stop before I howl.

All my love, my darling,

R.

6

The return of *The Dazzling Pilgrimage*

The rubicund, haginicholine face of Barnaby Freeth registered all the sense of revelatory alarm that must have been Ebenezer Scrooge's on Christmas morning. The bonhomous eyebrows were arched in astonishment, the bushy nostrils flared in anticipation, the bristles of his tough beard spurted in excitement.

Across the table O. Farr-Quinell of the World Banking Confederacy puffed quickly and with application at a very, very large cigar. Expertly, he studied the burning end.

'Farr-Quinell! You can't mean it!' said Barnaby Freeth. 'What was that figure again?'

'Ninety thousand pounds sterling per annum after tax,' said Farr-Quinell studying his cigar still.

He spoke without emotion. Barnaby Freeth was well known in certain circumstances for getting up like a whirlwind. This was one of them but, unfortunately, his emotions were so disarranged that he banged his knee on the underside of the desk and then cracked his forearm painfully, as he staggered momentarily, against its edge: so that his vigorous pacing, intended to impress the International Super Civil Servant with his dynamism and intensive powers of decision, was motivated as much by pain as by forcefulness, and a little lopsided.

Not only was Freeth disconcerted by the quality and nature of the amazing offer, but he was also slightly discomposed by the personality of O. Farr-Quinell, one of the most illustrious products of the Dragon School, Winchester, King's College, Cambridge, and the Europa College, Bruges, alumnus cum laude of Harvard, Bologna, Basle and Coimbra in record time. One of the highest paid of the founding Eurocrats, he had now, still aged only forty-four, become one of the elite knot of Cosmocrats with great power in the Western nexus and enormous influence outside it. Hardly a name in the average household, his was one the very whisper of which started echoes in the most deeply carpeted corridors of power, even in Paris. It was *whispered* frequently. All this careered through the mind of Barnaby Freeth as the pain in his arm and leg subsided and he paced with better equilibrium and more convincing energy; but it was the man's imperturbable confidence, the public school serenity, that somehow (as it always did in men far less awesome) got to him.

Farr-Quinell sat perfectly still and composed, except for moments of communion with his cigar. He was immaculately dressed in a fine fawn worsted suit with waistcoat, a pale green shirt and a brown and green bow-tie only slightly flamboyant. The crispness of his hair, which though frizzy would never fall out, matched that of his voice. His somewhat equine face might have been that of a comedian except that the eyes were bold, blue and penetrating. His blink-rate was low, as indeed was his pulse.

Barnaby Freeth wore good suits and went to expensive barbers, feeling he owed as much to the electorate; yet as he paced he was conscious of the balding spot upon his scalp and the creases behind this knees. Nevertheless, he must show decision and clout.

'You're asking me to make an enormous step in the light of the high responsibility I bear to the nation within Her Majesty's Government,' he said.

'Quite,' said Farr-Quinell, crisply.

'Special Contingencies Adviser to the World Banking Confederacy!' murmured Freeth.

'It's extremely challenging work,' said the Cosmocrat. 'Whenever any national economy got into a muddle, you would be called in to advise us. We consider that you know as much about muddles as anyone outside Moscow. We need expert opinion on the panic, confusion, vacillation that attend upon the train of economic misrule. I'm sorry to have to press you for a decision, but as you know the *fait accompli* is an essential aspect of World Banking operations if we are to avert speculative flux and reflux.'

He said something in a language Barnaby Freeth did not recognise.

'Beg pardon?' said Freeth.

'Heraclitus,' said Farr-Quinell.

'Oh,' said Freeth. 'I see.'

His jaws clamped together.

'I don't hang about when it's a matter of acting and when action, and prompt action at that, is called for,' Freeth said. 'Ninety thousand a year after tax. I accept.'

'Good. You'll tender your resignation as Chancellor today and apply for the Chiltern Hundreds.'

'Yes.'

'Excellent.'

The immaculate Super Civil Servant rose with quiet authority. He extended a long, well-kept hand:

'Freeth,' he said.

'Farr-Quinell!' said Barnaby Freeth.

'It's not so much a question, Augustine, of a nest of asps among which I am obliged to bare my bosom to the arrows of outrageous fate,' said Sir Hoke Dick, his strong voice trembling slightly with indignation, 'but that as custodian of this proud bastion of freedom against the darkening clamour of less happy lands, I feel a certain wrath on behalf of the people, those English men and women who never have and never will bend the knee to contumelious aliens.'

'I can understand how betrayed you must feel, Hoke,' said Augustine Cornflour.

He was still faintly uneasy when he addressed the Prime Minister by his given name.

'I appreciate that you can, Augustine. Loyalty is that precious commodity which though devalued upon the World Market, and even within the Community, flourishes eternally in the noble mind. And may I say, Augustine, since you have held office, I have been struck not only by the flair you have shown and the rapid grip upon the nettles of responsibility that you have exerted, but also by the nobility of your approach. You are on the way, my boy, to that magnaminity of outlook and commonness of touch that encourages the honest citizen to thrust forward his horny hand in instinctive trust and friendship.'

'Thank you, Hoke. Thank you very much.'

'Not only that,' said Sir Hoke Dick, pausing impressively. 'I have become aware, Augustine, that you have drunk deep at the Parnassian well. And at a time when ministerial proliferation, alas! alas!, only serves to increase the odds of betrayal, I have decided on nuclear government whereby a cabinet of a very few profoundly trusted men directs, through more junior ministers whom they themselves hold in the highest confidence, the affairs of the nation. These junior ministers reposit their belief in a handful of the most tried senior Civil Service. And in this way a lofty pyramid of faith will rise as a symbol of the will and purpose of the British race. To this end, my boy, I now invite you to combine in the new Ministry of Domestic Well-Being the existing Treasury as well as your own Interior (the working amalgam you have forged already), and to assume what the Press will call overlordship. It will make you quite a powerful man, Augustine.'

Neville Chamberlain Wynstanley filled a long glass with crushed ice and a round of lemon before splashing recklessly in some dry Italian vermouth. He went over to the drawer of his desk and took out a packet of Italian cigarettes which he bought specially in Soho. They were awful cigarettes, but

they evoked Italy. From another drawer he took a photograph of a great Italian film-star, dressed alluringly but
entirely decorously in a simple summer frock. Switching on
a slide projector he threw up on to the wall an image of
Cattolica, that vulgar, noisy, rapacious, colourful *Italian*
town.

From his armchair Neville Chamberlain Wynstanley
basked in the light and warmth of his evocation. His squat
slightly plump body became lean and sinewy, his pale round
face hardened and bronzed, his eyes undimmed, his moustache darkened and curved cruelly down around his thin,
hard mouth. The strings again crept in with delicate insistent
rhythm, once again the trombones throbbed Uwha Uwhawha
and in a silky languorous contralto the girl stepped out of the
picture frame and sang:

> *Permesso*
> *Just a smile and an espresso*
> *And two strangers in a Renaissance town*
> *Long after the sun was down . . .*
>
> *Va bene?*
> *Dreams that didn't cost a penny*
> *As two strangers on the isle of Capri*
> *Looked out on a starlit sea*
>
> *The crystal the wine the music were yours*
> *And mine*
> *Those sun-steeped days*
> *The sparkle the spray the magic is here*
> *To stay*
> *Now we've composed our Roman lays.*
>
> *Giulietta*
> *How my life is so much better*
> *Now two lovers in Verona share bliss*
> *In each sigh and tender kiss*
> *Such thrills I wouldn't miss.*

Wha, whaaaa. And a tripping four-note rising figure on the strings.

Neville Chamberlain Wynstanley was not entirely happy with the very last line of his lyric, but the pizzicato needed those extra six syllables to round off the song and make the artistic miniature whole. And he knew she would not mind if he changed the last line. He sipped his vermouth and smiled lazily back at her. . . .

Then the bloody telephone rang. Wynstanley thought that if this was Espadrille again calling him at home during his meagre and precious free hours, he would probably explode. He put on his spectacles, pushed himself out of the deep chair with a little effort and plucked at his small moustache rather petulantly as he went to the telephone.

'Wynstanley!' he snapped.

'This is Mrs de Wagram,' said that harsh, lubricious voice he so detested. How different from that lovely sound that he had been hearing a moment or two before, now far away fled!

Images of those loose, hideous, roseate knickers floated nauseatingly before Wynstanley's tightly shut eyes: brief yet voluminous disembodied knickers edged with black lace.

'Yes, Madam,' he said, bracing himself and choking back his bile.

'You must come here at once, Wynstanley. Something really urgent has come up. I can't talk over the telephone. At once, you understand!'

For as many as five minutes Mrs de Wagram had thought that she might actually have been hearing, for the first time in all her transactions with the paranormal, *real* voices.

Mrs de Wagram was making a few elementary preparations in the room at a South London municipal building, once an old somewhat rambling private house, when she heard what she first took to be a form of religious service. A single voice proclaimed something and many other voices made a fervent response. The only curious aspect of it was that the single voice was female and the other voices were predominantly male and Mrs de Wagram knew of few spiritual organisations in which women took a leading part. Then there was a certain amount of chanting and something like a hymn: but if the priestess or celebrant was a woman, it could not possibly be anything to do with the scattering of men in mackintoshes carrying little cases, whom she had noticed on their way to the hall and had taken to be members of some tacit brotherhood.

The suitability of the room to Mrs de Wagram's purposes rested on an enormous fireplace behind which there had been something resembling a priest-hole. It was doubtful whether it had ever been used by priests, since the house was early nineteenth century, built by a well-known South London eccentric prone to a variety of religious manias. Perhaps the intruding voices travelled from above or below by some acoustic freak occasioned by the idiosyncratic chimney arrangements. She slipped into the fireplace – now apparently boarded over with ochre hardboard – and listened.

She heard clearly the word 'Albion', reflecting with irony that this was the sort of word that acolytes of the Psychobolic Church were furnished with when concealed in that very aperture in order to enhance the atmosphere of a 'meditation' or 'seance'. The singing started again and there was something sinister about it that made Mrs de Wagram shiver: it reminded her of a thumping, romantic anthemry that had been so terrifying when she was a girl.

Uppermost in her mind, however, was the inconvenience of such interference during her forthcoming meeting of Psychobolic converts. Not only would their serenity be impeded by the rival ceremonies: they might also wonder (as she had) about voice-production and where they all came from. She decided to visit the caretaker and ask how long the meeting was likely to take and whether it might be possible to tenant an alternative room.

On the way down the grandiose and elaborately carved stairs, Mrs de Wagram happened to glance to one side at a strange stained-glass window on which was portrayed an intricate cabalistic design. As a result of some minor accident with a ladder one of the lights had been poked out and through the space Mrs de Wagram saw into the room below. She was transfixed with horror: there (in what was evidently the rally she had overheard) were ranged in paramilitary phalanxes fanatic-looking men in the identical uniform of dark, well-pressed trousers with white gaiters and well-shone service boots, gleaming white shirts of military cut, and identical armbands. They were being inspected by a slender woman, very striking in knee-length boots, riding breeches and a startling white shirt, carrying a short whip.

A terrible cold fear clasped at Mrs de Wagram's heart as she saw this revelation, but she was not easily a prey to panic. Her adroit mind flickered over the problem and she acted quickly, firmly and logically. She found the caretaker, made arrangements to move the meeting and telephoned the grotesque but absolutely faithful Wynstanley. A great rage which was the more dangerous because it was controlled, almost cerebral, possessed Mrs de Wagram: that England – tolerant mother of the various political parties, several religions and multifarious cults – should be menaced however distantly by this malignant growth.

Uneasy in spite of his comfortable surroundings and high position in the outwardly unprepossessing Department of Morale and Public Decency, Lord Spiedermann glanced furtively around the room. Elevated to the peerage in order to carry out his brief as a Minister of State on behalf of the powerful new domestic overlord, the Right Honourable Augustine Cornflour, CH, Spiedermann had, he supposed, achieved one of his ambitions. But it had been a sour triumph: he did not feel that he had been recognised for his intrinsic worth, so much as used for his expertise and mollified for his special intelligence about the new political meteor. And whereas his smooth manner and impeccable *savoir faire* allowed him to treat with moral vigilantes with perfect composure, and his early training enabled him to crack remorselessly down on the sophistries of pornographers and bent policemen, his own spirits were too low for him to attack matters of Morale with his former zest.

His telephone purred. The secretary announced that a delegation from the WRVS had arrived to see him. The appointment was one that he had forgotten, but it was obviously one that he must keep. The ladies were anxious to find out what part their service could play in contributing to national morale. He had received a stirring letter from one of the senior membership recalling the days of the Blitz and the Fall of France and the Nazi shadow. Lord Spiedermann combed his hair, tried out his voice and waited for them.

Three women in the distinguished uniform of the service were shown in. They were, thought Spiedermann, surprisingly young and attractive; not quite what he had expected. He experienced an uplifting of his mood at the thought that morale was already high enough in the country to encourage such well-set-up young creatures to voluntary service. He invited them to take off their coats. They did.

Spiedermann had always had a mild and harmless kink about women in uniform: in former days he had often been aroused by mere bus conductresses, and now was sometimes incongruously stirred by a traffic warden, given that she was already quite pretty. He turned from his desk with pleasant anticipation: to find the three women in the same kind of uniform, but not the kind he had expected. They wore rollneck sweaters, light skirts with deep slits on either side and (what he should have noticed) calf-length boots with sharp heels. Having not discarded the WRVS hats, they looked a trifle incongruous, but the automatic pistols held by the two flankers of the trio hampered Spiedermann's enjoyment of the situation. He recognised the standard Borgedici amazon's fighting kit: the provocative skirt, designed really to allow for complete freedom of movement in karate without detracting in any sense from its wearer's femininity on more social occasions; the snug boots with stiletto heels and metal toe points for close combat, with their concealed daggers . . .

'All aright, Sid,' said the middle woman.

He cursed himself for not recognising Lucrezia herself.

'Lord Spiedermann . . .' he said hoarsely.

'Sid Aperkins,' said the virago. 'I remember the awhole story about your early alife in Anewport, as clearly as I arecall your clammy ahand on my athigh! Now then, Lord Sid: Catherine says she awants the Cornflour photographs right anow or you're adead.'

'They're in a vault in a Swiss bank.'

'Get them by afour days from anow or . . .'

The two other women waved the automatic pistols in the air from side to side, slowly.

'All right,' said Spiedermann weakly.

'And one amore thing,' said Lucrezia Borgedici. 'I want to be invited to adinner at Number Ten Adowning Street by Sir Hoke Adick. Me apersonally.'

'He's not like that, Sir Hoke! He wouldn't look twice at an Italian. . . .'

'Yes?'

'At an Italian beauty like you. You're the flashing Mediterranean type: Sir Hoke is more for the English rose – but he is a man of iron control in such things.'

'Get me invited and don't ask abloody silly questions!'

Silently the three bogus voluntary servants donned their overcoats, buttoning them with menace, gazing at Spiedermann. Then they left.

The Minister of State sat down heavily at his desk and put his head in his hands. Not only would they use the photographs of Cornflour, they would then reveal to Cornflour the source. The Special Branch would take him off somewhere and grill him like Saint Lawrence. He was ruined.

Lucius reflected bitterly on the blandishments of status and position, so deeply inculcated into the underprivileged in British life and taken so for granted by their social counterparts. It was such goads to rank and apparent distinction that had poisoned his system with splenetic juices of revenge and subsequently made his lunge so intemperately for proffered honour from a man he might himself have exploited. Why had he not been content to realise his assets, retire to the French Riviera and amuse himself (and increase his capital) by finishing his autobiography, *The Gropes of Wrath*.

'Again,' said Arnold Espadrille, from the sound-proof cubicle, deep below the premises of the Maple Street Fresh 'n' Freeze.

The gas-masked, ear-muffed, rubber-suited figures in the interrogation studio wound back the tape of *These You Have Loved*, worked the bulbs of the sprays which emitted jets of cheap, pungent perfume into the already impregnated air, and ran (silently) on the giant screen the endless videotape of *Coronation Street*.

Espadrille pressed the key in the control-room and ordered with prodigious calm:

'The softener.'

It is not easy for men in overall rubber-suits with additional earmuffs and gas-masks to look doubtful about an order, but these three men, trained professionals that they were, did.

Espadrille remained immobile, implacable: his sallow face composed, a deep dull self-satisfaction in his inset eyes. The softener was his own inspiration, realised by top technologists in the employ of the security forces: a machine which captured in movement and vibration the noise sensation of five powerful pneumatic drills upon a granite surface.

Rufus Bushchat knew nothing about the softener, nor indeed about the tense secrets about which he was being interrogated. He was nevertheless *in extremis*. A master of psychological torture, Arnold Espadrille had quickly, after the initial selection test, charted Bushchat's areas of vulnerability. Out of a vast library of resource material, he had drawn items which he calculated would erode the very spirit of an intellectual and cultural snob.

Bushchat groaned and shut his eyes, clapping at the same time shivering hands to his ears, but he could not escape the cheap perfume or the vibrations.

'He's a tough one, I'll say that for him,' said Arnold Espadrille. 'If he doesn't break soon, it will have to be the LBC telephone programmes or *Thought for the Day* and provincial hotel frying-fat.'

He pressed down the key and said in his light, authoritative voice:

'Now, Bushchat, you have nothing to gain from stubbornness. Tell us about the master-plan. . . .'

'At the end of the day our strategy must be aimed at the ultimate erosion of the stranglehold imposed upon our legitimate aspirations by financiers and the moguls of international big business, said Griff Crabbe.

Bert Flexion gave him an alert stare and responded with an assenting and determined bite upon his pipe-stem.

'Not only my own members, but the great workers' movement as a whole, are entitled to expect from their representatives the deployment of initiatives, however ruthless, in the securing of a position from which to launch an unassailable negotiation in defence of their rights. It is the appropriate time for abandoning a posture of conciliation and boldly carrying the matters of unarguable principle into the enemy camp, plonking them firmly down on the table and saying: "Here we stand and we are not budging!" '

Nodding his head slowly, Bert Flexion removed his pipe deliberately from his characterful jaws. And then put it back again. Griff Crabbe proceeded:

'Split is our first target and the loathsome international web of Furgusson-Jungfrau, the monolithic symbol, if ever there was one, of the European profit-motive, against which,' his voice took on its dreaded scathing edge, 'the capitalist, anti-proletarian façade of puppet apparatchik, such as the Brussels commission, is as nothing. We must shrink from nothing. There must be no "Fair play, you chaps" about this. What is discreditable in his sybaritic life, lived at the expense of members' tears, must be disclosed to the working people through the powerful media which is exactly what we have on hand to hoist with its own petrard.'

He unlocked a drawer and drew out a brief-case with a combination clasp. He flicked the necessary sequence of numbers to open it and withdrew a thick file.

'The dossier on Split!' he said. 'We demolish this Titan and all the other minnows will be rushing for shelter as we demonstrate the resolution with which we intend to press this matter to a just conclusion. And, comrade, each step in the direction brings us closer to our friends in Soviet Russia and bears witness to our solidarity. What do you say?'

Once again, Bert Flexion removed his pipe from his mouth, upthrust his chin, placed it in an ashtray with care, unstrapped his watch and placed it on the table in front of him. As the second hand reached the minute, he began to speak – fluently and without hesitation. For two minutes and thirty-five seconds precisely, uninterrupted.

The nightmare was particularly dreadful for Lepidus Pounce, who had fallen asleep on his swivel chair at his desk, where he was putting in eighteen or nineteen hours a day. The Laureateship was vacant and in the brilliant time-space kaleidoscope of his dreaming (for although he dominated all his conscious material, even Pounce was not in control of the imagery of his sleeping moments) he was aware of meetings taking place all over London from which he was excluded: literary journalists in the upper rooms of pubs with gossip, ribaldry and malice; viziers of cultural administration in the latest fashionable restaurants with anecdotes, cultural 'change and tactical appreciations; academic berserks in bars at centres of broadcasting conspiring with

306

the media monsters against Culture. They were all determined to prevent him receiving the award that was his due.

So vivid was the dream that he was almost reaching for the telephone to seek reassurance from Branston Simcox, whom he did not like or trust but whose interests were coincidental with his own, when he was able to shake himself properly awake. He waited until his palpitations died down and applied himself once more to the draft rules for his Board of British Cultural Standards – to be ultimately formulated in the interests of consumer protection and public intellectual mediocrity.

Warrington Stokes was a little disappointed. He had now retired from the Premiership for over a year and so far there had not been a single honour that had come his way. No knighthood, no invitation to the Order of Merit, no directorships, not even a call to head a commission of enquiry into a suspect national institution. He knew that he had made many enemies, as who could not in political life; but he had never realized, when generous himself in office, how firmly established the dog was in the manger, how assiduously the grapes were kept from the fox, how stout the stable door was from the outside and how willing horses were very quickly put out to grass. '*That's it!*' He chuckled, with the triumph of one to whom everything comes with patience. 'I'll write my memoirs.'

Before the cameras, Deverell Pinpoint favoured Augustine Cornflour with the concentration of one about to pith a frog: a distasteful operation, perhaps, but necessary in the dissection of the central nervous system of a specimen – for the public good.

'Would you not say, Minister,' said Pinpoint, the lines of his forehead corrugating into isobars that foretold a

Force Eleven interrogation, 'that power is being over-concentrated in the hands of a very few people and that this is dangerous for democracy?'

'It depends on what you understand by power, Mr Pinpoint.'

'I know what I understand by power, Minister, and I'm sure that the television audience knows what it understands by power: what I am concerned to know is what *you* and Sir Hoke Dick understand by power.'

'The point is, Deverell, that I don't think you *do* understand what power is. . . .'

'With respect, Minister, I've sat in this chair for some twenty years asking the most eminent world statesmen about its various forms and I think some of their wisdom may have rubbed off.'

The humility of Pinpoint's words was accompanied by one of his wry triangular smiles, with its base along his cheek-bones and its apex at the top of the central cicatrice of his frown, by which he managed to convey a sense of humour without ceasing to look stern.

'With respect, Mr Pinpoint, if you will let me finish what I was saying. . . .'

'Please. . . .'

'I don't think you do understand what power is in Sir Hoke Dick's highly original interpretation of the nature of government. I think you have confused the Prime Minister's intention of streamlining departmental co-ordination, by making a few senior Ministers responsible for a broad spectrum of policy within certain confines, with the concentration of executive authority. . . .'

'I think I know quite well what I understand and what I do not, Minister, and I shall reserve the right to do so, as no doubt will the television audience who make up the British electorate: but is it not a *fact* – and I put it to you plainly – that home affairs, including the domestic economy, are under your personal diktat. As are European and foreign affairs under that of Les Wall, who happens to be Sir Hoke

Dick's uncle-by-marriage, and everything else under that of Doctor Simeon Sidestreet? Is this not so?'

'As usual, Deverell, you are over-simplifying a perfectly simple....'

'Is this not so, Minister?'

'Kindly allow me to finish, Mr Pinpoint. The three Ministers you have named have been given broad and solemn responsibility in the areas which you have delineated, and I think I speak for each of us when I say that we are keenly aware of it, and that we shall approach our duties with humility but also with zest. Dr Simeon Sidestreet is one of the brightest young stars in our firmament and Les Wall is one of the wisest old heads in our councils, who forges links with the great Fabian tradition and our grass roots....'

'We are not here to discuss the qualities of the men concerned, Minister: we are here to examine the dangerous accretion of power in ...

'I'd just like to finish what I was saying, Deverell. ... If it comes to that, Mr Flexion is still a member of the government and so is Mr Crake....'

'But no longer of the Cabinet! And Mr Flexion hardly carries the influence in the Department of Agricultural Implements and Social Equipment that you have in overall control of the Treasury, the Home Office, Economic Development and the Media. I put it to you: is that not too much for one man?'

'First of all, Deverell, let me remind you that the option of resignation is always open to Mr Flexion and Mr Crake, if they are discontented, which I have no reason to assume they are. Too much for one man, you ask? Never has a Cabinet been backed by such powerful brains as the present one. At my suggestion, Sir Hoke Dick has appointed an Intellect Reservoir to replace the archaic Think Tank of previous administrations. It is chaired by one of our most able civil servants, Rubicon Tweed, a man who knows the significance of every nut and bolt of power. We have the industrial know-how of Lord Steroid, the unrivalled experience in the power games of the mighty of Mungo Starveling, the vast grasp of multi-national economic truths of Anaximander Split and the aplomb of Reynard Tarsus, perhaps the greatest living expert on mass indoc ... communication.'

It was all that Deverell Pinpoint could do to maintain an expression of fearless independence and investigative determination, at the news.

'I put it to you, Mr Cornflour,' he said heavily, 'that the Intellect Bank, as you call it, might be seen as an Elitist Cabal, who ...'

'I put it to you, Mr Pinpoint,' said Augustine Cornflour, 'that you are arrogant and impertinent. I would remind you that I am a Minister of the Crown and I have no intention of allowing my motives to be impugned by a latter-day Herophile.'

No one had ever spoken in that way to Deverell Pinpoint before.

As they walked away through the morning sunshine after Mass, Catherine and Lucrezia Borgedici, suitably shriven and exalted, gave their minds once again to the business of the forthcoming week. They were a delectable sight for the connoisseur of female beauty: the elder sister voluptuous and confident in a close-fitting dark brown dress with a high neck, dark brown seamed stockings and very high-heeled shoes, with her fairish hair coiled in a magnificent chignon and her easy sensual movements; the younger sister, wonderfully proportioned in a pretty flowered dress and light blue-and-white shoes, flesh-coloured stockings, with her flowing black hair, her alarmingly blue eyes and the elegant controlled walk of a trained model which rippled around a magnificently rigid spine.

'It's perfectly simple,' said Catherine. 'Sir Hoke Dick drinks only lime juice. You put the capsule in his pewter tankard which he always uses. He will develop symptoms in the early morning and last the week. He should be at rest by the time we go to confession next Saturday.'

'And how are ayou getting on with Phase Atwo?'

'I am having lunch with Cornflour tomorrow. I shall have seduced him by fourteen-thirty, dominated him in the third or fourth coition by sixteen-forty-five and be his permanent mistress by the time I leave for our meeting at eighteen hundred hours.'

'And if not, the aphotographs?'

'This is more effective than blackmail. You have a lot to learn, *cara*. Your mind is crude. I used the photographs for reference – purely for reference.'

'That's as amay be. But you still aneed ame to do the abumping off.'

'You see!' said her sister, with an expressive Latin gesture. 'You make use of crude and out-of-date slang.'

Her eyes flashed. Lucrezia was subdued.

'Now then,' said Catherine Borgedici. 'Tell it to me again.'

'Steroid: curare; Starveling: abrake failure; Split: an accident while aswimming; Sidestreet: apublic disgrace and suicide; Wall: blood-pressure made acritically high by Clara and Valentina . . .' recited Lucrezia wearily.

'That will do for the moment,' said her sister. 'Oh – and Spiedermann. He knows too much.'

'How?'

'Electrocution in the Shepherd Street sauna. See to it.'

After the initial shock of Gina's revelations, Josephine Cornflour regained control of her emotions.

'I'm not telling you because of bitchiness,' said Gina. 'But I'm sick of it. And I'm not going to do it any more with anyone. I don't know what I'll do: whether to become a nun or enrol in the Open University. But I'm abandoning all *that*.'

Josephine felt deeply compassionate. The poor girl had been through so much.

'I'd like to help you,' she said.

'No,' said Gina firmly. 'Help England.'

She paused significantly.

'That's why I told you about him: because working in his office like I do, as the junior secretary – and that's only because he thinks I'll tell what I know and likes to have a bit handy, if you'll excuse that way of putting it – I hear all these things and see confidential papers and the rest of it. And I *know* there's a conspiracy to use him as the front in a dictatorship. And now there's this Italian woman who he's been seeing a lot and having lunch with tomorrow and a good friend of mine knows her from the past and she started off as a tart and is now a lady gangster, so he says. Your uncle's going to her place and God knows what she intends for him.'

'What do you think I can do?'

'Plead with him. Make him see what's right,' said Gina. 'You've got the brain and you've got the innocence.'

When Gina had rather tearfully gone, Josephine reviewed the situation calmly. Her conversations with Rufus Bushchat, now significantly perhaps disappeared, had alerted her to the sensitivities of the precarious political balance in the country and her own intelligence had worked out what forces were at work to undermine democracy. Now Gina's information had crystallised Rufus's theories and her own worries: she must, she resolved, save not only England but her Uncle Augustine.

The suggestion that she plead and argue was one she soon cast aside. Accustomed to the chicanery of politics and diplomacy, her uncle would soon be able to dismiss her feeble attempts as naive and untutored. But perhaps there was one way which, from Gina's account, her own shrewd observations, and a certain woman's instinct, would almost certainly succeed; whereby she might forestall the evil designs of the Italian woman and even establish permanent influence with her uncle for the general good.

Josephine blushed at the idea, but her excellent mind told her that it was necessary. And so determined, she went out to a certain shop she had noticed in Knightsbridge and made various purchases.

*

'The danger, as I see it,' said Rachel Bailey, 'is that we are turning, as a society, into soft-backed crabs. We want and expect protective legislation against everything: so that we're not deceived or cheated or fiddled. We are absolutely ripe for take-over: and when we go abroad, where no such legislation exists, we are taken almost every time.'

'I'm not sure that I agree. It might be construed as an extension of civilised English concern for those whom it's easy to exploit,' said Clodia Oricellari, smiling.

'Yes, but my argument is that we are over-protective and there is a mass of unnecessary legislation which accustoms people to accepting rules. We aren't robust and bloody-minded enough, as you are and as the French are. Especially the French.'

'I thought that one of the virtues the English most prided themselves on was bloody-mindedness. Was it not that quality, precisely, which won the war? The unbeatable combination of discipline and bloody-mindedness.'

'Discipline is all very well, but submission is quite another thing. If you extend the argument to preventative medicine, I'd contend that there again everything is being carried to excess, whether it's saccharine or cyclamates or cigarettes. I don't want people fussing about my health and I resent the infraction of my freedom of choice. It's all the little unimportant laws that make people amenable to the big and sinister laws. Disenabling legislation, in fact!'

'I don't think that there is much danger when there are people like you about in politics,' said Clodia.

'You're very kind. At the moment I don't feel as effectual and match-fit as I'd like to be. We're not as busy as we were in the last session, but it's still very tiring and I am missing my husband. Which is very adolescent of me, I suppose.'

'Why should it be? If I were married, I should want it to be that way.'

'Yes, I'm sure you would. But it's lonely sometimes, however busy one is.'

'Without wishing to seem unduly cynical about the circles you move in, I don't imagine you're lonely for lack of opportunity....'

'True,' said Rachel Bailey, wryly. 'Parliamentarians and journalists are a fairly virile category, or at least like to appear so. I imagine that you also have in mind some of the Highgates.'

'Let us say that I have been put in the way of temptation.'

'It has indeed been known. Unfortunately I am, from the evidence so far, by nature monogamous.'

'I don't think I am, particularly. Which is why I'm not married. At the same time I am not predatory. And I know from past experience what unhappy women can do when they are jealous, with or without cause. At first I was simply evasive, but I've now hit upon a really effective technique.'

'I'd be glad to hear it.'

'It's extremely simple and I can't imagine why I have not thought of it before. I assume, as the situation demands, a burning, passionate expression, or a melted, submissive one, or a look of frightening sincerity. Then I say: "Hugh, or Stanley, or Simon, or Jeremy...." '

'Jeremy!'

'Yes....'

'My God! Go on.'

'I take their hand and say: "I would love to have this adventure with you...." (I can't tell you how much I owe to the earlier films of Antonioni.) "*But*, if we are to be lovers, I want it to be something good, without shame. I will come to bed with you, but first you must tell your wife. I do not want there to be any deception, any lies, if we are to have this wonderful experience together." '

'Splendid! But you have a fairly Byzantine crew there:

314

suppose they promised you to do that, did nothing of the sort, and then came to collect?'

'It's all built into the pretty speech. "And don't think Stanley, or Simon, or whoever you are, that I will not *know*. Believe me a woman always does know. And if I thought that I too was being deceived, I should not only be sorrowful, I should also be angry. . . ." And a little grace-note of menace. It's really quite unflattering how easily discouraged some of them are.'

'I'm grateful for the tip. I'll bear it in mind for future encounters. As it happens, I am not specially bothered by the Highgates: they've got to take me for granted as they do also Sandra and Marie and each other's wives. I'm not at all surprised, though, that you and your sister should have created such a stir. And you have, there's no doubt about that!'

'Ah! I'm speaking for myself and not for Francesca. I don't know what her experience has been, or indeed how she has elected to respond. We are very different. By which I don't mean to imply that she is some kind of tramp. She is insouciant in all things which are not commercial.'

'She is an enviably beautiful woman.'

'Yes.'

'Er . . . tell me, Clodia, I know it's shamefully gossiping of me, but you did not mention Tony Connors among the contenders. He used to be among the more persistent.'

'So I understand. I have always found him a model of truth, honour and courtesy.'

'Amazing! I wonder about him. Perhaps you are altogether too confident. . . . Sorry, it's just a train of thought. I think his marriage had emotional repercussions. Then, on the other hand, he might be serious about the Taylors' daughter. Do you know her, the red-haired girl?'

'Candida. Yes. I've met her. She used to be a pupil of Roger Ingestre. Well, I hope that it works out for her. I have the impression that she is a little neurotic.'

'Is that so? It might very well be. I've always thought her

315

rather affected and I've attributed it, patronisingly enough, to growing up.'

'Charitably, perhaps.'

'I don't know. I think I was pretty trying at that age. Anyway, Jeremy's little attempt at . . . what was your word ? . . . an "adventure" with you might explain his unexpected acquiescence about his daughter and Connors. I must say, if I were a parent, which thank the Lord I'm not, I wouldn't be as sanguine about it.'

'Do you have any regrets ?'

'About children ? No. I don't think so. I suppose when we were first married, we had the odd sentimental moment when we thought how nice it would be to have a family. But nothing happened and with the endless hours Oliver had to work as a young doctor, I started to be active in politics and that was it. After that, it was already a matter of careers.'

'It's one of the reasons why I haven't married. I'm a Catholic, of course, and it would certainly have meant having children. I would be a very lousy mother.'

'And the other reasons ?'

'One I've already said something about in passing: I'm not promiscuous but I see no reason not to be, if I felt like it. And, obviously, I've never loved anyone enough to want to spend my life with him.'

'That, quite frankly, has its disadvantages.'

'Naturally.'

'If he's not quite as dedicated about spending his life with you. I'm not saying that's what it's like with Oliver and me. But I think there's probably that sort of imbalance in any marriage. D'you mean you've never thought of marrying ?'

'Oh, I had the usual infatuations. Usually with men a lot older than myself: so I can sympathise technically with Candida Taylor. Not otherwise. I once thought seriously about marrying Roger Ingestre whom I like very much: but it was purely a matter of convenience and civilised companionship on my part and I knew it would be very hurtful to him when I was unfaithful. As I should have been.'

'Yes, it would. Did you know Daphne?'

'I met her once.'

'A fine mis-mating. I'm very fond of Roger and I also find him an attractive man, physically.'

'Oh so do I! Don't mistake me,' said Clodia. 'There would have to be something of that. But he is too gentle for someone like me.'

'Connors was married to Daphne's sister, incidentally.'

'So I understand. Do you have any sisters?'

'No. Two brothers: one a dentist, the other a teacher. Comfortable wives and carloads of children.'

'At least in England you have a tradition of emancipated working women, whether married or not. It's not quite as acceptable, even now, in Italy. And people, especially other women, have the most extraordinary image of a career woman.'

'It's the same here. Make no mistake. Apropos of this general theme, one of my colleagues at the House who sits for a very working-class constituency in the Midlands tells me that thousands of his women are knocked out by Sheikh Youmani.'

'The Western world has never quite recovered from Valentino. Do you suppose that this is some kind of Jungian phenomenon? More to the point, *I* am knocked out by Sheikh Youmani at the moment and so must you be.'

'For standing out against the OPEC price rise.'

'Exactly. It's going to matter to us and to you.'

'Unquestionably. But it makes pretty fair sense to the Saudis and to the Emirates. They must be as anxious as we are not to weaken the free world economy, or to alienate the Americans. It's only a matter of time before the Russians have access to the Red Sea. I hope they appreciate the importance of Sadat. Not just *vis-à-vis* the Russians but also Qadhafi who is a jihadist. Isn't it incredible that so much power is now in the hands of people who are politically and ethically reactionary because of geological accident?'

'The more I pursue my life in the diplomatic service, the

more I recur to the existentialist despair of *mes vingt ans*: everything is accidental and all attempts at rationalisation are futile. It all helps. It allows a career diplomatist to serve on a day-to-day basis.'

'I think I remember something about cynics being preferable to fanatics in government, as well. Menken, perhaps.'

'I think I shall need all my cynicism. I think my next posting is Brussels.'

'I think I'd like that. I'm quite anxious to become more directly involved in Europe. Of course, it would be Strasbourg for me: if the opportunity occurs.'

'I like the idea of Europe. Naturally. But for an Anglophile to have to treat with the French, who automatically expect Italians to side with *them*, is going to try my Renaissance patience to the utmost. You're thinking of the Parliament rather than the Commission?'

'Yes,' said Rachel Bailey. 'I think that it's politically the most important development we can look for. And I'd like to have something to do with it. I believe that the new Europe, the potential of a new Europe, is almost evolutionary progress.'

'I agree. But I'm not committing my queen to any specific moves,' said Clodia. 'I think I'm sitting rather gloomily on a black square.'

'If that's where your money is, there you have to sit.'

'You're still an optimist. In spite of everything, Rachel?'

'What do you mean? In spite of my rocking marriage (as it seems to me at the moment)? Or in spite of the crumbling of our civilisation (as we think we know it)? Do you ever see "Kojak" on television?'

'I have seen one or two of them. . . .'

'Then I'll borrow their idiomatic formula: Life is just a bowl of jello – rough-hew it how we may. Baby!'

*

Endless people in and out and kisses and darlings; prettily

wrapped gifts, cheerful, cheerful chattery dinner and lunch and tea; champagne with cake at unlikely times. Visiting other people and strangers. Jessica being difficult and wanting her grubby friends in the kitchen. Or not wanting to go to lunch with people and then getting there and conning everyone with giggles. For once (even Jessica included) it would have been nice to go to Gloucestershire, to the cottage. Tony might have come and he would certainly now have been invited. But no: this year it was convenient for Barbara to be in London with endless people forever in the house, including the *very* famous people who seemed only to be available once a year at party time. Once she had been impressed: now she knew something of the realities of Parliament and public life. There were so many official goodwill sessions every bloody Christmas.

Tony was accepted: but there was unmistakable embarrassment, false heartiness. Barbara had asked him to spend Christmas with them and he had been there: distant, kind to her. There was all the stupid constraint that admitted her to their sophisticated social rituals (while Jessica could be stripping in the backyard) without ever being able to treat him, or he her, for what they were. Not that he seemed to want to. In telling Barbara, she had spoiled something that had been so positive in the Paris weekend. A stupid, immature reflex activated by Barbara's habitual condescension, a desire to show off. Or . . . Or a need to tie him down; make it difficult for him to discard her. Why should she have suspected that he might? She was surely over the jealousy. She had surely learned that futile lesson.

Calm. They were all so calm. Tony calm and Daddy calm and Barbara calm. And of course ghastly sniggering little sister knew, had to know and that somehow . . . yaach. . . . He too, Tony, was so cool. All right, that was what she admired about men of his age, even had admired about Roger Ingestre, kindly creased smile and gingerish aura. So different. Taken coolly that she had told Barbara and accepted it all. Daddy a little pale and shy, which probably fathers were when their daughters were first possessed by other men because they must know what the male sexual impulse was and how much was ravishment and how much or how little was the gentleness of love and . . . how much of it was rape. Rather surprised in fact at Daddy's almost apathy.

Tony never was angry and had not even hinted at resenting what she had told Barbara, but it was no longer the same. Now always a welcome guest, sitting at the other end of a sofa and embarrassed smiles, across the room, smoking a cigar and God knows what imaginings in their minds and in hers, but work meant he didn't come there often and although they met at his flat, it was much worse. A terrible strain on her nerves, with lolly-licking Jessica leering disgustingly at them. Oh fuck Christmas!

The twirl of twisted silver foil spun on its thread. Spinning and spinning and uncoiled, so that you could disappear in the spiral. Now more than ever. Lost in a cheap simple twizzle of light upon reflecting surfaces and circles of good cheer brought out to get by with merriment the yawning time. And coiled again. She watched it until her eyes blurred over. . . .

Sick, the excitement over Bukovsky, skeletal, arriving because some of them, who cared which, had demonstrated and written letters to newspapers and the authorities and did things for Amnesty. All self-centred. The poor sick man on the television with sunk, resurrected eyes. Fearfully ill-treated. And all *their* self-congratulation. Dissident. . . . Dissident. . . . And the eyes of that man who had been in one of their psychiatric prisons. The injections and humiliation and beating. The pain of a body going wrong and the terror of holding on to a good mind, always afraid it might be slipping away. That was what it was about and that was what this man knew about and they knew nothing. Nothing. NOTHING. She wanted to shout above all the smugness and self-satisfaction and nineteenth-century liberalism and idiocy. The of courses and in facts and quite franklys and honestlys. Because they were SICK.

Sunday had been *The Railway Children* and everyone (oh yes her too) (she yes) (bollocks) a bit pissed after claret and sickly Jessica boohooing alongside Roger Ingestre, streaming tears. Wisely smiled Tony and Barbara and Daddy sniffed as there was the Russian fugitive victimised (by the Czars, yes) for writing BOOKS. And the charming little girl (bloody Jessica-type) who thought it frightful that people should be so treated for Writing Books. Too good an opportunity for her to miss. And an interminable argument between them all including Rachel Bailey and her pretty round knees about whether it was possible to be liberal and militant. After the bloody RAILWAY CHILDREN. Boohoo, Boofuckinghoo!

She was sick and physically sick and went to lie down. And no one came to see how she was feeling. Jessica giggling and being tickled by Daddy and Tony's eyes on Rachel Bailey crossing her pretty round legs. I don't know. I can't tell the curtain-fold she said from the metal shade that burns my hand when I touch it, aaahwh. Hurt. It hurts and the grey rabbit's fur bloodies now. Small eye. Not like ours. The pigeons at my window seeing more than I can see. Shoo! pigeon! The crumbs are bread for little, pretty birds. I think frost is deliquescent and Orlando dredges the dim weather of what I would wish, she decided, to be. The frozen Thames and Gloriana upon a sleigh. Jingling bells, false Duessa with the rolled stockings thick upon his eyes. Oh Christ, didn't she know him. I do. Said she, bitterly.

She must have been briefly dreaming. Fallen asleep amongst them all. She looked for him and he gave her the slow smile of encouragement. And so did Roger Ingestre and so did Daddy. They must all have known she had fallen asleep and thought she was drunk. Except that she had gone away feeling sick and fallen asleep on her own bed. Where . . . Hurt, she said. It hurts. Poor Candy. Hand hurts. Something hurts. She hurts all over, Daddy, Please. . . .

Then Rachel Bailey came in with her soft deep voice and asked if she was all right, sorry for intruding but . . . Headache, she explained, and probably too much wine. Oh, cheerful sympathetic maternal noises. Chuck, chuck! Chickie-wickie! Little girl. And they must all know. All. Barbara she could imagine, with delicate eyebrows, joking. *Imagine*, darling! Little Candida. And *Tony*. Of all people. Veteran of every red-light arrondissement from Richmond to Stavanger. This was the real violation. She could feel their fingers and tits and gross pricks against and about and inside her, vicariously spoiling that intense and clear love she had shared with him. Whatever it had been. The desecration of herself in their diseased imaginations; male and female. Even her dear, loved Daddy, almost weeping through her defilement.

Oh it was bad. Then she had to return to find Tony and Rachel and Ingestre gone: but Ellis Fulford horribly there making Jessica raucous and everyone hruffing and spluttering stupid. . . . Then Marie White in three see-through layers sweating through *Je Reviens*. Never having said a truer word. Oh God! How long: intelligent conversation and Daddy's bargain claret and Jessica. . . .

Lived through, lost through. The whole Christmas farce. Remembering little snatches of poems about this day Christ was born. Moments with Tony and an obscene ritual under mistletoe with all the wrong jokes . . . aach. Retch of memory. . . . Reaching back into the acid throat, salt, salivating; wave of nausea at that foul mockery. And he did not seem to want to take time together, except for walking on the Heath. Throughout the days . . . the days. And it was possible to be liberal and militant. *Really*. Well, social democrat and militant? Was it? Was it? WAS IT?

Hours of the disillusion of Cyril Smith, the resignation of Prentice, the twenty-five Tribunites who voted against the Chancellor's package. Ingestre and Daddy exulting about a silly cricket match in India. Christ, if we can't beat bloody India. For once she was with Fulford. Everyone wants a broadly based centre party, but sure as hell no one wants *them*; including dear Tony. Oh God he hasn't touched me for so long. Jokes about Heath presenting a music programme on commercial. Onward and a dormant or dead butterfly in a corner of the room, under the mock and hideous mouldings. Ordinary white insect with perhaps faded, that is to say, yellowing, frayed wings. . . . Oh Rose thou art sick. The sweep of nausea again. . . . Candida, are you all right, darling?

Stand up and be counted, ye moderates. God rest you merry moderates, let nothing you dismay! Ding-dong. Tu-whit to-whoo. While greasy pots do keel the Joans and Jills and . . . Eeegh. Choking, dry nausea. Are you *sure* you're all right, darling?

Oh and the long, long holiday ahead and what will the righteous Germans think of us and our rotten, rotten workers, drunk for a fortnight in Dickensian gutters. They were all out walking on the healthy blasted Heath among the fens and vapours which I hope they get when she heard distantly the doorbell ringing and thought she was dreaming. She wondered about pretending to be asleep or out until she thought it might be Tony and it was. They were all out and away. . . .

Kissed him passionately and surged against him writhing breasts and hips, feeling him rise and stiffen hard hard against her, led him to her room the first time he had been there and threw herself wide open on her own bed asking him in a sob to be harsh and violent. And oh he was! Shrieking she remembered and his breath shuddering viciously as he drove into her hard until almost she remembered screaming at the highest pitch of her pleasure. . . . She thought as she moved her head struggling for breath that the door moved had forgotten to close it shut but there was no one in the house of course but when he had moved from her she pushed it firm shut and turned to him still erect and big knowing what he would like and went and knelt above him in her high stockings laughing as he whimpered in his kind of ecstasy. . . .

Then a better evening with the Italian women and an American to dinner all charm, outraging Daddy with right-wing opinions which made Tony the darling brutal wonderful lover whom she had at last had on her own bed laugh and there was a lot of hilarity and surface brilliance during which

Jessica sulked, drawing attention to herself and making Barbara think she was ill, looked certainly flushed. Just sulking. . . . Thought that Tony was being attentive to the younger dark Italian, girl that she remembered in a photograph on Roger Ingestre's desk the day I . . . Yes, Tony, unquestionably much too charming. Knocked a fork off the table and bent to pick it up, there the Italian girl's dress was pulled up on one side or disarranged she didn't know. It was hateful but the girl's beautiful face was calm and empty as usual though it was a beautiful face it was almost absolutely blank. The Italian girl stared once, almost a hint of humour in the blank beautiful face and her sister frowning slightly as though forgotten something, then once Jessica a look of venom that almost startled her.

Oh what a magnificent dinner, Barbara, so effortless. How many cordon bleu economists do you know, Roger? And now the evening was hellish again with Tony stroking the Italian girl's arm and it was obvious because she saw her sister the older nicer intelligent Italian watching them with narrow eyes no doubt she too found Tony very attractive. After what had happened that afternoon I suppose it's just a commonplace now for him as soon as it's over and Do you always eat as well as that? Why didn't Roger Ingestre interrupt them it was his bloody girl friend and there he was ineffectual as ever chatting some superior line to the American. Just for once stupid Jessica did something useful and broke them up having got over her sulks. Unusual for Jess to be so quiet: what's up, Jess? A hangover?

New Year's dreary party at Middleton's, which she hated because all the ritual of clocks and superstitious rigmarole made her uneasy and apprehensive. What did it matter, anyway, a passing of time one day much the same as the next and it was horrible because Tony could not come and the younger Italian wasn't there he said he had to spend the evening with his mother in Brighton but how could she be sure. One darkened room for dancing where beastly Middleton slid his hands on to her buttocks and stroked her all the time but she wouldn't let him kiss her and hoped his wife would see except I saw then someone else down her throat practically. Nor was Ingestre there but Daddy talking about the Honours List with boring Hay and never dancing. Barbara holding court in a sort of indoor patio with teenage idiots gaping at her foolishly. At the thought of what Tony might be doing with the Italian she drank too much and decided to go mad and play up to everyone who made a pass at her and gave some of them the shock of their lives dancing. And then humiliated herself by passing out but I don't care what they think. I don't care at all. Not at all. I DON'T CARE. She was deeply miserable. And no one cared.

*

I suppose I should feel ashamed at being surprised that I enjoyed Christmas at home: but if that's a symptom of intellectual snobbery, at least it stops there. As it happens, I had a thoroughly good time before coming back to London and a few weeks in the pub with Clifford and Teresa (reserved again, but not as stern-looking) before going back up to Oxford. Clifford was glad to have me for New Year's Eve and it's also convenient because Samantha is going back to Australia, where one of her parents is ill.

So now I feel relaxed and I ate too much and I've put on half a stone, which means some pretty energetic squash next term. Mum surpassed herself with all the Christmas food and I had a couple of very pleasant evenings down at the pub with Dad and some of his pals – even the political arguments! When I was a kid, I used to worry about being a copper's son a bit – as Fred Barton tells me he worried about being a parson's son – because it was different and in some way an interference in other people's lives. All nonsense, as I can see now, because the country policeman is as accepted for his own worth as anyone else. And it's good to see Dad welcomed by everyone in The Pony (including the villains. Villains!). It's also good to feel that Dad is reasonably proud of me and there's this corny but agreeable masculine thing of having a pint or two with the lad and a game of darts. Mum likes it too. Why don't you two get out from under my feet to the pub, so that I can get everything straight. I can't see many of the women I've met in London taking that line. Dad was very pleased and impressed about what I had to say about visiting the House and meeting various MPs. I thought he might have reservations about my opting for journalism instead of an academic career: but not a bit of it. He's now taking a close interest in the political columns and making informed comments. Ominously enough, he's started talking about the best chaps becoming interviewers on television and probably already sees me as the scourge of the next generation of politicians. The upshot is that I basked in a considerable glow of approval, because I worked hard quite a lot of the time and was seen to be working hard. It was all very satisfactory and there was also Wendy Parker. I'd forgotten about Wendy until the church dance. They evidently offer a very liberal education at physical training colleges!

Disloyal as it may seem, Wendy was very refreshing after Candida (whom I shamefully misrepresented as a steady girl friend). She has her own regular feller at her college, but very pragmatically pointed out that we were on holiday and on our own and that we had fancied each other at school. (I'd forgotten how much!) So short of actually going to bed, why not take a little healthy pleasure in each other's company. It wasn't *far* short but a lot of activity in the open-air kept it healthy. Well! Quite a girl: and there's a lot to be said for PE when it comes to body-building! No strings. No letters. Perhaps we'll meet again some time. That will be nice.

The glow continues here in London. Not quite as rosy as Mum and Dad, but Clifford and Teresa are full of benignancy in the dignified way that befits a host and hostess. And Clifford, aware that there are important exams coming up, never forgets to tell me to shoot off and hit the books when we're not busy. They are also delighted because

Candida has come to The Reeve a few times on her own. And they think she is suitable and are glad that, whatever our differences were, they have been patched up. Clifford lets all this be understood; Teresa is a little more explicit and perhaps a little more inquisitive as well.

I'm not sure, however, that things are particularly happy with Candida. Perhaps it's in contrast to the extraversion of Wendy: but she looks pale and has those same rapid changes of mood – from morose apathy to exaggerated high spirits, when she talks incessantly and to very little purpose. In fact, sometimes her brain seems to be racing and everything comes tumbling out in a tenuous chain of associations. The identity of her mystery lover is now revealed. Her parents know about it and it is all, apparently, all right. It turns out to be the MP I met with Rachel when I visited the House of Commons, Anthony Connors. He is a good twenty-five years older than Candida, but very handsome and charming. There's no reason that I can see why they should not have something serious going for them on mere grounds of age difference. Well, I couldn't compete with that sort of rival so it's just as well I'm getting over her. That may seem a bit faint-heartedly philosophic: but when I met him (although Rachel didn't show much enthusiasm) I was knocked out by the urbanity and style. And while I still like her a great deal I'm not as daft about Candida as I used to be. I doubt now that I was ever really seriously in love with her. I wanted to lay her and I still do, I suppose; and of course I'm very fond of her. But I wanted her much more when she was cool and quiet and disdainful than I do now, even though she is more vulnerable and consequently endearing now, and certainly a whole lot nicer to me. Again this may be the influence of a few trips around Wendy Parker and the benefit of sensible conversations with a thoroughly straightforward mind at other moments. Not that I could pretend for a moment that I loved Wendy (and I'm sure it was exactly the same for her), whatever we said at the time.

At the same time I feel concerned about Candida. The

problem, I'd guess, although she wouldn't dream of admitting it to me is that she doesn't trust this chap Connors and is fiercely jealous. (Well, I know what that used to feel like: but it must be worse for a young and not specially secure girl involved with such a very well set-up and assured man.) The woman she seems to be afraid of (understandably) is the Italian girl Ingestre sometimes entertains at Oxford. Again, she has said nothing directly, but she's talked of her once or twice with a scurrility that is quite unlike Candida as she used to be. It probably makes it worse, in fact, that her parents now know about it all. Admittedly they are a long, long way from Mum and Dad (for which I'm not actually sorry) and very sophisticated people; but I don't know – it must make things difficult where everything is cut and dried and rational and everything is discussed and explained. I can imagine what Wendy Parker's Dad would have said if she was involved with a man over twice her age. Or for that matter what he would have said if he had known what we were up to in the churchyard. Old Parker! (I don't suppose he's fifty yet – and yet he and my Dad and Mum all seem much older than Ingestre and Rachel and Ted White's mother. Especially sometimes Ted White's mother, I've begun to notice.) What seems particularly to have upset Candida was that she passed out at a New Year's Eve party and thinks she made a fool of herself. She says she behaved very badly, leaving the hint in the air that this was, in some way, with some of the men. I expect there was a bit of necking behind the rubber plants, or she let someone stroke her tits after a touch too much champagne. Still I mustn't be patronising. She's been having this full-blown affair with Connors and I can't see him stopping short of consummation. *That*'s a delicate way of putting it. I wonder though . . . Perhaps she hasn't been having any such affair at all and it's all an elaborate and real fantasy. That would be serious.

The last time I saw Ingestre, a day or so ago, he said very little about her indeed – except to ask if we'd met since I came to London. He said something vaguely reassuring (probably in the light of the chat I had with him at Oxford last term) about having seen her over the holiday, when she had seemed to be in good spirits. Nothing about Connors, which I would not expect. From Candida's account, he was playing it down: she said there hadn't been a moment's peace with people like Roger Ingestre and his bloody Italians in and out. It may very well be that Ingestre, having detected my recent despairing lovesickness, is anxious to spare me any upsetting details that I don't have to know. He switched to me and Schools and how work was going, calculating no doubt that, like everyone else, I am always more interested in myself than anyone else.

Rachel had told him that I was thinking of journalism. But he talked about scholarships to American universities and how useful that sort of experience could be and he talked with marked enthusiasm about graduate schemes in the EEC, well-paid important work. Knowing quite well that I haven't had anything to do with university papers, he asked how much experience I had of them.

This duty done, he moved on to things which interested *him* and the conversation took a turn for the better at once. He was a little disappointed that Prentice's resignation had not created more of a stir. True Dick Taverne had said on the radio that it was a brave and important step, that it was the moment for moderates to declare themselves and that an alliance of Social Democrats and Liberals would attract, would *still* attract (in spite of the by-election results), some rogue Tories. Ingestre too thought that *now* is the time for that alliance: but sees no hope as long as so many politicians are going to place ambition or self-interest or sheer survival before the recognition that a centre party is essential to the long-term, even the mid-term, maintenance of a democratic system in Britain.

Inflation, Rachel says, is still the problem, clearly believing that much of the optimistic noises we have heard over the past few weeks are meaningless. Singing in the dark. She invited me to tea in her flat in Bloomsbury, which is lined in every room with books and gloriously untidy. However much I was aware of her as a woman, I don't think such thoughts had crossed her mind and we talked about the pound and the apparent upturn in the economy. I happened to mention that someone I knew had been grumbling about the rotten behaviour of tourists in the London sales and she turned up a passage from a frightening book (which I have since read) about the German inflation of the twenties and how one of the first evil by-products was intense xenophobia and bitter, scornful envy of the rich foreigners exploiting a feeble currency and cheap goods at the expense of and to the envy of the native people. Although, she said, I will admit that I have never before seen notices in London explaining queueing for buses. And, of course, they are universally ignored.

I don't think I was as intelligent as I might have been because, being alone with her, I was somewhat over-aware of her inescapable femininity. I think I must have been watching her like some goon in a strip-show. Perhaps she decided not to be aware of it: but she was amused in that once-removed sexy way that older women have, which makes me never sure whether they expect and would like a breathless pass or not.

Back (from the erotic fail-safes) to Ingestre, slightly amused that I had tea with Rachel, in a different kind of once-removed way. The trouble with these people is that you never know what they are thinking, because when in doubt they look amused. Male and female alike. The first thing to learn is the slow, silent, generous, tolerant smile. Apart from politics, Ingestre is, as usual, obsessed by cricket, which I know very little about. Apparently we have beaten India spectacularly in a Test match, but the English captain has behaved 'egregiously'. Ingestre says that if I want to understand politics, cricket is very useful on and off the field.

He is also on some sort of archaeology kick and is angry about people with metal-detectors going treasure-hunting on real sites and digging indiscriminately and destructively.

This is obviously very bad. I have no pretensions to being an ancient historian let alone an archaeologist, but I hope I'm enough of a scholar to be saddened by any evidence lost. And I suppose that traces precisely my limitation as a scholar. I am saddened: Ingestre was (for him) furious.

He is often quite funny in a fairly quiet way, undeniably witty and unfailingly elegant: but on this Ingestre was almost poetic. Fragments of the pain and passion of individuals and all that is left of some attempt (however good or wicked or cruel or gentle) to make rules against which private grief and happiness worked themselves out. 'That's all it is, Steve. Not just the broken statues and battered books. Shards and chips of pottery and bones thrown aside, scrawlings and attempts at recording how it was or how it seemed to be or what it meant. At first hand, it's a desperate business. The longer I work at it, the more I am convinced I am a student of history, not a historian.'

The inevitable amused smile. At himself and at me. 'So, indeed, why not be a journalist?'

This took him to the earthquakes: the big ones in China and Turkey and the small ones around San Francisco. I have never been there, but he has and, in that mood, could imagine a sort of destruction that is quite beyond me. He related this to the CND days when he and Rachel and Ellis Fulford (who is often referred to) marched to or from or around Aldermaston. Ingestre can still talk of the holocaust. I wonder if it is a function of the intervening militancy, the chimera of the late sixties, that makes it less significant for us. We don't talk about holocausts. Was it simply that Ingestre and Rachel and the others felt righteous and helpless in the face of implacable governments? And that we don't? And would I have been a militant if I had been eighteen in 1968 and not twelve? I don't think so. But who would have thought of Ingestre marching to Aldermaston?

It's good to be in London again and in touch with all these people, for whom I have to thank Ingestre. Trumble called into The Reeve on his way to Candida's parents' place. (This impressed Teresa deeply because she had once seen him on 'Panorama': Trumble says he was pissed at the time.) He was in a very bitter mood and ticked off a list of strikes which are either on or pending. Rubery Owen have had three days in nine months without strike action in some form, making important components for the motor industry, and have just settled an electricians' strike on a technicality; Campbell Laird have a boiler-makers' strike on the grounds of some kind of demarcation dispute. The miners have been playing hard-to-get on the retirement issue with the Coal Board, so that Gormley is on and off television being hopeful and non-committal by turns. Most of the clients in the pub are less equivocal. Ted White is in Tangier, or we might have had a decent battle.

I've been trying to pack it all in by getting up at half past five or six, which bothers Teresa. It means I can get a good few hours in before I have to help with the morning chores, which gives me odd moments to keep up with the papers and my notebook of events. I don't think I've ever been more contented. Quite superfluously, I've no doubt, I have pangs of conscience about being so pleased with myself when Candida is probably having a bad time: but I don't see that I can do much. I could ask Rachel Bailey: but it seems crazy to ask an MP (whom I don't really know at all and who is being kind to someone else's protégé) to sort out some-one else's emotional crisis, when I can't even define its nature.

Candida came down to the pub on her own the other night and drank enough, obviously, for Clifford to suggest I saw her home before time was called. Very quietly. 'She's a bit upset, your girl friend. Probably a bit of a row at home. Often happens. You get around the other side and look after her. Go on.' I don't know what he really makes of it.

She had cut a cartoon out of the *Evening Standard* of a dismal-looking couple in a bedroom, one saying to the other: 'Let's face it, all we have in common is our commitment to Europe.' She said she was keeping it to edge in black for her parents' tomb at Highgate Cemetery and perhaps liberals would come from all over the Community to visit it.

I'm really very glad that I don't think, can't think, of my parents that way. I took her to the gate of her house and I think she wanted me to kiss her and whatever. It might have been easy and I might have passed up an opportunity not to be repeated, but it would not have been right somehow. You taught me a lot, Wendy Parker, and I am grateful, which is why I am sitting up half the night writing this. Sunday tomorrow: so I'll lie in.

*

Forty Years On, the Editor of *Tribune* says that things haven't changed all that much and that Capitalism is still the great enemy. It is disturbing, though, to realise how much further to the left some people in the Labour Party are since the days when Cripps, Laski, and even Bevan, founded the paper. Foot admitted on the radio that *Tribune* did not reveal as much as it knew of what was happening in the USSR during the thirties for fear of damaging the Cause. He also said this had been a mistake. All very well, after the event.

Although I seldom read *Tribune* these days, except on those occasions when there is some nine-day excitement, I remember it with an affection that is strictly retrospective in the days of the right–left argument of the fifties, when I joined the party and it was the hammer of Gaitskell and the Campaign for Democratic Socialism. How angry we used to get!

Kinnock, talking about *Tribune*, said it tried to stretch its readership by aiming above their heads a little. 'Aim at the belly,' he said, 'and they will think with their genitals. . . .' (On the face of it a somewhat paternalist sentiment for such a good socialist, I should have thought.)

Perhaps it is the consolidation of middle age working upon me, but I am increasingly aware of more and more people who seem to be 'thinking with their genitals'. Quite apart from Clodia's very amusing experiences, I noticed over the recent Saturnalia just how much was going on among the people I know in London. It is perhaps hardly surprising when at virtually every turn there is some reminder of sexuality – with proliferate sex shops, an astonishing number of magazines, films, books, advertising, etc. And among some of my contemporaries there seems to be a frantic determination not to miss something they believe is now freely available to their children, before they themselves grow old. I'm reminded of an aphorism which for the moment I'm not able to attribute: *The combination of a repressive political order with a permissive moral order is not unheard of in human history*. And indeed it is not. Less honoured in the breach, in fact. Perhaps this is not so under Communism, but I do not know. Occasionally one hears something about some kind of workers' crusade for purity against the vicious relics of Capitalism and Chiang Ch'ing (upon whom fresh odium is being garlanded) is thought to have scoured the Chinese of iniquity. Certainly some of the leftist clergy in this country think that Marxism would clean up Soho. What they ignore is that most people probably don't want it cleaned up. Such a massive pornographic industry does not thrive on a handful of rich decadents.

Anthony Eden is gravely ill, and once again those exciting years of passionate conviction and ideological argument are brought to memory. It seems strange now that the Suez operation caused such intense and spontaneous political feeling and ironical that Eden's name is always associated with that and not with his diplomatic successes. Political ambition is inscrutable. With the obvious exception of Churchill's leadership during the war years, Macmillan was the first really able Tory politician since Baldwin (and Baldwin is something of a curiosity). Chamberlain, Churchill in peacetime and Eden all had serious flaws as Prime Ministers, in each case because they were not prepared to acknowledge their own limitations. None of the Tories (again with the exception of Macmillan) had the all-round political flair of Attlee, Gaitskell and Wilson. Butler was never given the chance to prove it in the top job and Heath was prematurely cut off in his Premiership, having (until recently) been generally underrated. Even so, it could be argued that with a highly developed sense of politics, he would still be there. Once again one thinks of the old dichotomy between a statesman and a politician. Macmillan himself said 'when you're abroad you're a statesman; when you're at home you're just a politician', and the splendid Stevenson said that 'a politician is a statesman who approaches every question with an open mouth'!

Clodia Oricellari says that Anglo-Saxons, when they want to damn someone with the faintest praise while still appearing to be generous, use the word 'flair'. (I had said something about Rachel having a great deal of talent, but lacking Tony Connors's 'flair'.) Clodia also notes that we use the word 'clever' as a pejorative. 'A *clever* actress.' 'A *clever* poem.' 'Too *clever* by half.' 'Oh, that was a *clever* decision.' Always implying, in the case of the actress and the poem, a certain lack of sincerity, an effect achieved by trickery rather than honest passion; and, in the other cases, the deployment of cunning or, at best, the misapplication of high intelligence for slightly unworthy ends. I've been trying to list the words that I use in that way. ('Clever' isn't one of them: 'flair' is – I use it when I mean erratic aptitude which isn't backed by perseverance and industry.) It is quite difficult, because I think we conceal such routine hypocrisies from ourselves. Everyone wants to believe himself to be generous, whatever the world thinks.

It is noticeable that if you read people serious items in their own language when they are in some foreign place, they listen intently because it is *their* language and they are alert to nuances and subtleties that they would not usually trouble to notice. There is some satisfaction in understanding where other people can not. I have often found that when I am baffled by the banalities of a language and especially by its jokes, I give a lot more thought and attention to serious things. I've been thinking about all this in relation to the whole business of stretching people (and extending this scope beyond the readers of *Tribune*, who are a dedicated enough bunch already). On the hypothesis that people prefer to deal with difficult matters in what they regard as their own language rather than entertaining banalities in an alien tongue, the problem is to establish an acceptable language which will encourage people beyond their normal expectations of comprehension.

It is foolish to try to make serious things entertaining: and often irritating. (Compare the Galbraith programmes on the television screen with the text as printed in the *Listener* in the last couple of weeks.)

A basic principle of education, understood by the Jesuits and Communists among others, is that an appropriate language is established in which they talk *up* to their audience. The liberal fallacy is that people may decide what they wish to hear, and the language in which they hear it is then modified to the lowest common denominator of effort which they are prepared to expend. We are most of us lazy.

I tried an experiment with a second-year class of my own pupils in which I invited them to write, instead of the usual history essay, a historical dissertation on the theme that 'xenophobia in some degree is indispensable to national pride'. Two of them (both alleged Marxists) were delighted with the opportunity, a third objected on political grounds (which I do not of course mind in the least, although it was not very bright of her). What I did mind was the reaction of some of the others: who objected because it was not a proper subject, it wasn't history.

I asked them to consider what history is and how it relates to ethics and politics and all the other humanistic concerns. There was still discontent and one rather chirpy character, Marshall, asked 'how will it help me get a first?' I doubt very much that with such an attitude anything is going to help him. And yet these days who can tell? It is a problem that obtains at every level in the educational system.

And even more seriously throughout society, where language has been debased and deliberately misused with (as Orwell warned) an inevitable coarsening of political thought. The secretary of the Labour Party said some time ago (about social security fiddles) that: 'There are these people who are putting a sore thumb on the canker that does not exist.' Recently there was a report on a wireless programme in which a new information service was said to be 'anxious to be getting things across to the man in the street and not just the esoteric element and the media'! And 'there will be a great deal of horse-trading about who gets what in the final analysis'!

The long-range forecast is depressing! It was sickening, for example, when a few weeks ago Abu Daoud, said to be one of the Palestinian terrorists who organised the massacre of Israeli athletes at the Munich Olympiad, was arrested and immediately described as the James Bond of the PLO. How can the enormities of terrorism and the horrors of political violence mean anything when reality is so wilfully confused with escapist fiction.

I wonder when if ever we are going to grow up into even passably good Europeans. The economic problems of the French – unemployment, the aftermath of last year's drought, which hit them worse than it did us, and the quadrupling of prices – have brought out all Trumble's Francophobia and a working trip to the Berlaymont has done nothing to assuage it. Under the cynical mask, which one soons learns to make allowances for, he is normally a very reasonable and shrewd man: but about France he is absurd. As is Ellis Fulford about Germany and Bill Delahaye about Italians, except that Bill is buffoonishly exaggerating a comic prejudice because we have been silly enough to indulge it by laughing.

Trumble must realise that with France already running a substantial deficit they must be the next in line for currency speculation (especially after the Basle loan to safeguard the pound and decrease its international significance as a reserve currency). This would be very dangerous for French political stability, which in turn would be serious for Europe. In the same way Ellis's consistent pleasure in the many embarrassments of the Germans over security is simply childish. If the term, which we have heard so often in relation to Rhodesia, 'front-line state', means anything then Germany is the most important in the world.

Yet another example of fatuous use of language relating to a political theme, this time in connection with the continuing soap-opera of Andy Bevan and Transport House, where the National Union of Labour Organisers have refused to work with him because he is a Trotskyist. Up pops a Young Socialist in Bevan's defence to accuse them of being 'politically motivated'! *And dead seriously.*

All my third-year pupils and post-graduates seem to be in reasonable shape. Lumley has gone into over-drive and surprises me weekly with his ability. (Dreadful how insidiously one's own linguistic habits are polluted by cliché. At this rate, I shall have him powering through for the gold in no time at all. Sports journalists are the very worst offenders.) Kent maintains progress and seems to be in a very happy frame of mind, although he is still worried about Candida Taylor. I thought she was a little erratic on those occasions – quite frequent, I suppose – when I saw her at Christmas, but always in the company of others and usually with Connors somewhere around. He seemed to treat her decorously.

Fulford told me that she was cutting loose in no uncertain manner at the Middleton New Year party.

I feel relieved (thank Heaven) of some of the responsibility for that affair and her consequent well-being now that it is all in the open and her parents know about it. They seemed to take it extremely calmly, which is sensible of them. There was little else that they could do. I cannot believe that Connors, of all people, intends to marry the girl and sooner or later it must all end in an emotional mess. We must devoutly hope that it is later and that she will have had time to tire of him. In any event, I do not foresee the break being made without more than her fair share of histrionics. In the light of his desired appointment to the new Wardenship at Lamberhurst, Connors has behaved with much sobriety of late and it may not be impossible that Candida has something to do with it too. Yes: it is quite impossible: she is altogether too emotionally and intellectually fragile. Bearing that in mind, I must arrange to see her and make sure that all is well.

There was the expected rumpus over defence spending, with seventy-seven left-wingers challenging the government and demanding more cuts. Three right-wingers including Mackintosh (who gave adequate warning) abstained because they wanted more debate – as had occurred in all other areas where cuts have been made. Why (the right-wingers ask) are the Chiefs of Staff worried? Good question.

There is also a nice judicial row brewing concerning a Post Office Union decision not to handle South African traffic for a week as a protest against apartheid. The necessary futile gesture which has been taken to court. We shall hear about it for some time because it not only involves the unions and the judiciary again, but also the Attorney General who refuses to act against them, when they are in breach of the law which is (broadly) that the mails must get through.

There were vigorous scenes in the Commons which must have impressed the Russian dissident, Bukovsky, in the

Visitors' Gallery as a guest of the Liberals. There were some acrimonious exchanges concerning him, during which the Prime Minister was untypically unsunny.

Ford has bowed out of the White House to general praise after a reign which one American journalist described as 'elegant limbo'. Blakemore and I were entertained lavishly at the Connaught (Blakemore rather uncomfortable at such unrestrained hedonism) by James Lloyd Mitchell, who desired us to mourn in the Epicurean manner the necrobiosis of his country. It was an entertaining evening.

I suggested to Mitchell (who talked of Carter as if it were Herbert Marcuse entering the White House) that in spite of all the relentless battling, there was no discernible difference between the activities of liberals and conservatives in the United States and whoever was in power there was little fundamental change. He was pleased to enter into the spirit of the jest and so was Blakemore, now reconciled to truffled pheasant terrine, and such splendours, ordered for us by our host.

Mitchell explained to me that like so many European *socialists*, I thought that politics was a bread-and-butter business, whereas it was a battle for a nation's soul. 'And,' (said Mitchell) 'the powers of good have to contend in this Faustian imbroglio with the foolish dreams of men and the blandishments of the forces of vermilioness'. Blakemore agreed that this was a feasible reading of the American situation, but demurred at its application to Europe. Perhaps protracted exposure to Mitchell is making a radical of Blakemore. A radical conservative, of course! He chose to epitomise the difference between the power motive and the will to serve in a comparison of Lloyd George (whom he admitted to be the greater man politically) and Bonar Law, quoting Beaverbrook that Lloyd George had not cared which direction the car was travelling in, as long as he was in the driving-seat; and reminding us of Bonar Law's profound modesty: 'I must follow them. I am their leader.' Not surprisingly, both he and Mitchell deplored this attitude in a party politician and most of all in a chief minister or executive.

And so it went on through Mitchell's excellent dinner. The elaborate baiting of each other, usually in some area where expert knowledge was assumed, was a ritual of flattery, not uncommon among scholars who like those present, which is by no means always the case. It is harmless enough, but I sometimes wonder if it does not suggest to us an exaggerated idea of our own cleverness, which is eventually not desirable.

Trouble in Egypt is always worrying and there have been riots in Cairo over the price of food in the last couple of days, which Sadat has blamed on Marxist agitation. It is a dangerous situation, because he is accused of favouring the middle classes in his policies and from the various reports of correspondents and accounts from one or two acquaintances who have been to Cairo in recent months the anomalies between the poor and the relatively well-heeled are striking. A pro-Soviet Egypt would obviously make peace in the Middle East extremely uncertain, threatening not only Israel, but also the Sudan. With the Lebanon and Ethiopia in turmoil, any substantial Soviet progress in the Middle East and north-east Africa not only isolates Israel, but must put pressure on the Arabian peninsula and the Gulf states.

I was by no means reassured by a friend of Bridget Ross who lunched at the college, a full-blown and distressingly intelligent Marxist not given to that kind of hearty, knowing good humour which one used to recognise in evangelical Christians about the University, who had seen a great light and were filled daily with happiness. This man, Rigby, offered a convincing interpretation of what was happening and must in the long run succeed in Egypt, and indeed throughout Africa, on the usual lines of historical determinism, which are predictable enough, but seem to apply accurately to situations in Africa. Far from being pro-Soviet, Rigby took the line that what was happening quickly in certain parts of the world must be accelerated in others (such as our own reactionary corner) by vigorous collectivist policies, so that repressive proletarian regimes would be encouraged to become more attentive to human individuality when they were not under threat. (Out of nowhere I had a sudden image of the terrible fight between the dinosaurs in Walt Disney's *Fantasia* and what followed.) There is something alarmingly impressive about this kind of sane Marxist, for whom the idea of war as a means to achieve revolution is unthinkable and who seems to be possessed of enormous patience. He is prepared to work in a dedicated way to accelerate the process which he sees as inevitable, without at the same time expecting to live to see its final triumph – a socialist world alliance.

Bridget Ross attacked him, but not on the truistic grounds that Marx's materialism was one thing in the rapidly emerging nations of the Third World, and quite another in the poorer Mediterranean countries, each with a long and complicated experience of political vicissitude, let alone in the industrial states where there was also a strong tradition of parliamentary opposition in some form. Rather she suggested that Marx's idea of progress, which justified his own approval of the inevitability of the historical process, was entirely limited by his materialist premises. She acknowledged that other aspects of human activity were inseparable from the historical process, *but* claimed that Marx himself had neglected this inseparability in resting his argument upon economic conditions and ignoring political, ethical and even spiritual aspirations which were arguably not dependent upon the distribution of wealth and resources. I suggested that his 'accelerated collectivism' must be achieved at the expense of personal liberty and he retaliated with the view that there was no such thing as total individual liberty, nor was it desirable. Free-for-all liberty in wage-bargaining alone would indicate to our society its inherent self-destructiveness.

And at no time surely, he said, should the liberty of one man impinge upon the well-being of another. 'That's not Marx, that's Mill,' he added. An old trick. I pointed out that Mill's basic contention had been that an individual should not have the liberty *to make a nuisance* of himself to others. We failed to agree that this was not the same thing.

The Duke of Edinburgh whose wit and wisdom are always good for a laugh has suggested that there may be too much emphasis on the welfare state at the expense of enterprise and ability, which has upset the Apache nation who are whooping around the High Chaparral, sw1, again. Enoch Powell, who is seldom good for a laugh, has made yet another speech on race in his more virulent, but still quasi-logical, manner. Shirley Williams has repudiated the Trotskyists who have infiltrated the Labour Party and also attacked Powell in an excellent speech. Mr Crosland has said we are going to be 'rather definite and rather positive' about a new initiative regarding Rhodesia. An unrepentant Attorney General, Sam Silkin, has told the appeal judges they were wrong to prevent action by the Post Office workers against apartheid in South Africa and has warned them that 'they should not assume the mantle of Parliament'. Ellis Fulford says it is about time someone did!

Highgate meetings are well attended and there have been nibblings of late from increasingly significant people both in Parliament and elsewhere. The declaration-of-principles pamphlet is already in proof and reads very convincingly. Jeremy Taylor is evasive about Connors's chances of the European College appointment, but Rachel says that it is virtually assured. He has always tended to favour Rachel with his confidences; and it is also from her that I learn that he is not in the least put out about Connors and Candida.

*

343

My very dear love,

I am sorry: but I am also hurt and a little angry. In the first place I am deeply sorry for so completely misunderstanding that brief passage in your letter and I see that in so doing I must already have hurt you. Yes, it is difficult and of course we both know that we have a normal and lively interest in the other sex: but I'm glad that you, too, feel as I do. I know also that you are not something of a Puritan which I am – it's been a part of a rigid Protestant upbringing that I haven't been able to slough off – and I thank you and (in an old-fashioned phrase which most of our acquaintances would laugh at) I honour you for it. It would be dishonest and, I think, silly, for me to pretend, though, that I am not hurt and upset about the year in India after your American time is over. Surely you might have discussed this with me earlier: I can't help feeling it was on the cards when I was in New York and it is quite untypically devious of you not to have mentioned it until now, when it is as good as decided. I had hoped that you would be back in Geneva and that we might work out some means of being together more often.

Perhaps I am being childish and also selfish. I understand that it is only partly a question of ambition (and anyway who am I to quarrel with that: I have never been especially reticent in pursuing my own); and I know quite well that you have still your old idealistic desire to serve where you would be most useful, and it is one of the things I love about you. I am simply very disappointed that it didn't seem to you important that we should talk about it together: Heaven knows I should not have tried to stop you doing something that mattered. We have neither of us ever gone in very much for reproaches. So having said that, I don't propose to say any more and I intend to make the most of the three months we shall have in London before you to go India.

The sudden revelation about your suspicions of me and Roger Ingestre made me almost laugh aloud. Apart from being just a little pleased that you can still be slightly jealous about me, it is such a generally comic idea. I've always liked Roger a lot (and I assumed that you did). And he is, objectively, quite an attractive man: but the idea of arranging *any* sort of affair with him, let alone anything clandestine, makes me giggle even as I write. The idea of the whole civilised minuet, and the sarabands of conscience that would follow, is for me pricelessly funny: but not if you were worried. I like and value Roger Ingestre, but I can truthfully say that I have never, as you jocularly put it, 'fancied' him. Equally truthfully he has never shown the slightest interest in me, sexually. I think that he is in very good control of himself in such matters, although he is not in the least queer. I'm not *quite* sure what the relationship with the Italian sisters I've described to you is and I think the younger one is, or would be, quite receptive to him: but to all appearances he is remarkably aloof from country matters. (Incidentally, Ellis Fulford claims to have made a discovery that most of the people he knows who are homosexual are either Catholics or Anglo-Catholics and proposes that we collaborate on a tract entitled 'Mariolatry and Growing Boy: some Oedipal corollaria'. He is increasingly outrageous.) Anyway, that is how seriously I view even a notional liaison with Roger and I hope you'll also start enjoying the joke.

There were the usual parties and jollifications at Christmas and the New Year, which I did not much enjoy. In fact, I ducked out of most of them and spent a lot of the time, when I wasn't catching up on work, loafing about or reading. Bill Delahaye, whom I ran into in the lobby the other day, took me for a drink at the St Stephen's and thundered, if thunder stammers – and why shouldn't it? – about neo-Bohemian idiocies. I've always thought that Bill was a bit 'poor-cat-i'-the-adage' about these things, but he did seem genuinely angry about the way some of the younger ones are being corrupted. (He actually used the word.) I remember from my adolescence that moral indignation often walked hand-in-hand with covert lust (I think I borrowed that from Evelyn Waugh, somewhere), but Bill hinted that this Connors–Candida Taylor phenomenon (mentioned a few weeks ago) is not inhibiting his usual fieldwork. Candida apparently made a mild fool of herself, though obviously not in any way to worry her parents. I think our idea of *la vie bohème* is entirely different from that of the French, conforming with our idea of 'middle class' and their idea of 'bourgeois'. It is much more extreme for them because of that difference and in spite of the entirely ersatz image of swinging London that you so much disliked in the sixties, there is a lot more pantomime here than action. I'd say the real English Bohemian was not necessarily anti-social or wildly promiscuous but a sort of classless wanderer who won't accept a label and so tends to rebel against his early background and its assumptions, whatever it may have been. There are quite a few in our generation which I'd say was the one *entre deux bétises*, the fatuously posturing thirties and sixties: and the 'struggle' of the one and the 'pop revolution' of the other.

I have been fairly busy with constituency matters, but the late nights at the House and the hectic three-line whipping still goes on. There have been some very lively sessions, what with Bukovsky appearing during some exchanges on press censorship; the unions and the Duke offering succinct social commentary and recently, less diverting, Powell again on immigrants – which is as embarrassing for some of the Tories as it is odious to us. Some of his remarks were about 'civil war' and there has been some talk of prosecution which the *Sunday Express* says raises broader issues of freedom of speech, pointing to authoritarian forces in the government. I find this, as far as my own conscience goes, one of those old objective/subjective dilemmas, which are always a nuisance. Meanwhile the *Daily Express* has gone tabloid and has received itself rapturously.

There has also been a row between the Attorney General and the appeal judges about the Post Office workers being prevented from refusing to handle South African mail and so on, which is now dividing along party lines. That is a pity: because there is a serious constitutional issue involved that should be looked at dispassionately. Some legal experts say that Sam Silkin is entirely right in saying that the Attorney General is only responsible to Parliament. One of the problems of such tight divisions at the moment is that party loyalty enters into arguments that at other times would develop into serious and significant debates.

You will be pleased to know that Jack Jones has come out in praise of the Social Contract and that the Chancellor, emphasising its importance, says that industry and commerce can make or break the economy! J. Jones also says that without the contract there would have been a coup and some awkward sod asked pertinently who by: the Army or the unions? John Cousins, who is contesting the TGW succession with Moss Evans, says that the contract *hasn't* worked and that it is the duty of union leaders to represent their members and not to usurp the powers of Parliament by interfering in policy-making.

For comic relief, Harold Wilson appeared on television with the mimic (I can't remember if you've ever seen him) Mike Yarwood, who often gives impressions of him, in the Parkinson programme. He walked off with the show, very affable and telling very good stories brilliantly.

I went to Oxford last week to talk to the Labour Club. There had been a heavy fall of snow and it was incredibly beautiful, I thought. And very small. I was extremely happy there, even though we had not properly met and I regarded you as one of the wilder head-hunters of the same club whose guest I was. (Perhaps Eden's recent death reminded me of you thumping someone from Christ Church outside St John's during a Suez demonstration. I thought you were very impetuous, but rather heroic.) Of course, I am not unhappy now. Far from it; but I miss you very much. While I was there, wandering around, I couldn't help wondering whether I was remotely the same person as I was in those days. On the whole, I decided not. While I was there, I think I stayed pretty much the same, and even when I first started working in London: but part of a serious and successful marriage, as I believe ours to be, touching wood and everything else and

347

being most humble before the high gods, is changing and giving up something. Obviously I don't mean a career or an attitude or anything material: giving up something of yourself so that you are never entirely whole again without the other one and only feeling secure and happy as part of him.

I can't wait for May. Now that I've written this, I'm no longer cross about your going to India. At least, by the time you get there the dust will have settled, all being well, after their election. Mrs Gandhi is vindicated, after all, don't you think? I'd guess she must feel pretty confident about winning. The horrible thought has just occurred to me that *we* might have a bloody election in May or June. Not very likely: considering how badly the pound fell last year – we are only realising how badly now, when we see the effect on inflation of an extremely modest recent improvement – and how the government held on. It could be argued that Callaghan has the intention and the nerve to survive anything, contrary to many analyses, including the Highgate one. I don't want to lose my seat, but if I do at least I shall have the consolation of being on the next plane to New Delhi. I have every intention of taking the opportunity of visiting you and together we will make a tour of all the erotic artworks, in case we need inspiration. I am beginning to look forward to it positively.

Look after yourself and write soon. I promise to be more sensible and to remain as good.

All my deepest and wildest love,

R.

*

Good afternoon about education with splendid speech by St John-Stevas, very moderate and witty, quoting the vice-chairman of the Novosibirsk City Soviet of Working People's Deputies on finding and developing the gifted teenager. And interesting points about levels of proficiency (*All* secondary school teachers to have A-level maths? Surely not!); sixth-form colleges (not relating to Lamberhurst which would be

348

by its very nature highly selective) (Attention: Chickens!) (Achtung! Caution! Attenzione!); and a little bit of elegant figure-skating on his own part around examinations, where I don't think either Shirley Williams or Callaghan is very keen on some new general leveller, however many compulsory requirements there are. But just as any of our Education Secretaries have to be seen to be accommodating egalitarian doctrine, so the Tories must make noises and fret brows over science and manufacturing industry. (Though it is ridiculous, as everyone agrees, that we are indeed 'churning out' so many sociologists, psychologists, et cetera. Speculative head-counting, suitable for the academically moderate.) Good reply and an exhausting one by Shirley W., giving way often and dealing very neatly with everyone and, with two such performers, a genuine high level of debate. (Wish I could say the same for this one: think I'll take a trip up to the bar.) But there is an awful lot of vagueness about standards and the usual blurring of what they are about with talk of 'measured attainment' and 'qualitative' and 'quantitative' and once again the old subjective suspicion. And there is a certain dissembling in claiming that standards have gone up: when it must be true that the highest standards have gone down, and one per cent more passing something or other at A-level and ten per cent more at O-level does not compensate for the fact that passes are devalued and the quality of intellectual development has become worse.

I suppose I should feel some stirrings of conscience about just sitting on my butt and contributing nothing, but time has taken its toll and I'm not the bright-eyed *wunderkind* I once imagined myself. (Just as well when I look at some of the bright-eyed *wunderkinder* in the fifth and sixth decades!) Brevity, my Christ! On the motion for adjournment. What time is it? Half past eight. Yes: I'll stroll up to the bar. The honourable Member makes his bow to Mr Deputy Speaker and absents himself to the felicity of a large whisky awhile. I suppose that the best service my conscience can now per-form is to make me give way to someone who will serve, who

349

has not lost his political faith, who will have a safe seat and a reasonable constituency committee: and get on with a job for which I have enthusiasm. Honour no longer pricks me on. . . . Yes! In my case that is perhaps not a very fortunate choice of phrase. It has hardly been that since the divorce. Honour hath no skill in surgery. Who hath it? he that died o' Wednesday without his honourable friends noticing. A mere scutcheon. I too 'll none of it. . . .

. . . Hullo, Alan. Stretching my legs. These regional issues always bore me to distraction, so I'm just hanging about for the division.

Yes, I might as well drink with him in the press bar as on my own or with whoever else is hanging about. Interesting enough as long as he's not in a waspish mood. What was it someone said? 'The trouble with Trumble is he's a failed intellectual.' And the devastating answer: 'The trouble with Trumble is he's a failed alcoholic.' Not very nice. And not particularly fair. A heavy drinker with a conscience. A heavy drinker because of a conscience. Or disillusion. I've never been particularly bothered about drink. Other distractions. They seldom go together.

Usual run of conversation. Trumble suspects my party loyalty and is skilful at probing tender spots gently. Unlike most of the others who are disaffected, I don't want to stay in politics, certainly would not dream of crossing the floor, even if they'd have me. No. And in the Lamberhurst position, I could be useful and still contribute something, at least, to theory. . . . (Chickens!) Trumble makes no reference to that though I daresay they've been talking about it. Instead we pass harmlessly on to the Haines *Mirror* articles about life in the Cabinet below-stairs and the wilful behaviour of cook. Some have said it's a grave embarrassment to Downing Street and damaging to Labour. I can't see why. Much more damaging are the antics of the left. Trumble agrees. Sarcastic about the NEC investigating the extent of infiltration. Quotes Juvenal. To his grandmother, and translates it as: 'Who exactly is stirring up the custard?' Not bad, in fact.

There is undoubtedly a lot of the *quis enim* syndrome about these days. No less amused by the self-styled Social Democratic group who have declared Jack Jones, Clive Jenkins, Daly, Scanlon, Buckton and L. Murray himself to be influenced by a Marxist and pro-Soviet attitude. Delegates and representatives again. Is there any truth that the Manifesto Group are planning to strengthen the right of the party outside Parliament, something along the lines of the Campaign for Democratic Socialism. Part of my own salad days, he notes.

. . . I've heard nothing. As far as I know, it certainly isn't any official Manifesto Group line. I'd hazard a guess that one or two individuals who are in the group might be trying to organise something.

Yet another delay in the establishment of a centre party, Trumble thinks. Perhaps. It would not surprise me that things have already gone too far for any effective rehabilitation of the right in our party.

Leyland shop stewards give notice of strike action if there's no return to what he says Fulford calls 'freak electric bargaining'. (Fulford likes trying to do imitations.) Not only Eric Varley *but also* Scanlon and Jones given a rough time in a Birmingham meeting. And now the CBI up in arms about the Bullock Report on worker participation. Dissenting minority. Yes, the industrialists lined up against the academics and trades unionists. Watch that space too.

Uneasy times ahead. Especially as we near a Phase Three. Right now, I wouldn't give it a chance. My God! if there's one thing I am aweary of it's industrial relations. And it should not be difficult. There is the obvious example of West German arrangements and there must be some hope for a European model. There are certainly scores of good ideas at the Berlaymont. Trumble is pro-German? Yes. Thought so. Very Francophobe.

Ah well, inevitable if I say something like that we get on to private lives. Not looking forward to coming weekend in London with Candida. Worried too that I haven't been good for her in a vague sort of way. Used to be poised, clever, unobtrusively sensual: now over-excitable, demonstrative, possessive and very randy. No question of talking to Jeremy, or Barbara. In the circumstances. Certainly not Jeremy. I shall have to be very busy, a little distant and hope that she will tire of me. Natural wastage of affection. It's not a question of that, alas. No sign. And if she were properly upset I think there would be an almighty display of tears and temper. That would not go down well with Taylor and it would certainly influence his judgement.

Nod. Say how interesting all the gossip is. Trumble not really much inclined to it. Sandra. . . . Why did God endow one woman with such splendid physical equipment and such a totally addled brain. . . . Marie. . . . Always a word of affection for Marie. . . . Taylor family . . . the girls. . . . Clever application of electrodes, Doctor, but there's nothing registering on the little dial, is there? Just going through the motions. He doesn't care. Personal relationships are only interesting for him when they affect alliances, coalitions, pacts.

Back to politics. Can never keep off them for long. Understandable, like many others in his trade, seriously bothered about an NUJ closed shop and how it might operate. And there was a 'trades unions and the media' conference taking place today. (Forgotten about it.) Moss Evans (heir presumptive to J. Jones) was apparently floating the idea of a licensed press! God save us! Trumble reckons a threat to basic democratic liberties and is going back to Fleet Street to hear more. Might as well have a snack and get back to the Chamber. Aaaaargh! Don't know why I feel so tired. . . .

Curious message to leave with Jess. Arriving early. Why didn't she call herself? Essential to talk. Doesn't sound good. Unless young Lochinvar has arrived to snatch her away at last from the unworthy and decrepit tenant of the fair Ellen?

Don't know. I doubt it, but Candida would make the most of the dramatic moment and the message is consistent with that. I must be very serious and a little upset. Not too much. Just enough, rather sad that my advancing years can't quite compete with . . . (Chickens, again!) It could be some ghastly bout of nerves and hysteria, wanting to pack up Oxford and live with me and be my love. It has never actually come to that. Yet. And I've often thought that she's been on the brink. Perhaps she's worried because it's her final year and there's probably still that enormous pressure in the women's colleges. Wonder if the increasing number of mixed colleges will help diminish that. No: the competition is probably still as savage at the top. I was lucky about that. I never cared and was confident enough all along. In some ways, though, Languages are much less hit-or-miss than History or PPE. Of course, I worked: and I doubt very much that Candida does. Any more. That would certainly be indirectly my fault. . . . Really, I should worry a lot more about her. After all, I have felt very tender and affectionate and I'm being thoroughly cynical about it all when I know quite well that she has been . . . well, has believed she was . . . in love with me. Infatuation? Love? I used not to know the difference when I was her age. I must not just be seen to be kind. I must be kind. And very patient. Until she discovers herself. And I must try certainly to cool it. When we're alone as well. Trouble is that that is difficult, because she is so simply lovely physically and has learned (*mea culpa*, once again) to be provocative. *Amari de fonte leporum*. Perhaps a word with Ingestre, from whom I've been keeping a distance. That Italian girl of his is ravishing. Hope it doesn't turn out like Daphne. The other one, Clodia? yes, good name for her, is a wicked and cunning woman and no mistake, but Ingestre's is delightful. He should be so lucky. . . . Anyway, perhaps it'll encourage him to take a less pompous view than he otherwise might. I'll work on that. . . .

. . . Hullo, Jess, how are things. Thank you for the message. . . .

Odd. Candida not arrived. Missed her train and Daddy working late and Mummy with her Friday seminar. What a bloody nuisance! So I'll have to make do with her.

. . . Well, yes, of course, Jess. That'll be nice. When did Candida say she was arriving?

About eight. Another two hours. Bugger! I wonder if she plays chess. Doubt very much that I can find enough to talk to her about for two hours, unless Daddy arrives. Drink?

. . . Yes, thank you. What have you got? Gin and tonic? That will be fine.

Well-set-up little thing and beginning to be aware of it I'd guess as well. Some of these kids must be quite a trial to the more susceptible male teachers. The younger ones. She's better upholstered generally than Candida: she'll have to be careful she doesn't get fat. Young Italian figure.

. . . How are things at school? Enjoying A-levels.

Dear me! She's started making up her eyes. Bored with school, at least bored with talking about school.

. . . Ah, I see your father's chess set all prepared. Do you play?

No, she doesn't. Hum.

. . . Cheers. It's been one of those weeks. But they are all, aren't they? What are you up to this weekend?

No. That's the trouble at this age. They aren't really aware of their own bodies a lot of the time and they think it's dear old Dad across the room. Please, my dear, remember you're growing up and big girls don't sit quite as carelessly unless they have something in mind. God! Someone's going to be a lucky boy. . . . What! Oh for God's sake! When could that have been? Panic and general alarm, Tony, my boy. . . . Must have been that time at Christmas. She saw us and it excited her? Well, well it might. From what I remember it was pretty torrid. So now. . . . I can't believe this. All I need now is for Barbara to turn up in sequins and tights in the lobby and the whole family. . . .

. . . No, Jess. Sorry, Jessica. I think we should talk sensibly about this. I . . . er . . . understand that it was probably

354

something of a shock to see Candida and me like that and that . . . of course . . . it may have excited you, but . . .

She was sixteen last week! Heaven forfend. As soon as she heard Candida was going to be late. (She's lying. It's in her eyes. There never was any message.) And with everyone else out . . .

. . . Stop, Jessica. I find you very attractive: but you must see. . . . Don't do that. . . .

Taking off her blouse. Is she not perfect? I'll say she is but NO. NO. Standing up and very perfect, blushing but so aware of the splendour of her firm, taut young body.

. . . Jessica . . . if only I could tell you how much I would like to hold you now and make love to you or could make you realise how. . . . But it would be very wrong for all manner of reasons. Think of Candida. . . .

Yes. I should have known. She hates Candida. Obviously. So bloody supercilious about her and behaving like a whore herself. Well, Jessica isn't a whore and . . .

. . . Please, Jessica, button up your shirt again and let's talk quietly about this. Just something between you and me, but something we approach in a properly adult manner.

No! And moving towards me. What the hell is there to do now. I . . . The door. Jeremy's voice cracking. The girl shrieks. So bloody nearly do I. Oh sweet Jesus and everyone else. . . . Who is going to believe me? This is big trouble. . . .

7

'You look especially pensive,' said Clodia Oricellari.

'I was thinking about the events of the past few happy months and their effect upon the psyche of James Lloyd Mitchell,' said Mitchell.

'A good effect, I hope.'

'In some ways. This, particularly, is the zenith of his well-being – something entirely delightful, startling and unlooked for.'

'I should hardly say "unlooked for".'

'No: but attempted without any hope of success. I had obviously watched you very carefully and no one got close enough to lay a well-bred finger on you.'

'Carry on with the analysis of this strange character. He sounds like a successful executive in the mid-life crisis: that surely has nothing to do with you. You've never heard of such a thing.'

'I suppose you could call him that. He is a super salesman, as a lot of commentators are, with self-acclaimed mastery of different forms of communication. As with all the others, the product that he sells is himself.'

'Might the consumer say that she is satisfied?'

'Consumer sounds a little vampiric.'

'Black widowish. You have now been warned.'

'Well, the sort of spider that Mitchell is, spinning not daydreams but fictions which purport to be "the truth", is apt for sacrifice.'

'Is that the nature of his crisis.'

'No. That doesn't bother him. He is not oppressed by his own morality, however it is achieved. Mitchell, a paradigm of progress – one of the elegantly light-weight-suited, beautifully groomed, non-smokers, who might have once chewed a cigar in some thick natural fibre that sagged and stiffened – is faced with a crisis of conscience.'

'He is about to tell his mistress that he has a wife and pretty twins with blue eyes and yellow curls.'

'How you misjudge the conscience of such men. They do not trifle with minor peccadillos. Adultery would be nothing to people like Mitchell, who as it happens is quite truthfully unmarried. No. His conscience wrestles with mistier chimerae.'

'How terrifying!'

'It is. Our hero loses confidence. I came over here to write a series of well-paid articles and a book. There was also, and there still is, the possibility of making a couple of television programmes. I'm afraid that I had invested – and I hope this will not mar our wonderful new relationship – in European venality, corruption, sloth, failure of will, failure of nerve, moral disintegration.'

'Pretty comprehensive list of stock. It sounds like my family history. Or anyone's family history who has a family old enough.'

'Which is why you must suffer the brash confidence of men like James Lloyd Mitchell, whose family has not been going long enough to closet any skeletons.'

'I'll give it time.'

'Now, I'm not going as far as to say that I have not found in this temperate country, and in Europe at large, evidence that the stock listed above was not doing pretty well. But I have also found, especially in England, numbers of people behaving with doctrinal innocence and preparing for martyrdom.'

'Saint Roger Ingestre and his brethren.'

'As flies to wanton boys. Butchered to make a Marxist holiday.'

'Oh dear. And so all your fears about our decline in the West are realised.'

'I can't see any hope for Europe. The monolith in Brussels

357

is so readily adaptable to Communist bureaucracy. And as for the rest of us, in North America, I see an end of liberalism and a different kind of roaring capitalism, with attendant repression. The crisis for my conscience as a roaring conservative idealist is that I *need* the assumptions of liberal democracy to roar at. So perhaps you have some idea of the thousand indecisions afflicting me between the toast and tea.'

'Never mind. You've made at least one mermaid sing for you.'

'Unforgettably. And that song will never be done.'

'What happens if, instead, you freeze in the dark?'

'I don't think it will get that far. We are not that sort of people.'

'I'm surprised that it worries you. Surely you have always looked for the inherent flaws which will ultimately destroy the hubristic liberal. Doesn't it make your conservative Creon more self-righteous?'

'There is sometimes no comfort in being proved right. Who was it said "there is no virtue in history"?'

'I don't know. It might well have been Marx.'

'I don't think it was. From the purely selfish point of view, though, isolationism isn't as easy as it once was and we rely heavily on outside sources for energy. It would take a long time, but in an entirely inimical world, the North American continent (because the United States and Canada would have to act together) would either have to go to war or freeze into submission.'

'And it has depressed you?'

'Doesn't it depress *you*?'

'No. All times are the wrong times. There will be an Oricellari somewhere talking, smiling, negotiating or selling something. No child of mine: but Francesca's. My brothers' children. And their children. And then it will go through another cycle.'

'Or we blow up.'

'Or we blow up. There's always that.'

'Anyway, darling, I came with a pen filled with scorn and

358

what I find on the page is the ink of nostalgia for all the tolerance and idealism that is patiently awaiting its own destruction.'

'The obscure charm of the English middle-class, which they all affect to despise and to which they all tacitly wish to belong. But just accuse them of being bourgeoisie! Roger says that there are people who make a profession of being working-class, as there are professional Welshmen and Irishmen. This, you understand, is thought to be less dishonest than tedious.'

'They are quite different from the rest of Europe. Much less formality and dozens of unwritten taboos. It makes it more exciting, because more hazardous.'

'I think English women are certainly the most interesting,' said Clodia.

'I am not so foolish or ungallant as to agree. And as far as English men are concerned, I should have thought that you and your sister had first-hand evidence to the contrary.'

'You're observant, Jim.'

'I had every reason to be.'

'I accept the compliment.'

'Tell me: may I ask you something personal?'

'Why this sudden coyness?'

'Why should I be so lucky?'

'Another way of saying: what is so special about me?'

'If you like. But I didn't say that.'

'No. And it was unfair. Oh, I can tell you very easily. You are one of those men who are very sure of themselves. Right or wrong: decisive, uncompromising. I don't mean that you are conceited or overbearing or arrogant: just very sure of yourself. Unlike most of the men I meet socially. And since this has nothing to do with *machismo*, it is a simple matter of conquest. If you know what I mean.'

'Oh yes. I know!'

'There is that moment of conquest or surrender. . . .'

'Well, thank you. I don't know that I could have wished to hear anything better.'

359

'I'm not particularly trying to flatter you. My father, to whom I have always been close, is a rather gentle man who always thinks around questions and if possible never comes to a definite conclusion. I react a little against that. Francesca, who is less close to him, does not.'

'I've noticed that she seems drawn to Roger Ingestre.'

'And unfortunately Roger has not. Or, if he has, can't convince himself that she is not simply being "nice".'

'That could well be. I saw him the other day and his mind seemed to be devoted almost entirely to a centennial cricket game.'

'From what I know of it, a sport very suited to his temperament. Shall we have another drink or do you think it's time we started out for the concert?'

'We've a lot of time. It doesn't begin until eight. If we go by cab, there's no hurry. That's of course if we can find a cab!'

'Difficult, isn't it. It's all the rich foreigners.'

'Same again?'

'Yes. That was perfect.'

'I hope not. That would leave no room for improvement.'

*

Blue Champagne. . . . Cham/Pagne. Sham pain. . . . On no nothing sham about this pain. Real and like sap in the tree writhing along nerve-tracks to the ends of the body. If I could dissect a limb, I could show them pain. . . . Blue Champagne. . . . I do not know who next will talk, there is so much talk it is all talk and talking but it is sometimes only a dull ache and then a terrible stabbing of a thousand needles that I was frightened of when I was little and then too they were gentle. . . . Blue Champagne. . . . Transfer to what I wish I could make any kind of transfer: oh just a name that someone thought was romantic and I forget now whether it was a moment of truth on a ferry in someone's life. Who said so? Did he tell me? It was all moments of truth. Oh my head hurts where the needles are.

360

Candy . . . Candy! Poor little Candy hurt. Kiss her better. Daddy will kiss her better. Little girl. Little Candy. My name is Candida. . . . Suddenly I don't think I liked her, didn't want to be Candy who was sweet and happy little girl. Sister little baby sister and Daddy didn't kiss her better for that and Candy had to be good and little baby sister didn't have to be and was sick on things. No one cuddled Candida as they did Candy, pretty little Candy and so she had to grow up when they didn't cuddle her. Close harmony. I no we, they are not close. Nor particularly close as a family. What a good girl she is. She's very mature for her age. Oh Candida's no trouble and she's going to grow up into poor Candy a something of a beauty. Hurt and no one takes her on his knee to read stories about pigling someone and the naughty bunnies because of good books not baby books. Hurt, Candy hurts all over, Daddy. Kiss better. . . .

Champagne . . . Blue Champagne. . . . Notes bending to over backwards. No I don't hate him too. I forgive them. It was cruel to me and there is now this pain and he did hurt me because I wanted that too. Candida wanted to be bad. Bad and wicked and say dirty things and be grown up with Blue Champagne very sleek the stroking hand on silk and slobber of his thin mouth at her oh dirty excitement that she told him Naughty and grown up and tearing her so that she could scratch him and bite to also hurt Sophisticated too with him. What a bad girl Candida was and unhappy too, when Candy had been terribly happy and good in the sunshine and walking with Daddy holding hand on the fields in the Spring.

Blue Champagne . . . insistent sound. Beating against the pain, the needles. Little trembler shocks all over her once pretty body. Candida naughty and dirty and defiled with new pains. I don't know trembling and yet I can't see my hand moving. Just all real inside me and what I can see isn't what is happening because trembling inside and I can't see my pretty hands shaking. Make it stop, Daddy: the shivering. Candy.

Candy's cold. That is why she shivers and the baby is all snug and Candy has to walk. Tired and cold. But Daddy came to meet them and carried her. Can Dee. No, no. My name is Candida. . . . I don't like her because she is too happy and not serious: she won't grow up and be sophisticated with him. . . . I have forgiven him because he was cruel and hurt her. Not little Candy. No one hurt her: they were kind. Not her. The other one.

It is the television girl with the red pills again. Make me sleepy. Why? I don't *want* to rest. Go out in the sunlight on the grass with my Daddy. It is springtime now and not cold and there are leaves and soon there will be blossoms. Not tired now so don't want to sleep and be good. Good. Good? No. Candida must be good, be punished for saying dirty words and letting him defile her. And being *very* naughty. . . . Red pills. Go away, television girl. I know! I know! I know he is out there and you have only frilly knickers under that white coat and black stockings which he likes too. Oh, tell him to get up! So big she must be frightened of it. You can do what you like, television girl, with him and not be punished. Steal the baby and send it to the lost boys to look after. Slow champagne, running down sound like something slow on the tape recorder Daddy makes funny voices on for Candy. Pretty little girl. Slow where do they I don't forgive the baby good hate giggles and sick fat girl there it's not any more hand please for me Daddy.

*

I was right about Candida after all, which is certainly nothing to feel smug about. It seemed so obvious to me that something was wrong that I can't understand how anyone who knew her well and saw her often should not have noticed. It's quite possible that Ingestre saw her during good moments, but I should have thought her parents and some of her friends and surely the chap she was going to bed with must have been aware that she was in a very neurotic state. It may have been that she only showed this to me, which perhaps says something for our relationship: not much and not enough. The whole thing is still very vague, if not positively mysterious. She went to London for the weekend in the middle of term or thereabouts and has not come back. So she had the nervous collapse, or whatever it was, while there. Susan and the others say that since she had taken up with Connors (whom they know of only as an older man and suspected was already married), she had become very aloof and a little patronising. Ingestre asked me to call in and told me that she was ill. He said nothing about Connors (and I did not see how I could very well ask), saying only that she had evidently been under some strain and there had been a little trouble within her family. He said he blamed himself for not being as alert as I had been, looking very much as though he meant every word of it. Curiously enough, although I am deeply sorry for her and would do anything I could, the news has upset Ingestre more than it has me. It seems evident now that I could not have been in love with her and I find it difficult to understand how I could have deceived myself so completely and been so miserable. This does not mean that I am going to abandon her. At the moment I gather she is in a clinic and not able to have visitors, but I shall try to see her during the vac and if possible do whatever I can to help her get better.

It is depressing and a bit reprehensible how easily one forgets the existence of someone who once seemed to matter so much, although I don't think I'm particularly inhuman in this respect. The truth is that I have been so busy working, playing games to keep fit, and keeping up with what is going on in the world that I have not missed Candida very much and I now realise that we met, regularly and uneventfully, out of habit as much as anything: she needed company and male company, which I understand; and I liked being seen around with her and I'm afraid let people make assumptions that were quite false. Lumley gave me a lift to London the other weekend. I telephoned her house and spoke to her mother, who was every bit as calm and detached as Candida used to make her out to be. She thanked me for calling, told me that

Candida was making expected progress and was not yet well enough to see visitors. Kind, firm, polite and distant all at the same time. That was the most recent news I've had.

Alan Trumble gave me a standing invitation to call him when I was passing through on the off chance that he might be free. I was a little shy of doing so, but didn't think there was anything to lose. He took me to his club, mainly used by writers and artists of one sort or another, quite determined to be unlike the popular idea of such a place, where we had a pleasant boozy evening and were joined by Ellis Fulford (also a friend of Rachel's) whom I met last year. For all their determination to be unstuffy, the same rituals obtain, laced with rather more self-conscious ribaldry. I don't mean that to sound ungrateful, because I enjoyed the evening very much.

Much of the conversation was about politics. I've taken to reading Hansard regularly and was quite moved by the one which reported the death of Anthony Crosland, under the simple, dignified heading Death of a Member. I suppose it indicates how little I know, and how recent my interest in politics is, that I was surprised by the significance that both Trumble and Fulford attached to his death and their very real sadness. I had always thought of Crosland as a clever man, there or thereabouts: but Trumble says we cannot afford such losses in public life, especially on the Labour right where there are serious depletions. Fulford reckons that Crosland was one of the few men in either major party who could generate ideas and that his death, as well as being untimely, diminished moderate politics even more than Jenkins's departure for the EEC. He says Crosland was a 'right independent' in the Labour Party who had not lost the trust of many people on his left. 'They'll accept a gentle-man Socialist still,' he said, 'when they won't hear of a Socialist gentleman.' After Callaghan, they both thought he was the only remaining Labour leader who could have kept the existing Labour Party on a moderate course and by implication united. I'd heard from Candida and Ingestre about the centre pressure group that Candida's father was co-ordinating and knew that these two both belonged to it. I asked them if they would be sorry to see a big Labour split and they were both fairly evasive. I wonder, therefore, if much of this political activity is just chat. I think they would all be the happiest if there was a good British Social Democrat Party with a left-wing irritant and that they are, at least for the present, incapable of becoming Tories, while they dislike and fear the Marxist, neo-Marxist and sub-Marxist left. But this is rejection rather than positive conviction. They did not try to get away from the subject, but they talked around it. Benn, whom they would like to dismiss politically and can't (though they do intellectually), recently said that a middle course was no longer possible in British politics: it is either a question of Capitalism or what he calls Fundamental Socialism. At the same time Prentice had called, at a Taverne meeting, for the break-up of the existing Labour Party and the new central alignment that these two favour, in theory. (Surely these are the sort of voices that they want and need? Can it be that they are *already* disappointed in the response and the conspicuous lack of defectors to the cause?) At the same time there was gloom that Lever's constituency in Manchester was now in the hands of left-wingers. There was certainly no doubt in anyone's mind about his ability: and some enigmatic joking about some body of characters, of whom I hadn't until then heard, called the Bilderberg Group. (This just happens to include everyone important in modern existence – including Kissinger, Schmidt, Rockefellers, Rothschilds – you name him! Fulford said that he thought that their Highgate Group was important because it gave the Bilderberg perspective!) I suppose they were amused by my blissful ignorance, but I shall amuse a whole lot more people one way and another before I am a Trumble or a Fulford. The point at the moment is I think I could be better than either, even if less intellectual than Trumble and less intelligent than Fulford. I think I have certain qualities. One of these is that I *like* people more.

The jokes fell away quite suddenly and there you had the

responsible 'name' journalist and the missed politician, who might have been important in another party and who is now a very trusted administrator, talking seriously about how hard the politicians themselves work. I noticed how tired these men were about the eyes.And it was not the drink. I noticed too that they talked about work or politics (which is for them work), or theories about work or politics. And that was all. Fulford, now and then, said something that indicated other interests, but Trumble did not. No cars, women, football, religion, cricket (friends of Ingestre!), travel; no philosophy, literature, art (thank God!) or environment; no ethics, no morality. And yet in every exchange there was an underlying assumption that the cars had been driven (though not by Fulford, who can't drive), the women approached and sometimes achieved, the games played, the religion sadly rejected, the travel over. Also the impression that what an existing civilisation offered had been accepted gratefully and that their sadness (because they are both sad men) was of people who saw that civilisation was in decay, feeling as powerless as skilled surgeons over a bad gangrenous condition. (One of Dad's friends died because of gangrene and he hasn't ever forgotten it. Dad says a doctor told him: you see it in the eyes. . . .)

It was natural for men in middle age, neither of whom seems to have looked after himself well, to be talking about death. But the following day Shirley Williams on the Sunday 'World This Weekend' programme (which I heard at Ted White's – to a boring commentary from him) laid it on the line. And if I had some idea of how hard an MP worked, I had no conception of the work of a Minister. With very little respite from constituency duties. *Duties*. Long hours of sheer welfare work and sixty letters a day to deal with. And the very important point that serious consultation, at the highest level, is necessary before any big decision because the public are better informed and care more. I think she actually came out with the very words: the country is being governed by tired people.

Well, this exhilarated me. Not because people are tired and die prematurely: but because this dedication still obtains in a very tatty, commercial ambience and because it is appreciated by the not-*so*-tired, just exhausted, people who live around and with them. (Fulford said 'crocodile birds'.) I've often thought, working for Schools, how hard I drive myself. Now I am really learning. I am beginning to formulate ambitions, more purposive than getting a first, and I can see, from these two rather modest men, how much sheer industry is involved.

I was delighted when Fulford, who thought the talk was too staid for a visitor, started on newspapers and they classified their friends according to professional zeal (themselves); high moral fibre (Candida's parents); common pursuit (Ingestre and Rachel and . . . a pause and a look; does the boy know anything?); and so on. It did not matter, because they began to generalise about newspaper habits and the depressing evidence that most people in England take papers for everything except news. Until (said Fulford) they have *Pravda*. Then they'll miss the nude on Page Three and the Hickey column and all the people they cannot stand for one more instant-breakfast moment. I asked about 'quality' and Trumble said that of the Europa papers (*The Times, La Stampa, Die Welt* and *Le Monde*) only *Le Monde* made a profit and it was 49 per cent owned by the staff. . . . He left the question open. Fulford laughed.

I was a bit afraid of overstaying my welcome, although it was only just after eleven. I left them there and I was very bothered that I would be missing something until I realised that I had come to London to see what I could do to help Candida and had not given her a thought for hours.

After a lot of speculation about the Cabinet reshuffle, a Dr David Owen, who I had always thought was something vaguely to do with Health and Social Security, has become Foreign Minister, with enormous press attention. Dad thinks it's a good thing to have a young foreign minister because Anthony Eden was young and what Dad calls 'all there'. As far as he is concerned, you can be a bit over the hill to run the economy or the Home Office, or Number Ten: but dealing with these aliens you have to be 'all there'. Certainly Dr Owen has put on a fabulous burst of speed. Perhaps he's one of these British runners without a finishing sprint, who is just going to tire the field into submission.

Dad and the political discussions are becoming almost a nuisance because, where my opinion is sought and I try to offer it, it is really an opening for Dad to make heavy pronouncements, inevitably backed by facts. (None of your inspirational Kojak about Dad. He still prefers 'Z Cars' and is thinking of forgiving Watt and Barlow for doing entertainment programmes about Jack the Ripper and others. Destroys credibility that sort of thing!)

Having decided not to do a job during the vac I shifted a trunkful of notes and books home in order to get down to systematic revision for Schools. Everyone at home was impressed by this mountainous evidence of my industry: so let's hope it doesn't produce the ridiculous mouse. I've found that the very task of rationalising my notes over the last two years has helped me think more clearly and to order my ideas fairly well. In fact I feel much too confident and have to contrive all sorts of psychological hair-shirts as penance.

The wet weather and the absence of Wendy Parker skiing in Italy mean that there have been very few distractions, apart from the odd evening at the pub playing darts and shovers. I had been wondering how the splendid Miss Parker and I would view each other if we met this time around, feeling rather guilty about my incipient enthusiasm in the light of what's happened to Candida. God knows why. Conscience is a peculiar manifestation. If the friendship meant anything to Candida, which I believe it did, it was nevertheless no more than that. And if I felt no guilt around Christmas-time, when she seemed relatively well, why start agonising now? Furthermore, I had no way of knowing how Wendy would feel. (Trouble was I had all too precise a memory of that!) In the event, I had to make do with a post-card of an Alp and an ingeniously provocative message. I am pleased not to be forgotten.

I shall probably go up to London for a week or so. There are one or two things I want to look up at the BM and it will be a pleasant working break. I shall probably stay with Ted White and his mother, although Clifford and Teresa have said that they will always put me up if I just want to come and stay for a while. Perhaps I shall also see Candida.

I could never have guessed that things would turn out as they have. Ted White, having said that it was all right for me to stay with them, pushed off for Cuba after two days on some kind of special arrangement, leaving me in a slightly embarrassing position. I suggested moving out to The Reeve but his mother said there was no need to bother.

It's significant that I keep thinking of her as his mother – in spite of the latest developments. For some time I'd had a vague idea that she rather fancied me and dismissed it as conceit and a little wishful thinking. Then, the other evening, she came in from the theatre and started chatting over a drink. (I had been working on the Whig Oligarchy and rather enjoying it; but when she came into the sitting room it was obviously only polite to pack up.) We just talked generally and quite comfortably, although there was certainly a kind of sexual energy building up on my side of the room. She was wearing a black dress and was highly made-up and a study in opulent sophistication.

She put her glass down, got up and held out both hands to me. 'I think it's time for bed,' she said. It was as simple as that.

And it has remained so: as long, Marie says, as it does not interfere with my work.

*

Quite apart from my own sense of involvement and shame at what happened, the unpleasantness caused by that single incident between Connors and Jessica is still pervasive. What might have been seen (even by Jeremy) as a trivial enough event, had Connors not already been involved with Candida, is now regarded as a mortally wicked act. The consequences for Candida herself, whose psychological state was evidently more precarious than even those who thought her to be unstable would have guessed, have been deeply distressing. I have cursed myself a thousand times for my fatuously ill-considered remark to Connors on that hot afternoon and for my delayed return. (Not that it was easily to be avoided, as I recall.) Nevertheless I have to accept some blame, inescapably. So far I have not mustered the necessary courage to implicate myself to Jeremy and Barbara, though I feel sooner or later that I must.

The irony of it is cruel and the hypocrisy (notably of people such as Farrell and Middleton) is stultifying. These are the ones holding up their hands like pantomime Puritans and intoning that Connors has at least reaped the whirlwind of his lechery: hands quite often deployed for other purposes. Rachel and I are, as far as I know, the only two who believe his account of what happened, in which he claims that Jessica was entirely responsible for making the advances and that he was trying to repulse her as kindly and gently as possible when Taylor came into the room. Sandra Beeton has a predictable Freudian explanation, absurdly complicated. Fulford and Trumble are silent but contemptuous. Hay and Mears neutral. Other Highgates are less immediately involved being groupers rather than friends. Marie White, whose generous common sense and general experience in such matters might have been beneficial, has not been much in evidence.

Taylor is (I think) the only one who believes that Connors contrived to be alone with Jessica, who is herself extremely evasive about details, and naturally extremely disturbed about Candida's nervous breakdown. Jeremy's bitter anger suggests that if Jessica had not been just over the age of consent he would have looked for public vengeance, even though at no time has Jessica actually *denied* complicity in what happened. Rachel thinks it is entirely possible that she was being provocative and is now frightened of turning Taylor's wrath upon herself, and also being blamed for Candida's subsequent collapse. It is obvious that there must have been a wildly hysterical scene. Barbara alone has remained unemotional, going about her own work and supervising Jeremy's.

I believe that sooner or later Candida would have had some kind of emotional crisis and that the affair with Connors has simply precipitated it. I do not think this in order to exonerate myself in facilitating his original seduction of her. Far from it: such as admission makes that action all the more irresponsible and cynical. I am perhaps influenced by her initial attitude to me, though at something of a loss to relate the sexual impetuosity of both these sisters to the nature and lives of their parents.

Connors is being treated scornfully by almost all his former friends and viciously by some. Fortunately, in Parliament itself, they take a worldly view of personal lapses when it is not a matter for the yellow press and I do not imagine that many of Connors's fellow MPs, and so on, even know about it. It has, however, ended his hopes of the European College appointment, as Taylor would make it quite clear that he was not morally suitable for the guardianship of young people in their late adolescence. He has had a severe shock himself and must obviously be suffering terrible remorse about Candida. It seems strange in the circumstances to feel sorry for him, but I am.

Barbara has even called a meeting of the Highgate Group, which Jeremy did not attend. She excused his absence on business, made no reference to family troubles, but announced that they had been obliged by work commitments to ask

371

Mears and myself to be responsible for its activities until they were able to devote more time to it. All at once their co-ordinating enthusiasm and seriousness of purpose has become apparent. Outside Barbara's own specialisation in Economics, they relied for ideas on others and were putting their hopes on increasingly powerful backing among politicians and senior administrators: yet sometimes, in the last few days, I have found myself thinking that they were the only two Highgate people who actually had faith in an imminent and strong centre party.

The pity of the situation is underlined by a lot of talk about a General Election after a woeful piece of Parliamentary miscalculation by Labour managers refusing to vote on a technical amendment, which was lost by 290 votes to none. The Tories have, naturally enough, condemned the performance as disgraceful, and in many ways they are right. There is now much wagging of heads about a Lib–Lab accommodation, where in return for certain policy concessions the Parliamentary Liberals will agree not to bring down the government. This (to their credit) does not please many Labour left-wingers, who would prefer to lose an election on firm Socialist grounds than accommodate with anyone. It does not please many Liberals either, including Ellis Fulford who would have resigned his membership but for the fact that the party is doing so badly at elections at the moment. Ellis has an almost atavistic fear of having his motives misconstrued, even when it is a matter of principle.

Such are the political facts, however, that the Liberals must temporise to avoid annihilation at the polls. Some think this is inevitable anyway. I am inclined to think that only Grimond will hold his seat of the existing thirteen. It is equally true that if Labour did fight an election at the moment they would probably lose heavily and split the party.

Obviously this would be a very good moment for all the various dedicated centre groups, including our own, to rally in establishing a strong political entity. If the Tories had a walkaway majority, the chances are that they would attempt right-wing policies and suffer the disaffection of many of their moderates (except that one always has to take into account traditional Tory party-loyalty). At the same time, should there be another hung-Parliament with many more Scots Nats and a couple more Welsh, the appeal to right moderates, as well as left, of a strong alliance *not* a coalition, which would pursue moderate policies and recruit from a very wide electorate, might be considerable.

It will be a pity if the Highgate Group, which has produced a lot of ideas, fails to play any part in constructive work towards such an end – because neither Mears nor I have the basic tenacity and determination of Barbara and Taylor. I comfort myself, pusillanimously, with the cynical thought that the accommodation will occur and that there will be no election.

No prizes for being right. A weekend of Liberal self-justification, after Callaghan won the vote on an issue of confidence moved self-righteously by the Tories, followed by a highly conditional Budget, hitting only the motorist really hard and producing the first muscular twitches from the Liberals, desperately anxious to show what the new gymnasium is doing for their weakly frame. They suggest they will *not* support Healey's latest taxes aimed at the motorist. And now a sad day with Roy Jenkins's Stechford constituency lost to the Tories after a campaign with unpleasant racial overtones. A majority of 12000 turned into one of 2000 for the Tory. A Liberal debacle, beaten into fourth place by the National Front, who have improved their showing elsewhere.

There are the first tokens of celebration appearing in various pubs and restaurants for the Queen's Jubilee, an ironic occasion in view of the present state of the country economically, politically and even morally – though of course hardly

373

the fault of the Monarchy. It looks as though it will be a rather tatty festival because the British themselves don't really feel they have much to celebrate and the foreigners are here for Marks and Spencer's rather than Mountbatten-Windsor.

One can only feel sympathy for the Queen herself who has already been obliged to travel around the Pacific and suffer the excruciating wit of such people as Gough Whitlam and the endless ritual dancing of various tribesmen, and who will now have to do much the same sort of thing at home. There is, however, evidence of genuine affection for her which she surely deserves. Nobody can ever have been so relentlessly subjected to boredom as a matter of duty in virtually the whole span of history.

It is, at the same time, ridiculous to identify the spirit of the nation with whatever the passing show will be. People are short of money and patience and there is an undoubted crisis of identity. We have all the imperial deprivation symptoms and are not co-operating properly with the European therapy. Even in Brussels, some people are prepared to say who can blame us when one of the team of doctors shows such dislike of the patient. At all events, never has our taste and talent for pageantry seemed to me more inane and less symbolic of confidence, felicity and unity – whether federal or social.

Perhaps the sourness of my recent thoughts was catalysed by suddenly seeing Francesca Oricellari coming out of a Chinese restaurant one afternoon with James Lloyd Mitchell. Neither of them saw me and I did not call to them because they looked as though they were sharing some intimately happy moment. Well, why shouldn't they? It left me, nevertheless, with an obscure and imprecise sense of having missed something, the sort of nostalgia for what never was that I have so often dismissed, with a superior smile, as sentimental in others. Perhaps not particularly often, but I have certainly done so,

374

I had an idea, evidently erroneous, that Mitchell was more interested in Clodia than Francesca, though she has never talked about him. We went to the theatre the other evening and I told her in passing that I had seen them – to her slightly delayed but considerable amusement. On such occasions Clodia can make one feel unaccountably and uncomfortably naive.

For one reason or another, Rachel, Fulford and I were all on our own with no plans for the Easter weekend. Normally, this would not have bothered any of us: but we all seem uncommonly restless and so arranged to spend the Sunday together at Fulford's, a bright but rather cold day. The cooking was more recognisable than usual but no less excellent and Fulford insisted that we should watch 'The Life of Jesus Part II' made by Zeffirelli with an extraordinarily distinguished cast. Even Rachel's Protestant conscience was not proof against Fulford's hilarity. He decided, rather unfairly, that it was a 'spaghetti gospel' (complete with Herod Antipasto). He was also delighted by the commercial breaks, which had a strong Superman content, before which sundry significant characters in the story kept saying mystically phrases such as 'My time is over!'

At the moment Fulford is still possessed by the character of one Captain Triggers, who appeared in a splendid little series of which I saw too little, about First World War flying, entitled 'Wings'. The ostensible hero was a Sergeant Farmer, but not for Ellis. The episodes I saw in a thoroughly unpretentious way captured something of what rural England must have been like in the Edwardian and Georgian years, emphasising the dignity as well as the more unpleasant distinction between the different social classes. For once on contemporary television those not of the working class are not automatically riddled with some form of turpitude. There were quite pleasant squires and squadron officers (notably Ellis's Captain Triggers), as well as Sergeant Farmer's comely mother, his maimed veteran uncle who dumbly adores her, his freckled sweetheart and the sort of thick decent public school idiot who has been a part of life and literature since the gelding of the Danes (which Fulford says is his emotional equivalent to Marvell's 'conversion of the Jews'.) An evening with Rachel (and Ellis Fulford) seems to restore Roger Ingestre to a cautious optimism.

In such company, even the Gospel (let alone the story of the Royal Flying Corps) is only an intermission from serious matters, which is to say politics and industrial relations. After the engineers at Heathrow, after the electricians at Port Talbot (and their brothers rumbling under the not-so-red rock), after the torchlight red on sweaty Leyland toolmakers, Rachel sees the possibility of a Tory landslide. And she thinks that a confrontation with the unions a few months later is by no means inevitable, because modified monetarist policies, which allow for a fairly high degree of free bargaining, are likely to appeal to the Tory top five and to the rank-and-file of the unions. With the retirement of Jones and Scanlon, the air, she feels, will be less eager and nipping and she thinks that the ordinary union member will put pressure upon the leaders, so that more John Cousins will emerge in favour of top trade unionists representing the best interests of their members rather than meddling (I think he said 'usurping') the prerogatives of Parliament. She backs up her argument with evidence in her constituency and (she claims) elsewhere that many skilled and unskilled workers in what were once good jobs resent the soft options offered by the welfare state and are convinced the good intentions are being abused. She foresees a metamorphosis in union leadership and thinks there will be much more coherence between our industrial attitudes and those of Germany and Benelux. I am not sure how much of this is the consummation that we all devoutly wish rather than an imminent possibility; but I am inclined to agree that skilful Tory government, founded on an oil-based prosperity, might very readily co-operate with most of the big unions.

I called on Jeremy and Barbara ostensibly to find out how Candida was, but I think really because I intended to make some kind of confession about my part in setting up – there is no other word for it – her fateful meeting with Connors. Courage inevitably failed me: for, while Barbara is calmly practical and seems to have rationalised events to her own satisfaction, Jeremy is still extremely, almost inordinately, shaken. It would seem that his affection and protective instinct towards the younger daughter is especially strong and that this compounded with his remorse (perhaps) about what has befallen Candida has put him under severe mental stress. Jessica has been sent to Barbara's brother who lives near Bruges and is to spend a year at a school in Switzerland, a privately sponsored place. Candida has improved enough to be allowed out of the clinic and they intend to go to their house in Gloucestershire. It now seems that they both feel that they have somewhat neglected her, which Candida has always suggested, for Jessica who has the more appealing personality. They do not admit as much but they appear anxious to try to repair some of the damage that they have unwittingly inflicted. Taylor used the phrase 'offer the poor child some love at last'. And it was a moment of some pathos. I think that, if Barbara's practical plans are enhanced by Jeremy's kindness and consideration, in a year's time the whole wretched business will be just a scar on the memory which sometimes hurts but is healed.

Never an especially incisive thinker, Jeremy talked in a fairly rambling way about parenthood. He seemed to think it had been easier for his own parents' generation (my own, too, of course) than for his own. 'The trouble was that we both thought that Candida was such a sensible girl,' he said. 'I mean these days adolescents are given so much freedom, especially by the sort of people who live around here, whom

377

Candida went to school with. Barbara was even a little perturbed that Candida seemed to have so little interest in boys. . . . And then. . . . Jess was always wilder, as you know. But there's very little that one can do without making life thoroughly miserable for everyone or encouraging them to drop out. . . . You know I had an absurd notion that by sharing our own friends with both of them, very clever people and independent people and thoughtful people, we were storing up reserves of vicarious wisdom and experience for them, psychological and intellectual support for their inevitable emotional problems. And, of course, it did not work: a tolerant, moderately permissive outlook and intelligent company seem to be a poor substitute for affection and discipline. I was lucky in my parents, so was Barbara (although she claims never to have known her father): I don't think that Candida and Jess were.'

I suppose I was also lucky in my parents. Discipline was certainly unquestioned, but I was never especially undisciplined. My father's own self-respect made him quietly determined that I should at least be as good a craftsman as he was, but once I showed any academic ability there was no question about his support and, indeed, his tacit pride. Perhaps because of my own preoccupation with eighteenth-century Europe, I chose to interpret Jeremy's use of his friends in the light of the Emperor Charles the Sixth's pragmatic sanctions: making certain that his daughters had the friendship and goodwill of established allies, only to be let down by some of them. Fanciful. Shameful whimsy in the circumstances, even.

The trouble is that none of us, Taylor's closest friends or associates, have made a conspicuous success of our private lives. Connors, Ellis, Trumble and myself all divorced; Jock Hay, Bill Delahaye and Sandra Beeton all unmarried; Marie several times divorced; Farrell, Middleton and Mears all more or less living through their marriages until their grown-up children do them part; even Rachel separated from Oliver by the exigencies of their careers, and not happy. In fact Jeremy's and Barbara's is the most successful relationship in its rational, distanced way. In a way, the people who have been so successful and who have so much time to give to their varied interests are those who have nothing much else except casual friendships or love affairs. I thought, by contrast, of Blakemore with his five children. The discipline of the Blakemore household was something I had never considered, but it surely exists and his children have always seemed to be polite, happy and completely under-awed by Blakemore. Obviously, my reflections on parenthood are of very little moment: they have been prompted by a sense of pity for Jeremy Taylor and his bewilderment. On the whole, family relations, in my admittedly limited experience, are a source more of pain than pleasure when viewed with any honesty. Even the essentially benign Aristotle suggested that family life does children more harm than good; it is much the same for parents.

Thinking perhaps of the Taylor family in Gloucestershire and wondering how Candida was improving, I remembered my own last visit there, when we stopped at Avebury and I climbed Windmill Hill with Jess. (It's strange and unpleasant somehow to think of that bundle of high spirits suddenly becoming a would-be *allumeuse*; voyeuristic even – becoming aware that the tomboy girl-next-door has developed into a woman and watching her undress. Why should it be so? We are all sadly mixed up.) This is just by the way: what I recalled most clearly was that moment of young and genuine enthusiasm, when her imagination was working as she thought about the ancient people in that most ancient part of England.

Fragments. How we piece together the ordinary activities of vanished generations from scraps of metal or clay or bone and try to guess at their social structures, their politics, their early instincts for art and why they needed it, their first attempts at rudimentary technology. As later from what

379

is firm documentary evidence about policies and hierarchic systems and orders of government, we try to guess at the private lives and preoccupations of great and ordinary men and women at different times in the past. And in our own time, these same fragments are the lives, or what we see of the lives, of the people we know, or observe, or simply glimpse. How much of this civilisation (not entirely success-ful but not at all ignoble) will be guessed from physical fragments and how much from art and documents? Suppose it was only a private diary that survived, or a shopping list, or a catalogue, what would we be able to guess about the ideals and failures, miseries and delights of Declining Western Man? I suppose it is one reason why I make these disjointed, idiosyncratic notes, which I seldom bother to read again. Not that I expect them to be of anything but curiosity interest to myself when old and tired and full of sleep. A boyhood habit, unlike others, never discarded. I wonder if I shall be able to piece anything worth-while together from this disturbed dust and rose-leaves.

Returning to Oxford earlier than I had intended, I ran into Blakemore *passant gules*. He is always at his best when re-reading Tacitus: his spectacles glitter higher upon the noble brow, and the thin, long, straight, eloquent nose behaves more than ever sensitively. At such moments I am aware that Blakemore and I only ever hold conversations, while we should both claim to be each other's friend. I have no idea whether Blakemore is happily married: he does not know whether I am happily no longer married. It would be indelicate for either of us to ask.

Curiously I feel that he, Blakemore, might have been able to deal with the problem of the Taylor daughters in his way, as Marie White might have in hers. No doubt this is because they both remind me of my own inadequacies, representing in different ways the people who first enhanced and then dissipated my own young doubts and fears. It is an enormous lottery. I could have been wrecked by Daphne at a much more advanced age than Candida: I had the luck to be cerebral. Questions of self-preservation.

At lunch in the King's Arms opposite Blakemore, I dared to entertain such speculations about his own stoic privacy. He offered a short lucid criticism of any kind of idealism that was not strictly personal, though necessarily altruistic if it was ever to deserve the name.

It becomes apparent, though, that Blakemore is retreating. Despising all modern politicians, distrusting the administrators, the chairmen of commissions, yearning for some Platonic realm that never was, Blakemore is an archaism making a last Senecan grandstand play. He would not deny it. He constructs his threnodies upon a civilisation that was lost before ever he found it, or occurred in it; he waits. He assures me that nothing that I believe is wrong and that all my kind (and his own) are doomed. Ultimately, he claims, most men like most scholars are not wicked or even misguided: they are merely stupid: adding, with that refreshing malevolent gleam that they can never be as stupid as those, whether artists or scientists, who strive to be creative.

Candida Taylor has been found dead at the bottom of a quarry not far from the house in Gloucestershire. There is no way of knowing whether she killed herself. I shall have to tell Kent, who may be deeply upset.

*

Dear Rachel,

Perhaps it's time I wrote to you, a little apprehensive about Oliver coming back soon, a little afraid that it will no longer be possible to recreate something that once just happened. He will be here for a few months and then away again. How long can we survive these protracted separations? As soon as he is here again, with his laughter and confidence, I know I shall not have any doubts: but for the moment I am worried and I have drunk a little too much.

381

The daughter of friends, a pretty girl whom I did not know well and don't think I liked particularly, may have killed herself after a nervous collapse. A week or so ago there was a terrible air-crash at Tenerife after terrorist bombs had caused an aircraft to be diverted. I heard the cold news on the radio and felt frightened, sad, obscurely religious as I always do when there is some disaster which involves people I do not know. I heard about Candida on the telephone (from Connors, who was shattered); I felt numb because this sort of thing not only happens to other people but to the friends of other people. And there was also a disquieting thrill of excitement, that whiff of scandal and misfortune which seems to alert people when they are not immediately involved. What is left, I suppose, of a primitive cannibalistic opportunism which makes us respond immediately to the vulnerability of others. It is not pleasant to find in oneself, but it is not rational either.

Jeremy Taylor has always been quite a close friend, who has often confided in me. Barbara has never, I suspect, been close to anyone – except possibly her husband and Jessica. She and I have always been on excellent terms, but we are absolutely different. She would hate the constituency 'surgery', where you have to look directly at all kinds of ills as they work upon individuals, but she would work tirelessly at a microscope to isolate the various causes. I am not sure what, if anything, can be done to help them. Perhaps I can contribute to some corporate effort with Ellis and Roger Ingestre.

Connors is a different matter. It does not help that I do not like him and have always been pretty repelled by his automatic reflex lechery, but he is not a hypocrite and I do not think he is a liar. It does not seem to me that things are improved one jot by a campaign of vengeance against Connors now that the unfortunate girl is dead. He is resiliently intelligent and obviously responds to arguments that he cannot be held entirely to blame. I already know far more than I want to about what happened with Candida. The Jessica

382

incident is obscure, but I'm sure that it would be quite easy to get her to tell the truth. Well, it would have been. She must now be terrified and someone is going to have to do some plain talking to her, to Barbara and to poor Jeremy.

It is extraordinary that people's lives can get into such a mess. I don't think any of us are particularly nice but on the other hand we are not bad: we work hard, we are reasonably sincere and we try not to exploit people, circumstances, even those we love, for selfish ends. There is a certain amount of sexual manoeuvring, as there always has been and always will be. And there but for the grace of God. . . . Not really. After one episode which was initially painful and one lastingly painful adventure (but that was with a much older man too), I had the good luck to meet Oliver. And that was lucky! Over the last year I've had to dredge myself out of the sludge of self-pity a few times, but I wouldn't have it any different. I would not trade the shy rather dreamy girl I used to be for the woman married to Oliver. All right, I've lost something and I compromise every day with myself, with Oliver, and so on. But I will be loyal according to my conscience. And *I* know about my conscience and no one else does. Not even a putative God. I could still do something foolish because I am no more certain than anyone else how I should respond to this or that circumstance, but I know quite well what I should think about it and about me. The young Rachel was always yearning to live for the moment and to surrender herself completely to it and, apart from that one unhappy year, much too cautious to carry it through. Oliver's wife no longer wants to, aware (though not through her own experience) that the misery always outweighs the pleasure. I suppose I lost my essential innocence (nothing to do with virginity) before Roger or even Oliver, but I don't think I lost it so completely. Golden girls and boys all must like chimney-sweepers take a rational and responsible attitude to soot.

It still astonishes me that dear, lovely Oliver, who has never had doubts about anything should have had one about me and I am still perversely happy about it. If it had not been for him, I should never have become an active politician: always passionate, always for causes, the great bounding voice and the strong dependable arms and the laugh. How many of all the people who think him much too sure of himself would ever have guessed that there was that one tiny but vital area of uncertainty.

This is about us, Rachel: not about Owen in Rhodesia, and Gormley's cats in hell and Jimmy Carter Superstar and great national debates and Lib–Lab pacts. Like the man and his little horse I have miles to go before I sleep. (Literally true quite often! But Oliver has a way with insomnia.)

And it is not long now and I feel fatuously nervous about it. There is much to be done, and private as well as public obligations to be met. I cannot help wondering what Candida was thinking before she fell or let herself fall. And it is almost impossible to get near Barbara even now. Oliver might: he can surprise people with gentleness when they least expect it, because he is usually the one organising the games around the Christmas tree.

I'm not sure what this is about. I suppose if I could write poetry I would: perhaps I'll try one of these days. No: let's live the fair hours as they pass and not just talk about them. At least God and twenty-five years of the Queen have given us a respectable recess when Oliver comes back. I shall probably tear this up tomorrow when I am a little more sober. I do not want to disappoint. Soon I shall know that I don't.

Goodnight,

Rachel.

*

Surely not intended for me to hear. *And besides the wench is dead.* . . . Surely not. It would be very cruel, but then cruelty is one of the flavouring herbs here. How . . . I don't even know the fellow well and he could not know anything about my private affairs. Rumour and gossip. Often chuckled over some cruel little yarn myself in these same places. *And*

384

besides the wench is dead. Oh yes. She is dead, poor kid. And I have to live with that and the memory of her and the cynical shame of what I did for a few hours, added up, of gratification and pleasure. No longer even matters that Jessica tells the truth. Could they have meant that? Are they saying those things behind my back or just out of earshot or obliquely. I don't think I can ever be sure. . . . What is the point any longer: Jessica would only get herself into trouble. I suppose it *must* have disturbed her if she heard and saw us that day. Oh it was so bloody stupid! But Candida knew then exactly how to turn me on and the only saving grace is that I was not even tempted to touch Jess. . . . Why though? Asking myself thousands of times. Just as an act of spite, wanting what she thought was her sister's, or some kind of revenge. Candida was always jealous of Jess but there never seemed anything reciprocal until . . . I don't know: suppose for a young girl suddenly to see something as tearaway as that particular time would be seriously shocking, stimulating, what?

And Taylor's anger. It was more than natural, more than normal. Some brilliant sociologist on the 'Today' programme the other morning saying that incest was damaging to family relationships! Taylor would never admit it, never be honest with himself if he had desired one of his daughters and especially not Jess. Wonderful body which he must have watched so often. Those biting words to me. I didn't know that words could hurt as much. Suppose because there was something I recognised as the truth. And now . . .

We shall never know whether she fell or threw herself over. . . . Rachel is kind and Ingestre trying to be, but obviously blaming himself. *The wench is dead.* I wish they had perhaps let me see her. No: obviously there could be no question of that. How could they? Barbara was icy and rational and implacable. Taylor nearly mad. A dozen, a hundred times I crawl on my knees around these labyrinths each day, the penitent, the sinner. And will do for the rest of my life. Less often as time goes on: but always wondering how she died and what was in that wrecked distorted brain at the end when she fell. Or killed herself. Taylor is, of course, and must know it, partly to blame for making such a colossal row of it at the time when she came into the house that Friday from Oxford. God no! No! I've lived through that often. And the hysteria. . . . God knows how it stopped. I have no memory of it, just the noise and the atmosphere of near madness. And then those letters from him of corrosive hate. . . . I suppose I destroyed his family, as he sees it, when I was only the agent of their self-destructive impulse. Not making excuses. It's the truth and we all contain in us and in our relationships, *it is so obvious*, the elements of such self-destruction. And live on after the devastation and the pain and the pity. . . .

Cruel asides: the other country; now that we talk of dying. There was no scandal. . . . I must try to fight against this paranoid feeling of heads turning, voices lowering, sentences stopping abruptly, turnings away; blank misgivings. Rachel who always avoided me now makes a point of seeking me out. They seek me out who sometime from me fled. Secure now with Oliver back and in the knowledge that even I would hardly dare to make a pass at her *now*! Even the monster that I was. In fact that one left-cross was enough. I never did again. But since she has never liked me and once upon a time made no effort not to show open distaste, it is an effort of kindness that I cannot resent. And even now. . . .

. . . Good evening, Rachel. Paddling along. Can I offer you a glass of something.

Splendid. If we go on meeting like this my reputation will be ruined. Whimsical half-smiles, clearing of throats, sudden sidelong glances. You'd think that such a lewd and drunken and licentious assembly as Mr Paisley says they are would be more sophisticated. It's that old paranoid devil again. It must be controlled. Rachel chatters about the failure of the general strike in Northern Ireland and the Tory landslide in the local elections and President Jimmy Carter and the economic summit. These days she seems to think that if she talks fast enough and about as many subjects as possible she will crowd out of my mind any suspicion of why she is being kind and what it all refers to. The bar and Clatworthy bearing down on us. Oh God, I'm too tired: hope Rachel's on form.

. . . Hullo, Ieuan. Hunting prodigals again, are you? You have that honest pastoral beam in your eye.

Big Welsh smile. Extraordinary the number of horizontal creases the Welsh contrive around their eyes, giving them that benignly sly look. Perhaps it comes from practising Lloyd George faces when shaving. Yes, now look here, children *bach*, when are you going to see the error of your ways and be good socialists. And Jack Jones and Clive Jenkins and this business about direct elections that will make us the puppets of Europe. Now can I make you see sense then now, isn't it? Rachel won't be drawn on Europe, asks if Clatworthy has noticed that every time Jack Jones opens his mouth, the Bank of England has to do the footwork and what about free collective bargaining and the Scottish Trades Union Congress when the small unions threw McGahey's motion out? Oh well, it's the redistribution of wealth that we, as a party, are committed to, isn't it? And Rachel presents what she calls her St Augustine theory of trade union principles: make me restrained, Lord, but not yet. Alternatively, if the redistribution of wealth is Labour policy and the unions back Labour policy, what is all this stuff about a larger slice of the cake. Effectively, and she is now like a Spitfire around a Dornier, it means redistribute everybody else's wealth: but leave ours alone, which is the big battery argument and will lead to inflation of something like 30 per cent in less than a year. Clatworthy has never heard such a comical speech in years. Rachel, he says, is funnier than Mike Yarwood. And what about me? Surely I can see the folly of the European escapade. The devil is also citing scripture. Look at poor Tony Crosland and poor Peter Kirk: good men, boy! And gone before their time because of the strain, the additional strain, imposed upon conscientious men by the European Parliament, a work of the imagination at best. The point is (isn't it) that an elected Member of Parliament cannot properly represent his constituents at Westminster if he has to piss about (excuse my French, Rachel) in Strasbourg.

. . . I thought you people were more interested in being delegates than representatives, anyway, Ieuan.

The big Welsh smile. Aren't I a card? *Aren't* I! Isn't it terrible, the sly bastard says, to see a good socialist seduced by bureaucratic highlife. Daresay the word was carefully chosen. All I really want to say to these people is *Fuck OFF*. Instead, of course, I say:

. . . You having another, Ieuan?

He is not to be bought by a small whisky. Not by a long chalk, I should guess! (Marlowe, you're not human tonight.) The lady in white samite says it's her round and switches to the National Front and the politics of discontent. It is unbelievable. So we (I almost said they) barely held Grimsby: but Ashfield! and here is Clatworthy saying it is because the Midlanders know we have rejected *Socialism* and they want none of it. Rachel would rather be with Oliver and I would rather be somewhere, anywhere, else. Ah well, Anthony, no Bilderberg invitation for you. Last Year at Torquay. . . . *Paroles de* Dante Milton–Sartre; *Réalisation :* Sergei Hitchcock. *Avec* . . . *avec* . . . *avec.* . . . Kiss those dreams of dominance goodbye. (There was a very funny piece in the *Standard*. What's a *Standard*, Mummy? A newspaper, darling. What's a newspaper, Mummy? Oh dear, there is no end to that . . . no end.) Poor little Candida. All the expectations of real answers, offered only attitudes, paraphrases, evasions. And do I have the right to smile! I must have the glazed look. Someone has spoken and I have no idea what was said. Poor boy's been working too hard, says Clatworthy. I'll take a rain check, if I may, Rachel, *bach*. And departs, exaggerating his (industrial) limp. Well, we all have work to do. Rachel reaches forward and jiggles my hand, as you would comfort a disappointed reciter or half-miler. The optimism at the summit, the bad behaviour of the French. Callaghan the Leader of Europe (Carter almost *sic*): all good for a laugh. The pressure is building up. Send for Red Adair. The girl with red silken hair and a beautiful body and calm open eyes as she loved . . . lying, not yet (yes just) twenty, her neck or back broken, in a shallow quarry.

. . . No, of course. I'm waiting for the division. I shall probably catch up on letters. Thank you, Rachel.

Her pleasure? I don't think so. Not really. But in the great celestial lobbies I shall be for you, if it is ever put to the vote. Conscience: my vote flies up, my spirit soars below. I don't think I'm such a bastard . . . I don't think so. And yet I never had that part of conscience awakened until . . . until the wench was dead.

It is odd as the spring becomes summer and the girls start wearing their summer dresses and there are so many pretty girls in London always and the fashion this year is for very high, slim heels, so that legs and haunches are shown off and the young body swings and the breasts are held high and the fresh, fine hair swirls a little in the fresh spring air . . . it is odd to feel guilt and remorse, the waking agonies of last evening's folly before disgust at midnight and this sickly, parched, retching dawn. You wake always too early. With an unwanted erection. All those other forms of conscience are easy, once you have really helped kill someone and you can deceive yourself with self-pity as conscience. Why don't I go and work out a Theory of Descriptions or something? I don't even remember it clearly and I was never really quite good enough.

Oh dear . . . Rosemary. Why should I think of you? And whatever happened indeed to you at the bottom of a quarry lying distorted. Last heard of in Los Angeles. And Ingestre's wife, her sibling, on the shadier side of the Rüperbahn. *That's* for remembrance! No, honourable Member for Pisstrough West, I was not making a rude sign at you. The noble mind isn't quite yet *bouleversé*. Oh! Pphagh. He was probably thinking of something entirely different.

Come, come, Anthony. This will not do. I suppose I must let the dust settle on rumour and reputation, sit tight, vote, answer letters; and when the time comes remind the state that I have done some service and telephone some friends. Some passing acrobat, now at the BBC, once told me at Oxford that he would keep me in mind. God knows, I might yet need him!

It does not stop . . . it does not stop. . . . Will you play at conscience with me, Lord? Nay, fair lady, for your hands are much too white upon the board. That is almost. . . .

*

The Pilgrimage . . . falters

Josephine Cornflour. . . .

Oh alas no. Not tonight. Sorry, Josephine: you were intended to win. It doesn't work out often.

I am sorry, desperately sorry, Josephine.

Rest in peace: there can only be peace.

Call it a kind of domestic tear, if you will:
You are not beckoning me and I will not,
Would not, be beckoned. I am the stranger
And foreigner impertinent enough to compose
Your decent limbs, whatever happened. They were
All strangers and foreigners. Make no mistake
Whatever their apparel, however glib the talk,
Those that are most bleak will grieve an hour
And others will mourn a year and some a lifetime.
What ceremony else! I bow out, the churlish
Priest, who invited myself to your funeral
And was rude to the mourners. You were for me
Silly and delicate: I have known flowers so,
In springtime, and wished only to watch the folly.
The town is full of florists, after all. Let
Them now brawl about your grave, I am here
Uninvited to officiate, pretending nothing

390

But the compassion of my trade, dim and bitter
Clerk of their contracts. They would turn
On me as they turned away from you: so I must
Remain as obscure and churlish in your death
As I always seemed before. I did not love you,
Unfortunate young lady; I even borrow my grief,
Which is as futile as was my affection.

What happened to that fresh-faced, generous boy who,
Ingestre said, was deeply stricken by the young, cool and
(so they thought, so I thought) confident Candida? It is a
discomposing gift of the gods, comparable to the favours that
were bestowed upon Cassandra and Tiresias, that I am always
where I am not wanted with my indefatigable memory. Why
should I be at a scene behind the gasworks, fishing? Not my
sort of copy. And Marie White will let him return carelessly
and down lightly when the time comes, having the gift of
kindness, the emptiness of many bright and blowing days
in early spring, a private reliquary of flint and semi-precious
stones. Why should it matter?

It doesn't. Samson Carrasco, dedicated to saving virgins
and not concerned with demented chivalrics, mistook the
enchantress's castle for an inn and there was his own surplus
Dulcinea. But nice. Spring can really hang you up the most!

He will know, by this time, about Candida. He will have
wept and raged a little, got drunk, wept again against Marie's
soft white body: but now he must think about getting his
first. I wish him an elegant, colourful autobiography,
though I doubt he has the sense of style, however much
blessed by adventure. It was a happy fresh face turned to
Marie, holding her hand, there behind the gashouse, beside
the canal.

It's a pity that novel will never be finished and no one will
rescue Rufus Bushchat. I had thought of a suave trouble-

shooter operating under the cover of the first philosopher disc-jockey, bringing new horizons of enlightenment to Radio One. But Waverley Ferax and his daring rock metaphysics will now never exist. (Those programmes: The conversation with the flying Platos; You Kant, take that away from me; Sewing your own Rousseau; The Russell of Spring; Pet me, Popper – and all the others – all lost, lost!) And Bushchat will not even escape, let alone be smuggled to the blessed islands.

Poor old Bushchat. Not that he is aware of his predicament and the prison house he has carefully built around him. He smiles, he is easy and eloquent. His face in repose is tolerant and good-humoured. He is in good physical shape. The kind of don it is always pleasant to meet when one is a guest at his high table, charming and a good listener.

That is a good rule of thumb: the best minds are usually the best listeners, using silence creatively even if they are not paying much attention. There are enough of the other sort, beady-eyed expounders, full of paradox and counter-argument and contradiction and their own jokes, almost unable to co-exist with their own cleverness.

No, indeed: Bushchat is the best sort of fellow, the kind American visitors like to meet, and observe striding across the quadrangle, or sauntering in airy conversation on the ancient pelouses. They are seldom, if ever, aware that they are watching a species in grave danger of extinction: the last few liberal intellectuals who have a desire to serve without power – generous, altruistic, ineffectual.

Mears's organisation, Bushchat's energetic theorising, my tireless projections cannot bring to that group something that Jeremy and Barbara brought by emotional and intellectual commitment, respectively, when most of the members were doubting.

In different ways I think that Ingestre and I have both given up, although I doubt that he would admit it, because we no longer have the necessary respect for the nameless, unidentifiable public which provides the resonance for us.

I stopped writing novels when I no longer cared whether anyone read them and I now amuse myself and people like Ellis Fulford with fantasies, as Alan Trumble drinks, and Ingestre theorises. Politics for him is a hobby, as fiction is for me. We share a lack of ambition like a vitamin deficiency, a complex substance which makes good intention positive idealism.

Waiting for the end, boys. But not by any means sitting in cold fear.

This is the chief thing, Ingestre, be not perturbed.

Dear Rachel,

Of course I shall never send this letter and it would more appropriately be a poem, but I have failed to write it because it was not exactly a love poem and there is now no fashion for exercises in admiration or even expressions of kind wishes. In fact, I doubt that I would be writing it at all, but I had no heart for satirical fiction when the model for my heroine died. I always found her very beautiful. So far, I have not been moved to fresh malice or lust by anything in particular and so I am using the creative pause to write to you. It is, obviously, a testimony of my incompleteness as a person that I resort always to my typewriter and invent my own vicarious existence. As you know I am not a very good mixer and have always been thick of speech. It would not have been exactly a love poem as this is not exactly a love letter, because I am not and have never been exactly in love with you: I have imagined being in bed with you and I have thought about how pleasant it would be to share time with you and I have admired you. But that is not loving. (And I, God knows, am not Oliver.) It is rather another substitute for living the dark, unintelligible, sometimes lonely moment; another kind of catharsis.

Substitute lives are pretty commonplace: serial novels, the cinema, the radio, and now everywhere television, more real for some people than their own lives. It takes its most sinister cultural form in the popularity of inane give-away games and quizzes in which people make vicarious fools of themselves and indulge in surrogate venality and sado-masochistic pleasure. But that too is a catharsis and, in one form or another, there has always been a range of rich substitute existence for the educated classes, fictional and non-fictional. I have heard of one particular group of people who play a complex game in which they imagine themselves in certain historical or fictional situations and analyse their possible behaviour. Not dangerous as long as it remains cerebral.

Dear me: so far, this letter is either about me or my ramblings and it was to have been about you. In a way the poem that did not work was more successful.

I shall not dwell particularly on why I should like to make love to you. The reasons are obvious and you are so effort-lessly feminine that you must know exactly what they are. But understand that this is not the commonplace lust for the girl along the corridor in the office, or the ripened and worldly divorcée in the same block, or the girl on the maga-zine cover: it is a precise desire to communicate with your body; to express the admiration I shall speak of, in that way; perhaps it is a little too solemn. On the occasions when I have allowed myself to imagine it, it has had nothing in common with the crude passing fantasy.

When it comes to sharing time with you: this is simply an extension of the conversations we have had, the pleasing days or evenings when we have been guests at the same house. These daydreams are commonplace, even banal: merely sitting in silence, in the sunshine, at a table in a particular place, or being in the same room – what, as a single man, I imagine to be the unsung pleasures of marriage and com-panionship, the unremarkable affection that is understood between two people (which I presume to detect between you and Oliver and which seems to be very rare). That is all. It is something that I envy.

Lastly I admire you because, unlike Roger Ingestre and

394

myself, you have not lost faith in the survival of our kind and in the principles of politics and civilisation on which we have tried to base our usefulness and outlook. I also admire your loyalty, which must sometimes falter, to the underlying assumption of social democracy – that people are worth it; your refusal, in so far as I know it, to countenance the idea that tolerance and argument and unviolent government is doomed in the short-, medium- or long-term view. There are many things contingent upon this faith which I think I read in you that I also respect.

Alas, I do not like, let alone respect, many people and it is a pity that this letter will not be sent, because I should like you to know, at a time of uncertainty, when some have already admitted defeat and (as it happens) at a time when we and our friends have been closer to personal disaster than is usual, that I wish you much happiness.

Yours,

Bill.

They tell me I should be kind or at least understanding but I cannot find it in myself, for you have ceased to be a joke and I have always really loathed you. Opportunism without energy is a vice which deserves consignment to the same deep circle of hell where you would find the treacherous politicians. You would have made it in time, I daresay. Both in sexual and political opportunism, though, you managed to combine your achievements with indolence. You lived on your wits and charm and went for easy conquests; you hedged your bets and boxed your fences. Only when you were certain that there was no possibility of office did you show disillusion and pretended it was a crisis of faith. It will always be the same: you will bounce from pinging wire to pinging wire on the pin table, always managing to score. You will survive, you will adapt. You will never need faith or belief or even a set of political principles or private scruples. And if you had to choose between betraying your country or your friend, it would not be difficult, you would manage somehow to betray both! They tell me – someone tells me – that you were profoundly, drastically upset: I see no sign of it.

. . . Yes, Mr Connors, I am unusually silent: even for *me*.

The intention was for Josephine to make Cornflour realise just how rotten he was in time. . . .

Of course Mrs de Wagram's information led to the hunting down of Dahlia Dackord, who was immediately abandoned by Split. Griff Crabbe and Flexion planted evidence with such skill that they discredited Split himself, who was promptly abandoned by the KGB. After poisoning Sir Hoke Dick, Lord Steroid, and Rubicon Tweed, the Borgedici sisters were arrested on the evidence of Lucius Spiedermann who sold his autobiography to a national newspaper for a vast sum of money and went to live in the Bahamas.

Rufus Bushchat managed to escape from the cellars of Fresh 'n' Freeze and was harrowingly pursued throughout the home counties until, exhausted and at the end of his psychological endurance, he was picked up by a Rolls-Royce whose occupants saw his prostrate form at the roadside. The car belonged to none other than O. Farr-Quinell, the Supercrat, who had been Bushchat's junior at their public school, when the great international civil servant had been miserable and bullied and Bushchat was kind to him. Soon after Arnold Espadrille disappeared without anyone much noticing. Wynstanley's song was taken up by a popular television entertainer and he was able to retire from the Security Service.

During one of the very rare earthquakes recorded in England, Griff Crabbe, Bert Flexion, Lepidus Pounce and Branston Simcox were all crushed as a partly demolished abattoir fell upon them. They were all heavily disguised (for reasons of conspiratorial security), but this was misconstrued by the investigating authorities and the whole affair was hushed up, in the cause of Morale and Public Decency.

All the notes there. . . . Odd how amusing it seemed to be once and how bitterly futile it looks now. . . .

The intention was that Josephine should make Cornflour aware of just how rotten he was. In time.

'Well, this certainly is a lucky m-meeting. Cheers.'

'Cheers. Yes. I detest airports and my plane is always delayed these days. Nine times out of ten. Are you going to Brussels for your paper?'

'More or less. But to get background information m-more than to do a specific story. Are you just going to Rome for a holiday?'

'No! I shouldn't choose Rome for that. I'm due for a new appointment quite soon. So I'm going to talk about it.'

'We shall m-miss you.'

'That's very charming of you.'

'Is your sister still here?'

'Yes, She is. London agrees with her. And her business is thriving, it appears. Have you seen our friend Roger recently?'

'No. I missed the last m-meeting of that group which we both belong to, so we haven't met for about a m-month.'

'He's in a very serious state of depression. Apparently some of your cricketers have opted to play for what he calls a Circus, rather than for England! This obviously prefaces the imminent doom of civilisation.'

'It would. I'm afraid that is one of the impenetrable areas between Roger and me. I can't stand cricket.'

'Good Heavens, Bill! is that possible? To be a liberal in politics and a friend of Roger Ingestre and not like *cricket*?'

'Fortunately, we have other things in common. I suppose, when I think of it, m-mainly political attitudes.'

'I read one of your novels, *Mock Heroics*. I thought it was excellent. Roger lent it to me, which is why I mention it.'

'Thank you. That was a long time ago.'

'Roger says you've stopped publishing novels.'

'I've stopped w-writing them.'

'Why is that? It seems a pity.'

'Not really. I had a few ideas. Not many. But I once thought they were worth sharing.'

'And you don't think so any more?'

'N-no. I sometimes write to amuse myself, because I'm not a very fluent sort of person.'

'I've always thought you were shy. I was surprised when you came up to me now.'

'But I don't especially want to communicate any more, other than in my job on the paper. I think there's some point still in trying to present f-facts objectively, so that people know what's going on.'

'But not fiction?'

'Not serious fiction, which is what I tried to write once.'

'Why is that?'

'Oh, it's all very defeatist. The things I care about are held at a very low premium: art, poetry, fine workmanship. The guardians are usually people I more or less despise. It seemed to me more and more self-indulgent and when you lose interest in the people you once thought would read your work, you lose ambition. I have certain political preoccupations which I feel strongly about – none of them very original, but, all it seems to me, endangered. Apart from doing what I can in my work and outside to p-preserve certain standards in politics, I've decided to live as quietly and anonymously as possible.'

'I still think it's a pity.'

'Perhaps. I don't think it's particularly admirable. But I'm afraid that I am a cultural pessimist. Television, especially, has killed the possibility of a large audience becoming interested in any new minority forms, just as it has encouraged a particular type to emerge. If you are not good on television, whether artist or politician or journalist, you are rejected; if you are good, you are accepted quite uncritically and in the most vacuous way. Of course there will always be a very few who read books and so on, but they will get fewer and

398

fewer and they will, even these people, know less and less. And that bodes very ill for p-political trends.'

'You found nothing to encourage you in the Economic summit and the NATO conference?'

'I'm afraid not. It has been a summer of rituals, hasn't it? Both those events. And now the Jubilee. And then the Commonwealth Prime Ministers. All those smiles and handclasps and p-platitudes.'

'Yes, but there have to be platitudes. Or will you think me just another cynical diplomatist? Anyway, I don't think that there were all that many in the NATO meeting, even what we were allowed to hear of what passed.'

'There were enough in the other. Meaningless ceremonies to convince people that their wise men are in control.'

'I'm not sure. I think for the first time in years the West is showing a certain confidence. I also happen to think that Carter's approach to world Communism is refreshing and salutary. In fact, I was quite wrong about him. Then, as I'm always saying to Roger, I am an executive: not a politician, not a political theorist. Not a political commentator as you are.'

'I'm glad to talk to anyone who is hopeful. So here we are on the day of the third great ritual, flying out of London and away from celebration.'

'Yes, I'm rather sorry. You do festivals very well in England.'

'We do. We may be almost bankrupt, bitterly envious of one another and riven by all manner of group rivalries, not to mention regional and tribal discontent: but we do put on a good show. Only about a week ago one of the major political parties announced a policy of tolerance to people who are taking it over, as the declared enemies of the democracy it affects to preach: but everyone loves a good procession. When I arrive in Brussels I shall hear how impossible and self-seeking the French are, how treacherous they think we are, how the Germans are fed up with picking up the tab and how Benelux think we are all lousy Europeans and that we shall

399

never speak with one clear confident voice: meanwhile at home there will be endless pageants, tea-parties, walkabouts, futile sporting occasions and endless variety galas. Rain or shine, the Golden Coach will roll up and down today and people will cheer. The pubs will stay open late and there will be an extra day's holiday. People will cheer more and we will hear all about our rosy tradition of tolerance and our heritage of freedom.'

'And the struggle avails nothing. Perhaps we are all too old and too corrupt. Or perhaps you and I have lost heart, when nothing is yet lost.'

'Too late, Clodia. The old and corrupt may be moribund. But the surviving family have inherited the disease. Anyway, greetings on this auspicious day. I think they've just c-called your flight.'